HOLIDAY HEARTS SWEET AND WHOLESOME ROMANCE STORIES

VOLUME 2

JOSIE RIVIERA

INTRODUCTION

To keep up on newly released ebooks, paperbacks, Large Print Paperbacks, audiobooks, as well as exclusive sales, sign up for Josie's Newsletter today.

As a thank you, I'll send you a Free PDF ... The Beauty Of ...

Josie's Newsletter

Did you know that according to a Yale University study, people who read books live longer?

Holiday Hearts Volume 2

Copyright © 2019 by Josie Riviera

5 STAR READER REVIEWS

Amazon Review by J. Barr (Aloha To Love)
    5.0 out of 5 stars
"Really enjoyed this story because it follows a woman-Angelina and she's a writer and some of her script needs correcting before they can make it into a movie.

The scientific expert Caleb is on the cruise also and he conducts classes about his career choice. He knows a lot about volcanoes. She takes his classes and he helps her with the script-he playing the male part.

Love that he tells her, when he stops reading his lines, that a guy wouldn't say that. what was written. They improvise and get through the script and then some.

Story also follows Rachel who's pregnant and on her way to meet her spouse who's already on the island.

Love hearing of the events that take place away from the ship and all that is learned on the excursions. Good holiday romance."

Amazon Review by J. Y. (A Christmas To Cherish)
    5.0 out of 5 stars

"Emmanuelle has come to the small town of Cherish to spend Christmas with her friend, Dorothy, but she is also there to escape her abusive ex-husband. He has destroyed her confidence and her faith in God has been shaken.

Nicholas, Dorothy's brother, is a deputy in Cherish. When his bride abandoned him on their wedding day in a text message, Nicholas became embittered toward women and his bitterness and anger caused his faith in God to weaken. He and Emmanuelle were both very active in Dorothy's recovery and spent hours on skype talking with each other but now that she is inCherish, they are each uneasy that the other has romantic intentions.

This is such a sweet Christmas romance. It is a clean story with a message of faith and hope. It made me happy reading it."

Amazon Review by Sara (1-800-CHRISTMAS)
5.0 out of 5 stars

So far I have only read 1-800-Christmas and A Christmas to Cherish and wow, let me tell you, all the emotions running in this book! Love, happiness, fear, sadness, dread, joy. Makes you worry, laugh, cry and fall in love! Unexpected scene added in that I never would have thought. A definite must read book!!! I can't wait to read the other books in this collection! Well written, great characters and a wonderful story! A must add to your TBR list!"

PRAISE AND AWARDS

USA TODAY bestselling author

DEAR FRIENDS

Dear Friends,

A heartwarming story is the hallmark of a romantic holiday. Savor the magic with three joyful, sweet contemporary romances in my exclusive Holiday Hearts Volume 2.

Cozy up under a quilt, a cup of hot cocoa and lose yourself in this wonderful season of love.

Aloha to Love

Goodbye has never been this hard...especially when love is saying hello...

Screenwriter Angelina Conte has been butting heads via email with the studio's unbelievably nitpicky scientific advisor, volcanologist Dr. Caleb Sloane. Between his scheduled lectures aboard a Hawaiian cruise, she intends to prove that she's no Tinseltown hack.

Caleb had planned on using this Christmastime cruise to adjust his workaholic attitude. A tough assignment when he tangles with the movie studio's surprisingly stubborn scriptwriter.

Startlingly, their chemistry is off the charts. But when the studio gives Angelina an ultimatum, she remembers why she put love on the back burner—and why, for her, happily-ever-after was never in the cards.

A CHRISTMAS TO CHERISH

There's nothing a Christmas kiss won't cure. Except perhaps a shattered heart...

When Emmanuelle Sumter steps off the train in Cherish, South Carolina—a town simply glowing with the promise of Christmas—she finds herself praying God will help her find the broken pieces of her life. Shattered, like her beloved harp. Her dreams. And her trust in men.

Not long ago, while Nicholas' sister was in rehab, Emmanuelle's voice and smile on his Skype screen held him together. After that, she seemed to disappear, an absence he felt keenly when his ex-fiancée left his faith in God dented but not broken.

Now she's in Cherish, even more stunning in person. Yet she's holding tight to a private pain she refuses to reveal. Nicholas resolves to be patient, vowing that he'll never let anyone hurt her again. Even when her past rears its ugly head to destroy what's left of her heart.

1-800-CHRISTMAS

When two hearts get in a jam, it'll take more than whiskey cake to sweeten the deal.

Keiran O'Malley is back in Roses, North Carolina, lugging his own shattered dreams of home and family. Until he's on his feet and ready to open his own Irish pub, serendipity finds him an attic apartment in Desiree's fixer upper in exchange for his remodeling skills.

Roses is all polished up for the holidays, but nothing

outshines the Cinderella beauty who owns the house. The spin of warmth between them is instantaneous...but their broken hearts may not be strong enough to build happiness on, especially when the past shows up to demand its share.

Aloha to Love
Hawaiian Holiday Series

JOSIE RIVIERA
USA Today Bestselling Author

This book is dedicated to all my wonderful readers who have supported me every inch of the way.

THANK YOU!

ALOHA TO LOVE

BY
JOSIE RIVIERA

CHAPTER 1

*A*ngelina Conte stood along the railing of the *Bird of Paradise* cruise ship as the achingly familiar Los Angeles, California, skyline disappeared from view. The ship's horn blew, and people waved madly from the shore.

In the deepening dusk of a glorious December day, the intimate ship began cruising the sparkling Pacific Ocean waters, leaving San Pedro Bay far behind.

Sipping her refreshing glass of iced tea, she turned and gazed through the glass doors of the grand atrium, the center of the ship. A sweeping spiral staircase, bedecked with brilliant red poinsettias, commanded attention, and the bubble elevators eased passengers up and down to the various decks with amazing efficiency.

Every detail of the cruise shouted "Happy Holidays" and high living, and she would have loved to savor the experience. There was a catch, though, and a big one. Unexpected script changes for her screenplay, *Aloha to Love*, had to be fixed by January first. And all these fixes were because of one man, the eminent volcanologist, Dr. Caleb Sloane.

Partridge Production Studios had paid for her cruise

under the stipulation she attend Dr. Sloane's lectures on board the ship. The studio had hired him after she'd handed in her screenplay, and he had problems that the studio insisted she discuss face-to-face with him.

"Dr. Sloane insists that correct details are equally as important as your story," her boss, Devon, had quoted. "Working with him directly will give you a better grasp of the destructive nature of volcanoes."

"I know, I know," she murmured, although it was difficult to abandon her view of the stunning scenery to go below deck and plug away.

She scanned the red-and-green flowered garland strung along the deck railings. A gigantic gingerbread display had been set up in the main lobby, and each guest had received a celebratory tote bag upon boarding. On Christmas Eve day, church services would be held. The most important part of Christmas, she mused, was what one of her favorite pastors had once said, a quote she'd seen many times: "The child of Christmas is God."

She set her iced tea on a side table as a woman who appeared to be in her forties rounded the corner. Her head and face covered by an impossibly broad fedora straw hat, she had graying red hair, wore a flowing sun-flowered caftan, and was noticeably pregnant.

"Hi. I'm Rachel Olson. Or rather, aloha." The woman took a bite of the chocolate ice cream cone she held in one hand while extending the other for a handshake. She apparently had come from one of the numerous ice cream bars. "The cabin steward described you to me when I dropped off my luggage, so I presume I'm your roommate for the next few days. Did you know that most people think that *aloha* means both hello and goodbye in Hawaiian?"

"I didn't, but now I do," Angelina said with a smile.

"Although people use the term for both greetings," Rachel

licked her ice cream, then finger-quoted, "Aloha really means 'something that genuinely comes from the heart.'"

Angelina's smile was now largely from relief. Because the studio had had to book her berth at the last minute, she had to share her cabin with a complete stranger. Fortunately, she immediately liked Rachel Olson.

She shook Rachel's free hand. "I'm Angelina Conte."

"Is this cruise a last-minute decision?" Rachel asked.

Before Angelina could answer, a voice came over the loudspeaker and Captain Jorgen Berg extended a welcome greeting. An acquaintance of Angelina's had taken this cruise before and had told Angelina that the wild-haired, thick-browed captain was known for his humor. She wasn't surprised when he ended his message with a joke.

"Now if I can find the manual on how to steer this ship, we'll get underway."

With a hearty laugh, Rachel turned back to Angelina. "Most people book their cruises months ahead of time," she said. "From the small size and low deck location of our cabin, apparently not you?"

"My boss reserved this cruise for me a couple days ago." Angelina kept from glancing at the woman's pregnant belly by focusing on the people queuing up for the departure buffet in the Hibiscus Star, one of the main dining rooms. "At least we have a porthole window."

"True."

"Are you alone?" Angelina asked.

"My husband and I are moving to Hawaii. He has family there. I was supposed to travel with him but last-minute details kept me at my office longer than I expected. Rather than fly, he insisted I enjoy a little luxury and cruise to Hawaii." The words tumbled from Rachel's lips in an unending rush. "He arrived in Honolulu a few days ago. Hilo is our first port on December 25 and Honolulu is our second port on

December 26. Happily, Fred and I will celebrate Christmas together when the ship docks, although I'll be a day late."

Christmas. Happy celebrations. Once upon a time.

Memories flooded to the surface of Angelina's mind. A tiny evergreen tree set up in an equally tiny living room in the first apartment she and Jake, her late husband, ever shared. The burned turkey she'd served on Christmas Day—and the good-natured ribbing that followed.

How long had it been since she celebrated Christmas? Certainly not since Jake had died.

Rachel went on. "I'm officially retired from my demanding job to assume my new role as a stay-at-home mom. Thus, I'm eating for two." She lifted her ice cream cone for a last bite. "Fred and I have been married ten years and are finally expecting our first child."

Angelina picked up her glass to toast the expectant mother. "Congratulations."

"Thanks. I'm proof that miracles can happen at any age."

This was the part where Angelina should say something about experiencing her own miracles, or at least smile politely or murmur agreement. But a miracle had never happened to her.

A Christmas marvel, during God's most joyful season of the year.

Fanciful hopes. Fanciful dreams.

Rachel gestured toward the sunset—cotton-candy pinks and oranges canvassing the sky. "Nothing is as enchanting as a Los Angeles sunset. Especially when you're saying good riddance."

Angelina blinked. "I'm sorry?"

"Don't be sorry. I'm certainly not."

"I take it you don't like California?"

"I'm tired of all the noise and traffic. It's not good for me or the baby." Protectively, Rachel patted her stomach. "Are you a California native?"

"Yes." Angelina again put her glass aside. "I live near Hollywood."

"Lucky you." Rachel made no attempt to hide the sarcasm in her voice.

"It's not bad. I'm used to the buzz and in-a-hurry life-style." Angelina propped her elbows on the railing and took in a breath of fresh sea air. "Both my parents were involved in the acting business, so I'm used to it."

"I've always been enamored by Hollywood. Can I tell you a secret?"

"Let me guess. You wanted to be an actress and ended up bartending instead? That's the story I hear most often."

Rachel laughed. "No, I'm an accountant."

"So, what's your secret?"

"This was all Fred's idea."

Angelina snapped her head around. "The baby was Fred's idea?"

"Not the baby." Rachel's green eyes twinkled with mirth. "We're thrilled about the baby. I meant moving to Hawaii, although now I'm glad he talked me into it—a thrilling new adventure." She pulled her cellphone from her caftan pocket and scrolled to a picture of an older man sporting a gray mustache. "This is Fred."

"He's ..."

"Older than me. Yes. He's twenty years my senior. He was my professor in grad school and ever since we met we've been madly in love." She batted her eyelashes in playful coquetry, then sobered. "Fred's grandmother lives in Honolulu." Rachel inclined her head toward the miles and miles of ocean. "You mentioned your boss booked this cruise. I assume you're traveling on business?"

"I'm a screenwriter, and got a coveted assignment from a colleague to write a romantic comedy about Hawaii."

"Lucky you. Screenwriting must be very interesting—rubbing shoulders with all those famous actors and actresses."

"I've never met any of them." Angelina gave a helpless laugh. "Although screenwriting is my passion."

When she wasn't punching a clock with Mr. Stick-in-the-Mud Volcanologist.

"While you're on board, make time for fun. Cruising is so romantic." Rachel flashed a wicked grin. "Where's your flower, by the way?"

"What flower?"

"I don't see a flower tucked behind your left or right ear."

Enjoying Rachel's teasing and personable humor, Angelina teased right back. "I don't see a flower tucked behind your ear, either. And I confess I don't know the difference."

"If a woman is taken she wears a flower behind her left ear. If she's not, she wears a flower behind her right ear. It's part of the Hawaiian culture. When I get off the ship to meet Fred in Honolulu, I'll wear a flower." Rachel sighed dreamily. "Please forgive me for prying, I'm a hopeless romantic. There's no special man in your life?"

Somehow, Angelina knew Rachel didn't want to be forgiven as long as she received an answer. "I'm not convinced I need romance," Angelina said. "I was married … once."

Rachel was quiet, studying her. "And now you're divorced?" she finally asked.

"And now I'm a widow." Angelina choked back a sorrow that never went away. All the heartbreak returned in a rush—the familiar pressing ache in her chest, a soreness in her lungs that never ceased.

"I'm sorry for your loss," Rachel said. "You must have been devastated."

"I was." Angelina swallowed. "We were only married a short time."

Gently, Rachel touched Angelina's hand. "I don't know what to say."

"Thank you. It happened a long time ago."

"With your good looks you're probably fighting off hordes of men."

"I'm not interested in dating." Self-consciously, Angelina moved away. "I'm focused on establishing my career. Screenwriting is highly competitive."

Lately, though, she questioned whether perfecting a screenplay about Hawaii hadn't been done a hundred times before. Devon had insisted she explore ways her story could have a greater effect on her audience when it was put on film. A different pitch, he insisted, to add a hook to her romance.

Rachel tucked a silvery-red strand of hair behind her ear. "Screenwriting is an enjoyable and lucrative field?"

"Enjoyable, yes. Lucrative? Well, hopefully. The movie is just about ready to shoot and we'll see how it's received by audiences when finished."

"And you didn't have any family wanting to come along for the cruise?"

Angelina smiled at the abrupt change in topics. Rachel would certainly prove to be an interesting roommate.

"I wouldn't have time to spend with them," she said. "Plus, the studio is picking up the tab. My mom is touring Europe for the holidays, and I'll phone my dad on Christmas Day."

At Rachel's inquisitive expression, Angelina further explained, "My father recently got married again and fancied spending a few days alone with his new wife, Delphine."

His *third* wife, but Angelina didn't add that part.

Don't judge, she told herself. *If Delphine makes Dad happy, then I should be happy for them.*

And she was, although the empty days between now and New Year's would be difficult to fill, even if she was occupied with a romantic screenplay and on-board Christmas entertainments and exotic Hawaii. Still, she didn't have any siblings, so she was used to being alone. She could even say that her childhood had been a lonely one.

"There's lots to do before we reach Hilo, our first port," Rachel said. "Christmas movies will be shown by the pool, and a Hawaiian dessert-making class is slated for Christmas Day. Plus, there's a Santa parade for the little ones."

"Yes, the ship's holiday calendar is remarkable." Angelina took a final swallow of her iced tea. "There's even a carol singalong at the Anthurium Theater."

"Do you like to sing?" Rachel asked.

"I love to sing."

"You look like an angel and you probably sing like an angel."

"Hardly, but my singing is passable. Thanks for the compliment, though."

"Count me in for the informative presentations. And …" Rachel gave a wistful glance toward the ice-cream bar. "I'm debating about eating another cone."

Angelina laughed. "It's up to you."

"I'll wait." Rachel blew out a sigh. "What was I saying?"

"Informative lectures."

"Oh right. I can't believe Dr. Caleb Sloane agreed to give on-board lectures. He reserves his speaking engagements to overseas assignments and was in Malaysia recently."

Angelina held up a hand. "I know all about Dr. Sloane."

The corrections he'd initially sent her were a little too terse for her liking. Afterward, the tense emails and texts they exchanged confirmed her opinion. She got the feeling

Dr. Sloane assumed she was uneducated and unconcerned about scientific accuracy, especially if it got in the way of a good story.

Thankfully, they only needed to dig away at her screenplay for a few days.

"He's one of the world's leading volcanologists and a noted scientist." Rachel peered longingly at the buffet offerings in an adjacent dining room—a pasta and pizza station, meat carvery, and an assortment of desserts. Then her gaze swung to a group of people standing across from them on the deck. "Angelina, there he is. I recognize him from his picture on the promotional cruise materials. And wow, look at him." Rachel gestured toward a tall, handsome man. His dark hair was shaggy and pulled into a short ponytail at his nape.

Angelina studied him. "That's Dr. Sloane?"

"Yes. I thought you knew all about him."

"Just through emails and texts." Angelina set her empty glass on the table. "I'd never even heard of a volcanologist until I started this project."

She glanced back at him, briefly catching his cool gaze. So he was the man who made her feel uneducated and inexperienced? She'd expected a short, balding fellow sporting a polka-dotted bowtie and tweed jacket. Instead, this man was certainly good-looking, in a rugged sort of way. Despite herself, she kept watching him. He wore khaki pants and his collared navy polo shirt hugged his broad shoulders. He was trim and fit, most likely from all the climbing and field research that went along with his job.

"He's the most eligible bachelor on this ship," Rachel said.

An unexpected shiver of attraction went through Angelina, and she willed it away. They'd be working on a special project together and this was a professional relationship. That is, if they didn't kill each other first.

He was speaking earnestly with a perky brunette who seemed to hang onto his every word. Seeming to realize Angelina continued to stare, he glanced up. Briefly, he met her gaze with an extremely blasé one of his own, and her self-assurance slipped a notch.

I don't want to be here, his demeanor seemed to shout. *Get me off this ship.*

This wasn't her fault, Angelina wanted to shout back at him. He was the brainy professor the studio—and the cruise ship—had endorsed, and the reason her script was delayed.

He went back to talking with the brunette, and Angelina went back to her iced tea before she realized she'd finished it. She scowled at the empty glass.

Okay, Dr. Sloane. Any fascination she may have felt toward him certainly hadn't been reciprocated.

"Are you listening to me?" Rachel asked.

Angelina met her inquiring stare. "Yes. Well, no, actually."

"I asked if you planned on attending Dr. Sloane's lecture tomorrow morning?"

"I have no choice. He's the reason I'm on board."

"He's written scores of research papers that have been published in leading scientific journals." Rachel grinned, and the numerous freckles on her cheeks seemed to pop. "Fred's a geology enthusiast, and I'm somewhat of an expert myself. Dr. Sloane is the most knowledgeable man on the planet when it comes to volcanic research."

"Yes, yes." Angelina nodded. "Good to know." Although she already knew, thanks to the movie studio's accolades.

"I'm glad we're going to be roomies." Rachel patted Angelina's hand. "And just think … we reach our final destination in only a few days."

Angelina opened her mouth to remind Rachel the cruise was roundtrip for everyone except Rachel. And Dr. Sloane.

Devon had told Angelina that Dr. Sloane was taking a new assignment in Hawaii.

"I wanted to stay up for the buffet, but nowadays I'm tired all the time," Rachel said with a sighing laugh. "I can always order room service if I get hungry."

"I'll leave now too. I can't get oriented, and I've already gotten lost a couple times."

"Aren't you hungry?" Rachel asked.

"Here? On the *Bird of Paradise?*" Angelina pointedly looked around at the different food stations. She was about to comment on the overabundance of food when her cell phone buzzed inside her purse. She pulled it out and clicked on a text message from C. Sloane:

I understand you're in need of my assistance. Please attend my lecture tomorrow morning at eight a.m. in room 104. Plan on meeting with me afterwards.

He didn't ask. He simply stated.

Annoyed, she began texting a sharp reply.

She paused. No, that would never do. She was a talented, experienced screenwriter who'd done a sound job on her research. And she'd begin their face-to-face work relationship by proving she was a true professional.

I'll be there promptly at 8, she texted back.

She tucked her phone in her purse and met Dr. Sloane's stare from across the deck. He gave a quick nod, then turned on his heel and strode in the opposite direction.

So he had recognized her. How had he known what she looked like? And why hadn't he come over to personally introduce himself rather than send a text message?

The answer was simple. The man was beyond impossible. Thankfully, once they parted ways when they reached Hawaii, they'd happily never see each other again.

CHAPTER 2

*C*aleb Sloane organized his notes one last time in his deluxe suite on the upper deck of the *Bird of Paradise*. He appreciated the fresh orchids in his bathroom, the oversized basket of native Hawaiian fruit—mango, pineapple, and papaya—on the coffee table, and the Swarovski Optic binoculars.

And, of course, he was flattered that Devon, the producer of the highly-acclaimed Partridge Production Studios, had called him personally. Caleb was reviewing a movie script about Hawaii for accuracy, and the woman who'd written the screenplay would be attending his on-board lectures. The cruise line had offered him a generous salary, which coincided with his plans to accept a new position on Maui. Plus, he had a second cousin on the island whom he hadn't seen in years. He planned to visit him and his wife over the Christmas holiday.

Sometimes things worked out perfectly.

Caleb had just finished spearheading a project studying Mount Rainier, a dead volcano, while working as a professor at Washington State University. The Hawaiian Kīlauea volcano, which was near Maui, was very much alive. He anticipated continuing a fulfilling career with his research in Maui at Haleakala crater, currently a dormant volcano. Measuring ten thousand feet, it was Maui's highest point. Of course, with the ever-active volcanoes in the Hawaiian islands, he would travel wherever he was needed.

Nothing wrong with spending Christmas in one of the most beautiful places on the planet, he rationalized. And perhaps, just perhaps, he could finally make peace with his failed marriage.

Because some things didn't work out perfectly.

He set down his notes and stared out the expansive window of his suite, the sliding glass doors, and the balcony beyond. The sun had risen, and the day boasted a resplendent blue sky.

For the thousandth time he wondered how Mona, his ex-wife, could have found science boring. At the end of their marriage she'd actually told him how much she despised his long-winded technical explanations concerning his latest studies.

Prior to the divorce, he had been focused on becoming the greatest volcanologist the University of Washington had ever hired. However, these past few months he'd begun to wonder if Mona had been right. Perhaps he was too focused on his occupation. Perhaps he needed better balance in his life.

Do something different. Meet new people. Shed his stuffy reserve.

He uncapped a bottle of water and took a sip. Well, this was the time and the place. He was moving to Hawaii to begin a new chapter in his life.

He adjusted his tie, picked up his notes and briefcase, and strode down the hallway and a flight of stairs to the lecture room. Although he never presented his research to the general public, he assumed this audience would be respectful, at least those few who might attend. The cruisers he had observed the previous evening had seemed more interested in entertainment: food, dancing, and casinos. Consequently, he didn't expect a crowd, especially at eight in the morning.

A lecture about volcanoes, violent eruptions and sulfuric acid entering the stratosphere? The only person who should be in attendance was Angelina Conte, the screenwriter who didn't seem the least bit interested in accuracy.

He hoped there was a pot of freshly brewed Kona coffee in the lecture room. The delicious, rich coffee was served everywhere on the ship—a reminder of an upcoming excursion to the coffee farm on Kona, one of their last stops.

He'd skipped breakfast because he hadn't been hungry. The constant motion of the ship had doused his appetite. All part of getting his sea legs, he supposed.

He strode into the air-conditioned lecture room and ensured that the slide projector and handouts were set up. After a brief meeting with Angelina, he'd grab coffee, return to his suite, and wrap up a final paper to be published in an open-access journal.

A particularly strong wave rocked the ship, and he held onto a chair until the motion subsided. He blew out a breath and steadied himself. These up-and-down, side-to-side movements were never-ending.

Contrary to his expectations, the room filled quickly, and he took his place at the front behind the podium. A pregnant woman occupied a seat in the first row and smiled at him. He acknowledged her smile with one of his own. He'd noticed her the previous evening chatting with Angelina.

Promptly at eight o'clock, he greeted the attendees, introduced himself, and turned off the lights. His first slide showed the earth's crust and he went into a lengthy explanation about its cracks and weaknesses. Then, he expounded on density and pressure.

"And," he said, gesturing toward the slide screen, "although numerous factors can trigger a volcanic eruption, the most important three are—"

Someone knocked on the lecture room door. Before he could move, the pregnant woman in the front row stood, flicked on the lights and opened the door.

"Excuse me," the lovely woman with curly blonde hair whispered as she slipped into the room.

Angelina Conte.

He greeted her with a grim smile. "Please come in. We started without you."

"I apologize, Dr. Sloane." Her blue eyes were wide and unassuming, arresting against her delicate features. "I'm usually never late and—"

"No problem at all." His irritated tone completely belied his words. "Please find a seat." He gestured toward a vacant chair in the back of the room.

"Thank you."

Somehow, she managed to disrupt every person in the last row before finally settling in.

She looked at him and mouthed *sorry*.

Pointedly, he peered at his watch, then at her. Half past eight. This was his first lecture, and she'd already missed half. She was putting in her time, as the studio directed, although she obviously had no intention of taking his suggestions.

For a long moment, he said absolutely nothing while he continued to gaze at her.

She carried a half-open briefcase and her hair was still wet—presumably from a quick shower. Her pale ringlets were pinned into a messy bun, and tendrils escaped with every turn of her head.

He went back to his slide presentation. His concentration had been ruined, though. Three times in three minutes, he lost track of what slide he was presenting. Decidedly distracted, he still finished his presentation promptly at nine o'clock to enthusiastic applause. In his haste to organize his notes in order to meet with Angelina, he almost missed the line forming to speak with him.

He set down his notes. As was his custom, he allowed time to talk with anyone interested in his field. After some minutes of discussion, the pregnant woman came forward.

"I'm Rachel," she said. Although she'd been seated in the front row, she now stood with Angelina at the rear of the line. "My husband and I respect all you're doing, Dr. Sloane. Volcanic exploration has always interested us." She stepped aside to allow Angelina space to come forward. "And you already know my roommate."

"Ah, that explains the connection." He crossed his arms. "Can someone please explain to me why one roommate is punctual and the other is late?"

"I got lost." Angelina tossed her head, sending blonde curls around her face. "Rachel and I are on a lower deck, and my sense of direction is lousy."

"Going from the first floor to the second floor is difficult?" He collected his notes and gave them a crisp thump before placing them in his briefcase.

Her full lips curved into an unrepentant smile. "It's a big ship."

"Fortunately, you now know the way to the lecture room. Can I assume you'll be on time tomorrow?"

"I'll draw a map." Her smile lit her bright blue eyes, reflecting a hint of mischief.

Her blunt reply made him laugh. "I'm pleased to finally meet you in person, Mrs. Conte."

"Call me Angelina. I'm not married."

"Angelina it is." He held out his hand. "By the way, you're looking a bit pale, Angelina."

She accepted his hand and shook firmly. "And so are you, Dr. Sloane."

"Caleb."

"Alright." She hesitated. "Caleb."

"I'll blame my paleness on seasickness. What's your excuse? Partying until dawn?"

"You're right about the partying, although it wasn't me. There's a nightclub, Coconuts Disco Bar, directly above our cabin." She glanced at Rachel who affirmed her words with a nod. "I was working on my script until very late to the pounding of a disco beat. Before you assume things about other people, you should—"

"How fun that you two will be working your fingers to the bone together on *Aloha to Love*," Rachel interrupted with a cheerful smile.

"Yes," Angelina said. "Our mutual boss, Devon, is a stickler for accuracy."

"As well he should be." Caleb still held Angelina's hand in his. Her soft, lovely hand. "Your boss promised me the world in order to get me on this ship, and offering lectures is an added bonus for me."

"Cruise ships aren't normally your thing?" she asked.

"All this extravagance? No. I'm more suited to geology and digging rocks."

She grinned. "Well, then, welcome to the world of Hollywood."

He couldn't help responding to her smile. Nor could he help noticing that her figure was tall and straight, her face heart-shaped. Her flowery dress, a light powder blue, enhanced her bright eyes. She was pretty and slender, shoulders firmly back, yet something in the way she carried herself reminded him of an elusive bird.

Rachel cleared her throat. "I'm heading for the breakfast buffet and will catch up with you later, Angelina." She looked meaningfully at Angelina's and Caleb's hands. They were still joined.

Angelina flushed and pulled her hand from his. "Shall we begin, Dr. Sloane?" She set her briefcase on the table next to his lecture materials.

The ship took that moment to execute another slow roll, and he briefly closed his eyes. Although he'd set up this meeting, he realized now was not a good time. If he could go right back to his suite, he could rest for a while, and then he could finish his journal submission.

"Actually, I'm not feeling well," he said. "What do they prescribe—"

"For seasickness?" She gave him a knowing look. "My father got seasick on more than one occasion after he bought a sailboat. His sailing adventures did not last long."

"Or yours?" Caleb asked.

"Or mine." She smiled. "The ship's medic will give you a tiny pill. It will help, although you may feel a little fuzzy afterwards." She picked up her briefcase and matched his stride as he headed for the doorway. "In the meantime, I can fetch you a glass of ginger ale. Or tea? It's no bother."

He nodded. "Thanks for the offer, but I'm fine, really."

He certainly didn't want this woman, with whom he would be collaborating, to see him vulnerable. "Since we're on a tight time schedule and the studio needs the script, can we meet for dinner instead?"

"Where?"

"Santorino's Italian Bistro on the upper deck at seven? Nothing too fancy."

"Your treat?" She grinned.

He chuckled. They both knew there was no charge for meals on the all-inclusive cruise.

"Absolutely," he said. "As long as you treat next time."

"It's a deal. See you tonight, Caleb."

"I'll look forward to it, Angelina."

A slight swing graced her steps as she walked away.

He smiled at the bizarre about-face of his opinion toward her. Never in their correspondence had he visualized this beautiful, competent woman—part spitfire and part angel.

He mounted the steps back to his suite.

Angelina Conte. He'd treated her with impatience, but within the next few days, he'd try to make amends.

CHAPTER 3

*T*he food at Santorino's Bistro matched the culinary quality of the entire ship, Caleb decided. The cuisine was five-star. Hungrier than he'd anticipated, he savored the meal, as well as enjoying the company of the delightful woman sitting across from him at the cozy, checker-clothed table.

"A Michelin chef supervises and cooks at this restaurant," Angelina had told him when they entered the sun-dappled outdoor terrace, where he pulled out a chair for her. "Which translates to we're going to be fed superbly."

More than an hour later, he wholeheartedly agreed. When their tiramisu and the excellent Kona coffee were nearly finished, she drew her laptop from her ever-present leather briefcase. Eyebrows furrowed, she clicked keys and studied the screen for a couple minutes, then looked up at him.

"Your background is stellar, Caleb, although I already knew about your research in Washington and Mount Rainier." She swiveled her computer toward him.

He examined the screen. "You looked me up on

Wikipedia?"

"Why not?" She moved her coffee cup aside. "I like to know who I'm collaborating with, although the word is out" —she tapped the screen—"that you're a genius."

"Don't believe everything you hear." Thoughtfully, he swirled the last drop of coffee in his cup. "Should I look you up on Wikipedia?"

A beaming smile lit her features. She was so pretty when she smiled.

"You can, but I won't be listed. I'm just an ordinary day-to-day struggling screenwriter hoping *Aloha to Love* is a huge success." She tilted her head. "Is your research in Washington finished?"

"Yes. I've been offered an interesting and rewarding position in Hawaii."

A waiter wearing a black collared shirt and black pants approached the table. At Caleb's dismissive shake of his head, he soundlessly withdrew.

"So," she said, "this screenplay project worked out well for you because you were traveling to Hawaii, anyway."

"Perfectly." He set his white porcelain coffee cup down on its saucer. As Angelina had predicted, the ship's medic had prescribed a pill for his seasickness and the cure seemed to be on track. His brain was still foggy, though, especially after a heaping plate of pasta. Managing a smile, he tried to concentrate on her words.

For dinner, they'd relished a wide range of Italian dishes, including antipasto, homemade pasta and fresh fish. They had eaten on the terrace overlooking the ocean. Now the sun had set and moonlight gleamed silver on the ocean's swirls. Angelina's blonde tendrils blew around her face in the gentle nighttime breeze.

While he listened to upbeat Christmas music provided by

an unobtrusive pianist, he relaxed in his chair and gazed at her.

She presented an enchanting picture. Her flawless, creamy complexion glowed, and her blue eyes gleamed. She was a woman of contrasts, which fascinated him. In the course of their association, she'd treated his emails with cool professionalism, switching to indignation when she disagreed with his changes to her script, and then her teasing cheekiness when she'd checked out his Wikipedia page.

Each facet of her personality was utterly charming. And she was a good script writer, although he hadn't complimented her. Not yet. First, he'd ensure her script evolved from Hollywood nonsense to a smart, factual story.

Over a last bite of biscotti, he found he couldn't concentrate on anything except the smidgen of basil on her cheek.

"Caleb?" she asked.

"Hmm?"

"Shouldn't we discuss the first scene in my script that needs to be fixed?"

"Certainly." He finished his coffee and folded his hands, definitely feeling better.

Their waiter discreetly removed plates and silverware, then freshened their cups of coffee.

"Have you read my script?"

He reached across the table and lightly brushed the offending basil from her cheek. "Most of it."

A strong wind gusted, sending Angelina's striped green scarf fluttering around her shoulders. She retied it and smiled cautiously. "Then you know that in the first scene, the heroine is researching an exotic yellow-headed bird, found only in Hawaii's volcanic areas, for a weekly blog on Hawaiian birds. The name of this particular bird is the palila."

He fixed an encouraging smile on his face. *"Loxioides bailleui."*

"I'm not putting that long name into the script." She drew back. "The actors will never be able to pronounce it, so I'm sticking with palila. The bird only lives on the dormant Mauna Kea volcano in Hawaii, correct?"

"Very good." He nodded approvingly. "So, you've done a little research."

"More than a little, and I'd appreciate if you didn't insult my work ethic at every turn."

"My apologies for my rudeness, past and present." In the spirit of relaxed friendliness, he added, "Although your motto should be, 'accuracy at all costs.'"

"Apologies accepted, and I'll consider your motto as long as it doesn't derail the entire story." She graced him with a poised smile and again swiveled her computer so they both could read the screen. "In the first scene," she repeated with emphasis, "the hero owns property at the base of the Mauna Kea volcano and the heroine needs his permission to be on the property to continue her study there."

"Mauna Kea is a very tall mountain."

"Yes."

"And the air at the top is very thin."

"Yes."

He folded his hands. "First, owning property near a volcano is risky. What does your hero do for a living?"

"He runs a successful restaurant. However, he inherited a plot of farmland at another volcano nearby from his father. The hero is having second thoughts about the restaurant, because he's beginning to feel that farming is a real part of his heritage. That's the root of the story, and that conflict will be resolved in the final scenes."

Caleb nodded. "Will there be an eruption at this other volcano?"

"Yes, to add drama, although the aftermath won't affect the main characters. However, I'll treat the scene carefully. I know and respect the devastation a volcanic eruption can bring to people living nearby."

For a moment, he was quiet.

"Do you?" he asked softly.

"I've seen the evacuations on television." She studied him. "Are you all right?"

"I've also seen the evacuations, but first-hand. The widespread panic and devastation ..." He shook his head. "The flow of red-hot lava came within only a few miles of the small village near my hotel."

"I'm so sorry." She kept her gaze on the computer screen, then took a deep breath and turned to him. Her eyes gleamed with shiny tears. "I'm trying to bring love and laughter to the big screen so people can forget their problems, at least for a little while."

Caleb's annoyance at what he perceived as her flippant attitude toward volcanic eruptions faded. He had told himself two dozen times to be patient with her when they'd corresponded by email. Now, noting her quivery smile, he saw his patience had been worthwhile. She was astute, had done due diligence, and—contrary to his earlier opinion of her based on her script—she cared about other people's suffering.

"Please continue," he said.

"The hero's refusing because he's been scammed before by a woman and has trust issues," she said. "Subsequently, he's being difficult." She cast him a sidelong grin. "You know how men can be."

"Do I?" Surely she wasn't insinuating *he* was difficult.

She continued grinning and didn't answer his question. "Anyway, the hero finally grants permission, and the heroine finds the birds' habitats—"

"Which will be near impossible. The palila is almost extinct and your heroine would be forced to hike the mountain to the upper slopes to find it, which we've already established is a very tall mountain and, incidentally, can get snow in the winter. One estimation is that there are only 1300 remaining palila birds in existence." He leaned close to her. "And do you know why?"

"Because of the volcano?"

He shook his head. "Mauna Kea's last eruption is estimated to have occurred 4500 years ago."

"Then why?"

"Because of the mamane tree."

She typed the word into a search engine. "The birds are becoming extinct because of a tree?"

"If you completed your research, you'd know the trees are eaten by feral goats and sheep. They ate all the mamane at the lower levels, forcing the birds to move to the upper slopes."

Her gaze swung from him to a group of guests admiring the restaurant's tasteful design. Like the décor of the entire ship, Santorino's was lavishly adorned with pots of red poinsettias. Sprigs of red holly berries weaved through linen placemats, all lending festive color and merriment to an already warm, inviting place.

She turned back to him. "Caleb, what does all this mamane information have to do with the heroine?"

"The heroine is searching for a bird she'll never be able to find, at least not realistically."

"I thought you were a volcano expert, not a bird expert."

"It's your script." He shrugged. "But anyone who is familiar with the palila will know your scene isn't correct. Don't assume your audience is ignorant to scientific facts."

"I've never assumed anything of the sort." Frowning, she glanced from her computer to his face. "What are you suggesting?"

Their waiter appeared again, and Caleb signaled to pour them both a glass of water. "Change your scene to something your heroine can credibly search for."

"If every line in a movie is changed because of all these endless details, then no movie would ever be made."

He remained silent for a beat. "You mean no movie of *quality* would ever be made." He smiled. He was feeling better and better.

"The arts are equally as important as science."

"I'm not refuting you. I appreciate the arts, as I assume you do."

Her smile was wide, reaching her expressive eyes. "What would the world be like without artists and musicians and writers? I imagine it would be quite dull."

He nodded in agreement. A part of him wanted to become reacquainted with theater and opera, reading popular fiction versus research reports, watching a movie purely for enjoyment. He wondered if those interests had anything to do with the entrancing Angelina, or were instead part of his new motto to shed his reserve.

Both, he supposed.

After his divorce, he had limited his choice of women to those who weren't complex. He wanted zero claims on his feelings. However, intuition voiced a clear objection in Angelina Conte's case. Nothing about the woman was simple, and her tug on his emotions was surprisingly real.

"Well, Mr. Volcano Expert?" The woman in question lifted her small, delicate chin and regarded him. "Any ideas?"

"On what?"

"On another bird the heroine can search for."

"She can research a native Hawaiian forest bird." His hand paused in the act of accepting the water glass the waiter offered. "For example, use the apapane. The bird is bright crimson and easy to spot."

Quickly, Angelina shifted her computer in order for him to see her type in the bird change. "Better?"

Satisfied, he prompted her to lift her water glass. "Good. Now we're both on the same page."

"Literally." She clinked her glass against his, then stared, trancelike, at the endless ocean waters.

He watched her and pretended he didn't. Completely unexpected, this attraction.

"Caleb?" She set down her water glass and tapped her computer screen with her tapered fingernail. "Will you read the end of the first scene with me?"

Spurred on by the pleasant feeling prompted by the tiny pill and a plateful of carbohydrates, he felt positively benevolent.

"I'm at your disposal. Let's go to a corner booth in the neighboring lounge where it's quieter." To illustrate his point, he gestured toward a large group of cruisers being seated at a table near them.

With a smile, Angelina agreed.

He helped her collect her computer and handbag and then tucked her hand into the crook of his arm as he led her from the restaurant.

Once they were seated in an empty alcove in the adjacent outdoor lounge, Angelina requested two glasses of water and a bowl of macadamia nuts. "I love these nuts, and the ship gets them fresh." She popped a handful into her mouth and then positioned her computer in the middle of the table. "Now I'll be the heroine. Her name is Angela. You can be Charles, the hero." She pointed to the computer screen. "I'll go first. All you have to do is read Charles's lines."

"You're the boss."

She lifted a delicate blonde eyebrow. "As you're most

certainly aware, you've become the go-to person for this entire project."

"Surely you can agree that we're all tired of Hollywood movies using a veneer of science and getting too many details wrong."

"Yes, of course. Okay, now. Here goes." She sat straighter, her demeanor changing as she assumed the role of Angela. She zoomed in until the dialogue showed clearly.

"'Charles,'" she began, reading the script, "'please permit me to research the apapane for my blog.'"

"The heroine has a blog?" Caleb asked.

"Yes, a Hawaiian bird blog."

"Only Hawaiian birds? Why not all birds?"

"She's not Audubon, Caleb." Angelina changed the wording in the script. "But yes, sure, she can blog about all different types of birds."

She cleared her throat to continue. "'Charles, I realize I'm on your land, but I'm asking you just this one time.'" Slowly, she raised her eyes to Caleb's, her expression full of expectation.

His composure briefly cracked.

"Your turn, Caleb."

He dragged his gaze from her face and read the next line. "'I'm considering your proposal, Angela. However, I'll need a little more persuasion. May I suggest you move your chair a little closer?'"

She frowned, looking from her screen to him. "That line isn't in the script."

"It should be, considering what happens next."

She didn't follow his prompting, turning her computer away from him.

"Before we continue," she said, "I'm double-checking the primary food source."

He recognized the flower as soon as it appeared on her computer screen.

"How do you pronounce the name of this flower?" she asked.

"The lehua is the official flower of Hawaii, and it's pronounced just the way it's spelled. The flower comes from the 'ōhi'a tree, and it's the food source for the apapene when in bloom." Quickly, he added, "Just remember, the flower isn't in bloom all the time."

Angelina typed the name into the script. "The bird's primary food source is the lehua, a flower." She looked up and gave him a warning frown. "And we'll assume the flower is in bloom, so don't give me fifty reasons why it can't be."

"I bow to your superior judgment."

"Yes, yes."

He lifted his shoulders. Genius, she'd called him. Well, he wasn't conversing much like a genius now. Surely he could do better.

"Try again?" she prompted.

"Certainly."

She expelled a breath and resumed her role as the heroine. She feigned picking a flower and sniffing it as the script dictated. "'Oh, Charles, the scent of the lehua flower is so sweet.'"

Caleb nodded curtly.

"Your turn." She cut her gaze to the computer screen.

"I won't read the next line. A man would never say that."

"Then make something up, Caleb. This is the end of the scene and it's all leading up to the hero and heroine's first kiss."

"So if you put your lips on mine, I can respond however I'd like?" He straightened, giving his best impression that he was about to call the entire scene off if she didn't agree. He kept his expression bland while inwardly grinning.

She crossed her arms and looked him in the eye. "Yes, although you should stick to the script!"

He gazed back. The more time he spent with her, the more he liked her. Sure, she was a knockout, but she was also out of the ordinary in other ways. She didn't fit the type of woman who usually appealed to him, the brief dates that lasted only an evening. He wanted to spend time with her because he was interested in learning everything about her. Even chancier, she compelled him to show more about himself. Yes, precarious indeed. Most likely, she'd quickly become as bored with him as his ex-wife had.

"Well?"

"We'll resume where we left off."

"Take three," she announced. Smiling, she reassumed her role as Angela. "'Oh, Charles.'" She paused dramatically and sighed. "'The scent of the lehua flower is so sweet.'" She feigned sniffing a nonexistent flower and then pressed a chaste kiss on Caleb's lips.

Immediately, she pulled back.

The kiss had been featherlike and flickering, yet warm and inviting. Her lips were moist and soft. And being this close to her was tempting. Before this went any further, he stopped himself, bringing up the familiar shield protecting his heart.

"If that's the way your heroine persuades the hero," he said, "it's no wonder he doesn't offer to help her."

"Excuse me?"

With deliberate disinterest, Caleb sat back and inspected Angelina's face—her pert, turned-up nose, the color in her high cheekbones amplifying her scarcely hidden frustration. The shining moon gilded her blonde curls to a golden glow. And she looked unbelievably gorgeous in a silky forest-green sundress. A solitary, flawless rose in a sea of loud tourists and over-the-top Christmas decorations.

She waited a millisecond. "I can't help it if you're a lousy actor." Her face reddened, her expression positively indignant. "You could attempt to cooperate and make things easier."

He gave a lazy shrug. "Shouldn't the heroine's job be to motivate the hero? He needs a good incentive to trust again if he's been scammed."

Her eyes blazed. "I can do better if you can." She pulled her chair an inch closer, and her slim bare leg brushed against his. "I'll just pretend you're someone else."

"Really?" He stiffened. "Who?"

"Anyone on board this ship will do." She gestured to the stout, balding bartender at the adjoining bar.

"Oh?" Caleb considered her as an idea formed. Her attractiveness now aggravated him, rather than delighting him as it had done earlier, particularly since she was now examining her manicure.

Angelina Conte was definitely in need of a lesson, he decided. He'd finish the scene, but he was going to show her that a kiss was much more than a casual, calculated brush of the lips. Then, when he evoked a response, he'd separate himself and walk away.

"Shall we try again?" he asked nonchalantly. He leaned across the table, his mouth hovering over hers. This near, her scent reminded him of fragrant wildflowers.

"Take three," she said with a seductive half-smile. Her hand glided across his shoulders. "Or is it take four? What take are we on, Caleb?"

"I've lost count."

"I'll assume take four." She took a deep breath and again feigned a sniff at a non-existent flower. "'Oh, Charles, the scent of the lehua flower is so sweet.'"

She pressed her lips to his, drawing out the kiss, encouraging him to respond.

He shadowed her lead. However, whenever she drew back, so did he.

She tried to kiss him again. When he didn't respond a second time, she dropped her hand and sat back, visibly upset.

"I should have known you'd make even a simple scene difficult," she said.

Her words made him upset too, but not at her. He was upset with himself. For the first time since forever, he'd been dangerously close to losing control. The innocent brush of her lips against his, her light caresses across his shoulders, had nearly toppled his attempts to curb his instincts, which was to take her in his arms and thoroughly kiss her back.

"Shall I assume you're giving up?" he asked.

"I didn't give up." She drew a torn, frustrated breath. "I just got your message loud and clear. We're done."

She pushed back her chair, about to stand.

"You're a quitter?"

When she didn't answer, he pressed, "Are you?"

"Never."

He glanced at his watch. He wasn't in a hurry, but she didn't need to know that.

"Then finish the scene, and we can both get some rest."

"I warn you, this is the last time." She shot him a murderous glare. "Take five."

She feigned picking a flower, although she yanked the flower instead and then pointedly threw it over her shoulder. Like an accomplished actress, she flashed him a dazzling smile and transformed into Angela again.

"'Oh Charles, the scent of the 'whatever-it's-name' flower is so sweet.'"

He grinned. Merriment danced in her eyes.

He tipped up her chin. "Like you," he whispered. Unhurriedly, inch by inch, his mouth drew closer to hers.

She blinked. "I thought a man would never say anything like that."

"I changed my mind."

Yes, that was his genius side again. Scintillating conversation.

"Isn't changing one's mind a woman's prerogative?" she asked.

"Not when I'm the boss."

"I never said you were the boss."

"You most certainly did."

She gave a hard shake of her head. "Even if I did, that line isn't in the script, either."

"No, but this is." His hands moved from her chin to frame her cheeks. She didn't pull back. She simply considered him, inciting an unrestrained impulse. He pressed his mouth to hers, kissing her thoroughly. She tasted delightful, the tang of coffee and cool, creamy tiramisu lingering on her lips.

Faintly, she inhaled. "Caleb."

"This scene is getting better and better," he murmured.

She placed her fingers on his chest, a wedge between them. "This type of kiss would never happen in a first scene."

"Why not?"

"It's too ... too ... passionate. The hero and heroine have only just met."

"Then you'll have to rewrite the scene. You want it to be perfect, right?"

With a sigh, she whispered something about him being impossible and she wouldn't be rewriting the scene.

His mouth brushed against hers again, growing bolder. When her lips parted, he drew her into his arms and deepened the kiss.

CHAPTER 4

$\mathcal{T}$he following evening, Angelina secured a corner booth at O'Reilly's Irish Pub located on one of the cruise ship's upper decks. She ordered a glass of fresh-squeezed lemonade with a salt trim, the pub's signature drink. Despite her interest in attending the Christmas singa-long in the Anthurium Theater, she decided to work on her script instead.

While she waited for her lemonade, she went over her day, which had begun with attending Caleb's lecture. She'd been punctual, sitting at the front of the room with Rachel, and she'd asked a number of questions. His answers were professional, although he'd hardly spared her a glance while he went into detailed explanations about the movement and formation of molten rock beneath the earth's surface. By his anything-but-subtle disinterest, he told her in no uncertain terms he preferred their relationship continue on a professional level only.

Despite the kisses they shared the previous evening. The kisses she hadn't stopped thinking about. The feel of his mouth pressed to hers, his hard, muscled chest beneath her fingertips, brought her feelings to life. Feelings that had been dormant.

As she attempted to analyze her thoughts, she tried to come to terms with her reaction to him, because she hadn't stopped him from kissing her. And despite her reprimands to herself, she hadn't been able to stop thinking about him.

She touched her lips, recalling how he'd kissed her casually at first, then confidently. Why, oh, why had she returned his kisses? Had she done the right thing, acting out a romantic script with him?

Inwardly, she groaned. No, probably not. But the truth was, she had wanted their kiss to go on, go deeper, because it felt so right. Unfortunately, they'd been in a very busy lounge where the kiss couldn't continue.

Or rather, fortunately.

Because if they'd been somewhere else, what would have happened?

"Nothing," she said firmly. They were strictly coworkers.

Besides, she'd given up on men long ago. And in Dr. Sloane's case, her mind issued a firm warning: *The man is impossible. You know that. In addition, you'll only be seeing him a few more days.*

Therefore, the developing relationship, if anything in fact *was* developing, would soon be over.

So then, why had he kissed her so passionately? To follow a script he constantly disagreed with?

Exasperated, she blew out a breath. He certainly wasn't interested in emotional involvement.

Yay. Great. Because neither was she.

A waitress served her lemonade. As Angelina tasted the delightful salty and tart combination, she daydreamed, hardly noticing that the pub had become busy. A patron put a coin in the jukebox, and "Rockin' Around the Christmas

Tree" blared, bouncing against the bare wooden walls and jarring her back to the computer and her script.

She was tempted to plug in Caleb's name on social media. She brought up her favorite browser, typed in his name, and speculated whether or not he had a Facebook page as she waited for the results.

No, no, no.

She quickly logged off. Clearly, his presence on the ship wasn't helping her to get any work done.

Despite her intention of dismissing anything Caleb related, her thoughts stubbornly disobeyed and drifted back to him.

That morning when his lecture had finished, she'd hurried from the room while several class members had surrounded him. Changing into tennis shoes, yoga shorts, and a stretch knit T-shirt, she ran five laps around one of the ship's lower decks, despite a relentless wind, determined to push Dr. Caleb Sloane from her mind. Done. Move on. His life as a volcanologist in Hawaii was as far removed from a Hollywood scriptwriter as a walrus was from flying to Venus.

She drank more lemonade and told herself—again—to get back to work. Yet when she tried to focus on her script, she couldn't resist bringing up Caleb's Wikipedia page for a quick peek.

"Hey, Angelina."

As Rachel marched over to Angelina's booth, Angelina switched to her screenplay with a guilty start.

"I'm glad I found you," Rachel said. "You disappeared after the church service. Merry Christmas Eve." She squeezed into the seat across from Angelina. She'd purchased a one-shoulder blouse in hot pink from the ship's expensive gift shop and paired it with black chiffon palazzo pants. Both shirt and pants complemented her round belly shape.

"Merry Christmas Eve," Angelina echoed. Being on the ship, with the sea surrounding them and no snow in sight, there was a sense of timelessness, with one day already melting into the next.

Rachel ordered a glass of iced tea and a plate of potato pancakes from the chirpy waitress. After a few minutes of chatting about her latest email from her husband and what she was planning on ordering for dinner, she leaned close and asked, "Did you see Caleb slip into the church service? He sat in the back and knelt almost the entire time. Obviously praying."

Angelina had noticed. He obviously had God in his heart, which made him even more attractive. She'd always believed that God would lead her to the right man, and he had, her husband Jake. Surely, one love was enough for one lifetime.

The volume level in the pub increased as an Irish Celtic band took the stage and lifted their instruments—a flute, whistle and accordion.

"Wow, I came at the right time," Rachel said. "I love Celtic Christmas music!" She had to raise her voice to be heard above the din, and her over bright smile warned Angelina to brace herself. "As I was saying, I'm glad I found you. Are you intending to work late?"

Angelina massaged her temples. "Yes. Nonstop."

"On Christmas Eve?"

"I have no choice."

"But you're still attending the Christmas singalong with me tonight, right?"

"I can't." Moodily, Angelina contemplated her lemonade glass. "You know I can't."

"It'll be fun and a great way to usher in Christmas. Besides, the entire show lasts less than two hours, and the advertisement stated that everyone in the audience will leave"—she made finger quotes in the air—"'overflowing with the holiday spirit.'"

"The show will be delightful, I'm sure." Angelina drained her lemonade. "Although, as you know, my script is a few days away from being due."

The waitress set a pitcher of iced tea, an empty glass filled with ice, and an overflowing plate of potato pancakes on the table.

"I'm *always* hungry," Rachel said, as if she'd just noticed. "Eating constantly is common in the second trimester … and the first trimester. And most likely the third trimester. Besides, I'm eating for—"

"Two," Angelina finished. "I've never been pregnant, so I wouldn't know."

Rachel poured the iced tea. "How long were you married?"

"A little over a year." Angelina glanced at the musicians tuning up their instruments. "Jake and I wanted children, but our careers came first. We thought we had time."

Thoughtfully, Rachel chewed a pancake wedge. "You met with Caleb last evening for dinner." Her face registered no particular emotion, although her tone brimmed with excitement. "I noticed when you came into our cabin after midnight you were humming."

And that was the reason, Angelina realized, why Rachel had found her at the pub. It had little to do with girl talk or potato pancakes or a Celtic band playing Christmas music. Rachel wanted to discuss Angelina's work date with Caleb because she was an incurable romantic.

"I thought you were sleeping. I'm sorry." Unsure how to evade Rachel's statement, Angelina decided to deflect. "Did I disturb you?"

"Hardly. I'm so uncomfortable, I rarely sleep more than a couple hours at a time." Rachel patted her stomach. She did that often. "You have a lovely voice, by the way. I read an article in the newspaper that music will spur creativity."

"Which means?"

"Which means the Christmas singalong will be a perfect diversion for you." Rachel reached for three sugar packets and stirred them into her iced tea.

Angelina went back to her script.

After several gulps of tea, Rachel set down her glass. "Also, Caleb was looking for you this morning after you left the lecture so fast. He asked me where you'd gone off to."

Angelina's head snapped up. "Really? I doubt he even noticed I was there."

"He noticed, all right." Sagely, Rachel nodded. "He couldn't keep his eyes off you the entire sixty minutes of his lecture. And at the church service when he wasn't praying, I might add."

Angelina chewed her bottom lip, uncertain. He must have been watching her when she'd been taking notes. During the service, he'd sat behind them. Leave it to Rachel to check him out.

Noting Rachel's piercing gaze, Angelina drew a breath.

Should she confide in her new supporter and tell her that likewise, Angelina couldn't keep her eyes off him? Rachel would be thrilled that an exotic love affair on the open sea was brewing.

Although it wasn't.

Still, hadn't Rachel already declared that Caleb was the most eligible bachelor on the ship?

Angelina picked up her lemonade glass and circled the salty rim with her finger.

Contrariwise, if she told Rachel she had no interest in becoming romantically involved with any man because of losing her husband all those years ago, Rachel would sympathize. If Angelina revealed she felt like an adolescent schoolgirl around Caleb, but as a woman in her mid-thirties had no intention of acting like one, Rachel would commiserate.

She decided to say nothing and set her glass aside.

"You'll come with me, right?" Rachel forked a bite of potato pancake. "I don't want to attend a Christmas sing-along all by myself, especially on Christmas Eve."

The woman's eternal optimism, her enthusiasm for all things Christmas, seemed to increase with each passing hour.

Thanks to Gabriella De Luca, Angelina thought. Gabriella was the exuberantly sunny cruise director who drove the upbeat atmosphere of the entire vessel. And, of course, the hilarious Captain Berg, whose frequent updates, broadcast over the ship's loudspeaker, were a highlight of the day.

Angelina poised her fingers above the computer keyboard. "Are you certain the performance lasts under two hours?"

"I'm positive." Rachel finished her iced tea and poured another glass. "Bring your computer back to our cabin, and I'll meet you in front of the theater in thirty minutes. It's a couple decks below us. Please don't get lost."

* * *

EXACTLY THIRTY MINUTES LATER, Angelina arrived at the theater. She'd changed into a decidedly feminine lacy navy-blue sundress, high-heeled sandals, and a white linen cardigan. She assumed the theater was air-conditioned, as most public spaces were, and she didn't want to freeze.

Gaily, she mouthed a sunny aloha to Rachel as she made her way through the overcrowded theater. Then, in the act of waving, her hand stilled. Standing beside Rachel, and looking impossibly handsome in a white cotton shirt that complemented his tanned face, stood Caleb.

He smiled as she advanced, his white teeth gleaming. His

slim, stone-colored chinos fit the contours of his hips and legs to perfection, and her heart did a double-flip. Frustrated by her reaction, she attempted a cool, unflustered demeanor. Falling for a guy like him, any guy actually, wasn't part of her future. Adding to her discomfort of being around Caleb was the fact that her emotions had been colorless for years, no highs and no lows, even when she dated nice, attractive men. To her, those men were like white bread, flat and uninteresting, whereas Caleb reminded her of a good wine—concentrated, bringing out powerful feelings best buried beneath her work.

But suppose, just suppose, she could no longer shove those feelings to a side burner?

Certainly, her marriage to Jake had been happy, although perhaps too happy. Either way, she didn't intend to fall in love again. The agony of being left behind after the loss was too great. Remembering that sadness, she efficiently resurrected the safe, protective barricade. She had no intention of moving out of the comforting familiarity of the life she had built for herself.

"Surprise!" Rachel exclaimed as Angelina reached them.

"What's he doing here?" Angelina directed her question to Rachel.

"A little rude, don't you think?" Rachel asked bluntly, glancing at Caleb's frown. "Caleb and I ran into each other in the lobby as the cruise director explained shopping in Hilo. Then, when Gabriella announced the singalong would begin in fifteen minutes, I invited him to join us." Rachel beamed her brightest smile. "So now we're a threesome. I figured you both needed a night off from working."

"Thanks," Caleb and Angelina said simultaneously.

"Merry Christmas Eve, Angelina," he said. "I saw you at the church service."

"Merry Christmas. I saw you too."

The flickering of the lights signaled the show was ready to begin. She accepted a program from an usher dressed in a red velvet Santa hat and rubber elf ears, and chuckled. The *Bird of Paradise* deserved an award for the most festive yuletide celebration cruising the Pacific.

"I'll bet that Angelina is an excellent singer," Rachel remarked to Caleb as she led the way into the theater.

"And an excellent conversationalist," he said. "I've found her both of those things, and many more."

Angelina shrugged, then quietly thanked him. He was always generous when he referred to her.

Rachel twisted to Angelina. "Besides being an expert on volcanoes, Caleb's knowledgeable about everything Hawaiian."

"Believe me, not everything," he said.

"He was telling me he has extended family in Hawaii. A second cousin," Rachel added brightly.

If ever there was a matchmaker contest anywhere in the world, Angelina decided, Rachel would win first place hands down.

They jostled through the crowd and found seats with an excellent view of the stage while the enormous theater filled to capacity. Caleb sat on Angelina's right, Rachel on her left.

"You have a Hawaiian cousin?" Angelina shook the wrinkles from her lacy dress, then sank into the comfortable red velvet seat. "You never told me."

"Last evening, the subject of our extended families never came up." He carried off a dismissive shrug, his grin almost boyish. "As I recall, we were diverted by a particularly important scene in your script that took priority."

She searched his handsome face for signs of mockery but found only sincerity. Secretly pleased he remembered their kiss and was no longer acting as though she didn't exist—or worse, that she was an unmotivated science student failing his class—she ducked her head to hide her smile. Soon he'd learn she was determined to get every scientific detail right.

"Which proves you don't know everything about me, Angelina," he added. "I could be part Hawaiian."

"Are you?"

"No. I'm Scottish and Irish. You?"

"Mostly Italian. Although I know more about you, thanks to Wikipedia."

"Touché. However, I may have been checking you out on the Internet."

"Were you?"

"Is this confession time or showtime?" He gestured toward the rising curtain, then leaned back his head and laughed, a deep, throaty laugh that prompted a surprising warmth through her veins.

"Caleb told me Hawaii is the only state that grows coffee commercially," Rachel said.

Angelina slanted him a wry smile. "All this information is just floating around in your mind?"

He grinned. "Is that a compliment?"

His gentle teasing made her feel churlish because of her initial reaction when she saw him. Sighing, she accepted the fact that she liked being with him.

"Yes," she replied truthfully.

"And you look lovely tonight."

"Is that a compliment?"

Keeping his gaze locked to hers, he said tenderly, "Yes, and I mean every word."

"Let's all go for coffee after the concert," Rachel piped in. "There's a first-rate champagne buffet served all night on the observation deck. I can't drink because of my pregnancy, but I like buffets."

"I'm in," Caleb said.

Since Gabriella was on the stage introducing the

performers, Angelina only nodded agreement to both Caleb and Rachel. She hoped the observation deck wasn't too high, because sometimes she felt disoriented and dizzy when she was too far off the ground. Her mother blamed it on a senseless fear of heights.

When Angelina's emotional right-side brain agreed with her fear, it triggered anxiety. She combatted the fear by focusing on her left brain's intellectual ability, reassuring herself nothing was going to happen.

The singalong commenced with a hilarious rendition of the "Twelve Days Of Christmas" sung a cappella by twelve energetic singers. They were colorfully dressed as elves, in green velvet pants, jackets, and striped socks. Within seconds, the audience was joining the chorus with a rousing, "And a partridge in a pear tree."

Angelina sang every holiday carol, from a buoyant "Jingle Bells" to a German rendition of "Silent Night," letting the music wash over her. Rachel tapped her feet to the cadenced beats, her tone flat and out-of-tune, for which she apologetically shrugged and then sang with even more abandon. Enthusiastically, she pumped her fist in approval at the end of each song.

Caleb merged his rich baritone voice to the harmonies and winked appreciatively as Angelina belted out the melodies.

"I'm very impressed with your singing," he whispered between refrains.

"With me or with Rachel?"

"You, but don't let Rachel know," he teased.

"I heard that!" Rachel joked, attempting to look scandalized. "But no offense is taken."

"Your enthusiasm makes up for everything," Angelina said. "And I enjoy hearing you both."

Caleb touched her arm, fleeting and spontaneous, yet causing a flutter in her chest. "And I love hearing you."

"Thank you. Music is a passion of mine."

"Mine too, once upon a time." He nodded slightly. "I forgot how much I like to sing."

"And *you're* perfectly on pitch." She tried to speak matter-of-factly, tried to retain a dispassionate response to his smiles, but how could she when he sat so close with his arm touching hers, his soft breath stirring her hair while he sang? On the surface, he seemed remote, almost removed from the world. But the way he laughed with her, sang with her, she knew he wasn't cold or remote. For whatever reason, he was merely guarded.

"You're a better singer. Your voice is like an archangel's," he said.

"An archangel?" She grinned. "Well, that brings my voice to a whole new level."

He nodded. "And that's because an archangel is the chief messenger of God and higher than an angel." Before she could remark, he added, "I figured you liked to sing after our discussion yesterday and assumed you might attend the singalong this evening."

Hmm. Was that why he'd attended the show, because he hoped to see her? She mulled that over as her heart did a flip.

Perhaps.

She caught the sly, piercing look the eavesdropping Rachel gave her, and they exchanged smiles. Ever the romantic.

During intermission, Rachel excused herself to snag a bag of popcorn at the concession stand, while Caleb and Angelina chose to stay in their seats.

"Can I tell you a secret?" Caleb asked Angelina after Rachel had squeezed past them.

"Please, be my guest."

"I sang in the church choir when I was young." He bent his head, his warm breath tingling against her ear.

"I also sang in the church choir."

After a long, comfortable silence, he said, "So we've agreed on something else."

"We didn't *agree* to sing in the church choir together. That's a commonality between us, something we both did when we were children. Not an agreement." She scratched her cheek. "What else do you and I agree on?"

"The *Loxioides bailleui* bird."

"You mean the palila bird."

"Either name is correct, although mine is more scientific."

She laughed but declined to touch that loaded subject. Instead, she said, "I've never played a musical instrument, although I always wanted to learn how to play the piano."

"I'm a fairly competent pianist and took piano lessons for ten years. I'll teach you."

When? she wanted to ask. The ship would reach Hilo by morning.

Their conversation was interrupted by Rachel, who wedged around them while they stood to let her by.

"I can't play any musical instruments, either," Rachel remarked, obviously overhearing the conversation. Settling into her seat, she zeroed in on the large monitor positioned above the stage and the lyrics to the next Christmas carol typed in boldface. "This monitor helps. I always forget the third and fourth verses of "Jingle Bells," as well as all the other songs."

Caleb chuckled. "We all do."

As the second act began, Angelina tapped her feet to the easy 2/4 meter of "The Little Drummer Boy," enjoying an extraordinary moment of contentment while Caleb harmonized with the baritone part. The advertisement had been right. Christmas music, an energetic choir and merry decorations were ideal holiday inspirations, especially on Christmas Eve.

Of course, she couldn't discount the effects of having the jovial Rachel on her left and the good-looking man on her right, who made her forget everything she was going to say whenever he smiled at her.

She glanced at Caleb's chiseled profile—his straight nose and well-defined cheekbones. He was certainly a man of startling contradictions. Not only was he well-versed on volcanoes and Hawaii, he also appreciated the arts and was a fine musician. Irrationally, she was eager for the singalong's finale so she could talk more with him over coffee.

When the performance ended to wholehearted applause, Rachel quickly stood. "Let's head to the observation deck. Is anyone hungry?"

No one focused on food as much as Rachel.

To beat the other theater-goers, the threesome rapidly threaded their way through the jam-packed lobby and took the lift to the circular observation deck, soon finding seats around a sleek silver table. As Rachel had noted, the upper deck boasted an all-night buffet, and a disco bar was situated on a tier above it. Rachel excused herself and headed straight for the hamburger and French fry station.

Caleb made his own food foray, returning with a tray laden with two cups of coffee, a plateful of chocolate doughnuts, a bowl of macadamia nuts, and a glass of sparkling champagne.

Angelina surveyed the tray. "Only one glass of champagne?"

"Yes, and it's for you. I don't drink. I wasn't sure ... do you?"

"Only on rare special occasions." And this being Christmas Eve and the fact she was spending it with Caleb was one of them.

He inclined his head toward the swarm of people bearing down on the buffet and filling their plates with enormous quantities of steaming roast beef, meat loaf, and mashed potatoes.

"Not traditional Christmas Eve food," he mused.

She sipped her champagne. "What do you usually eat on Christmas Eve?"

"It's a low-key celebration for us Scots. Turkey, hot chocolate, eggnog." He stared again at the buffet line. "How do you normally spend Christmas Eve, Angelina?"

Alone, she wanted to say. Instead, because they'd been talking about established Christmas traditions, she said, "I'm Italian, thus in the past I've enjoyed the Feast of the Seven Fishes."

"Sounds awesome. What type of fish?"

"Shrimp, calamari, cod. Whatever's available."

"I'm interested in learning all about your Italian traditions. Perhaps you can show me."

When? When he taught her how to play the piano? Their time together was only a few short days.

He picked up a doughnut. "It's a good thing we arrived before the onslaught of the entire theater mob. Unfortunately, our conversation will be limited by all this commotion."

"By all these festivities, you mean." There was always tomorrow, Christmas Day, she told herself, and she'd appreciate tonight for what it brought—Christmas music, a fast friend in Rachel, and a chance to be with Caleb.

She sampled more champagne, savoring its warm path from her throat to her stomach. "Tell me about your Hawaiian cousin," she prompted.

"Not much to tell. We've corresponded quite a bit. He's a distant cousin on my mother's side."

"And your mother? Where does she live?"

"Both my parents are deceased, and I'm an only child. What about you?"

"I'm an only child too. My father recently remarried. My parents divorced years ago." Her tone faltered at his inquiring glance. "Long story."

In truth, her father had gone into a tailspin after the divorce, buying and selling land, two apartments and a sailboat. Her mother had labeled it a midlife crisis.

"And your mother?" Caleb asked.

"She's on a quest to see every country in Europe and is currently on a riverboat cruise in the Netherlands. And that's more information about me than you'll ever find on Wikipedia." She dismissed any further references to herself with a wave of her hand. "On which island does your cousin live?"

"He and his wife live on Maui, and I'm meeting them on December twenty-ninth. In fact, I rented a place there, as I'll be doing research at Haleakala, a dormant volcano." Spotting a quick-footed waiter, he stood and handed the waiter their empty tray, and then he slid neatly into the booth beside Angelina. Nonchalantly, he stretched his arm around her shoulders.

She opened her mouth, preparing to point out there was no lack of comfortable seating around the table. Therefore, he didn't need to sit an inch away from her.

Rachel returned, her tray overflowing with a heaping order of French fries, a double cheeseburger, ketchup packets and a tall glass of water. "Fred and I are making our new home on Honolulu near his grandmother's house." She gazed in astonished appreciation at how close Caleb and Angelina were sitting. "Sorry. I didn't mean to eavesdrop, although I seem to do that a lot, don't I?" Without waiting for an answer, she took the seat across from them. "What's your cousin's name, Caleb?"

"Kapena. Somewhere along the family tree a cousin of

ours married a Hawaiian woman. He and I have emailed many times. Until a few years ago, he was a confirmed bachelor."

"Was?" Angelina asked. "I sense an 'until' coming."

Caleb raised his coffee cup to his lips and regarded Angelina over the rim. "He met Zoe and his life changed. He described their first meeting as being hit by a lightning bolt."

Her eyebrows rose. "How did they meet?"

"Through an online dating agency." He grinned. "Zoe lived in Iowa and moved to Hawaii to marry him."

Rachel sighed languorously, then bit into a French fry thoroughly smothered in ketchup. "How romantic."

"A lightning bolt," Angelina said, "isn't the least bit romantic-sounding to me."

"Love at first sight," Caleb said. "The French have a saying for it—*le coup de foudre*—because love is a delightful shock to the system."

Two hours later, the threesome had laughed and eaten more than Angelina could ever recall in her life, and she'd already determined it was the best Christmas Eve she'd spent in years. She was now on her second glass of champagne and had eaten at least four chocolate doughnuts, and vowed to run ten laps around the deck in the morning. Feeling animated and unquestionably lightheaded, she decided the entire cruise had been an excellent idea and nothing could diminish her happy mood.

During a rousing conversation about why the wind blew east to west in Hawaii, four women converged on their table. One was the perky brunette Angelina had observed the first evening on the ship.

"Hi, Jillian." Caleb stood to greet her and the other women. Jillian was lushly dressed in a burgundy bodycon tank dress that clung to her full figure. A glittering gold clamp secured thick hair away from her face. Laughingly, she returned Caleb's greeting, then pointed across the room to a slender, curvy woman with long black hair.

"We just took a selfie with Lauren. She was the woman caught on the kiss cam saying no to a marriage proposal at a Pittsburgh Penguins game in L.A. The video went viral. The hashtag was #kisscamgirl."

"I hadn't heard," Caleb replied, and Rachel and Angelina concurred.

With a refined elegance, he fulfilled his role as host and led the women in exchanging greetings.

"May we join you?" Jillian asked. She plucked glasses of sparkling champagne from a side table and handed one to each of her three friends.

With a glance, Caleb deferred the decision to Angelina. Having little choice, she inclined her head. Rachel responded with a dispassionate nod of assent.

He waited for the women to be seated, then canvassed the deck for another chair for himself. Finally securing one, he carried it to the only available space around the table, which was across from Angelina.

Soon afterward, Rachel pushed to her feet. "I'm grabbing another plateful of French fries to take back to our cabin." She looked meaningfully at Angelina. "Although I assume you're staying here?"

Angelina glanced at her watch. "Only until midnight."

"We're all on this cruise to celebrate turning twenty-nine." Jillian gestured to her friends, then downed her champagne in one gulp. "And I can stay all night. Besides, it's Christmas, the most special time of the year."

Angelina looked around at the four women. "You're all turning twenty-nine, not thirty?"

"We're saving the really big celebration for next year." Jillian swiveled in her seat and snatched another glass of champagne from a passing waiter. "We're high school buddies and graduated together." She raised her glass, prompting the other women to do the same.

"Cheers!" they chimed together. "To twenty-nine!"

Angelina sipped her champagne and glanced at Caleb. He was now deep in conversation with a blonde woman who had asked him a question about volcanic eruptions.

She took another swallow to dull a surprisingly sharp ache of jealousy. The blonde was hanging onto his every word, as if volcanoes were the most interesting subject in the world. Of course, she was also interested in the fact that Caleb was heart-stoppingly handsome, and urbane, and a perfect date for the upcoming shore excursions.

Didn't he realize how calculated some women were in their efforts to entice a man?

Angelina set down her glass and regarded Jillian. "How long have you and Caleb known each other?"

"We met the first night we boarded, and just ... you know ... clicked." Jillian snapped her fingers, then lifted her face to gaze in apparent rapture at the silver design of stars twinkling in the night sky. With a dreamy sigh, she refocused a telling look toward Caleb. "I realized who he was and immediately introduced myself. I've always been fascinated with science."

Uh-huh.

Or, Angelina supposed, Jillian was fascinated with a presumably wealthy, well-known scientist.

Jillian pressed her lips together, then subjected Angelina to a penetrating look. "May I ask you a personal question?"

"Of course," Angelina replied.

She eyed Angelina with a mixture of guarded speculation and superficial pleasantness. "How old are you?"

Angelina was momentarily stunned by the other woman's colossal nerve. With this assembly of attractive, vivacious women, she felt old and dowdy and unsophisticated.

Caleb turned toward her, evidently interested.

"I'm thirty-five," Angelina said.

"And you, Caleb?" The attractive blonde patted his arm and beamed up at him.

"I recently turned forty. But Angelina already knows that, thanks to her researching me on Wikipedia."

He grinned at her, but Angelina didn't grin back.

Although she tried to conceal her embarrassment beneath an impartial expression, she knew she blushed furiously. The other women surely would think she was stalking him on social media.

Rubbing a hand through her hair, she inhaled, and then exhaled. She'd pictured sitting alone with Caleb, leisurely talking and bantering, admiring the starlit sky, celebrating the coming of Christmas Day. They'd sip coffee and eat too many doughnuts and gaze at each other.

However, surrounded by this group of loud, clamoring women, he seemed completely at ease. The women flirted flagrantly with him, breaching the bounds of correctness, anything to keep his concentration on them. And there was no question that Jillian, as well as the blonde, were sizing him up as a potential romantic encounter for the duration of the cruise.

Good luck with that. Angelina frowned darkly at the thought.

Baffled, she continued to watch him. He had seemed interested in her when he kissed her during their script-reading, then had blatantly ignored her in the lecture room.

And now? Well, clearly now he was having a grand time with the other women.

At the blonde's childlike plea to learn more about Hawaii, he began a lengthy explanation regarding the Dole Planta-tion's pineapple maze, and how it was the world's largest maze and listed in the 2001 Guinness Book of World Records.

Angelina shook her head, reverting to her former opinion of him.

The man was impossible.

With her, he assumed the serious professor role, constantly correcting her script errors.

That is, when he wasn't singing Christmas carols with her.

Or kissing her.

CHAPTER 5

*B*efore sunrise the following day, Caleb selected a cup of black coffee, declined a serving of scrambled eggs, and grabbed an apple Danish from the dining room's breakfast buffet. Then he claimed a café table on the airy outdoor deck. Like clockwork, The *Bird of Paradise* catered to every customer's schedule, and a superb assortment of appetizing food had been set up before five a.m.

Dawn changed the sky from charcoal to a rich, dusty gold while he dined. A low-hanging mist in the air refused to let go, covering the world with a white-veiled haze as far as his eyes could see.

Today was Christmas Day, although there was little difference between this and any other day. The past couple years he'd spent the day alone—usually grabbing a meal in downtown Medina, then returning to his condo to immerse himself in a project.

He found he got a lot done in the quiet hours before dawn, and this morning he intended to prepare for his morning lecture. Despite the holiday, he'd continue with the volcano series for any interested guests.

In the afternoon, he'd booked a Hilo excursion for himself and Angelina. What better way to spend Christmas than on a helicopter tour, "flightseeing" over the Kilauea volcano? Nothing would give her a better understanding of the power of a volcano than to actually fly over one so recently active.

Surely she wouldn't refuse, and he planned to inform her about all the details after he saw her at his morning lecture.

He scanned his notes. Today, he'd discuss volcanic eruption while stressing the fact that eruptions were never associated with the weather. Perhaps the information would help Angelina finish her script, as she had mentioned a rainstorm occurred in the last scene. With the knowledge from his lecture, she wouldn't assume—in case she did—that a driving rain prompted a volcanic eruption. Perhaps she thought an eruption would be a perfect, dramatic ending to her story. This way, he'd save her hours of rewriting.

A waiter passed his table carrying a steaming coffee pot, and Caleb indicated to him to freshen his coffee.

He gazed around the deck. Because the ship was scheduled to arrive at Hilo by midmorning, a scattering of diners occupied seats near the railing, ready to greet the first Hawaiian island on the itinerary.

Grateful for the solitude, Caleb opened his laptop. A particularly interesting article by one of his colleagues on ash dispersal from highly explosive volcanic eruptions caught his interest. He sharpened the screen and began reading.

"Dr. Sloane?" a woman's voice interrupted.

He looked up and spotted Jillian waltzing toward him. She wore a white see-through coverup over a black bikini, and he wondered if she'd actually gone swimming in the adults-only pool, although she didn't look wet.

"Merry Christmas!" She glided into the seat beside him. "May I join you?"

He minimized his computer screen and managed a cordial nod. "Merry Christmas."

"Are you the type of man who buys Christmas gifts?" She smiled into his eyes.

Good breeding dictated he answer. "Sometimes," he said offhandedly.

He hadn't bought a gift for Angelina. He wanted to. He should have.

But why, exactly?

Because ... because of their work association, and because he genuinely enjoyed being with her. He pondered whether the gift shops were open, then decided to buy her something special from one of the islands.

"Caleb, will you get me a cup of coffee?" Jillian bobbed her head toward the buffet table.

Obligingly, he stood, fixed her coffee and brought it back to the table.

After his conversation with Jillian and her friends the previous evening, he feared she might assume he was interested in a shipboard romance. Certainly, he had fulfilled his role as the attentive gentleman, but he'd left the observation deck shortly after Angelina retired.

"We'll be docking soon." Jillian touched his arm. "I can't wait to spend Christmas in Hawaii and explore the little shops there."

How things change, he mused. Until a couple days ago, he enjoyed Jillian's attractiveness and seductive ways. Now, he found her tiresome and predictable.

He smiled politely and stared into his coffee cup as she chattered nonstop about her low-fat breakfast and tanning regime.

After several minutes, she wagged a finger at him. "Caleb, I'm not boring you, am I?"

He raised his cup to his lips and didn't bother to reassure

her, nor reward her with the compliment she obviously sought for eating blueberry … something for breakfast.

The more she went on, the more he regretted the time he'd spent with her and her twenty-something schoolmates. Time he could have spent getting to know Angelina better.

Believing Angelina might find him boring, he had tried a little too hard to shed his normally reserved behavior. And now, ironically, Jillian had asked if *she* was boring *him*.

Sure, the attention from the women had been enjoyable, but they all had major shortfalls. Beginning with the fact that their eyes weren't a warm cornflower-blue. They didn't disagree with him about his research, and he doubted they'd return his kisses with an emerging passion that couldn't be hidden.

He glanced at Jillian—the coquettish way she touched his arm, then compared her small hands to his large ones.

She was too available, too keen to entertain him. She wasn't quick-witted and gorgeous in a natural fresh-air kind of way, breathing new life into his world-weary soul.

She wasn't Angelina.

He sighed.

The day before, he'd attempted to ignore Angelina during his lecture. Their paths wouldn't cross again after he reached his cousin's port, he had reasoned. Consequently, what was the point in beginning a relationship? It would only make their unavoidable farewell more challenging.

Nevertheless, he hadn't been able to help himself. He'd attended the Christmas singalong, assuming, hoping she would be there.

She was constantly in his thoughts. She made him laugh, made him care, striking a heartfelt chord in his chest. She made him want more from life than interpreting clues from rocks or trying to understand an ever-changing earth environment.

He scowled at the thought of something, *someone,* being more important to him than science. That had never happened before. Ever.

With a long exhale, he came to terms with his feelings. At forty years old, he was falling hard for an impudent, dazzling woman who calmly incurred his displeasure and refused to yield to his opinions if they didn't suit her.

How had this happened? He couldn't afford a complication. Besides, no one fell that quickly for someone they'd only known a short while. They had just met, although their tense email exchanges had begun weeks before.

Still, every time he was with her he melted a little more. She was having a huge effect on his every thought, and he couldn't stop himself from wondering what she was doing when he wasn't with her. She was captivating and charming. And yes, sometimes exasperating.

Knock it off, he told himself.

Maybe—if her sweet smile didn't warm his soul, or she didn't blush so gorgeously while she laughed at his jokes.

Abruptly, he set down his cup and stood.

"Jillian," he adopted his most polite tone, "I must prepare for my lecture. Enjoy your day and … Merry Christmas." Without another word, he darted for the nearest exit.

* * *

ANGELINA HUNCHED OVER HER COMPUTER, pointedly ignoring Rachel's attempts to get her out of the cabin. Rachel sat on her berth tying an oversize, bright-purple caftan over her maternity capris, all the while humming "We Wish You A Merry Christmas."

"Angelina, you can work upstairs on the deck until Caleb's lecture," Rachel urged. "Savor the fresh ocean breezes. Enjoy Christmas!"

Angelina didn't have the heart to tell Rachel that she wasn't attending Caleb's lecture. She'd learned enough about volcanos, more than enough to finish her script accurately. If he wanted to meet with her, he could text her. Until then, she didn't plan to see him. The fact that it was Christmas Day didn't change anything.

Besides, the most important part of Christmas was the church service, and she'd attended an inspiring, uplifting service the previous day.

"Will you be taking any Hilo excursions today?" Rachel asked.

"No."

"I signed up for the Lava Falls tour. The excursion bus leaves at eleven o'clock, which gives me time to call Fred and wish him a Merry Christmas."

"I'll phone my dad in a little while," Angelina replied. "I called my mom yesterday, because the Netherlands is twelve hours ahead of Hawaii."

"In the meantime, you can work on deck." Rachel offered a heartfelt smile. "The scenery and endless ocean views are stunning."

"I'll never get anything done if I'm distracted by the scenery," Angelina countered. "Besides, it's not just this screenplay I'm working on. There are numerous other projects I need to look into if I want to keep my career on the right track."

"No businesses will be open on Christmas Day." Rachel looked very determined. "And this sudden desire to spend all your time in the cabin doesn't have anything to do with Caleb's behavior and those twenty-nine-year-old women from last night, does it? I heard you return to our cabin well before midnight."

"They were all having a grand time. He didn't need me around."

"You couldn't be more wrong." Rachel made no attempt to hide her scoff. "Anyone can see he's completely infatuated with you. Last night on the observation deck he watched your every move. And at the singalong, he couldn't lean close enough to you while you sang."

"We were harmonizing."

"Uh-huh. And now it's time to get out of this cabin."

Before Angelina could open her mouth to object, Rachel glanced at her watch. "I give up—at least for now. The breakfast buffet has started without me, and there might not be any food left."

"We wouldn't want that to happen," Angelina joked as Rachel scurried out of the cabin.

After a couple hours of aimlessly scrolling through her screenplay, Angelina shut her computer. She called her father in California to wish him and his new wife a Merry Christmas, and accepted their offer to celebrate Christmas together when Angelina returned from Hawaii.

She glanced at the time on her cell phone. Of course, she was being ridiculous about Caleb. Rachel was right. She should work in the fresh air, not holed up in a 160-square-foot cabin. She certainly didn't want him to think she was hiding to avoid him.

Placing her computer in her briefcase, she decided to go to the Irish pub. Besides being deserted in the morning hours, the pub was a place Caleb wouldn't hang out. Most of the cruisers aimed for the main dining room's breakfast buffet.

After a quick shower, she dressed in a cherry-red sundress and matching red sandals. She secured her unruly ringlets into a semblance of order with a faux-crystal hair clip and applied a red lip gloss. Although she always wore sunscreen, the sun had obviously found her, and her skin had taken on a warm rosy hue.

At a quick pace, she hurried through the hallway and peered right, then left. Now, if she could only remember which deck the Irish pub was located on.

* * *

AFTER HIS LECTURE, Caleb sat in a shady alcove on the upper "serenity" deck, intending to graze on a bowl of seasonal fruit and read a volcano excursion pamphlet. However, he ate little of the apples and oranges seasoned with honey, and what little he did eat, he hardly tasted. He was too preoccupied in figuring out a way to ask Angelina to go with him without appearing too anxious.

She hadn't attended his lecture. Therefore, he hadn't been able to tell her about the helicopter tour he'd booked for them.

He thought about phoning her, then paused when a text message from his Realtor in Washington flashed across his screen. Mentally, he worded and reworded his Realtor's description of his condo before emailing his approval. The Realtor was a go-getter, in full swing on Christmas Day. But then, Caleb's two-million-dollar condo in the trendy Medina area was a plum listing.

He ate a spoonful of fruit, then did a double-take as Angelina walked swiftly past his table. Not once, but twice.

Where could she possibly be going?

He set down his spoon, wondering if he should call out to her.

Hmm, probably not a good idea. She certainly hadn't been in a hurry to attend his lecture, which had finished over an hour ago.

He'd worried she might not be feeling well, but she certainly looked fine as she rushed up and down the same hallway. More than fine, he corrected. Intriguing, beguiling, and absolutely stunning.

As she scurried past again, he held back a grin. Her sense of direction was beyond poor. He, the other cruisers, and especially the captain, the distinguished Swede, Jorgen Berg, should be grateful she wasn't steering the ship or they might have ended up somewhere in the Atlantic rather than the Pacific Ocean.

In any event, he couldn't deny he was happy to see her.

When she darted through the hallway a fourth time, he rationalized he couldn't keep letting her walk around in literal circles. Besides, he couldn't take her on a helicopter tour of the island if he didn't invite her.

He grabbed the pamphlet and strode quickly toward her while she hastened to the elevator.

"Angelina?"

She stiffened a brief second. He was positive she heard him, yet she kept walking.

"Good morning, Angelina," he said, louder. "Merry Christmas!"

Gracefully, she turned. "Merry Christmas." Her blue eyes darkened as she regarded him with astonishment, then ill-concealed annoyance.

"Where are you heading?" He used a friendly smile to cover his disappointment to her less-than-thrilled reaction at seeing him. "I assume you're not rushing to hear my lecture because you most decidedly missed it." He considered checking his watch, but he'd already done that once.

Instead of giving him a multitude of good excuses why she hadn't attended, all of which he had already decided he would benevolently accept, she said nothing.

At first.

Then she declared she didn't need any more volcano

information. To add to his mounting frustration, she refused to meet his gaze.

"Oh, really. Why not?" he asked.

She stepped into the empty elevator. He filed in beside her.

She ignored him and his question. The elevator stopped at the floor she'd punched in. Deck four. Briefcase in hand, she advanced into the hallway. Then she took a breath, eyed the signs mounted in the corridors, and pivoted. "Because I needed a break from ..."

You, he thought, finishing her sentence. She needed a break from him.

He rubbed his forehead and briefly squeezed his eyes shut.

"Volcanos and research," she finished. "My muse yearned for creativity. Good day, Caleb."

Good day? Good Christmas Day? He was taken aback by her polite, measured smile.

He came from the elevator and faced her. "And you found this ... muse by walking around in circles?"

"I'm still finding my muse."

"Then may I suggest we do something besides work today? I'm sure you can agree Christmas is a special day." His disappointment, his confusion at her coolness toward him, reduced his voice to a plea. "The cruise director listed the events for today on the ship's TV station. This morning, there's a culinary demonstration in the Aloha lounge given by a noted Polynesian chef. Would you join me? I've always been interested in cooking."

She looked as surprised as he did for blurting out something he hadn't even given the slightest thought to until a moment ago. He couldn't recall the last time he'd cooked a meal for himself, much less tried out a new recipe. Calling for takeout had always suited him perfectly.

Angelina hesitated, considering him, then inclined her head. "All right. I like learning new recipes. And if it's Hawaiian, I may be able to use it in my script."

"Let's go, then. The class starts in ten minutes."

First, a morning cooking class, then an afternoon helicopter ride. He'd ease into things slowly.

* * *

ADORNED IN A WHITE apron and chef hat, Angelina couldn't keep from staring. Standing in the ship's spotless culinary kitchen filled with stainless-steel appliances, she watched Caleb vigorously stir coconut milk, sugar, salt, and cornstarch in a pan on a large stove, waiting for the mixture to thicken.

The ten other participants, all husband and wife teams, joked with each other, and she and Caleb added to the merriment. Listening carefully to the chef, each couple learned how to make haupia, a delectable dessert and ideal for Christmas.

Leaning closer, Angelina admonished Caleb to be careful not to burn the mixture, or himself; and he smilingly assured he had things well in hand because he was familiar with the recipe.

Although he didn't look as if he'd ever donned an apron before or, for that matter, ever switched on an oven, he was an active, willing participant while she preferred to cheer and encourage from the sidelines.

"You actually cook Hawaiian food?" she asked for the third time in as many minutes. She could only picture him at a desk or podium, thumbing through piles of research papers scattered around him.

"Kapena has emailed me many recipes over the years."

"Did you actually cook any of them?"

"No, but I looked them over." He grinned, that boyish grin that made his impressive looks even more appealing. "I'll be interested in how haupia tastes."

"So will I, if you don't burn it."

Laughing, he shut the burner off, and they turned their attention to Elikapeka, their chef instructor. She looked decidedly Asian and strikingly exotic, her straight ebony hair pulled back into a long ponytail.

"Pour your haupia into the pan. Once it's cooled, we'll refrigerate it," she instructed the participants. "When it's solid, we'll cut the dessert into blocks, so come back later."

"Thus, haupia is a coconut gelatin," Angelina murmured.

"Yes, Mrs. Sloane."

Angelina turned at Elikapeka's voice. "I'm sorry?"

"Aren't you husband and wife?" Elikapeka's gaze swung from Caleb to Angelina.

"No, we're merely … coworkers," Angelina finished, as Caleb said, "good friends."

"I assumed you were married because you two look very natural together …" Elikapeka smiled, her white teeth flashing against tanned skin. "In any event, *ohana*, which means family, because in Hawaii, we are all family."

Caleb removed his apron and hat, then fixed his sleeves, which he'd rolled up for the cooking class. "Well, Mrs. Sloane," he said, smiling at Angelina, "do you agree we should set aside Christmas as a non-work day?"

"I can't," she said, as they stepped out of the kitchen. She looked wistfully about the picturesque outdoor deck. "Business before pleasure, I'm afraid."

"How about combining business and pleasure?" he asked. "We've reached the first port, and I booked an excursion in Hilo I know you'll appreciate."

"The production company didn't pay for anything extra."

"This excursion is my treat. Are you interested in a helicopter ride?"

She lifted a brow. "Where?"

"Over one of the most active volcanoes in Hawaii." He glanced at the blue sky. "The weather looks promising, so the excursion won't be canceled. Although we won't be able to fly too close, you'll get a clear idea of what a recent major eruption looks like." His gaze drifted toward the island, swaying palm trees in the foreground with the black outline of the volcano beyond. Quietly, he added, "A much better idea."

"Caleb, I—"

"Are you afraid of heights?"

She was, sometimes. Okay, oftentimes, but she wouldn't admit her fears to him. Left brain, she told herself. Be an intellectual like him.

"I can't," she began. "The expense ..."

"Of course you can. And I'm paying, remember?"

"Why? I—"

He halted her objection by pressing a finger to her lips.

"I'll give you a simple answer. Because the helicopter ride above the Big Island will give you an overview of the landscape and you can chalk it up to research. Wear a dark-colored shirt, bring your camera and I'll meet you in the lobby at two. We'll need to arrive an hour before takeoff, and the helicopter leaves at half past three."

"How long is the tour?"

"The flight takes about an hour. We'll fly southwest over the volcano and waterfalls, see the jungle over the coast, then back to the airport."

He waited expectantly, and Angelina finally nodded. "Okay. See you at two."

*A*ngelina stared at her reflection in her cabin's bathroom mirror as she combed her hair into an upsweep, adding a celebratory red organza bow for Christmas. As Caleb had requested, she wore a dark-colored V-neck T-shirt and decided on cropped skinny jeans and sensible leather flats.

Armed with a dose of an anti-anxiety drug prescribed by the ship's medic, she met Caleb in the lobby at two.

He gave an appreciative smile. "You look lovely."

"Thank you." Her face heated. Another compliment. Although his flattery was more unassuming than others she'd received from men through the years, Caleb's praise meant more to her. Curiously touched, she changed the subject. "Why did you suggest we wear dark colors?" She gestured to his dark-gray polo shirt, noticing that his dusty-blue shorts revealed a good length of his muscular legs. Around his neck hung a small black camera bag.

"Wearing dark colors helps when we take pictures." He guided her down the gangway to the excursion bus waiting at the port. "Light colors will reflect off the helicopter windows."

She hid her smile. He thought of everything.

If someone had told her when she had boarded the cruise ship that the man she'd exchanged such tense emails with would be a man she wanted to spend every waking moment with, she would have discounted the conversation with a wry smile and a shake of her head.

But Caleb wasn't the stern, stuffy volcanologist she'd pegged him as. Instead, he was helping her write a more effective screenplay.

His dry humor matched hers. And he was a gentleman—pulling out chairs for her and standing whenever she entered a room. Plus, every time she saw him, he seemed to become more recklessly handsome.

"I wasn't sure if you preferred a doors-on or doors-off helicopter ride," he said.

"What's the difference?"

"Doors on means exactly what it says." He regarded her with teasing indulgence. "The helicopter doors will stay on during our ride."

"Then doors off means ..." She took a step back. "Are you some kind of thrill seeker? If so, you should know I'm exactly the opposite."

"Nope, I'm fairly cautious. However, I am a scientist, and I've learned you'll see more and get better pictures with the doors off. Besides, I'll keep you safe. Honest." He grinned as her brows furrowed. "Don't worry, you won't fall out of the helicopter. The seat harness holds you firmly in place."

"Let me guess," she said. "You prefer doors off. However, what if—"

He slid an arm around her. "I used to own a private plane, and I've flown doors-off hundreds of times."

She hesitated. He watched her.

"However, if you're afraid ..." He coaxed. Or was he clarifying?

Firmly, she shook her head. Left brain, left brain. Be logical about your fear of heights. Ignore the negative movies playing through your head.

Besides, enough of the 'what ifs'. She'd show him once and for all she was serious about getting her story right.

"Doors-off it is." Jaw set, she pushed her shoulders back and adjusted her crossbody purse. "I wouldn't have it any other way."

"That's my girl. Never afraid of a challenge."

My girl? Her throat went dry, and she couldn't respond.

He gave an appreciative smile, dropped his arm from her shoulders and took her hand. Together they strolled from the ship amidst a children's choir from a local cathedral singing Christmas carols.

Angelina slowed her steps, spellbound by the island's natural beauty. She'd never traveled much. In fact, she'd never been to Hawaii. Lush greenery covered the landscape, interspersed by patches of rainbow-colored flowers and sparkling golden sand. The crystal-blue ocean stretched in every direction and the fresh, humid air teased her nostrils.

"Breathtaking," she murmured, and Caleb wholeheartedly agreed.

Together, they boarded the bus to the heliport at the Hilo airport.

A half hour later, a petite woman with dark hair and tanned skin greeted them and asked for their height and weight. Angelina listed hers—five feet eight, one hundred and thirty pounds, while Caleb added his on the following line. As she estimated, he was six feet tall, one hundred and eighty pounds.

"Knowing our passengers' heights and weights are safety features to balance the helicopter," the woman explained, when Angelina asked why the company required personal information.

She assigned Angelina a seat in the middle of the helicopter next to the pilot. Caleb helped her in and settled beside her. "I normally sit harnessed with my feet dangling out of the helicopter," he said. "However, I'll face front this time. I want you to feel safe."

She raised her eyebrows. "Should I be appreciative?"

"Absolutely. I like watching your reaction to new things. Your face is so expressive."

"A doors-off helicopter ride is definitely new for me. In fact, I've never been in a helicopter."

"I hope you'll enjoy it as much as I do," he said. "I took the liberty of booking a private tour. Hence, no one will be joining us."

"You also took the liberty of booking this very expensive excursion without asking me first."

"It's well worth the money."

Her gaze narrowed. "Suppose I'd said no?"

"Then I would have used all my persuasive powers to change your mind."

"Which are?"

He leaned in. "I'd remind you about your screenplay and how this excursion will enable you to get a first-hand appreciation of the power and devastation of an active volcano. It's much different from a movie script or anything you've seen on television." He pointed out the mountainous volcano in the distance. "Eruptions are serious natural disasters that affect many lives and communities. Believe me, I've seen heartbreaking situations."

She glanced uncertainly at him. His tone had become grave, his features expressionless.

"When?" she asked.

"When I worked in Malaysia a few years ago with a team

of volcanologists. Despite all our scientific and seismic information, a volcanic eruption caught us by surprise. Many lives could have been saved if only ..." His voice trailed off, his gaze darkened. "The volcano was so quiet, then erupted with no warning. I've climbed numerous slopes and crept into deep craters to take measurements. But that time, all my years of research weren't enough. I held onto my faith in God to move me forward."

There were moments when emotions left you speechless. This was one of them.

Lightly, she touched his hand. "The eruption must have been horrible."

"It was." He pulled away from the consolation she offered and stared straight ahead.

He was such an empathetic man, she thought. A good man, a brave man. More important, he embraced God and was humble enough to realize it wasn't all up to him. A hard realization to face, especially for a man who relied on facts and statistics.

Once they were strapped into their seats, the pilot climbed into the helicopter and furnished them with headsets. "Merry Christmas! I'm Pika, which is the Hawaiian name for rock." He took off his fuzzy Santa hat, replacing it with a helmet. "Your headsets will make it easy to communicate once we begin flying." He primed the engine and engaged the rotors. "Any special requests?"

Angelina tried not to look terrified and gripped her seat with both hands. "No."

"Then let the fun begin."

"Brace yourself." Caleb grabbed her trembling fingers and squeezed reassuringly. Warily, she peered through the large opening of the helicopter on the far side of Caleb, feeling every thump and bump as they ascended and the spectacular scenery below grew smaller.

"That's our cruise ship." Caleb pointed, enabling her to get her bearings.

"And directly below us is the Mauna Loa Macadamia Nut Farm." The pilot gestured with his chin. "When we fly over the volcano, our air space is very limited because of the massive recent eruptions."

Caleb's grip tightened around her hand. "There's the Kilauea volcano. See the smoke and fire?"

Stunned at the reddish-brown ash plume ascending into the air, she heard her own intake of breath. Sharp fragments of gas shot a column into the sky.

"Lava flows are erratic," Pika explained. "However, today I'm able to fly within a reasonable distance around the crater."

"The spilling from the recent eruption destroyed hundreds of homes." Caleb sucked in a breath and turned to peer down at the scene. "This destruction is horrific."

"Flames spewed from the volcano and lava rolled down the streets," Pika said, his smile grim. "I even saw a car being swallowed by fire. I live nearby and visited every day. It smelled awful—like sulfur and burning trees."

Angelina leaned her head back against the seat. "Yet people still live here and are rebuilding their homes. Why?"

"Land is cheap," Pika said. "You can buy a small lot for less than ten thousand dollars although the landowner won't be able to get insurance on it."

"Then why live here, of all places?" she repeated.

"This is their home. Residents understand the risk and what they're getting into," Pika said. "And I believe, as do many natives, that this land belongs to Madame Pele."

"A fire goddess," Caleb furnished.

Although Angelina knew who Madame Pele was, she allowed Caleb to explain. She liked it when he shared his knowledge with her.

"She cleanses the land," Caleb continued. "She teaches the people how to live in harmony with the earth as well as staying connected to their ancestors."

"So, she's a myth?" Angelina asked, hoping she wasn't offending Pika.

"Yes, although the premise is sound." Caleb paused, his expression grave as he surveyed the scene below. "Humans need to respect nature and live in harmony with the earth's elements. Not only is that an admirable premise to live by, it's common sense." He turned and bent forward, snapping a series of rapid photos with his high-quality digital camera. "Eventually, there will be excellent farming here because the land is fertile. Volcanic soil is known as andisol, which is formed from volcanic ash."

He paused as they both surveyed the uneven tracks of vehicles trekking through the lava flow. Angelina wondered if they had been residents returning to view their destroyed homes.

"As you mentioned," Caleb continued, "many people own restaurants and shops near these areas because of the tourism trade. Thus, another answer to your question of why people remain at the foot of a volcano."

Aside from the sight of the awe-inspiring layers of ash and rock below them covering the natural landscape, Angelina felt something deeper. Her chest ached. Her vision blurred through hot tears.

So deep in thought over the loss of lives, the incalculable damage, she couldn't pinpoint exactly when Caleb's hands began to caress her sweaty ones. She just knew she was grateful for his sensitivity. Unashamedly, she grabbed onto the comfort he offered and coiled her fingers tightly around his.

"Thousands of people were forced to evacuate." He

nodded to a spot below them. "See there? Those are minor outbreaks of lava seeping through the older lava flows."

"I never comprehended how treacherous a volcano is. Or I thought I did, but I really didn't, not without seeing it for myself." She focused on the in and out of her breath to steady her breathing. "How does something of this magnitude happen?"

"This eruption was triggered by a series of earthquakes that pushed the lava into new chambers underground," Caleb said. "The increased lava flow forced a section of the volcano, which is already active, to become even more so."

"How long has this particular volcano been active?" she asked.

"Since 1983. And the magnitude of the earthquakes opened additional fissures." He shook his head. "Countless families were affected by this disruption. It will take years to rebuild their homes. I'm fortunate to be in a position to help see that this never happens again."

His deep voice, full of sadness, carried through her head-set. Profoundly touched, she shared in this complex man's compassion for humanity. His gifted scientific mind, his relentless research, his empathy, was appreciated by all who knew him.

Sitting so close in the cockpit, his warm body pressed against hers, made her heart skip a beat. He was strong and fearless to confront these natural disasters—all in the name of making the world safer. But there was much, much more to him.

Sidewise, she glanced at his handsome face, his pensive expression.

Caleb Sloane had a vulnerable side. Beneath his walled exterior, he was sensitive and socially conscious. And he was the type of man she could easily fall in love with.

"There's the hidden waterfalls over Waimanu Valley." Paki

shifted gears to rotate the helicopter's rotors and hovered over the waterfalls. "The cliffs are over 2000 feet high."

"I'm ... bedazzled," Angelina said. She'd never used a word like that before. She was a writer, and this scene left her grappling for words to describe it. The rushing waterfall poured off a tall sea cliff, in sharp contrast to the fiery activity of the volcano. Mesmerized, she shot several photos with her cellphone. "Hawaii is almost too magnificent to describe. I've seen photos of the white sand beaches, the tropical scenery, but this ..." She placed a hand over her heart.

"Is paradise," Caleb finished.

A few minutes later they landed, thanked and tipped Pika, and wished him a Merry Christmas.

She righted her unruly hair and accepted Caleb's hand as they walked back to the bus. They looped around a couple of talkative cruisers and secured seats in the back of the bus. The driver cranked up the volume of the holiday music, and "Deck the Halls" began.

Caleb draped an arm around her. "What are you thinking?"

"I have a new and better appreciation of a place I've never visited."

And a new appreciation for him.

He kissed her forehead. "Merry Christmas, Angelina. I wanted to buy you a gift, the perfect something, but I don't know. Is there anything special?"

"Merry Christmas, Caleb." She leaned her head against his shoulder. "Truly, nothing can be more extraordinary than this day." A thought occurred to her, and she blurted it out loud. "This entire cruise has been nothing like I imagined."

He cupped her chin in his hands and gazed into her eyes. "In a good way, I hope?"

"In a very good way."

His deep-brown eyes, so intense, reminded her of the rich

soil that came out of the volcanic ash, only his eyes were flecked with pure honey-gold.

"This Christmas has been special for me too." He flashed her one of his jaw-dropping grins, and her pulse gave a decisive lurch.

"Wanna see the pictures I took from the helicopter ride?" She dug her cellphone out of her purse and scrolled through the pictures.

"There are others?" he asked, as she continued thumbing through them. "I see one of the ship before we departed."

"I always take before and after shots. It's surprising how different things look depending on the time of day. This picture was taken at noon, when I arrived at the cruise ship terminal."

He studied the picture. "You're a very good photographer."

"Thanks." She shot him an unconvinced look. "I'm strictly an amateur and will stick to screenwriting."

"Believe me, you're excellent at both." Seeing the affection in his eyes, she felt her cheeks flush.

He grinned and lightly kissed the tip of her nose. "Once we get back, we'll check our haupia. It should be firm enough after being refrigerated for several hours." He grazed his lips over her hair. "We can bring it up to the observation deck and eat our coconut dessert with a cup of Kona coffee, which has become my personal favorite. But first, we'll eat a proper Christmas dinner with roast turkey and mashed potatoes."

"I want to see the gingerbread village the chefs displayed in the grand foyer. There's supposed to be simulated snow too."

"We'll see everything, all right?" He drew her closer. "This time I promise we'll spend the evening alone."

"We won't be inviting Rachel?"

He chuckled. "We won't be inviting anyone. Just you and me. And ..."

She knew he was making amends for the previous night when Jillian and her friends had arrived at their table.

She slanted him an impudent grin. "And what?"

"And your laptop." He flashed a roguish smile. "I believe we can make some definite improvements to your opening scene."

Her eyes widened. "We've changed the name of the bird. What else do you want? I can't keep making all these changes."

"Yes, but this change is very important." He brushed a kiss over her lips.

"The kissing scene?" An involuntarily provocative smile formed. "I told you the scene can't end with the hero and heroine passionately kissing. They only just met. In fact, they were probably arguing about something."

"Except this isn't the first scene anymore." He gave her a warm, sweet kiss on the lips. "It's the second."

CHAPTER 7

*A*ngelina sat with Rachel inside their cabin and gazed out the porthole. The cruise ship had arrived at the second port on their itinerary, Honolulu. Red and green Christmas lights twinkled from a tour boat berthed near the terminal. The entire harbor sparkled as if it had been sprinkled with holiday fairy dust, the sun scattering diamond patterns across the ocean's surface.

Angelina had skipped Caleb's morning lecture again, sending him a quick text that she wanted to spend the last few hours with Rachel before she left for good.

"How was Christmas?" Rachel asked. Between questions, she hummed "I'll Be Home For Christmas" off-tune. "And how did the helicopter ride with Caleb go?"

She scooped up a bright-yellow caftan and stuffed it into her suitcase. Although she had invited Caleb and Angelina to accompany her when she disembarked and reunited with her husband, Caleb had declined, saying he and Angelina were going on an excursion. He hadn't told Angelina which one—only that she should wear closed-toe shoes with proper traction, ankle-high socks, and comfortable clothes. He encouraged her to wear a hat too, and she'd borrowed Rachel's broad-brimmed fedora.

"How was the helicopter ride with Caleb yesterday?" Rachel repeated, raising her voice. "And how was Christmas?"

Fabulous, Angelina thought. Memorable. Wonderful.

The non-work day had left her refreshed and invigorated, and allowed her to make excellent headway on rewriting and tightening various scenes in her screenplay the night before. Finally, she was beginning to find balance in her life. When Caleb had suggested another excursion, she'd readily agreed.

"I've never spent a Christmas Day quite like that one," she said aloud. "How was yours?"

"Very pleasant." Rachel pointed out the porthole to the harbor. "If I was going back to California, I'd say I'd miss Hawaii, but I'll be living here permanently, so I don't have to say a thing. It seems surreal after living on the mainland my entire life."

"Yes, the islands are otherworldly," Angelina agreed. Images flashed through her mind of waking up every morning to the soft murmurs of the sea, scuba diving and exploring colorful coral reefs with Caleb, walking along a sandy beach, a salty breeze tingling their cheeks.

The idea of leaving, and the loneliness that would invade her once the cruise was over, ran deep. So far, the week had been wonderful. The thought of leaving was agonizing. She sighed and ran her fingers down her cheeks. More and more, a part of her wanted to stay in Hawaii. More than a part, if she were honest with herself.

However, she was a practical woman, earning a living, independent and finally on track after the heartbreak of losing her husband. One way or another, her adventure would soon come to an end.

She squared her shoulders and checked her appearance in

the full-length door mirror—twill shorts and a rounded neck T-shirt in a dusty pink color, which complemented her rosy cheeks. She'd gotten entirely too much sun, she decided, and quickly applied sunscreen.

Fastening a daypack around her waist, she said, "Yesterday, I learned so much about active volcanoes."

Equally important, she'd learned so much about Caleb. His explanations about the volcanic eruptions were interesting—thorough, intense, and yet animated, providing her with ample information for her script. They'd finished Christmas Day on the observation deck savoring sweet, coconutty spoonful's of haupia while "Have Yourself a Merry Little Christmas" played in the background.

She liked him.

She liked him a lot.

After dessert, they had reviewed her script.

"Every act in a movie relies on sight and sound," she explained to him. "Pack as much emotion as possible into every scene."

He had agreed, referring to the scent of the lehua flower before his mouth met hers.

Sighing again, she smiled.

Rachel cocked her head. "Daydreaming about a certain famous and thoroughly handsome volcanologist?"

Angelina blinked in startled confusion, then tightened her smile. "How was the Lava Falls bus tour?"

"Due to safety precautions, some of the areas were closed, although the bus was able to drive through historic old town Hilo. We toured Liliuokalani Gardens too. Those were so peaceful. With all the arched bridges and pagodas, I felt like I was in Japan." Rachel ran her fingers across the curved handles of her suitcase. "Still, I missed not seeing Fred on Christmas Day."

"You'll see him today."

"Yes, finally. Although I'll miss not seeing you anymore." With tears filling her eyes, Rachel embraced Angelina in a warm hug. "Aloha, my dear friend."

Which meant far more than hello or good-bye, Angelina had learned. *Aloha* meant a genuine love and respect for all people.

"Aloha," she said in reply, her voice choked.

She'd become enchanted with Hawaiian culture and beliefs. Their philosophy about life—what they called *Huna*, or inner knowledge of energy, love, happiness—was highly respected and passed down through generations. Plus, the entire pace of the islands was more relaxed. She was thoroughly interested in their Polynesian customs, which were as varied as the people.

"I'll miss you too." Angelina hugged Rachel in return. "I promise we'll call and text each other."

"And you'll return to the islands, right?" Rachel let go of Angelina and patted her stomach. "To see the baby and me and Fred, and Fred's grandmother ... and to return my fedora hat."

Angelina laughed. "I'd love to. Maybe one day."

"You must come back." Rachel gave the cabin a last perusal and tucked a purple orchid behind her left ear. "In the meantime, I want updates on your dates with Caleb."

"We're not dating."

"Of course you are." Rachel didn't attempt to hide her smile as she swiveled to close her suitcase. "You've both developed a genuine fondness for each other."

Developed a genuine fondness?

Angelina grinned. Yes, her every moment with Caleb was fairy-tale-like, and she couldn't deny the happiness lighting up her mind, her days, each time she saw him. But Caleb was part of a make-believe world, much like the magnificent tropical scenery surrounding them.

Sure, they spent hours bantering and were never at a loss for words. And she'd be the first to concede that each minute spent with him was a fascinating glimpse into his brilliant mind and academic world.

However, she'd also be the first to acknowledge that a future with him was impossible given their jobs and lifestyles. The distance between California and Hawaii was twenty-five hundred miles, which was not exactly an easy commute.

Firmly, Angelina shook aside any whimsical hopes of a future with Caleb. She needed to set Rachel—and herself—straight.

"It would be more accurate to say he barged into my life, and that because of my job, I've been like a puppet on a string, acceding to his every suggestion."

Rachel whipped around. "Oh, really? You may have felt like that before you met him in person, but I know you don't feel that way anymore." She held up a finger to prevent Angelina from speaking. "You care about him more than you're admitting because you're in love with him."

"Love?" Angelina backed up a foot. "You're joking, right? We just met."

A knowing gleam reflected in Rachel's green eyes. "Why don't you tell him how you feel?"

"I most certainly will not!" Angelina adjusted her hat, then picked up Rachel's suitcase to carry it to the dock for her. "A romance can't develop in such a short time. Everyone knows that's impossible."

Rachel's soft voice checked Angelina as she yanked the cabin door with a boisterous click. "Nothing is impossible when two people are falling in love."

* * *

TEN MINUTES LATER, Caleb met Angelina on the departure deck as she wiped tears from her eyes.

Whenever she saw him, she couldn't tamp down her reaction—the bewildering flurries of excitement in her belly, the way her heart rate quickened. He was so fine-looking, so self-assured. So utterly masculine in his chambray shirt and chocolate-brown cargo shorts.

He carried a backpack over his shoulders, and the thought crossed her mind that his broad shoulders were strong enough to carry any burden.

He offered his usual heartfelt smile and gave her his full attention. "Why are you crying, Angelina?" With his forefinger, he caught an errant tear running down her cheek.

"Off Rachel goes on an adventure of a lifetime and I already miss her." Angelina waved a final aloha as Rachel climbed into a waiting taxicab. "In a short time, we've become best friends."

"She's a fun, outgoing woman. Sounds like she's married to a great guy and will soon be mother to an adorable baby. You can visit her when you return to Hawaii."

"Who said I'm returning?" Angelina countered. "My life is in California."

"We'll have to force you to come back here, then." He grinned. "Although forcing and Hawaii have little in common."

He was teasing, and she wanted to laugh. Instead, her stomach clenched. She needed to come to grips with the fact that this magical place, this superb man, this festive cruise ship, would soon be a distant memory. Certainly, Hawaii was gorgeous. Nonetheless it wasn't home, because home was in California.

Wasn't it?

The deadlines and traffic and stress ... Wasn't home supposed to be somewhere peaceful and serene?

"Rachel and I promised we'll email or Skype every week," she said.

For a moment, he kept silent, eyeing the bustling activity of the harbor, the tour boats and tugboats.

"Email and Skype are not the same as experiencing life together, in person," he finally said.

He was right.

She blew out a breath, then rallied by offering a small smile. "What's on tap for today?"

"Still a surprise," he said. "I will tell you I packed rain ponchos, bottled water and snacks. But first, mosquito repellent." He fished in his backpack and removed a spray can, instructing her to spritz her arms and legs. When she finished, he did the same. Then he steered her toward a waiting excursion bus, past the shopkeepers setting up their wares—handcrafted wooden bowls, packages of macadamia nuts, and baskets woven from coconut fronds.

"I looked over a whale-watching leaflet," he said. "As much as I would have enjoyed sharing that particular adventure with you, my seasickness has only just abated and if the seas are rough ..."

"Perfectly understandable." She shaded her eyes and peered toward the sun-drenched city's downtown district. "So what did you book instead?"

He slipped his arm around her shoulders, and she rested her cheek against his soft shirt. Although the weather was warm, gentle trade winds brought a welcome cooling effect.

She glanced at him, his firm jaw, one hand shoved into his shorts pocket, the tiny creases at the corner of his eyes. He was a man who was extraordinarily intelligent, passionate about helping people, and generous with his time. In turn, he made her feel secure whenever she was with him.

"I booked a hiking venture for us." He paused to pull a brochure from his shorts pocket and read aloud. "'Discover the hidden treasures of Oahu's volcanic rainforest on this moderate two-mile round-trip hike.'"

"A hike? Who classified it as moderate? You, the mountain climber?"

He laughed. "I was assured by our illustrious cruise director, Gabriella, that this is a non-strenuous hike." He handed Angelina the brochure. "The exact description reads 'journey through the past and present'. I figured a hike would give you the chance to experience a real rainforest. If my memory serves me correctly, the third act in your screenplay is set in one. Doesn't the hero sprain his ankle and the heroine saves the day?"

"So you did read my entire screenplay?"

He winked. "A considerable portion, yes."

She winced. "How many errors did you find in the rainforest scene?" In her mind's eye, she visualized the many hours she'd spent writing and rewriting.

He slid her hand into the crook of his arm as they continued walking toward the bus. "After we finish our rainforest exploration, you tell me."

"Will we be gone long?"

"Four hours."

He pushed a dark strand of hair from his face. Offhandedly, he'd remarked the day before about getting a haircut when he reached Maui. She preferred his hair long. It went well with his university-professor image.

She forced herself to stop staring at him and concentrated on the brochure.

"Don't worry," he teased as they boarded the air-conditioned bus. "At least this adventure is on the ground."

* * *

THE TOWERING waterfall cascading down the mountainside, Caleb thought, was a true testament to the splendor of Hawaii. Unspoiled and natural. Exquisite. However, all that beauty was no comparison to the stunning woman standing beside it.

They had split from their excursion group with the promise they'd meet at the edge of the rainforest within the hour. Twisting vines, giant leaves, and gargantuan boulders made it seem like they were deep in the jungle, although they were only a couple hours away from the cruise ship.

Which gave him additional time, he reasoned, to feast his eyes on Angelina. When he explained the native plants to her, her engaging smile warmed him to the core. Whenever she grabbed his hand to steady herself, her touch brought tingles to his skin. Genuinely engrossed, endlessly enquiring, she delighted and captivated him, something no woman had ever done before. And lately, he couldn't fathom a life without her.

She struck a silly pose beside the waterfall as he snapped photos of her. Laughing above the sound of the thundering water, she held her arms beneath the fierce spray.

"The water's warm! I thought it would be freezing," she said.

"Wanna go for a swim?" he joked, gesturing to the glistening pool at the bottom of the waterfall. They hadn't brought their swimsuits, and now he wished they had. He'd never been one to give in to impulses, but he wanted to plunge into the clear waters with her, hold her in his arms and listen to her lilting laughter as she shook the wetness from her hair.

Next time, he told himself.

Although there wouldn't be a next time. That clear, shattering reality left him with a feeling of panic. Time was slipping away.

With quick, sure footsteps, she crossed a muddy trail leading to a small stream. Standing on tiptoe, she examined the bright red berries of the strawberry guava tree.

"*Psidium cattleianum*," he automatically supplied.

"I smelled the fruit's aroma from the waterfalls," she said. "I didn't realize the trees grew so tall."

"They look harmless." He was prepared to launch into lecture mode, explaining how guava fruit was causing horrific damage to the forestland. She forestalled him.

"The guava tree is a killer," she said, "and the major degradation of Hawaiian forests."

Surprised, he stared at her. "How did you know?"

"How do you think?" she asked with a grin. "I'm no fly-by-night screenwriter who hasn't done her due diligence." She picked two pieces of fruit from the tree, both the size of large marbles, and handed him one. He took a bite, savoring the sweet-tart taste. She watched him before taking a bite of her own.

"Don't spit out the seeds," she warned as they both chewed.

Silently, he applauded her. Apparently, she'd already researched the Hawaiian flora and fauna information that he'd expounded on during their hike. She hadn't interrupted him, despite the many minutes he'd spoken. Instead, she had seemed genuinely engaged.

"Consequently, you understand," he said, "that thousands of Hawaiian acres are covered with strawberry guava?"

"I do. And I also know that this fruit can't keep growing at this pace. Endangered species—both plants and animals—depend on a sound ecosystem. Unfortunately, this plant spreads very quickly and chokes out other forms of plant life."

He lifted her hand and kissed it. "I'm impressed."

"Thanks. I've been researching the details of my screen-play for many months."

He nodded. Still holding her hand, he motioned toward the lush vegetation. Not far from them, a spectacular water-fall plunged at least fifteen feet. "I meant I'm impressed by not only your work, but you. You're breathtaking in this tropical setting."

Self-consciously, she pushed a curly wisp from her cheek. "Even with my hair going every which way and my sunburned nose and sweaty arms?"

He reached for her. "Especially so. And I love seeing you happy."

For only an instant, she tensed before he pulled her into his arms.

"Caleb, you're getting off the ship in a couple days," she said.

"I'm very aware of that fact, Angelina."

"You say it like it doesn't matter." She focused on the guava tree. "Coupled with …"

His gaze on her sharpened. "With what? We can't deny what's happening between us. We're so good together. Surely you must agree."

She still wouldn't meet his eyes.

"Yes, but it doesn't change anything." Finally, she gazed up at him. "Sure, I look around at this picturesque setting and think, whoa, stop my California life because I belong here in this unbelievable paradise." She pulled off her hat, ran a hand through the offending blonde curls. "Can you believe my work has been exceptionally productive on this cruise, and I've accomplished more in a few days than I have in the last month? I've woken up in the middle of the night and prayed, asking God if I'm foolish for believing there's truly such a thing as a happily ever after."

"A happily ever after with us?"

"Yes."

"And what did God say?"

"He said I'm perfectly rational."

He held her closer. "Then listen to God."

"I do, at least I try to." She broke from his grip. "But still, you and I don't know each other well enough."

"I know everything I need to know about you."

"No, you don't." Her mouth tightened. "I'm perfectly happy pursuing my career, and dating isn't a part of my life."

"It should be. You're young and vivacious and—"

She shook her head. "And I'm a widow."

"What?" He paused. "I … I didn't know." There were no trite phrases he could utter, no shiny remarks. A heavy feeling hit his stomach. "I'm sorry for your loss."

She'd told him she wasn't married, and he had wondered why a woman like her—witty and vibrant and gorgeous—wasn't taken by now. But he'd kept silent and hadn't asked, assuming there was an unhappy breakup or divorce in her past. Ex-husbands were one thing. But the death of her husband left him with a loss for any words that were heartfelt enough.

Tenderly, he brushed her hand.

She shifted a couple inches away. "My husband died unexpectedly. We weren't married long. He was a fine man—morally upright and generous. He had a smile for everyone."

Numerous beats passed, the silence awkward.

"What happened?" Caleb asked.

"He was hit by a drunk driver while crossing a street in LA. It was an accident." She hesitated. "It's been almost six years."

Caleb reached for his water bottle in his backpack and offered her a drink. She refused.

"Wouldn't your husband want you to move on with your life?" he asked softly.

She turned to stare at a native fern, the *palapala*, a favorite fern to make leis. Somehow, Caleb was sure she already knew that. Her screenplay was well-researched, a great deal more so than he'd initially realized. She knew her craft and was a hard worker.

"Let's just enjoy the time we have left together," she said.

He'd become fairly adept at keeping his dating life casual, but with Angelina Conte, he didn't want an off-the-cuff romance with no promises or commitments. With her, he wanted an agreement and an assurance.

And then what? They'd agree to continue their relationship long distance?

He couldn't leave his new post in Hawaii. He was needed here. There was much to do, especially with a violently dangerous volcano. Many peoples' lives and livelihoods were at stake.

"Did you know a volcano is considered active if it's erupted in the past ten thousand years?" he asked.

"No, I didn't."

He blew out a breath, took a sip of water. Everything he wanted to say to her was coming out like an inane spouting of facts that had no importance, no bearing on the real truth.

And that truth was an intense, no-holds-barred attraction he couldn't deny.

He became conscious his gaze had been fixed on her all this time, and he prompted himself to concentrate on what she'd said—the devastating loss of her husband, and that she wanted to enjoy the time they had left together.

"You make me wish this cruise wasn't coming to an end," he admitted.

He watched her exquisite features, full of sadness, and decided he wouldn't push the conversation any further. Soon, they would be pulled apart by hundreds of miles. He'd advance to his new position in Hawaii, and she'd return to California.

He scrubbed a hand over his face and peered at the setting sun starting its descent. Their shadows were beginning to lengthen. "We'd better get back to our hiking group. Otherwise, the crew will organize a search party for us."

"I can't imagine the distinguished Captain Berg traipsing through the rainforest with a flashlight," she said.

Caleb placed the water bottle in his backpack and offered his hand. "Especially when we're scheduled to arrive at Kauai by midmorning tomorrow. The captain will be too busy steering to be delayed by two missing passengers. And do you recall what he announced over the loudspeaker two days ago? If people don't make it back from their excursions on time, he hopes they have a fabulous camera to take a picture of the ship sailing away."

He was heartened when she grinned, and even more so when she accepted his hand.

"I do recall him saying that. I also read in The Coral Chronicle, our ship's newsletter, that one of tomorrow's excursions is a river cruise and luau on Kauai."

He steered her toward the bamboo trail leading to the edge of the rainforest. "Good, because we're going."

"Caleb, I can't." The grin fled from her expression. "I'm revising the last two scenes of my screenplay."

"You can work on your screenplay after we have dinner." He broke her objection by taking her in his arms and pressing a light kiss on her forehead. "Didn't you say your writing has been more productive these past few days?"

Her brow furrowed. "Yes, although I need sleep, and the last scene isn't going to write itself."

"Maybe I can help."

She sighed. "Unless you're a farmer, I highly doubt it."

She looked so breathtaking he was loath to let her go. "Do

you like steak as much as you like sleep?" he asked. She nodded. "So, we'll dine early at the Cattlemen's Club, and end the night eating dessert at one of the many ice cream bars. Chocolate, vanilla or strawberry ice cream?"

She laughed. "Neapolitan."

"All three flavors, then." He smiled.

He hadn't yet bought her a Christmas gift and recalled several high-end boutiques were located near the steak restaurant. Perhaps she could choose a gift in one of the boutiques. He'd never been proficient at buying gifts for people, and dinner and ice cream provided by the ship didn't count.

Although she deserved a special hand-picked gift, a surprise, something that meant … something.

"Tomorrow I'll come to your cabin after my lecture is finished. Unless, of course, you're attending?" He raised his eyebrows in a teasing look. "I missed you yesterday and even more so today when I took roll call."

"You've never taken roll call." She grinned as she jabbed him in the ribs.

"I could."

She swallowed a chuckle. "Since you're bent on being an upstanding professor, do you also give out grades?"

You're an A, he thought, thinking of their kisses.

"So tonight and tomorrow are settled," he said. "You'll have more than enough time for your screenplay."

And time for me.

She hooked a hand on her hip. "Are you always this organized?"

"Always." He bent his head to kiss her, and she raised her lips to his.

More kissing, he decided, was a very good thing.

CHAPTER 8

"*A*loha, everyone. The *Bird of Paradise* has docked at Nawiliwili Harbor, which is on the southeast side of Kauai. If you're booked on the Wailua River day tour, meet in the theater at eleven and wait for your group to be called." Gabriella DeLuca's cheery voice echoed from the loudspeaker in the hallway outside Angelina's cabin. "The cruise is an hour and a half. Afterward, you'll enjoy a luau, one of the most celebrated in the world, and finish your evening in authentic Hawaiian style."

Angelina half listened to the cruise director's message while typing a run-on sentence—a breathless bit of dialogue for one of her characters. Surely, the hero and heroine needed a happy ending. Surely, nothing would keep them apart, not even the complication of a volcano.

She clicked off her computer and pushed out a long breath. She was grateful her deadline wasn't until January since she was now spending every waking minute with Caleb.

And why not? Their days were limited, and the cruise was

a once-in-a-lifetime experience. At least, that's what she rationalized whenever she started to feel guilty.

Daily, she emailed Devon, her boss, to keep him up-to-date on her progress. Unfortunately, the Internet connection was slow and she hadn't received a response for a few days. Of course, with the Christmas holiday, everyone at Partridge Production Studios would most likely be out of the office until after New Year's.

Gabriella's announcement had scarcely finished when a text from Caleb slid across Angelina's phone screen.

Good morning, gorgeous.

Good morning, she typed back.

You heard Gabriella's announcement?

Loud and clear.

Then I'll be knocking on your cabin door at 10:30.

Her heart quickened.

Stay calm. This entire cruise is about finishing your screenplay, not a flirty exchange with a scientist who's too handsome for his own good.

Are you still there? Is that time suitable? he asked.

"Suitable?" she questioned the empty cabin. Any time was "suitable" if she had the opportunity to see him. The earlier, the better.

She wondered what he was wearing while he texted her, and if he'd just gone for a vigorous swim. He'd mentioned the swim had become part of his morning routine after his daily lecture. She visualized him with his shirt off, his strong body slick with clear drops of water running down his chest, a towel slung around his broad shoulders.

Oh, my. She swallowed.

10:30 is perfect, she texted. *See you soon.*

She took a swig from a bottle of water on her small night-stand and went to her closet.

What did one wear for a river cruise and luau? She sorted

the question in her mind while ranking the handful of clothes she'd brought with her. She held up a vivid turquoise sundress, took a picture, and texted it to Rachel, asking for her opinion. Rachel replied that because the luau was on a beach and the group would be sitting at picnic tables in the sand, a dress wasn't the best option.

Angelina agreed. She noticed that Hawaii was extremely casual and decided on lightweight Capri pants in a deep-rose, paired with a ruffled sleeve top in a garden floral design.

"Sand in my toes," she mused, slipping into breezy flip-flop sandals before giving herself a final perusal in the mirror.

Her bright blue eyes glowed back at her, her cheeks flushed pink with excitement.

At exactly ten thirty, Caleb rapped lightly on her cabin door.

"Aloha." She greeted him with a welcoming smile. "I'm ready."

He gave her only a second to admire his appearance—white polo shirt and khaki shorts—and then he was reaching for her, pressing her body close to his. She twined her arms around his shoulders. His hands slid down her spine, and he nuzzled her neck as she rested her head against his chest.

Beneath the cotton of his shirt, his chest was broad and comforting, his heartbeat strong. She was glad he wasn't wearing a typical Hawaiian shirt like most of the other men —short-sleeved button-downs imprinted with palm trees or coconuts. Somehow, that style didn't fit Caleb. He was staid and steadfast, not flashy, sporting a classical style of men's wear that suited his self-confidence.

He tipped her chin up and said quietly, "I missed you."

"We were together until midnight."

"Which wasn't nearly enough time to spend with you."

They shared a silence for several beats. "You should know, Angelina, that all of this is new territory for me."

It was on the tip of her tongue to ask him what he meant, but she knew. Yes, she definitely knew.

"It's new territory for me too." Guardedly, she laid an unsteady hand on his jaw. He'd grown a slight beard since the cruise had started, the dark stubbles prickly beneath her fingers.

"I should get a shave and haircut once I reach Maui," he said.

She considered voicing her opinion again. Both his full thick hair and stubbled chin were wildly appealing.

Her feelings for him had grown with such force, she hardly had the resources to breathe, to say nothing of having a chat about his choice of haircuts.

Before she could reply, he twirled her around. "Did I wish you good morning and tell you that you're a knockout?"

She laughed. "No, but good morning to you, and a sincere thank you for the compliment. You don't look half bad yourself." Her laughter receded. "Did your lecture go well this morning?"

"The room was filled to capacity, and many people asked questions. I assured the attendees I'm always available and provided my email address. As you know, my last day on the ship is nearing. I heard a flower specialist is replacing me for the morning lectures."

How could she forget their time together was coming to an end?

And then ... what? Silent nights and hundreds of miles between them.

She worried the thoughts around in her mind. When it was over and he was gone, she'd nurse her wounds and be thankful she'd known him. Besides, the wall around her heart was impossible to breach, and somehow, she felt he was keeping any promise of commitment in check by not talking about the future.

Choked by a silent sob, she paused to gain control of her voice. "Many scientists are standoffish. You're generous to provide your personal email to strangers."

"The more people learn about volcanoes, the more they can become proactive," he said. "Giving of my time and expertise is the least I can do. Knowledge saves lives."

* * *

An hour later, Caleb and Angelina, along with a score of cruisers and their tour guide, boarded a flat-bottomed river-boat at the Waialeale crater. Preferring to stand by the windows rather than sit on one of the long benches, Angelina noted with appreciation the lush grasslands bordering the riverbanks.

The river was a lengthy and meandering one, the guide explained, and the only navigable river in Hawaii.

They glided past several kayakers, and Caleb identified Mt. Waialeale, a cloud-covered, green mountain range, in the distance.

"Waialeale means rippling water in Hawaiian," the guide continued, "and this mountain range sits in the middle of the island. Although it's been called the wettest spot on the planet, it's actually the second wettest, as a range in India claimed first place."

"Waialeale receives around 450 inches of rain per year." Caleb bent close to whisper in Angelina's ear, and she felt the caress of his soft breath. He always smelled of mountain air and a hint of coffee. Earthy and woodsy, like the outdoors he loved.

He shifted to stand behind her. As the boat passed a

particularly barren place, he indicated where a recent tropical storm had removed the trees and topsoil.

Enchanted by the sights and sounds of the hula dancers and ukulele players on board, the sensation of her hair being tossed by a sultry breeze, she relinquished the last of her restraints.

Why not? The islands followed their own path, and she embraced the magic.

Caleb's arm circled her waist, and she leaned against him, relishing his nearness. Did he realize just how perilous this all was for her? The last time she'd given her love to a man, he'd died, leaving her desolate and abandoned.

Given her love to a man? Her eyes went wide.

Who said anything about love? Caleb had only said they were "good together" and that this was "new territory." He'd offered no promises to see her after he settled in Maui.

Leisurely, he twined her curls around his finger. "What are you thinking?" he murmured.

"Something about this trip makes me want to reexamine my priorities and what's really important. I thought it was—"

"Work?"

With great effort, she didn't respond except for a slight nod.

After a thirty-minute stretch, the boat reached the landing for the sacred Fern Grotto, a lava rock grotto covered in tropical ferns.

Caleb and Angelina turned to view their guide as he explained that they would be serenaded by customary, native songs at the grotto. "One of which," he emphasized to the couples lining the open-air deck, "is the 'Hawaiian Wedding Song.'"

"A wedding song," Caleb mused. "Should we get married?"

She contemplated his face, attempting to read the inscrutable. Sometimes, she couldn't tell whether he was serious or joking. She curtailed the conversation by following the couple in front of them off the boat. How else could she possibly respond to him?

"You're discussing marriage to the wrong woman, Caleb," she said over her shoulder. "I'm focused on my career."

He didn't answer, didn't attempt to question her.

When they started for the planked path leading to the grotto, he held her hand, his expression again giving nothing away.

The Fern Grotto was at the end of a short nature walk. Fragrant native flowers—yellow and pink ginger, stunning orchids forming along long tree spikes, tall red flowers the colors of a burning bush—enhanced their steps. Tropical zebra plants and towering palms ruled the walkway, a teeming, diverse array of vegetation and wildlife. To her delight, Caleb recited the Hawaiian names, as well as the medicinal, religious, and cultural value of various plants.

When they reached the end of the walkway, he indicated the ferns growing upside down, while their guide added that the ferns were formed millions of years ago.

Angelina lifted her face to the sun, soaking it all in. She felt utterly swept off her feet by the aloha spirit—the charm, warmth, and harmony of the Hawaiian people.

Caleb took her arm, moving her a little way away. "Shall we venture closer and explore this famous grotto where numerous couples are married every year?"

Agreeing, she adjusted her sunglasses and walked with him. She was too happy not to enjoy this fantasy, because Hawaii made her feel alive. Thanks to Caleb, she was emerging into the writer she'd always aspired to become. Well-traveled, well-informed, and creative.

This was another reason why she needed to return to California to see the production of her screenplay through from beginning to end, or however long fickle Hollywood might take.

But when Caleb gazed at her with his dark eyes, smoky and dangerous, she forgot her complex world, her impossible deadlines, the accolades of success, because nothing mattered except him.

"Ready to be serenaded?" Caleb asked.

When the musicians finished, several couples attempted to hula dance with their tour guide, and Caleb and Angelina cheered them on.

As the guide led them back to the riverboat, Caleb stood aside so Angelina could walk ahead of him back along the narrow walkway. The perfect gentleman as always, she thought. She welcomed his unstudied social graces, the sincere thoughtfulness in his gaze when he listened to her. All these attributes were a matter of course for him, simply a part of who he was.

Yes, she was excited by his every touch and intrigued by their lengthy conversations about everything and nothing. Each moment with him was sweet and memorable.

She'd never felt like that before with any man, and the realization left her breathless. Perhaps her memories of Jake were enhanced by rose-colored glasses, and it was time she slipped those glasses off. Recollections of who he had really been were elusive, refined by wishful thinking and the exhilaration of being newlyweds.

Whereas with Caleb, her feelings were grounded in reality.

* * *

"HERE COME MORE SPELLBINDING VIEWS!" their guide exclaimed as the riverboat docked at the luau facility. The cruisers disembarked and were quickly transported by tram to a sandy beach overlooking the ocean. Following a script, the guide read, "'This luau honors Polynesian traditions and features local, delectable delights. Afterwards, you'll be treated to a hula and a Samoan fire-knife dance.'" He lowered the script. "For a final tidbit of information—our luau location was once a place reserved for Hawaiian royalty."

Caleb slung his arm around Angelina's shoulders. "Shall we, your majesty?"

Angelina smiled. "I'm as ready as you are, Prince Charming."

Greeters draped colorful purple, green, and white leis around their necks, and a photographer asked to take their "remembrance photo", which would be available for purchase in the ship's gift shop the following day.

Driven by the enthusiasm and excitement of the evening, they agreed.

Scents of roasted pork and charcoal permeated the air, while a gust of wind from the sea carried a whiff of seared grilled fish and the bright white flesh of fresh coconut.

"The process is called *imu*," Angelina said, gesturing to the pit where the pig was being roasted. "The pig is wrapped in ti leaves and cooked underground, then served on banana leaves. Think of the pit as an earth oven."

"For a minute," Caleb said, "I had a flare of hope that I might actually know more about a luau than you do."

"Not a chance." Her eyes sparkled. "My screenplay features a luau scene, and I spent a lot of time researching it. I couldn't write about a Hawaiian feast without grass skirts and cooked taro leaves and octopus appetizers."

"Heaven forbid," he teased.

They both declined offers of wine, beer, and mai tai, opting for cold glasses of juice. Within the open-air dining facility, they found a picnic table with seating for eight people. Caleb recognized a husband and wife team from the haupia cooking class and greeted them with a smiling aloha.

"Quite a feast. We'll make a dish and sit here," Caleb said.

The abundant, mouthwatering buffet was loaded with professionally cooked meats and vegetables, and they piled their plates with kalua pork, beef teriyaki, chicken adobo, and sweet and sour mahi-mahi.

"*Kau kau* is another word for food in Hawaiian," Caleb said as they wended their way back to their table.

She grinned. "I knew that too."

Before eating, she bowed her head and whispered a prayer of thanks to God. He did the same, reflecting that this was one of the many reasons why he was attracted to her. Outwardly, she was a shimmering diamond, brilliant and sparkling, feminine and appealing. Inwardly, where it truly mattered, her spirit was humble. The manner in which she conducted herself, the way she rested her faith in God, was truly inspiring. As was her nature, she was kind and gentle, sincerely interested in the people around her.

When they finished praying, the couple sitting across from them murmured their approval.

Angelina scooped Hawaiian sweet potatoes off her over-flowing plate. "I'll be dieting for a month once this cruise is finished. I haven't tasted any kau kau I haven't liked."

Caleb agreed. "Speaking of food, if we leave the ship as soon as it docks in Maui, you can meet my cousin and his wife for lunch, and then drive with me to my new place." He stretched out his long legs. "It's near the Haleakala crater, and the sunsets are on many people's bucket lists."

"I'd like that."

"Is that a promise?"

"A promise to what?"

"To see the sunsets."

She attempted a smile. "Someday, perhaps."

"Someday," he said quietly. He scrubbed a hand over his face. "In any event, we can spend the day exploring the island and seeing my new home. I rented a villa along the shoreline of the Pacific Ocean, and the views are supposed to be amazing."

"Sounds lovely."

A rush of hilarity from the table across from them briefly distracted her, but then she turned back to him and said, "You haven't seen your new home yet?"

"Only the Internet photos. I secured a two-year lease. Now as I was saying ..." he watched her closely, "I'd like you to meet Kapena and Zoe. If we're lucky, he'll cook for us."

"I'd like that," she said softly, and then looked away.

A sadness he could hardly explain burrowed deep into his heart. He tried to let go of it. Her career came first, she'd informed him. His career did too. He hadn't told her that. Or had he, in so many non-words?

When the plates had been cleared and the entertainment began, he and Angelina swiveled on the picnic bench to view the performers. Three Polynesian musicians wearing Santa hats, one of them strumming a candy cane, the other two playing a bongo drum and ukulele respectively, belted out the Hawaiian carol, "Christmas Luau."

Angelina clapped and sang in time to the cheerful music. "Caleb," she said, leaning close to him, "I've heard this song a hundred times this week on the ship, but I never get tired of the fun lyrics."

He listened, nodding to the beat. "Me neither."

She swayed to the melody and sang, "'The tables were loaded with plenty of kau kau ...'"

He pressed a kiss on her hair and drew her to him. Her voice was exquisite. He'd never grow tired of hearing her sing. He'd never grow tired of Christmas. He'd never grow tired of her.

When the song ended, she twisted to face him, her gaze lifting to his, and the gentle yielding in their blue depths was almost his undoing. He wanted to stay immersed in her gaze, to leave the luau and be alone with her, to ask her to stay with him in Maui, at his rented oceanfront villa that he'd never seen. They'd take long drives and see Haleakala's sunsets. Some people waited a lifetime for that otherworldly experience, to stand on top of the world, enveloped by a sense of the mysterious and the remote.

"You're talking about marriage to the wrong woman, Caleb. I'm focused on my career."

Her remembered words brought his fantasy to a crashing halt.

When his marriage ended, his wife had packed her suitcases and articulated in no uncertain words that she'd met another man—someone who was entertaining and stimulating. Someone, she insinuated, who was the complete opposite of Caleb. Furthermore, she was making time to pursue her career as a lawyer rather than follow him all over the world.

If he'd ever been searching for an ego-deflating letdown, then that was it, her clear judgment that he wasn't "all that special".

As the music continued, he and Angelina were quiet as they listened. From behind came the sounds of the sea, the surf crashing along the beach. The sun had begun its descent and drenched the sand in golden light. Torches were lit on long wooden poles, and flickering plumes of fire weaved a dreamlike spell over the entire gathering.

During a break between songs, Angelina fingered the lei around her neck and murmured, "Caleb, can I ask you a question?"

"Certainly."

"I know you were married."

"As were you."

"I told you about my marriage."

"And now you want to ask me about mine."

"Yes."

This was as good a time as any. He tried to remember what his ex-wife looked like, smelled like, her mannerisms, but nothing came to mind.

"I'll give you a shortened account of our three years of marriage. In summary, Mona was bored with me and my work."

Angelina frowned. "I don't understand. Your work is fascinating."

"To you. To some people." He paused. "Here's the thing—Mona wasn't entirely at fault. I was caught up in my research, and I ignored her for a good amount of those three years. I traveled to Malaysia alone, and when I completed my research there, I asked her to come with me to the state of Washington, my next assignment. She refused. I tried everything to persuade her—flowers, fancy dinners, a promise of an extravagant vacation. You see, my career was on an upward swing."

"An exciting time for you, Caleb, I'm sure."

"For me, not Mona. And in the end, nothing I could do persuaded her. Shortly afterward, she filed for divorce. I willingly signed the papers."

"A failed marriage is always sad," Angelina said, quietly touching his arm in sympathy.

"Even before Malaysia, Mona and I weren't compatible," he said. "Neither of us could handle being together for long periods. We never laughed, never really talked. Or rather, I suppose I talked too much about ..."

"Volcanoes," Angelina said, the heat of indignant color spreading across her face. "And saving peoples' lives with your research."

Odd, he thought, that he could have a heart-to-heart with her, speaking without anger or regret over his failed marriage. Angelina was truly caring and thoughtful.

"And your marriage ended for entirely different reasons," he said.

"Yes. After Jake died, I didn't function for a long time. Finally, I'm standing upright and I intend to make a success of a creation I've worked on for many months. Screenplay writing is the stuff of dreams."

"And soon you'll be famous."

"If only fame was that simple." She chuckled. "Once *Aloha to Love* is completed, my production company will apply to the screenwriters guild. If the application is approved, my name will roll along with the actors in the credits."

"Impressive."

"More important," she continued, "I'll be eligible for healthcare and a pension and guaranteed a minimum salary for my writing."

He nodded. "I'm sure the application will be approved."

The musicians ended their set, and he and Angelina held a collective breath while the thrilling Fire Dance—all exhilarating emotion and fiery action—hushed all the lighthearted conversation on the beach. Nervousness took root as the audience flicked worried glances at the artful knife throwing, acrobatics, and twirling and catching of the long-handled knives. Rings of fire flew through the air.

"Let's give these men a round of applause for their heart-stopping performance," their guide announced at the end of the dance.

Angelina pressed a hand over her heart. "Heart-stopping is a justified description. Wow! These fire dancers are amazing."

Hula dancing came next, and Angelina persuaded Caleb to follow her to a private area on the corner of the dance floor. Laughter trembled on her lips as she shadowed the Hawaiian women's graceful demonstration.

"Bend your knees, keep your hips loose, and move two steps to the right, two steps to the left," one of the women instructed. "Now raise your arms to correspond with your leading foot."

Caleb leaned against a makeshift pole, watching Angelina's hips sway and rock to the lyrical beat.

Never had she appeared so radiant, so utterly beautiful, laughing with joyful abandon while she quickly learned the dance. She was a shaft of sunlight dancing in the center of an enchanted world. And the happiness they shared sent a poignant longing through him. He'd been searching for her his whole life.

There was still tomorrow, he reminded himself. Still tomorrow before they were forced to separate. They'd be together all day because he'd booked an excursion to the island of Kona. Did she need to live in California to write? Or could she submit her screenplays long distance? He didn't want her to lose her job, and he anxiously filed through a list of possibilities.

Conceivably, she could work for another movie company. Producers made movies here in Hawaii, didn't they?

If that didn't come to pass, maybe she could commute to California on occasion.

And if she couldn't ...

Or refused?

He frowned. The balance of their relationship hung on her decision, for their growing romance had to continue here in Hawaii. Because of a dangerously active volcano, he wouldn't be able to move back to the mainland for a long time.

CHAPTER 9

*I*n her bed near the porthole in her cabin, Angelina leisurely opened her eyes.

Kona.

Caleb had booked an excursion for them to tour the island of Kona that day.

"Because you love coffee," he had teased, before giving her a final good-night kiss at her cabin door the previous evening. "It's highly prized and grows in the hills above Kailua-Kona."

Blinking at the bright sunlight filtering through the sheer curtains, she stretched her arms over her head. She smiled, reviewing their day in Kauai—the riverboat cruise, the luau, the sweet and spicy delicacies—all the wonderful memories.

And Caleb, always Caleb. When she wasn't with him, she yearned to be near him, but then chastised herself for her yearning. In a few hours, she reassured herself, she'd see him again.

Her blue-lit clock on the nightstand flashed eight a.m., and she sat up. Morning was well underway, and she felt the vibration in the ship's thrusters as it docked.

The night before, after Caleb had left, she'd switched on the cruise ship's television station. Gabriella broadcasted a thorough overview of Kona, which wasn't an actual city, but rather a region. They'd anchor at Kailua-Kona Bay, and the passengers would take tenders to Kailua Pier.

Gabriella had gone on to say it almost never rained in Kona, and guests should expect sunny and dry weather conditions. Besides coffee growing, the island boasted white and black sand beaches, and Caleb had suggested that he and Angelina walk along the shore after the coffee tour. If they were lucky, he said, they might spot humpback whales and sea turtles.

Too excited to stay in bed another minute, Angelina swung her legs around and went to the porthole. The sky was lit in mellow pinks, orange tangerines and vivid blues, blurring together to create a picture of paradise. The vast sea caught sparks of brilliant sunshine just as Captain Berg's hilarious daily announcement sounded from the hallway's loudspeaker.

"This is your captain from somewhere above you," his deep voice boomed. "I've dropped the anchor and told the ship to stay. Usually she obeys me, so keep your fingers crossed. Enjoy Kona today, and don't forget to use sunscreen. Oh, and drink a cup of coffee for me. I've had my quota for the day."

Angelina smiled in a state of pure happiness.

After a warm shower, she donned a pair of slim sage-green twill shorts with a wide cuff, and a heather-gray top with a ruffled peplum. She packed her bikini and cover-up, hoping she and Caleb would be able to swim in the crystal-clear ocean. They'd agreed on a ten AM departure, giving Caleb time to present his lecture and then go for a swim.

Room service dropped off her breakfast tray consisting of fresh-squeezed orange juice, black Kona coffee and a croissant. Angelina broke the buttery croissant in half and closed her eyes as she chewed. Everything on the *Bird of Paradise*— the decor, the entertainment, the five-star rated food—was divine.

As she savored her creamy-smooth coffee, she curled her bare feet up on her chair and contemplated the splendid day ahead in quiet solitude. When she finished her coffee, she spent an extra few minutes taming her thick curls.

She glanced at the clock. Nine forty-five. She had a few minutes, so she pulled out her cell phone to read Caleb's texts again.

Every night since Christmas, he'd sent her a text at bedtime. The night before, he wrote, *You're the reason this cruise is so perfect. You make me smile.*

And then, just before she drifted to sleep, he texted another line: *You have my heart, Angelina.*

At first she didn't reply, hesitating, fearful she might tell him too much.

And then she did, because he was the man she adored. He was Caleb, and she could tell him anything. Around him, she didn't need to hide her feelings.

And you have mine, she texted.

A quick ping in return featured a heart emoji, and her pulse quickened with joy.

Since then, although she'd checked her phone numerous times, he hadn't texted.

Deciding she'd spent far too long fixing her hair and acting like a schoolgirl with a crush on her professor, she switched on her computer to check emails.

To her surprise, an email from Partridge Production Studios was in her inbox, with the subject title, URGENT. Quickly, she scanned the body of the email.

The producers had accelerated their schedule and demanded her finished script in twenty-four hours, Devon wrote. The script needed to be received by eight a.m. on December twenty-ninth.

In shocked despair, she read between the lines. There was a veiled threat that if she couldn't meet the new deadline, they would hire someone else to finish the script.

Her heart stopped beating.

"No." She put a hand to her mouth. "I'll lose all the credit for my screenplay if that happens."

She pushed back her shoulders. Well, it wouldn't, because she would succeed.

Rationally, she prepared her strategy, taking into account that California time was three hours ahead of Hawaii. Now close to ten where she was, it was nearly one p.m. in California.

She dropped her head into her hands. Why had she lost focus of her career, even for a few days, when it meant so much to her? Thoughts of failure hovered anxiously in her mind. She fidgeted and watched the clock tick away another minute.

She read and re-read Devon's email.

Although she could think of nothing as inviting as another day spent with Caleb, the email was proof that romance didn't belong in her life. Someday? Yes, sure. Maybe.

Once her career was established, she could think about a relationship with someone.

But now? Definitely not.

"Angelina?" Caleb's voice came from the other side of her cabin door. "Did you hear me knock?"

"It's open," she said in a strained voice.

He stepped inside. "Are you ready to see Kona? The tender is leaving soon, and the excursion bus to the coffee farm will be waiting when we arrive at the pier. I brought my binoculars to get a better view of the whales." He scrutinized her features. Three swift strides brought him to her side. "What's the matter? Are you sick?"

"No, I'm ... Please, no hiking or helicopter or boat rides today, okay?"

He stood motionless. "You love coffee as much as I do, and the whales are supposed to be migrating along the coast. I saw Gabriella in the hallway just now, and she said there are sometimes hundreds of whales at sunset."

Angelina pointed to her computer screen. "I've got to work. My screenplay needs to be completed by tomorrow morning, California time." She heard her tone, distant, formal. Already she felt herself pushing him away. "Devon emailed me."

A frown darkened Caleb's face. "Your screenplay is due in January. They can't do that."

"Hollywood runs on their own schedule." She stood and turned her back to him, pretending to focus on the stunning view outside her porthole. "To make it worse, I'm having difficulty writing the last scene."

"Angelina ..." He captured her elbow and drew her to him.

If only she could hurl herself into his strong embrace and blurt out her frustration. Aware she couldn't, that there was a screenplay to be finished, she stepped away.

Caleb stared at her back, her posture rigid, forbidding. He wasn't going to let her push him away like this. He moved closer.

"Angelina, let's find a place to work together. I'll help you. Everyone will be off on one of the Kona excursions, and the ship will be nearly empty."

"No." She sighed. "I prefer to plug away in my cabin."

"Really?" His mind was already made up, and he challenged her. "The ocean breezes and scenery will encourage your muse to work overtime, which is exactly what you need right now."

"You sound like Rachel," came her clipped reply.

That wasn't good. He wanted to be more than just a friend.

Initially confused and annoyed by her tone, he reminded himself to understand the tough spot she was in. He'd offer his support and expertise. And then, unless he received an invitation to stay, he'd leave her alone to finish.

After further persuading, she finally agreed to work with him, and slipped on her sandals and seized her laptop. When they reached the quiet lounge near Santorino's Bistro, he ushered her into a corner booth.

"Kona coffee?" he asked, beckoning a waiter.

"Yes, I'll need at least a pot," Angelina muttered. She opened her laptop and began typing madly on the keys.

When she turned the computer toward him, he skimmed the scene on the monitor. "This is after the hero and heroine settle the dispute about the bird?"

"Way after. This scene is near the end. The hero has given up his restaurant to farm the plot of land he inherited from his father. The question I'm stuck on is whether the heroine will join him or continue her blog on birds."

He gave her a look that meant she couldn't really be stuck on such a question, and said quickly, "She can write her blog anywhere there's an Internet connection."

Her brows drew together in a frown, and he realized he'd misunderstood the problem. Reminding himself how distressing this all was for her, he softened his tone. "Maybe that isn't the question you should be asking."

"Caleb, you haven't read the updated version of my script. I appreciate your assistance but—"

"Stop for a minute." He forced himself to speak slowly. "The hero's restaurant is at the base of Mauna Kea, correct?"

Angelina sat still and placed her hands on her lap. "Yes."

"Mauna Kea is dormant, but the plot of land the hero inherited is near an active volcano." He reached for his coffee and sipped.

Because of the new deadline, she wouldn't be able to see the Kona coffee farm. Not today.

Not ever?

A sharp stabbing pain pierced his heart, and he shoved the coffee aside. "So, has the active volcano in your script erupted?"

"As a matter of fact, yes. That happens in one of the earlier scenes."

"Then the hero's farm won't work."

"Six months has passed in the story." Angelina stared at him, stared at her steaming coffee cup. "The volcano cleanup has been finished."

"Even so, there wouldn't be any significant land at the base to farm."

"You mentioned andisols on the helicopter ride, and that volcanic ash made the soil very rich and fertile." She flopped back against the booth. "I assumed the land would be ideal."

"Yes, but not in a matter of months." He reached for her hand, but she jerked away. "It all depends on how much rain falls. On a dry portion of land in Hawaii, it could take up to ten years. In fact, there's a side of Hawaii where lava flowed a few hundred years ago, and there's still hardly any grass growing at all."

She passed him a look of frustrated annoyance. "Luckily, I'll set this volcano eruption on the wet side of Hawaii."

"If the volcano is anywhere near Mauna Kea, which I assume it will be given the setting of your screenplay, the volcano is located on the dry side of the island. Furthermore, two years will have had to elapse for the volcanic ash to settle. Maybe a little less time, but not much."

Caleb treaded carefully in offering his opinion. Stick to the scientific facts, he told himself. Nothing else.

He wanted to tease her, get her to relax, take a breath, enjoy this process of finishing the screenplay. The accelerated deadline had obviously upset her, though, and she was focused on meeting that deadline with single-minded determination.

Rubbing the back of his neck, he gave a heavy sigh. Were the producers really going to review a script before New Year's?

"What about the hero's aspiration of becoming a farmer?" Angelina fired back at him. "The whole point of this script is for the hero to follow his dream with the heroine by his side."

"Your hero still can. Just extend the time frame."

"I will, as long as they can be together at the end." Pensively, Angelina seemed to set aside that thought and give her full attention to a new one. "What kind of crop could the hero cultivate if his farmland is affected by deposits of ash?"

"Coffee." Caleb smiled and clinked his cup to hers. "Volcanic soils are extremely compatible for coffee trees."

* * *

AN HOUR LATER, Caleb pushed back his chair and stood. "Did you need anything else from me?" he asked.

Angelina blinked up at him. She'd been so immersed in rewriting the final scenes, she'd forgotten he sat across from her, quietly staring out at the sunlit turquoise water.

"No," she said. "Thanks for helping me, but this deadline is ultimately my responsibility." She checked her watch. "If you hurry, you might be able to catch the next tender to the island."

He shrugged indifferently. "I'll keep that in mind."

"Caleb … I prefer to finish the script alone." She eyed the

food he'd brought to the table: salmon and tomato salad, a slice of Hawaiian bread topped with butter, and a dish of macadamia nuts.

He looked at her, looked at the spotlessly clean deck, the staff plumping up sea-green pillows on the teak lounge chairs. She followed his gaze.

"You'll eat eventually, yes?" he asked.

"Absolutely." She bit into the bread, her mouth filling with the rush of sugary, yeasty flavors. "Enjoy your day. I'll be working quite a while longer."

"Sure. You too. If you need anything, text me." With a curt nod, he quit the lounge.

Her spirit bleak as he walked away, she turned back to her computer.

The morning had long passed when she glanced up again and eyed her wilted salad.

How wrong she'd been, she thought. Working quite a while longer? Hah! How was she supposed to finish in mere hours what should take several days to accomplish?

Daylight had faded to dusk when she retired to her cabin. She checked her phone, half-expecting a text from Caleb asking how the script was progressing, or if she needed moral support. Or more macadamia nuts.

Her phone screen was blank, any new texts non-existent. Apparently, he'd gone off to Kona after all, undoubtedly using his binoculars to view the humpback whales while he stood on shore with the other tourists. Perhaps Jillian and her twenty-something friends had met him along the way, sliding up beside him, and they were all relishing the end of a sun-filled day on the island.

Angelina's heart squeezed. A premonition of failing—at her job, at any further connection with Caleb—vibrated through her. If he truly cared, he wouldn't have waited for her to contact him. He would have at least sent an encouraging text or stationed himself on the deck beside her.

The caring, teasing Caleb had evaporated. A polite stranger had taken his place. Still, in typical Caleb-like fashion, he had offered a scientific, yet practical solution to her plotting problem.

Coffee. Of course. A grin touched her lips. The perfect crop.

Yet, she was perversely angry at him.

You told him to leave, her conscience reprimanded.

Alone in her room, she accepted a turkey sandwich and fruit cup brimming with fresh pineapple and coconut from room service, and texted Rachel while she ate. She was pleased to learn that Rachel loved her new home, Fred's grandmother was "the bomb" who cooked the tastiest poi, a traditional starchy dish, and Rachel was living the Hawaiian dream.

How are you and Caleb? Rachel asked.

Busy day, Angelina answered, neatly navigating around the subject. *My production company demanded the screenplay rewrites ahead of time. While I'm texting you, I'm looking at how much work I have left.*

Excited to see your finished product.

Me too.

Tomorrow is Maui, right? Rachel asked.

Yep.

You really need to live here in Hawaii once your screenplay is done. Fred and I will show you around.

"Subject change, subject change," Angelina muttered. She texted: *Well, as soon as the disco lounge finishes the next set, I'm either going to join the upstairs dancing or call it a night.*

LOL! It's so peaceful here in our little cottage. Fred calls it magical! We even have a small sandy beach overlooking the ocean, and our kitchen cabinets are made out of bamboo. I'll text pictures soon.

Can't wait to see them, Angelina replied, and then tossed the phone onto her bed.

Sighing, she looked around her empty cabin. "I'd be delighted to see Rachel's magical cottage." Of course, she never would. Already, she'd spent way too long dwelling on a fantasy life she would never know.

* * *

DARKNESS HAD SETTLED when the ship hit a huge wave, almost knocking Angelina out of her chair. She rubbed her eyes and peered at the time. Almost midnight.

Her gaze shifted from her nightstand clock to the view out her porthole, the sliver of moon weaving beneath a thin line of clouds. They'd departed Kona hours ago and were sailing toward Maui, the final destination.

Undeterred by the wave, Coconuts Disco Bar had gone into high gear. Apparently it was '80's night, and her ceiling vibrated with the bass guitar thumping of Billy Joel's, "It's Still Rock and Roll to Me".

Perhaps a change of scenery would help her write faster. Hadn't Caleb suggested that earlier … something about her muse?

She picked up her laptop and made her way back to the lounge adjacent to Santorino's again. Her stomach growled at lingering scents of tomato, basil, and garlic as the waiters cleared the last of the tabletops.

After pouring a glass of iced tea for herself, she observed the vacant tables. Directly opposite her was where she and Caleb had worked on their first evening together, discussing her script, rehearsing the kissing scene.

A tear trickled down her face as she stared blankly at the couples strolling along the deck, arm in arm, chatting and laughing. She pinched her lips together, furiously wiped the tear away and squinted at the computer screen. The minutes were marching on, and there was no time to dwell on the past.

She pushed her glass aside. She wasn't thirsty after all.

"Yes, I will finish this," she said clearly. Leaning in, her muscles stretched in readiness. Finally, she was rewriting the last scene.

As the hours crept to early morning, her words became a blur. The lull of the sea, the rocking sensation of the ship, the gentle breezes, prompted her to lay her head back against the booth and drift off. Just for a moment, she told herself.

* * *

"ANGELINA?"

She awoke to the sound of Caleb's deep voice, his gentle touch at her elbow. "I texted you several times, then went to your cabin. When you didn't answer, I started searching for you."

Startled and embarrassed, she smoothed her green cargo shorts and gray T-shirt, now hopelessly wrinkled.

"What time is it?" She peered around. Save for the soothing sounds of the ship—subtle creaks and groans, the muted rumble of the engine, the lounge was completely silent.

"Three o'clock in the morning." He studied her laptop, the darkened screen, her unfinished glass of iced tea. "Did you complete your screenplay?"

"Almost."

She stared at her watch. She had two hours until the California deadline. Shaking away the pressure, she switched on her computer, acutely aware Caleb was staring at her. She tried to ignore him, but couldn't keep from glancing at him. She was heartened when he offered an encouraging smile.

"I'll stay with you." Quietly, without fanfare, he was offering his support. "That is, if it's all right."

"Yes. I ... I appreciate the company."

Scarcely breathing, she spent the last two hours typing, painstaking in her detail, muttering aloud the dialogue that forced her hero and heroine to part, and then the words of love they exchanged when they came back together.

At the stroke of five, she attached the screenplay to her email to Devon. With cautious hope, she licked her bottom lip, pressed the send button, and turned to Caleb.

He offered the same charismatic smile that always brought a shiver of excitement down her spine.

"Done?" he asked.

She locked her hands together, forcing herself to remain still. "Done."

"Excellent. Congratulations."

"It might be a little soon for cheering."

"I have no doubt your screenplay will be well received by Devon and the production company." Rising from his chair, Caleb pressed a kiss on her forehead. "You've had quite the exhausting day. I'll walk you back to your cabin so you can rest. If it's okay, I'll call you midmorning."

"Of course it's okay." The next moment was stilted, but she couldn't resist asking. "How was your day in Kona?"

"I never went. I stayed in my suite catching up on emails and wrapping up loose ends in Washington. My Realtor has a buyer already for my place there."

"Oh." There was so much about him she didn't know, so much she *wanted* to know. Another stilted moment. "You should've taken the excursion to the coffee farm. You were looking forward to it ... I mean, we both were looking forward to it."

"I'll be living in Hawaii for two years, so I can visit Kona any time. I wanted to be on the ship near you, in case you texted."

"Why would you ever waste a beautiful sightseeing day waiting for me?"

His dark gaze held her bound. "You really have to ask why?"

When she didn't answer, he cleared his throat. "Tomorrow, or rather, today, the ship drops anchor in Maui. If you'd like to spend the day together, I'll introduce you to Kapena and his wife. Time permitting, I'll show you my new home. However, it's almost a two-hour drive from there. Remember, it's near the Haleakala crater." He pushed out a breath. "It will be too early to view the sunset from the crater, which I really wanted to see with you. However, you promised me that someday ..."

Had she? Promised?

Someday.

Glancing tentatively at him, she was surprised to find he was gazing at her with thoughtful intensity. She favored him with a slight nod, all she could offer.

Drowsily installed in her cabin a few minutes later, Caleb's words ran through her mind:

However, you promised me that someday ...

Keeping the thought close, she fell into a drained sleep.

CHAPTER 10

*A*ngelina awoke to a heavy anchor being dropped and knew they'd reached Maui. Groggy, she rolled over in bed and opened her eyes. She blinked and regarded her nightstand clock. Only eight a.m. Having gone to bed at dawn, she told herself it was okay to drift off again.

When next she woke, the ping of a text prompted her to grope for her cell phone. She squinted at the bright sunlight streaming into her cabin and realized her head was pounding from the stressful, sleep-deprived night.

Have enough shut-eye? Caleb had texted. *It's nearly noon, and I'm hoping you and I can get our first glimpse of Maui together.*

So he'd waited for her all morning, postponing seeing his cousin and the place Caleb would call home for the next two years. Surely that counted for something.

Come to my cabin, she replied. *I'll be ready in a half hour.*

Can't wait to see you.

She pushed the covers off and scrambled from bed. Well-versed on the ship's itinerary, she knew they'd be docked in

Maui until five o'clock in the evening. At most, she'd be able to spend only a few hours with Caleb.

She recalled that sometime the previous evening, as they'd steamed toward Maui, the ever-cheerful Gabriella had given a preview of Maui over the loudspeaker, describing it as "the trip of a lifetime with one hundred and twenty miles of coastline." She had said something about docking at both Kahului Harbor and at Lahaina, a historic town with plenty of restaurants and shopping.

Angelina quickly showered, leaving her hair to air dry into a mass of curls. Deliberating, she chose one of the only outfits left in her closet she hadn't already worn—a floral pink sundress and matching sandals, complemented by a woven-straw clutch purse. She was looking forward to meeting Caleb's cousin and his wife, but deeply regretted that there would not be enough time to drive to Caleb's new home.

She let out a sad, tight breath. She had wanted to, but she'd slept too late.

Would Caleb ask her to visit him once she left Hawaii? Would he offer to fly to California on occasion?

She wasn't sure. He kept a fragment of himself removed from her—more than a fragment. He was tormented by an unsuccessful marriage with its own set of heartbreak and difficulties. She got that. Devoted to his work, he blamed himself for the divorce.

To be fair, she kept a part of herself from him too.

With good reason, she reminded herself. She wouldn't permit her heart to be broken again. What if anything ever happened to Caleb? A volcanologist frequently found himself in dangerous situations. How could she cope with a painful loss if the man she loved was taken from her a second time? Her chin quivered, and she blinked back tears.

She checked her appearance and decided she was ready to

go. So, one more thing to do. She turned on her computer and checked her email. She had a message from Devon.

"Received your screenplay. Will let you know what the producers decide. Thanks."

* * *

TRYING to match Caleb's upbeat mood, Angelina slid into the front seat of his rental car, a highlighter-green Mustang convertible. She laughed as he joked about the car being an attention getter and that the interior reminded him of a cockpit. As they buckled their seat belts, he rolled the top and windows down so they could have the best view of the numerous beaches and waterfalls they'd pass along the way.

He fired up the engine, kept his foot on the clutch, then comically lifted his brows at the loud exhaust as he shifted into first gear. The rumbling V8 under the hood prompted a chuckle from them both and a thumbs-up from several onlookers.

They'd been greeted at the dock with alohas and a draping of orchid leis around their necks. Angelina fingered the fragrant flowers and sank back into the Mustang's leather seats. The view out her window offered glimpses of a breath-taking tropical island, fringed by white sand beaches and acres of coconut palms.

Still worried about whether or not the producers and Devon would like her script, she fixed her gaze on the bumper-to-bumper stream of traffic ahead of them.

"Gorgeous weather," Caleb remarked.

She looked up and inhaled the moist air. The blue sky promised another dazzlingly sunny day.

"Apparently the word is out that Hawaii is paradise," she replied.

Turning to him, she admired his strong profile—defined

cheekbones and firm jaw—and his muscular form clad in a cream-colored polo shirt and navy-blue shorts.

He caught her looking. "Do I meet with your approval?" he teased. "You certainly meet with mine. You look beautiful today."

"Thank you. And yes, you do … meet with my approval."

He gave her a startled smile before his gaze fixed on the car in front of him. He released the clutch, his foot hitting the accelerator as traffic started to move.

"Have you ever bodysurfed?" he asked.

"Um, no." She sat upright, turning to him in bewilder-ment. "You can't mean we're going—"

Ruefully, he shook his head. "No, we only have a few hours, and my cousin and his wife are expecting us. Perhaps, one day?"

One day.

She tried to keep her tone neutral. "You really are a thrill seeker."

"I'm not. It would just be something fun for us to do together."

When? When he taught her how to play the piano, or relished an Italian Christmas Eve feast with her?

"We'll have a quick bite to eat at Kapena and Zoe's condo," he was saying. "After that, we'll need to turn around to get you back to the ship before it sails."

"I'm looking forward to meeting both of them," Angelina said.

Did she really have to say goodbye to Hawaii, the laid-back lifestyle and perfect weather? And to Caleb? Falling back against the luxurious seat, she squeezed her eyes shut in desolation.

There were words she wanted to tell him—how much she cared, how much she adored his company—subjects she needed to discuss. How could she talk to him when he was treating their last day so upbeat? Evidently, he wanted to end their parting amiably, as good friends.

"Kapena and his lightning bolt wife," Caleb said.

His playful tone roused Angelina from her unhappy thoughts.

"Lightning bolt," she repeated. "Love at first sight. *Le coup de foudre.*" She put on her best breezy smile. "The term didn't resonate with me the first time I heard it, but it does now."

"Especially when it's said in French," Caleb quipped.

Two hours later, after visiting with Caleb's cousin and polishing off a wonderful meal, Angelina and Caleb were quickly closing the distance back to the harbor where the tender was docked.

As the wind glided through her hair, Angelina realized her headache had abated and she could better appreciate the warm golden sands of the numerous shores they passed. The scrublands and crescent-shaped beaches entertained sun worshipers, as well as stand-up paddlers in their slender canoes, gliding through the glistening waters.

Caleb draped one arm out his open car window and regarded Angelina. "Did you enjoy meeting Kapena and Zoe?" he asked.

"They were delightful and fun and complement each other both in personality and appearance."

Like Caleb, Kapena was tall and muscular, and Angelina had loved the head lei he wore. Zoe was slender and petite, and her flaming red hair defined her—adventurous and unrehearsed.

"Their condo is lovely and their outside Christmas decorations were great," Angelina said, "especially the palm tree lit by white twinkling lights, and the barefoot Santa."

"*Kanakaloka,*" Kapena and Zoe had greeted them when she and Caleb entered their tiled foyer. Baked ham and sweet potato casserole roasted in the oven for dinner, as Caleb was celebrating the Christmas holiday with them.

When they'd arrived, he'd brought his sparse amount of luggage into Kapena's condo for safe-keeping. Knowing Angelina wouldn't be joining them for dinner, Kapena had set out a lunch of *manapua*, barbecued, pork-filled buns, and sushi.

As they ate, Kapena and Zoe described their Hawaiian wedding on the beach. Their attire had been bathing suits and flip-flops.

"Getting married in Hawaii is fast and easy," Zoe noted. "There's no waiting period and very little red tape. Kapena and I are *aloha nui loa*." Her fair, freckled face glowed as she laughed at Angelina's perplexed look. "That means we're madly in love. Since moving from the mainland, all these Hawaiian words are starting to rub off on me!"

Caleb sent Angelina an oddly challenging look. "Very romantic," he said softly.

Angelina changed the subject, remarking on how well Zoe's Santa hat matched her plaid red shorts. As soon as they were done eating, she jumped up to go into the kitchen with Zoe to help serve the homemade fruitcake.

Caleb followed, carrying dishes. "You're avoiding me," he whispered, coming up close behind her.

She didn't turn around, uncertain what to say.

He pressed a kiss on her hair, his lips gliding down as he murmured in her ear, "Everything's romantic here. Haven't you accepted that by now?"

She shivered, savoring his nearness. Filled with an ache she couldn't explain, her brain argued he was very wrong, while her heart argued he couldn't be more right.

Now, two hours later, they were headed back to the *Bird of Paradise,* the top still down on Caleb's rented Mustang. The invigorating whiffs of salty sea wind, green bamboo, and lush floral invited her to breathe it all in. She wanted to capture the sultry, blissful scents and keep them in a safe place near her heart.

"So, you'll be leaving in a couple of hours," Caleb said, stirring her from her musings.

Although it was only a statement, her heartbeat tripled. A wild fantasy, one that had played in her mind ever since she met him, assured her he was going to ask her to stay. Not his usual off-the-cuff joking, but a clear invitation.

"As you know," she said, "Captain Berg runs a very tight schedule."

"Perhaps we can get together in the New Year."

Get together? So casual?

Automatically, her mind combed for a suitable response. "Where?" She ran a hand through her hopelessly disheveled curls. "Hawaii or California?"

He didn't answer.

Because he didn't understand.

If she was going to allow romance into her life, it would be 100 percent, not a casual, long-distance relationship. Didn't he know that by now?

He navigated the car along the narrow roads, shifting from one gear to the next, before pulling off at a deserted beach near the harbor where the tender waited. The ocean swells were up, the outcropping of rocks slick. Beyond, picturesque cliffs overlooked the seashore.

"Angelina," he said, his expression serious, "you have to trust your feelings."

"I do."

"You'll never be able to see the Haleakala crater if you're not here. It's supposed to be awesome at sunset." He took both her hands in his, and she stared down at them.

Beats of silence hung in the air. If he was asking her to stay, he was doing a poor job of it.

Beyond them, the Hawaiian sky was painted in cotton-candy pinks against a dark blue, signaling the approach of sunset.

Another minute passed, neither of them speaking.

"So, I assume this is goodbye, then," Caleb said curtly.

She sat ramrod straight, strong and proud, and met his probing gaze head-on. "Yes."

He angled his head toward hers. "Then a proper aloha kiss is in order." He brought his lips to hers for a sweet, tender kiss. She slid her hands upward, along the fine cotton of his polo shirt, and her arms wrapped around his neck.

She'd always remember this, she thought. Kissing him at the edge of the harbor as the sun reached the horizon.

Endless minutes later, he tore his lips from hers, and cradled her cheeks between his hands.

Attempting to memorize his features, she leaned her head back and focused on his almond-shaped eyes, his male-model good looks, the outward manifestation of his inner compassion and empathy. And she faltered.

A firm reminder came to the fore. Their lives were separate. The week had been wondrous, but now it was over.

Without warning, he dropped his hands, as if he could read her thoughts. He kissed her forehead, then rested his chin on her hair.

In the distance came the sounds of a conch being blown and the rhythmic beat of a large pahu drum, the enchantment of a melodic incantation. *Oli*, she thought, the highest form of the Hawaiian language, reflecting a people keenly attuned to creation.

Loneliness and sadness crept over her as she uttered the words she knew she must. "I love the sights and sounds of Hawaii." Her voice wavered, and she couldn't help it.

He nodded, his expression becoming unreadable. Without another word, he drove to the pier where the tender waited. As he walked her to the boat, he held her hand, turning to gaze at her from time to time, mentioning how he was beginning his new assignment researching the Haleakala crater on January first. She murmured that *Aloha to Love* might begin filming soon in California if her script was picked up.

"Can I text you?" he asked.

"That wouldn't be a good idea."

"Okay, I'll call you."

"Don't. You're so busy, and so am I."

"How about—"

"No. Sorry." She attempted to nod brightly to soften her words, although a heavy weight sat solidly in her chest. "Be careful when you climb that crater. I know the volcano is dormant but—"

"I will. I'm a volcanologist, remember? That's my job."

He put his life in jeopardy, she reminded herself, to help keep that wall firmly erected around her heart.

"Safe travels, Angelina," he said softly. "Aloha."

Hello or goodbye? In this instance, the word meant goodbye.

"Thanks. You too." Somehow, she managed a cheerful tone despite the catch in her throat. "Goodbye, Caleb."

She forced back the memories—his affectionate kisses, his good-natured banter, his fair and honest spirit.

"A wedding song. Should we get married?" he'd asked her at the sacred Fern Grotto.

If he cared for her as much as Rachel believed he did, then surely he would say something before she boarded.

He didn't.

With great effort, Angelina kept her chin high as she climbed aboard the tender. She embarked the cruise ship just as a long horn signaled its departure. Standing by the railing, she shaded her eyes with her hand, looking for a brilliant-green Mustang and a tall, handsome man standing beside it.

He wasn't there.

Her hand shook violently as she lowered it, and she gulped in a ragged breath.

Already, he'd driven away to begin a new chapter in his life.

Pushing back tears, she wandered through clusters of cruisers heralding the beginning of the early dinner buffet. She searched the deck to be sure she avoided running into Jillian and her twenty-something friends.

She intended to be alone. She needed to be alone.

She'd find her balance again, she promised herself. If she continued to block out a pair of deep-brown eyes, tousled dark hair, and a kind smile, she might even forget Caleb Sloane someday.

CHAPTER 11

*S*o this marks the finale of a Christmas cruise, Angelina thought, re-reading the New Year's Eve celebration itinerary in The Coral Chronicle. Balloon drops, a DJ, high-energy live entertainment—the staff promised merrymaking, all in the company of family and friends.

Eligible men on the ship she hadn't noticed before had appeared at her side, and one even escorted her to a holiday show in the Anthurium Theater. Before intermission, several members of the audience requested a Christmas song, and a barbershop quartet ended the first half with an a cappella rendition of "The Little Drummer Boy". As tears welled in her eyes, she remembered Caleb's baritone voice, his perfect pitch as he sang in harmony with her on Christmas Eve.

Feeling as though she might be as seasick as Caleb had been at the beginning of the cruise, she began to stand in the middle of the performance, prompting her escort to inquire if she was ill. She scolded herself to remain in her seat no matter what, but when the curtain rose for intermission, she made her excuses and hastened from the theater.

Although Caleb had texted, emailed, and called her, she

refused to reply to his messages. After all, what would she say? His farewell words had troubled her:

You'll never be able to see the Haleakala crater if you're not here. It's supposed to be awesome at sunset.

Aloha.

By now, he would have celebrated Christmas with his family in Kaanapali. Kapena had mentioned midnight fireworks were held on New Year's Eve if Caleb decided to stay with them until then.

From Rachel's text, Angelina learned that Rachel and Fred and his grandmother were still celebrating the Christmas holiday, but were planning to ring in New Year's in the usual Hawaiian style and Rachel's favorite activity, by eating a bountiful feast.

And for Angelina? Well, she preferred to be alone.

Although the helicopter ride with Caleb on Christmas Day was memorable, she hadn't experienced the Christmas of her dreams—decorating a fresh pine tree in her own living room, the inviting smells of an Italian Christmas Eve dinner, and attending a midnight church service.

Sure, her father had invited her to celebrate the holiday in California with his new wife when Angelina returned to California. But still, it wasn't the same. More and more, Angelina wanted a family of her own. She wanted to create her own special celebrations.

The only bright spot on the return cruise was that Devon and the producers had been thrilled with her script. Devon had forwarded the film's shoot schedule, which would begin soon after she docked in California.

To keep busy, she'd begun writing another script. After all, *Aloha to Love* was officially finished and would only take a few short weeks of filming.

Each night since she and Caleb had parted, she'd fallen into bed, fatigued from another day of writing. She hadn't decided on a title, but knew that although this would also be a romance, the story would be different and innovative. If only she could determine the proper setting for the hero and heroine, although she wanted to begin where *Aloha to Love* had left off—in a rainstorm.

New Year's Eve arrived with a black-tie dinner and ball held on the lido deck. As she handed out horns, hats, and blowers, Gabriella insisted Angelina attend. With Rachel and Caleb gone, though, Angelina preferred to remain in her cabin, so she pleaded tiredness.

How could she attend a festive gala when her heart was breaking?

"Nonsense," Gabriella said, giving Angelina a high-five. "Everyone on the ship is attending, and you are too, even if I have to tromp to your cabin and drag you to the lido deck myself."

Not doubting Gabriella would make good on that threat, Angelina dressed in the formal black gown she'd brought for the event, and sat between the buoyant Gabriella and the Hawaiian chef Elikapeka, who greeted her with a heartfelt exclamation of, "Ohana! My family!"

Captain Berg even made an appearance, greeting the cruisers with a jolly hello. When asked who was manning the ship while he joined the New Year's festivities, he looked puzzled for a moment, as if he really wasn't sure. Then, his blue eyes twinkling with glee, he held up his cell phone. "I have an app for that," he said.

At midnight, amidst the revelers watching a fireworks show over the water, Angelina felt her phone vibrate with a text message. Pulling it out of her beaded black bag, she read the sender's name. C. Sloane.

Happy New Year. I assume you're still awake.

Feeling churlish if she didn't respond, she texted: *Happy New Year.*

It's midnight here in Maui. I'm in my home, staring out at the Pacific.

I had dinner with Gabriella and Elikapeka—sashimi on a bed of lettuce. She paused, then asked: *Did you end the year by watching a Haleakala sunset?*

Not without you. I miss you.

She didn't reply. She pictured him, striking and straightforward, and her throat swelled with tears.

I miss you, too, she thought.

Slipping away from the cruisers celebrating the New Year, she took the elevator back to her cabin.

This cruise had taken her on a voyage she never anticipated. A man she'd formed a negative opinion about before they even met had become her true love.

Her true love. Not a memory. Someone real, whom she could share her life with.

She entered her cabin and sat in silence for several minutes.

"I'm sorry, Jake." Tears came down her cheeks. "You're not here anymore, but I am. I need to open my heart again in order to find joy. I can't worry about danger and loss. That might happen, but I won't be afraid anymore."

She loved Caleb, and she was going to fight to reclaim the relationship they'd begun together. As soon as the ship docked in California, she'd call Devon and work out the details. Then she'd give her notice on her apartment and pack her things.

Hurriedly, she logged onto the Internet and booked a one-way plane ticket from LA to Maui, leaving in three days. Shelving any unconstructive thoughts, she changed out of her gown and began packing.

At 9:00 on the morning of January second, Captain Berg's yawning voice sounded from the hall's loudspeaker as the ship cruised into San Pedro Bay port.

"Folks, I hope you enjoyed your cruise to Hawaii. I, for one, am very tired, and I'm retiring to my cabin to take a long nap after wallowing in all that sun and sand. It's been my pleasure to be your captain on this voyage, and on behalf of the staff and crew on the *Bird of Paradise* Hawaiian cruise ship, we wish you a fond farewell. Oh, and there's a tipping jar by the doorway. Make out any checks in my name. Just kidding. Aloha!"

Angelina chuckled, then peered out her porthole as the terminal came into view. She hoped the disembarkation process would be as easy as the initial check-in.

Meticulously dressed in slim-fitting ankle pants and a lilac blouse, she debated about stopping at Devon's office first before returning to her apartment. Both the office and home were thirty minutes in either direction from the terminal.

She envisaged her studio apartment—the organized galley kitchen and pull-out couch. Tidy but small, it was all she could afford in pricey Hollywood.

As she reclaimed her luggage and stepped onto the sidewalk, she wondered when the tar-black clouds had rolled in. Her thoughts had been far away from any weather forecast, because she was thinking about Caleb.

She sent him a quick text:

The Bird Of Paradise just docked in California. She took a photo of the ship, attached it to her message and pressed the send button.

There. A trip to and from Hawaii, the full circle.

She hung back on the sidewalk, deliberating whether to go back into the terminal to avoid the impending shower or continue walking to the cab station. Spotting a taxi, she raced across the busy street, luggage in tow, only to have the taxi accept another passenger and drive away.

"Come back!" she shouted, then blew out a breath.

The wind howled, giving a short warning before rain began falling like heavy stones.

She huddled near the entrance to a coffee shop, under its burgundy-striped canvas awning. The owner stepped outside and quickly moved tables and chairs together to keep them from getting wet.

She gazed up and read the shop's sign.

The Ground Café, a coffee chain started in Ireland, complete with a pot of gold logo. She'd heard the coffee was excellent and wondered if the taste could compete with Caleb's beloved Kona coffee. From the online reviews she'd read, the chain was distinctive and new in the coffee landscape.

A man's voice spoke from behind her. "I'm assuming you're in need of my assistance."

Expecting to see the coffee shop owner, she turned to thank him for allowing her to stand near the doorway.

With a swift intake of breath, she stepped back in disbelief.

"Caleb?" Incredulous, she touched her throat. "H-How?"

His expression solemn, he closed the distance between them in two strides. "Aloha."

"Aloha." She heard the quaver in her voice. "I thought … I thought you were in Maui."

"I boarded a plane bound for California yesterday evening. With the time difference and the delays we encountered because of the storm moving in, I got to LAX a little while ago. I was afraid I wouldn't get here in time."

Falteringly, she smiled as the shock of seeing him started to wear off. "I sent you a text message not five minutes ago."

"I read it while I was searching the terminal for you." He steered her farther under the awning to shield her from the blowing rain. "Then I walked to the entrance and saw you racing across the street for a cab."

"Why are you here?" Her breath hitched. "You're supposed to start your new post and—"

He pressed a finger to her lips. "I'd much rather start a new life with you."

Up close, she took in his wrinkled sports shirt and jeans. He obviously hadn't gotten a haircut in Maui because his hair was still shaggy, and the rain had plastered it to his forehead. Sleek, glistening drops of water had settled in the corner of his eyes, and she brushed them away with her fingertips. Then she laid her palm against his strong, stubbled chin.

He desperately needed a shave.

And he'd never looked more devastatingly handsome.

"I hope you didn't quit your job." She attempted to control the tremor in her voice. "I know how much the work means to you."

"I didn't, but I asked for a personal leave. I love you, Angelina. You left Maui, and we're supposed to be together. If you want me to stay in California, I'll look for a post here." He kissed her hair, her face. "I'll do whatever it takes ... I just don't know the right words."

The naked emotion in his voice brought fresh tears to her eyes. "Yes, you do. You said them. And I love you." She linked her hands around his shoulders and buried her face in his warm chest. "I love you very much."

He tipped up her chin and kissed her, tender and sweet. She wanted to stay like that, in his arms, disregarding the rain.

"Shall we go inside?" he murmured against her lips. "I'll get your luggage."

"I can manage. It's only one suitcase and a carry-on. Besides, you have your own."

Agreeing, he opened the door for her and followed her inside to a corner booth.

When they were situated with their luggage stowed safely

beside them, he reached into his briefcase and held up a large red plastic flower. "Did you know that in Hawaiian mythology, picking a lehua flower can cause it to rain?"

She watched the water coursing down the café's windows. "Well, imagine if your flower was real. Then we might have a monsoon on our hands."

He handed her the flower. "This is for you."

"A lehua?"

"The official flower of Hawaii."

"Thank you." She accepted the flower, went to sniff it, and grinned. "But plastic?"

"The airline won't allow fresh flowers on the plane."

"Caleb, I—"

"You want to stay in California. I get it. You've worked hard and it's understandable."

She glanced up and saw the aching tenderness in his gaze. "I booked a one-way plane ticket to Hawaii."

"You did?" His eyebrows lifted at her angelic smile. "What about your screenplay?"

She laughed. "While you were booking a flight to California, I was booking a flight to Maui. Sure, work is important, but I wasn't going to miss my chance at love."

His strong hands cupped hers. "You're going back to Maui."

"Yes, I'm going back to Maui. I can write my screenplays anywhere, and if I need to fly to California now and then, it's less than a five-hour flight."

He leaned across the table and kissed her. His fingers stroked the curls around her temple. "I love you," he said hoarsely.

"And I love you."

"There's another Hawaiian tradition that's more important than any of the others." He plucked the flower from her hand and tucked it behind her left ear. "You're taken, Angelina."

And this, she realized, was her aloha to love. Not the end, only the beginning.

THE END

HAWAIIAN HAUPIA RECIPE

Haupia is a simple and delicious recipe, and a dessert that can be made during the holidays or any special event.

Cooking Time: 10 minutes, then refrigerate for 2 hours
Serving size: 16 squares

Ingredients:
- 1 14 oz. can coconut milk
- 4 tablespoons cornstarch

- 5 tablespoons granulated sugar
- 3/4 cup water

Instructions:

1. Place coconut milk in a small saucepan over medium heat.
2. Combine sugar and cornstarch in a bowl, add the water, and whisk until combined.
3. When the coconut milk simmers, add the sugar and cornstarch mix, then whisk until the mixture thickens and appears translucent, approximately 10 minutes.
4. Pour mixture into an 8x8 pan and cool on counter.
5. Refrigerate until solid and completely cooled. Cut into 16 pieces and enjoy!

A NOTE FROM JOSIE

Dear Reader,

Thank you for reading *Aloha To Love,* my holiday romance set on a cruise ship bound for beautiful Hawaii.

I've always wanted to visit Hawaii, and even more so after writing this book. Several cruise line websites and pamphlets, plus talking to people who visited Hawaii, were the inspiration for this romance. Plus, I've always been fascinated with screenplays and, of course … volcanoes! In the course of writing *Aloha To Love,* I learned so much.

Angelina is a smart, independent heroine. And Caleb, the hero, sets out on one adventure, only to encounter the woman of his dreams.

Despite their differences, Angelina and Caleb were fun and engaging to write!

If you loved this sweet romance as much as I loved writing it, please help other people find *Aloha To Love* by posting your amazing review.

Aloha To Love is available in ebook, paperback, Hardcover, Large Print Paperback, and audiobook.

I'd love to meet you in person someday, but in the meantime, all I can offer is a sincere and grateful thank you. Without your support, my books would not be possible.

As I write my next sweet or inspirational romance, remember this: Have you ever tried something you were afraid to try because it mattered so much to you? I did, when I started writing. Take the chance, and just do something you love.

My Spotify Play List for Aloha To Love is here.

With sincere appreciation,

Josie Riviera

Love sweet romance Christmas stories? Be sure to check out my book bundles:

Holiday Hearts Volume One

Holiday Hearts Volume Two

Holiday Hearts Book Bundle Volume Three

Holiday Hearts Book Bundle Volume Four

ACKNOWLEDGMENTS

An appreciative thank you to my patient husband, Dave, and our three wonderful children.

ABOUT THE AUTHOR

Josie Riviera is a USA TODAY bestselling author of contemporary, inspirational, and historical sweet romances that read like Hallmark movies. She lives in the Charlotte, NC, area with her wonderfully supportive husband. They share their home with an adorable shih tzu, who constantly needs grooming, and live in an old house forever needing renovations.

To receive my Newsletter and your free sweet romance novella ebook as a thank you gift, sign up HERE.

Become a member of my Read and Review VIP Facebook group for exclusive giveaways and free ARCs.

To connect with Josie, visit her webpage and subscribe to her newsletter. As a thank-you, she'll send you a free sweet romance novella directly to your inbox.

josieriviera.com/
josieriviera@aol.com

USA TODAY BESTSELLING AUTHOR

JOSIE RIVIERA

a Christmas to Cherish

A SWEET AND WHOLESOME
HOLIDAY NOVELLA

PRAISE AND AWARDS

USA TODAY bestselling author

CHAPTER 1

Emmanuelle Sumter surveyed the picturesque town of Cherish, South Carolina, brightly lit in crimson and green holiday decor. The town looked as if it had emerged from a Christmas card. Glittering frost framed bare tree branches, and local artists were setting up their canvases for an art walk. The coldness in the air was soundless and serene, comforting in its own way.

She exited the Cherish Central train station, zippered her cobalt-blue puffer coat to her chin, and stepped onto the curb.

Who believed an actual, breathing town could resemble a holiday snow globe?

Evidently, her friend Dorothy did, considering her enthusiasm whenever she described her idyllic South Carolina town.

Emmanuelle stood on the curb and shoved her hands in her pockets. A cold December gust slapped her cheeks, sharp streams of frigid air. She swept a wisp of hair from her cheek and searched for Nicholas, Dorothy's older brother. He was supposed to pick her up. People were shouting greetings, kissing, cooing over babies. A teeming mass of humanity.

But no Nicholas.

A taxi's horn spiked. Emmanuelle jumped, an involuntary nervous reaction.

Take a deep breath. Relax. Dorothy had assured her Cherish was a safe haven, a harbor in a storm.

Repeating her mantra, Emmanuelle hailed the black-bearded taxi driver parked at the curb. She still didn't see any sign of Nicholas, so she'd take the cab.

She handed the driver her suitcase, then slid into the backseat and gave the address of Dorothy's music store, Musically Yours.

They passed charming shops decorated in glittering lights, and a sign advertising a historic home tour. A few minutes later, the driver pointed at the Musically Yours lighted outdoor sign and idled at the corner of Myrtle and Magnolia Streets.

"The store's two hoots and a holler away, ma'am." He hoisted her suitcase from the trunk and set it on the side-walk. "We've reached your destination."

Destination. Was this where her journey ended after a year filled with pain and abuse? Did hope and encouragement wait for her in this little town?

A new life. With perseverance, she could start fresh.

"Thanks." She climbed from the taxi, paid the driver and grabbed her suitcase.

Daylight faded as dusk crept in, and she tipped her head to take in Evergreen Street. Family-owned businesses had switched on their storefront lights, transforming the town into a fairy-tale sparkle of miniature white lights. The tanta-lizing scent of honey roasted almonds wafted through the air. Boughs of fragrant holly tied with red velvet bows hung cheerily from tall solitary lampposts. Bright-faced children skipped by, lifting their faces skyward to catch a sprinkling of snow. Their conscientious parents followed close behind.

"Emmanuelle! You arrived right on time!" Dorothy flung open the door of the music store and pressed a welcoming kiss to Emmanuelle's cheek. Dorothy's brown hair was swept up in a French braid, her creamy complexion glowing with an enthusiasm Emmanuelle didn't recall from their days working as struggling musicians in New York.

Dorothy had lived there before moving back to Cherish, her hometown, and marrying her high school crush, Ryan Edwards. He had been an opera star in the making and had given up his touring career to settle in Cherish. They were newlyweds. They were in love.

Love. The beginning was always so alluring. It was the end Emmanuelle feared.

Dorothy regarded the departing taxi. "Apparently Nicholas didn't pick you up?"

"I didn't see him so I took a cab."

Emmanuelle turned from Dorothy and admired Musically Yours' frosty window display, bedecked in an infinite array of treble clef signs. A pine wreath, embellished in antique ornaments—tiny pianos, violins, and harps—adorned the front door.

"It's wonderful," she said. "You've worked so hard to set this up."

"Thanks. Ryan and I are still learning the business, and we're inspired by anything musical."

Emmanuelle smiled, but then shivered. "It's colder here than I expected. At least the blizzard that threatened to shut down New York never came."

"The storm hit after you left," Dorothy replied. "You escaped the worst of it."

Did she? She couldn't answer at first, finally whispering, "Hopefully."

Dorothy raised a delicate eyebrow, but Emmanuelle didn't elaborate. Sure, she'd escaped the snowstorm. An escape from George, her ex, was yet to be determined.

Please God, be with me now in my dark season, when I'm so out of place. The world around me is glowing with the promise of Christmas and I feel dark and empty inside.

She leaned forward to admire two animated polar bears sitting amidst the treble clef signs in the shop's window. Beneath a starry sky, the bears tapped drums to the tune of "Jingle Bells."

"Very clever." She couldn't help a grin. "Thanks for the invite to Cherish."

"We're thrilled you agreed to join us for Christmas." Dorothy grabbed her hands for a reassuring squeeze. She was so pleasant and gracious, Emmanuelle thought. So jovial.

On the other hand, Emmanuelle felt the opposite. All she had become in twenty-five years—a dependable, straightforward woman as well as an esteemed harpist—she'd lost in six months to George.

She'd once been like Dorothy, resilient, independent and a woman of God.

Her ex had taken it all away.

Deep in her coat pocket, her fingers worried an angel ornament she'd purchased at the New York airport. For her, the ornament symbolized the sacred Christmas season, its optimism, dreams, and promise.

She hadn't taken it out of her pocket yet.

"You've been difficult to reach these past few months." Dorothy studiously appraised Emmanuelle. "You hardly ever answered your phone."

"I've been busy with concert engagements." Emmanuelle forced her features to remain blank. "You know, musician stuff." It was a lie, and with the lie came heaviness, a wide band of disapproval. Where had her sense of decency gone?

She tightened her paisley scarf around her neck. Although the violent purple and yellow bruises had faded, she still felt self-conscious.

Dorothy guided her into the music store. "My brother will blame his forgetfulness on his new job, or that gigantic puppy he adopted at the animal shelter. You'd think he'd know better at thirty years old."

"He's a good guy," Emmanuelle said. "Nicholas and I Skyped every night for months when you were in rehab."

"Thanks to you both, I'm better." Dorothy smiled. "And most important, thanks to God."

Once, Emmanuelle would have readily agreed. God was her salvation, her refuge. Now she didn't know how to answer because her faith had wavered.

Truly I tell you, if you have faith as small as a mustard seed, you can say to this mountain, "Move from here to there," and it will move. The verse from Matthew 17:20 came to her mind, a reminder of her strength. All she had to do was reach for it, if she was brave enough.

Inside the store, Dorothy ran a finger along one of the shelves, grinning when she was assured it was dust free. "Ryan and I purchased a cottage-style bungalow four blocks from here and there's an extra bedroom."

"This is your first Christmas as a married couple." Emmanuelle set her suitcase out of the way of a passing customer. "Please celebrate the holiday without me in the middle."

"I insist you stay with us."

"For an entire month?" Emmanuelle shook her head. "Insist all you want. I booked a room at the Cherish Hills Inn. You raved about the inn's accommodations being top-quality when you returned to Cherish for your brother's wedding last year."

"The wedding that didn't happen." Ruefully, Dorothy

sighed. "Nicholas is still healing from the embarrassment and heartbreak."

The ending stages of love. Dreams shattered.

Without warning, the front door burst open. Instinctively, Emmanuelle held up a hand, shielding herself from view.

A heavy-set woman, her hair helmeted in a tight gray bun, ambled inside. She called out a jovial hello to Dorothy.

"Be with you in a minute, Mrs. McManus." Dorothy gave a flap of her hands, and then turned back to Emmanuelle. "Sorry. What were we discussing?"

Emmanuelle blew out a breath. This uneasiness, this fear of being followed, had to stop.

Still shaken, she kept her focus on a Mozart statue topped with a red plush Santa hat sitting on the counter.

"We were discussing the wedding that didn't happen," she replied. "Whenever Nicholas and I talked when you were in rehab, he always reminded me we should place our trust in God."

"Sadly, people change, beliefs change." Worry replaced Dorothy's earlier smile. "Hard knocks can shake the faith of the most devout. I pray he'll go to church again because he's faltered since the breakup."

Suggesting Emmanuelle put her suitcase behind the front counter, Dorothy led her past a display table. As Dorothy paused to rearrange two pairs of oboe earrings so they lined up side by side, she said, "God had other plans for him and for me. I believe things work out for the best."

Emmanuelle frowned and nodded, aborting both actions.

For Dorothy, perhaps. For Ryan. For anyone in this idyllic snow globe town. But not for me. And apparently not for Nicholas.

Her cell phone buzzed. She retrieved it from her tote bag and scanned the screen. *Unknown caller.* Her heart stopped. A telemarketer? A wrong number?

"Who is it?"

Looking up, she saw Dorothy was studying her with keen interest.

"No one." Fumbling, Emmanuelle tucked the phone back into her faux leather tote. "You're right. People change for many reasons." And she'd changed most of all. She'd been a competent, successful woman. Now a chill crept up her spine when a door opened into a harmless music store.

"Are you okay?" Dorothy asked.

"I'm fine, just tired from traveling." Emmanuelle's eyes welled with tears, and she averted her gaze. She'd applied makeup, the first time in months, attempting to conceal her sleep deprivation. The endless worrying and crying had taken a toll.

"We're organizing a concert in the town square the weekend before Christmas," Dorothy was saying. "I meant to ask you to bring your harp—"

"My harp weighs nearly eighty pounds." She picked up a pair of piano earrings and fingered the tiny keyboard. "It's in New York."

Broken. She wouldn't reveal how George had destroyed her harp in one of his lightning-fast rages. The memory caused a block of ice to form in her stomach, a block that she knew would be slow to thaw. She hated the thought of her beloved instrument, splintered into pieces, lying on a New York curb under a pile of snow.

Better the harp than you splintered into pieces.

But his shouted insults and rough slaps had been her fault. She'd provoked him.

No, no, no. Her inner voice took on a sharp edge. That was the old Emmanuelle talking. The new Emmanuelle knew she wasn't a dishtowel to be thrown around on a whim. In hindsight, she should have known George was abusive. The warning signs were there.

She blew out a breath. She'd resolved to find peace and comfort in this holiday … in this town … somewhere … and find her footing again.

"Enough about me." She set down the earrings and dismissed herself with a flutter of her fingers. "Where's Ryan?"

"He's rehearsing in nearby Stanley Valley today and will arrive this evening. He'll be singing 'O Holy Night' for a Christmas Cantata service. He gives so freely of his talent." Dorothy's smile was as radiant as a Merry Christmas bouquet. "He's featured throughout the Carolinas in many guest appearances. Plus, the Atlanta opera house asked him to perform the role of Zoroastro in Handel's opera, *Orlando*. I'm incredibly proud of him."

"You should be." Dorothy's smile was contagious, and Emmanuelle managed a warm grin. "He's famous and extremely talented."

"And you? Any upcoming concerts?"

"None." She answered in a firm tone that she expected would discourage her friend from probing. Judging by the way Dorothy's eyebrows drew together, she'd succeeded.

Fortunately, an acoustic guitar arrangement of "Lo, How a Rose Is Blooming" piped in the background, the ideal holiday music to smooth a lull in the conversation.

"I'm sure you're keen to check in." Dorothy broke the silence. "I'll deal with these last few customers, close the store, and give you a lift. Unless you'd rather walk the three blocks to the inn?"

"No, no. I'll wait for you."

She'd never walk alone again. Not in New York, not in Cherish. Not anywhere, because she'd never feel safe again.

Dorothy gestured toward the front of the store. "If you care to browse, the Christmas music section is on your left. There's a lovely harp arrangement of *The Nutcracker*."

"Thanks. Your store is a music-lover's dream."

Intrigued, Emmanuelle stepped past a buyer laden with music bookmarks and made her way to the sheet music. She thumbed through endless arrangements of Christmas solos, wondering what madness had brought her to this town. She didn't belong here among all this gaiety. Her sadness was a burden refusing to go away.

Disheartened, she stared, trancelike, at the display window. A whimsical model train circled the polar bears, and the sight was enchanting.

Beyond, past the cheery town, past the exuberant children and the enormous Christmas tree illuminating the town square, a darkened sky had followed dusk.

CHAPTER 2

*A*s he entered his apartment, Nicholas Thompson pulled off his deputy badge and set it on a table in the foyer. Except for one traffic violation, a minor fender bender and endless meetings, the day had been relatively calm for a newbie deputy.

He looked forward to relaxing in front of the TV with a good cup of coffee and a chocolate-glazed doughnut. Ever since he'd become a deputy, he'd acquired a taste for both.

All fifty pounds of his six-month-old golden retriever greeted him with an energetic stretch. He'd purchased the dog from an animal shelter in Stanley, two weeks to the day after his fiancée, Alice, had broken up with him. The dog surveyed Nicholas with expectant black eyes and a fiercely wagging tail.

"No, Molly Belle, I'm not taking you for a—"

The dog ran in circles around him and barked.

Nicholas groaned. He'd no sooner walked in and he was forced to turn around and walk out again. "All right, take a tater and wait a sec." He weaved around a mountain of laundry and strode to his bedroom. His bed was unmade, an old sweat-shirt tossed over a side chair. He removed the gun from his holster and locked it in his bedroom closet's safe. Then he loosened his tie and changed out of uniform—white shirt and khaki pants—dragging on jeans, a long-sleeved T-shirt, and work boots. Pausing, he ran a critical survey of his apartment, particularly the coffee table piled with remote controls and junk mail and old catalogues. The large sofa begged for a skilled reupholster, and his sister, Dorothy, had admonished him countless times to hang curtains on his bare windows.

He darted a glance at the motorcycle calendar propped on a shelf. Today was December first, and Christmas was less than a month away. At the very least, the season merited a Christmas tree in the corner and a wreath on his apartment door.

Nope. Not this year.

Despite Molly Belle lightening his days, Nicholas didn't have the heart for celebrations and feasts. What other man in the state of South Carolina had experienced the humiliation of his fiancée leaving him on their wedding day? And by text, no less. Not even in person.

The dog's impertinent barking prompted him to grab the leash, button his navy pea coat and open the front door. With an eager yelp, Molly Belle ran ahead, down his short flight of stairs and onto the sidewalk.

"Slower, girl." The dog, as usual, didn't obey and tugged harder on the leash. Nicholas made a mental note to sign her up for obedience classes.

His cell phone buzzed. He hoped it wasn't a call to drive back to the police station. Relieved to see Dorothy's caller ID, he clicked on.

"Nicholas, are you through with work?" she asked.

"Yes, I just got in." He restrained the dog from sniffing

every blade of glass in a neighbor's garden. "I'm taking Molly Belle for a walk."

"Emmanuelle arrived an hour ago. Did you forget?"

He sighed and slapped a hand to his forehead. He forgot a lot of things lately. "I got sidetracked by last-minute meetings at the police station. Please tell her I'm sorry."

"You can tell her yourself. We're at the Cherish Hills Inn and she's unpacking. Meet us here, then join us at Frank's Pizzeria for a slice. It's your favorite restaurant."

His first response was *no* before he thought better of it. He should extend a polite apology, considering he'd forgotten to pick up the woman. He'd swing by and make his amends and then leave.

As he and Molly Belle neared the inn, it was all he could do not to reverse direction and head back to his apartment.

He could work. He could take care of his spirited dog. But he didn't relish small talk with a woman, especially a woman he'd grown close to during their many phone conversations. What would he say to her after all these months?

"Oh, by the way, Emmanuelle, do you remember me talking nonstop about Alice, my fiancée? She left me the day of our wedding."

Molly Belle ignored his command to walk slower, nearly choking on the leash as she lunged forward.

CHAPTER 3

*B*attling for control of the leash, Nicholas strode into the Cherish Hills Inn's lobby. Briefly, he admired the boxwood wreath hanging on the wooden door, the lighted village scene on a round cherry tabletop in the foyer. He greeted the white-haired innkeeper, Tom Canning, with an apologetic shrug and lifted the dog's leash.

Tom scowled. Crevices grooved the sides of his mouth. "No animals."

"Just this once—for someone you've known your entire life?" Nicholas asked. "For a man who upholds the law in our town?"

Tom sighed, unbending a bit, and peered at Nicholas above the cheaters perched on the bridge of his nose. "Go ahead, deputy." He rewarded Nicholas with a brief nod, but raised his index finger to issue a one-minute warning.

"Thanks." Nicholas strode across the wide plank floors to the parlor where a fire blazed in the stacked rock fireplace, so large an ox could stand upright inside it. On the center of the mantel sat a handsomely carved Nativity set in burnished wood. Artistically arranged seasonal fruit—oranges and apples and pears—were loaded high in a wide pewter bowl on a side table.

He directed his gaze toward Dorothy, who stood near the fireplace, and that was the last thing he remembered.

The undeniably beautiful woman who stood beside Dorothy, clad in a white lace sweater dress, resembled a dainty, sweet confection. Her complexion was pink, her dark lashes slightly lowered, her lips plush and generous. A puffy blue jacket was slung over her shoulders, and she held a tote bag close to her side.

His mind reeled with memories.

Emmanuelle Sumter. They'd Skyped many times, so he'd known she was attractive, but in person she was positively breathtaking. Silky blonde hair rioted around her face in impossibly tight curls, and her huge blue eyes acknowledged a tentative welcome.

"I assume you remember me." He fumbled with Molly Belle's leash as the dog sniffed the rug incessantly. "You look … different in person." *Better*, he amended to himself. *She looked better. More than better.* He extended his free hand. "Please accept my apologies for forgetting you."

"Apology accepted." She placed her small hand in his large one. "How could I forget our nightly conversations? You guided Dorothy through a challenging season in her life."

Emmanuelle's features were so petite, her fingers so fragile. "And you were the friend she counted on." He tightened his grip and vigorously shook her hand.

"You were the person who prayed with her every day." She pulled away, politely, decisively. "You encouraged her."

"Hold on you two, I'm right here!" Dorothy laughingly stepped between them. "Are you competing in a compliment contest I'm not aware of?"

Emmanuelle's dimples winked in a slight smile. "Your brother's the winner."

"Please don't boost his ego, or he'll expect you to treat for pizza." Dorothy chuckled. "Frank's Pizza is within walking distance. They advertise the best pizza in town."

"Because they're the only pizzeria in town." Nicholas helped Emmanuelle on with her coat, then swung Molly Belle's leash up and down. "Unfortunately they don't allow animals and I won't be able to go."

Molly Belle responded with a defiant stare and Emmanuelle leaned down to pet her. "Aww, your dog is so friendly." Soon, the dog was lying on the rug legs up, outstretched in doggy ecstasy while Emmanuelle crouched to rub her stomach.

"You said you'd just gotten home from work," Dorothy said as she encouraged Emmanuelle and the dog to stand, then steered the threesome to the doorway. "Have you eaten dinner, Nicholas?"

"I'll whip up something." He couldn't imagine what although there was a slight possibility a frozen pizza sat in his freezer behind a carton of peanut butter ice cream.

Molly Belle had different ideas, having decided Emmanuelle was her new best friend. With a wiggle of glee, she changed direction and hurled straight into her.

Emmanuelle fell back and Nicholas let go of the leash to stop her fall. Freed from her leash, the dog shot in another direction and knocked over a crystal vase filled with red roses. The vase shattered on the floor.

Tom, eye-glass cheaters in hand, tore into the parlor. His face colored to a beet-red as he tapped his watch. "Your one-minute dog visit was up five minutes ago, Nicholas."

"Sorry. We were just leaving." Nicholas righted Emmanuelle as Dorothy picked up the roses, then he dashed forward to retrieve the leash.

"Shoo, all of you!" Tom said. "I'll clean up the mess."

The women followed Nicholas. They exited to a whip of

icy wind that blew Emmanuelle's curls around her face. Nicholas lifted his hand, an automatic response to protect her from another gust. She flinched, tightened the pink paisley scarf around her neck, and moved a step away.

He tossed an inquiring glance toward her. She ignored him.

As if by mutual agreement to cover up Emmanuelle's skittish behavior, Dorothy began talking about every holiday event scheduled in three counties between Christmas and New Year's.

"Frank's boasts an outdoor enclosed eating area," Dorothy continued, talking in a loud voice to drown out the quiet. She stopped briefly to commend the florist shop's front window decorated in scarlet-red poinsettias and twine wreaths. "I'm sure Frank's will allow Molly Belle inside, Nicholas. She's leashed and we'll take an out-of-the-way table."

Before Nicholas could comment, Dorothy's cell phone pinged. She grabbed it from her tote bag, read the text, then extended an unapologetic grin. "Ryan returned early from Stanley. A few weeks ago, he bought a cookbook called *Southern Charms* at a fundraiser for encouraging women empowerment, and he's been learning to cook gourmet. He's preparing a romantic dinner of rosemary chicken and pasta salad and he wants me to come home now. He has a surprise for me."

"I applaud your husband for buying a cookbook and supporting a beneficial cause." Despite his words, Nicholas sent his sister an exasperated glance. "So, you invited me to join you for dinner and now you're leaving?"

If she was trying to fix him up with Emmanuelle, he refused to go along with it. From what Dorothy had revealed, Emmanuelle had accepted his sister's offer to visit Cherish for the holidays primarily to get away from New York. The result of breaking up with a man. It was always because of a man, he thought, reflecting on his cheating fiancée and her new boyfriend.

He wanted to extend a sympathetic ear, for surely Emmanuelle wanted to talk at length about the break-up, although he wasn't in the proper frame of mind to attend to anyone's problems other than his own.

Yes, he'd gotten along well with her. They had talked nightly for months because of their shared interest in Dorothy's welfare, plus their unshakeable faith in God. But his life was different now. His faith teetered. If he had to define it, he'd say his faith was lukewarm.

He tuned back in when he heard Emmanuelle say, "Don't disappoint Ryan." She put her hand on Dorothy's arm, then flashed a look at Nicholas. "I'll double back and finish unpacking if you don't mind walking me."

This was his out. A polite response and he'd be sitting in his recliner watching television within fifteen minutes flat. Instead, he found himself saying, "We're almost at the restaurant so we might as well enjoy dinner."

Besides pizza, the restaurant had good coffee.

"Perfect! You two go on without me. I'm sure there's a lot to catch up on since you haven't talked in a year." Dorothy tucked her brown hair under the black wool cap she produced from her handbag. With a satisfied wave, she swung in the opposite direction.

"This way." Nicholas touched Emmanuelle's arm. She sidestepped him and ran a hand over the zipper of her jacket. Although she appeared to be an elegant and poised woman, she was as edgy as a newborn fawn.

Perhaps there was nothing left to discuss? Dorothy, their commonality, no longer required their help, and he obviously wasn't interesting enough for pretty and popular Emmanuelle. The thought left him maintaining a chilly and reserved silence as they walked toward the restaurant.

His gaze landed on two tow-headed toddlers running ahead of them. They pointed to the fairyland of Christmas lights in the town square and the sight made Nicholas smile. He loved children, although now he'd never have any. He'd never subject his heart to another battering. He'd successfully barricaded himself behind a solid, protective shell.

Lonely? Sometimes.

Safe? Definitely.

He headed Emmanuelle and Molly Belle toward the next block.

Molly Belle had a mind of her own, though, wanting nothing more than to loll on the sidewalk and hug the ground. He encouraged the dog with an assurance of a treat, and Emmanuelle added a "C'mon girl."

When they resumed walking, he asked, "Are you still the principal harpist for … I forgot the name of the symphony. It was in a town somewhere outside New York."

"No, I'm not playing the harp anymore. It's gone." Stillness reigned for several beats after her self-deprecating laugh. He recognized the defeat in her shining blue eyes, and sympathy flickered in his hardened heart.

"What about you?" The audible stress in her tone made him hesitate. "I remember you were studying for an important exam."

"The police academy. I passed and I'm a deputy."

Her eyes widened. "A—a deputy …" She blanched and missed a step.

"And here I thought congratulations were in order," he half joked.

"Yes, of course." She clutched her tote bag and kept her head down. "Umm, congratulations, Deputy Thompson."

Something had happened to her in New York. Something bad, although he couldn't offer any support because he was empty. The woman whom he'd thought had loved him had left him flat. He'd been a blind fool while she'd deceived him for months, but he'd learned a painful lesson and he'd learned it well. Relationships with women were well off his radar, especially when a woman clearly had a hang-up about men.

Bachelorhood was serene. Naught to fear, because nothing—no hearts, no feeling, no plans—would be broken. Besides, a dog was excellent company.

Despite himself, his gaze lingered on Emmanuelle's profile, her slim figure she kept well-hidden beneath her winter jacket and high boots.

Molly Belle barked a little too enthusiastically, prompting Emmanuelle to jump when a black lab trotted past.

"She's high-spirited," Nicholas offered as an explanation.

"Who's in control here?" she asked him. "I used to work around dogs. They were a big part of my life." She patted Molly Belle's head, then smiled when the dog put a wet nose in her hand.

"I'm considering dog obedience classes. Do you think it's a good idea?"

Emmanuelle opened her mouth, closed it again, grinned. "Yes, it's an excellent idea. In the meantime, begin with simple commands like *sit* and *wait*. Can you do that?"

"Certainly. I'm the master."

An irreverent chuckle burst from her lips and he fought the insane impulse to kiss her.

He knew her through those lengthy phone conversations, and every night he'd looked forward to their discussions about God, and their everyday lives, and their pasts. Their comfortable hour-long chats had become easy and familiar. If he hadn't been engaged to his fiancée at the time, he might have admitted the attraction he'd felt for Emmanuelle.

This stiffness between them was foreign. She had frequently sought his advice, the comfort of his faith coinciding with her hard-won beliefs. She'd been orphaned when she was in her teens, but she had persevered, studied hard, and become a virtuoso harpist.

They walked the last block to the restaurant at a quick pace. Her knee-length dress glided along her legs and her suede boots fit high above her knee. Nicholas kept stealing glances at her. The self-sufficient woman he'd known had evaporated. She'd become breakable, her voice soft, her movements hesitant.

They walked up the steps to the pizzeria's entrance, and he reached around to open the door.

"I'm ordering Frank's deluxe-meat lovers special," he said. "Are you the salad type?"

"Salad? Salad is for vegetarians." She walked past him into the restaurant, her expression amused. "I'm the barbecue and corn fritters type."

CHAPTER 4

$\mathcal{T}$he next day was Saturday, and Nicholas worked a half day. The morning had started with an arrest for drunk driving and ended in the police station with multiple copies of blank forms to fill out. He loved his job, but he could do without the written procedures and minute details.

When he returned home at noon, he changed out of his uniform and into jeans and a shirt, a white pullover hoodie, and running shoes. He dashed off a reminder note to price affordable curtains over the weekend, then leashed Molly Belle for a quick jog.

Ryan's surprise for Dorothy the previous night had been tickets to a tuba Christmas concert in Stanley, and Dorothy had given Nicholas the not-so-subtle hint that Emmanuelle would be spending the day alone. Despite telling himself a firm *no*, he found himself veering toward the Cherish Hills Inn.

Their dinner at the pizzeria had ended abruptly when Emmanuelle had pleaded tiredness soon after he began telling her about his job as deputy sheriff. He'd started off by regaling her with amusing tales of some of the absurd arrests he'd made. One had been for drunk and disorderly conduct when a spectator ran onto the field of a high school football game declaring he was the sixth offensive lineman. On another occasion, he'd walked an eighteen-year-old home to face his parents after a keg party had gotten out of control, only to have the boy get sick on their front lawn.

As he talked, Emmanuelle's shoulders had tightened and her hand quivered as she'd pushed the barbecue around her plate. Her fear was tangible, stretching across the red-checkered tablecloth, and the pizza set neatly in the center of the table.

He got the hint and stopped talking about his profession altogether, carrying on instead a reasonably normal conversation, albeit one-sided, observing the average winter temperature in South Carolina and New York.

The inn neared, and he closed the distance to the porch steps in five long strides.

He leaned forward to catch his breath and wipe his brow on the sleeve of his hoodie. Wide-slatted rocking chairs were assembled on the expansive front porch and evergreen garland and holly berries were strung across each window.

Although he normally would simply walk into the inn, after the mishap the day before, he thought it best if he knocked first.

Pushing his cheaters down his nose, Tom Canning peered through the entry's side glass, glowered, and flung open the door. "No dogs allowed inside, Deputy Thompson." He tried to sound polite, but there was no mistaking that he was issuing an order. "No exceptions."

"I'm sorry about yesterday, Mr. Canning, and I'll be happy to pay for any damages."

"Good. I'll write up a bill for you."

"No hurry. I mean, please do." Nicholas kept a sneakered

foot in the door as the innkeeper attempted to shut him out. "Will you let Emmanuelle know I'm here?"

Tom took off his cheaters and polished them. "Is she expecting you?"

"Probably not."

"Hi Nicholas." Emmanuelle appeared at the bottom of the curved staircase, looking bewitchingly beautiful. Her blonde hair was piled high at the crown, her ever-present pink scarf around her neck, her puffy blue jacket all zippered.

"I guess she was expecting you." With a conspiratorial half grin toward Nicholas, the owner ushered them outside, then slammed the door, leaving Emmanuelle and Nicholas standing on the porch with Molly Belle.

Annoyed, Nicholas fixed his gaze on the door. "I thought everyone loved animals. Apparently, Tom doesn't like dogs."

"His reasons are excellent." She didn't withhold her chuckle. "That vase of roses spilled water across his rug and cost him thirty minutes of clean-up, not to mention the cost of the vase and flowers."

"I offered to pay for the damages." Nicholas inspected her trim, shapely form. Today, black jeans and high boots accentuated her long legs. A green sweater peeked from beneath her winter jacket. "Were you … expecting me?"

The color on her cheekbones rose to a flattering blush against her creamy complexion. The afternoon sun gilded her blonde hair to streaks of platinum, and he favored her with an unabashed smile. She was stunning.

She stretched on a pair of pink knit gloves that matched her scarf. "Dorothy mentioned you might stop by."

"Several local booths in the town square are selling Christmas items. Are you up for some last-minute shopping?" He was prepared for her to refuse. However, he didn't expect the wariness on her face, the absolutely motionless air between them.

"I have no reason to shop. I'm not buying any Christmas gifts this year." She focused a pained stare on the mixed greenery placed around the white rocking chairs.

An unexpected fury flowed through his veins at whoever had hurt her. When? Where?

"Surely there's something you'd like." He grinned, an attempt to disarm her. "The locals sell handmade jewelry and artwork and leather goods. And I have it on excellent authority that one of my friends, who owns a restaurant called The Grill Room, set up early this morning and is smoking South Carolina barbecue as we speak."

She considered her watch. "It's a little late for lunch."

"It's just shy of two o'clock. We'll call it an early dinner." He hooked his thumbs in the back pockets of his jeans and felt the leash go slack. In an instant, his dog had raced off the porch in a mad chase after a squirrel.

"Molly Belle!"

What happened next occurred in slow motion.

The dog ran into the road. Brakes squealed. A sickening thud.

"No!" Unmindful of traffic, Nicholas dashed for his dog, seeing only Molly Belle's limp body lying helpless in the middle of the road. Blood seeped from her stomach, matting her glossy golden fur. He sank down, right there with his dog, and did something he hadn't done since he was a child.

He cried.

CHAPTER 5

$\mathcal{E}$mmanuelle sat in the passenger seat of the innkeeper's lime-green Volkswagen and held the dog in her lap while Nicholas drove. She controlled her voice as she rubbed Molly Belle gently behind her ears. She'd secured a makeshift muzzle using the dog's leash, assuring Nicholas even Molly Belle, a sweet dog, could lash out when she was in pain.

"Looks like a surface wound," she said. Carefully, she lifted the dog's lip, murmuring about capillary refill time. When Nicholas didn't seem to hear her, she added, "Fortunately, the driver stopped in time."

Everything had happened in a blur. Visibly distraught, the driver had burst from his car in a frenzy and groped for the words to apologize. Tom Canning rushed out and offered Nicholas his car, and then dashed to the inn. He was back almost instantly with sterile gauze and a yellow crocheted blanket an instant later. A bystander stopped traffic, which allowed Nicholas and Tom to use the blanket as a sling and carry the dog to the car. Emmanuelle placed gauze over the dog's stomach and applied pressure, murmuring relief when the blood didn't soak through.

Nicholas drove quickly and silently to Cherish Animal Hospital. She took in his granite profile, his short blond hair shoved back from his forehead. He hunched behind the wheel stuffed into a car not made to fit his six-foot frame.

"She doesn't appear to be in shock." She kept her voice quiet and upbeat.

His dog might not be in shock, but Nicholas was. He had taken immediate action, though, and had phoned the animal hospital to tell them they were on their way.

"You don't know that," he finally responded.

"Yes, I do. I've been around plenty of sick dogs."

When they arrived at the hospital, Nicholas parked near the entrance. Once more using the blanket as a sling, they carried the dog past a red-haired receptionist who announced that her name was Scarlett Evans.

Dr. Judson Troutman, the veterinarian, waited for them in the examining room. Nicholas had mentioned to Emmanuelle that Dr. Troutman had been widowed two years earlier.

Slim, serious, and sandy-haired, the vet was casually dressed in khaki pants, a button-down shirt, and a white lab coat. After brief introductions, he checked Molly Belle's lungs with his stethoscope and confirmed Emmanuelle's evaluation. The dog wasn't in shock.

"My father was a veterinarian," Emmanuelle said. Reverently, she ran a hand along the stethoscope after the vet had laid it to one side.

"You learned well, Emmanuelle." His deep-brown eyes were kind, his demeanor innately gentle. He angled toward Nicholas. "I'm going to give Molly Belle all the time she needs, Deputy Thompson. After her fluids are stabilized and the diagnostics run, I'll give you an update. For now, there's nothing else to do except sit and wait."

Scarlett ushered them into the reception area. A nervous-looking woman in her fifties cradling a quivering black dachshund bobbed a brief hello.

Emmanuelle slid onto a thinly padded chair and nudged aside a half-finished cup of coffee set on a corner table. She rubbed her arms and then dropped her head into her open hands. Now that her adrenaline had settled, she felt chilled and kept her jacket and scarf over her shoulders.

Nicholas paced the hallway for several minutes before coming to sit beside her. "I don't know why I wasn't paying attention and didn't hold onto her leash tighter. If only I had …" He stared down at his hands.

She scanned his clenched fists, the skin bunching at his eyes. "Molly Belle is blessed with the ability to love life. You're the most important part and not to blame. She's always on a leash and you do all you can to keep her safe."

Her quiet reassurances seemed to help, for he sat straighter.

"Still, I was lax. Will she ever forgive me?"

"Of course."

She didn't know where to put her hands, so she rested them on her lap.

Scarlett ushered the nervous woman cradling the dachshund down the long hallway. A door banged shut.

"The accident should never have taken place." Nicholas scrubbed his fingers over his face. "I can't make sense of it. Lately, I can't make sense of anything that's happened to me."

"Everything in our lives is a result of God's favor."

"Favor? What favor? My cycle of believing has been broken."

"So was mine. Whenever I think about the person I became these past few months, it makes me sad."

"What happened, Emmanuelle?" He studied her expression. "When we last spoke on the phone you were so upbeat."

She chewed her bottom lip. "A lot happens in a year. Don't ask me about the in-between because I'm not ready to talk about it." Mentally reliving George's abuse, a heavy despair settled in her gut. Whenever he'd banged her body into a wall, he screamed that they belonged together, and he was trying to teach her who was the master. No one had ever hit her before. She'd come from a kind and loving home.

"You were only meant for me, Emmanuelle."

The psychological, and then physical, abuse was always worse after George drank. The sharp smell of whiskey on his breath predicted the flashes of unpredictable anger sure to follow. A familiar sweat of panic slid down her neck. On a jerk, she swung her gaze from Nicholas and locked the terrifying remembrances in a safe compartment in her mind.

"Emmanuelle?"

She faltered, found her axis and drew a fortifying breath. "Dorothy stopped by the inn this morning."

"Why?"

"To talk. And she reminded me I shouldn't rebuke myself for past circumstances. She encouraged me to keep my attention on God and not dwell on myself."

"How can a memory upset you if it already happened?"

"Now there's a question I ask myself. Memories can only upset you if they have your attention. The key is to focus on what really matters." Despite her brave declaration, she couldn't meet his probing stare. Instead, she eyed the white-lighted snowman, accented with sheer purple ribbon, hanging on a far wall.

After breakfasting with Dorothy in the inn's sunny conservatory, Emmanuelle had confessed the beatings she'd suffered while tears had streamed down her cheeks. With every frightening scene she confided, heavy chains had been lifted from her heart.

Dorothy was kindhearted and understanding, a true friend, her intentions always in the right place.

Emmanuelle's rapport with Nicholas was different. He had commended her on her talent and independence, complimenting her on countless occasions. What would his opinion be if he learned she had been foolish enough to allow a man to control her?

She released a sigh and hid her face in her hands. She carried a shame she couldn't describe, not even to herself.

"Care to discuss what happened to you, Emmanuelle?" Nicholas repeated. "You can trust me."

He stared at her. She stared at the snowman.

She could hear a cell phone ringing in the hallway. She could smell the cold, stale coffee on the corner table.

Yes, she trusted Nicholas, even as she feared his admiration would change to disapproval once he understood her situation.

Why hadn't she left George sooner? She'd asked herself the same question more times than she could count.

"Because, Emmanuelle, you were meant only for me."

She shuddered, recalling his bloodshot gray eyes, as he was liquored up more often than not. When had he changed? He'd been so charming at the outset of their relationship, wooing her with lavish dinners and dark chocolate truffles and evenings at the theater.

"Emmanuelle?"

Despite her resolve to start a new life, she pressed her lips tight and didn't acknowledge him.

"You know," Nicholas went on, "I once was a person of great faith." He inclined his head and spoke softly. "This dejection I've felt ever since Alice—"

Emmanuelle's words came quick with no apology. "Your sister said, "'If you despair, you will live in despair.'"

"Dorothy is admirable and Ryan has taken her lead. Together their faith is anchored in God. I want to trust in the Lord again, I really do." He lifted his hand and cupped her chin, raising her face to his, forcing her to meet his gaze.

She didn't flinch, knowing that he needed a fresh start, needed her full attention.

"Begin by reaching out in prayer." She took his hand, holding it as he bowed his head and whispered praises to God. Silently, she joined him.

Scarlett strolled over, stacking used coffee cups and folding morning newspapers. "Do you two want anything? There's coffee in the vending machine."

Nicholas looked up at her. "Is it any good?"

"No. It's instant, and cold, and shuts off sometimes. Often, actually." She grinned. "Anyway, I brought in extra junk food from home. You know, candy and cupcakes, bottles of soda. Want anything?"

Emmanuelle smiled. "We're fine, thanks."

"My motto is to embrace life and indulge yourself."

Scarlett's full-figured form, Emmanuelle noticed, was pleasing and curvaceous. She was empathetic and sunny, a person who saw the bright side, even on a bleak afternoon. Upbeat, she finished cleaning up the waiting room and retreated to her desk.

As afternoon slipped into evening, Dr. Troutman emerged from the hallway. He drew up a chair to sit across from them. "Delightful news, Deputy Thompson. Surgery isn't necessary. There's no internal bleeding, organ damage, or broken limbs."

"She's going to be all right?" The guarded hope in Nicholas's voice prompted Emmanuelle to place her hand on his arm.

"Molly Belle will be fine." The vet came to his feet. "You can take her home tonight. Find a comfortable spot and get her settled with some heating pads. Given time, she'll heal with no scars."

"Thank you, doctor."

"Clean the wound and apply an antibiotic cream. I gave her an injection for her discomfort." Dr. Troutman rooted in his lab coat for a pad and pen. "I'm prescribing an anti-inflammatory and I recommend not leaving her alone for extended periods of time."

Nicholas's face paled. "For how long? A week?"

"Recovery time varies. She's a young bouncy dog, and I predict she'll be fit in a few weeks or less. Incidentally, she might be a mixed breed. Although she's mostly a golden, I'm thinking there's a bit of yellow lab mixed in." He scribbled the prescription and handed it to Nicholas. "I'll ask Scarlett to schedule Molly Belle for a check-up next Saturday."

"Are you sure I can properly care for her at home in the meantime?" Nicholas hesitated before starting for Scarlett's desk. "If it's safer, please keep her overnight for observation."

"Nothing to observe. You and your girlfriend are quite capable," Dr. Troutman said. "She knows her animals."

"I'm not Nicholas's girlfriend," Emmanuelle clarified, quick to get to her feet. "I learned a tremendous amount when I helped my father. We lived in Remsen, a little town outside of New York. For years, I visited his office every day after school."

From the corner of her eye, she saw Nicholas's thick eyebrows raise as he busied himself with paying the bill.

"How far outside of New York is your father's office?" the vet inquired.

The memories flickered, faded, a million miles away. Once, she'd felt safe and happy, living like other people. How easy it had been when she was a child.

"He died ten years ago when I was sixteen." She spoke carefully, not letting her sense of loss, her free and easy childhood, creep into her voice. "He was a highly regarded veterinarian in our little town. Cherish reminds me of Remsen. Without Remsen's snow."

"I've never been to Remsen," Scarlett chirped. "I bet it's pretty there."

Dr. Troutman gave Scarlett an indulgent smile, then turned back to Emmanuelle. "A small town's down-to-earth values and its focus on what matters most in life ... Well, there's not much that can beat that."

"You're absolutely right." Emmanuelle extended her hand. "Thank you."

Over at the reception desk, Nicholas handed Scarlett his credit card, then peered over his shoulder at Emmanuelle. "All those hours we spent on the phone and you never mentioned your animal expertise."

She shrugged. "There were more serious topics to discuss."

Saying he would get Molly Belle, the vet walked down the hallway. He and Nicholas transported a muzzled Molly Belle to the rear seat of the Volkswagen using a large dog crate.

On the drive to Nicholas's apartment, Emmanuelle pondered what to do. Torn between the belief that helping for a week wouldn't matter because she had no other plans, and the fact she'd be immersed in his personal surroundings, she considered how to word her offer before she spoke.

He needed help, especially when he reported to work on Monday. Yet, he hadn't asked for any. A proud, stubborn man, Dorothy had once described her brother when she'd become frustrated at his inability to talk about his hurt after his marriage plans fell apart.

"Once Molly Belle is situated tonight," Emmanuelle began, "I'll stay with her while you fill her prescription."

"I appreciate that."

Guarded, yet so polite.

"Once Monday rolls in, I'll watch her while you're on duty, deputy."

"Wouldn't you rather kill time checking out the Christmas markets and visiting Dorothy and Ryan?"

"I'd rather kill time being of some use."

"All day nursing a sick dog isn't a vacation." His expression indicated his willingness to accept her offer, although he kept his tone carefully noncommittal.

"Who said my visit is about a vacation? Christmas is the season for giving."

What else could she say that was a reasonable justification for offering to help? She simply *wanted* to because Nicholas and Molly Belle had become important to her, but she certainly couldn't say that. "I have experience tending to sick animals."

"I'll pay you." He offered a quick, grateful smile.

"Do you cook?"

"Do frozen pizzas count?"

"You're describing the extent of my cooking skills as well." She grinned. "Fortunately, Ryan is learning gourmet cooking so I'll throw out some hints. Or better yet, I'll borrow his *Southern Charms* cookbook."

CHAPTER 6

*W*ith Molly Belle settled on a blanket near the recliner in the living room, Nicholas went off to get her prescription. Emmanuelle applied a heating pad to the dog's belly, where it seemed she had the most pain. When she was assured the dog rested comfortably, she removed the heating pad and waited for Nicholas to come back with the prescription.

Dr. Troutman's injection had made Molly Belle drowsy. Her brownish-black nose pressed upon the blanket, and her sides rose and fell as she dropped into in a deep, sound sleep.

In the solitude of the quiet room, Emmanuelle set to work tidying the coffee table. She boxed up old magazines and catalogues that lay scattered in a mismatched pile beside five remote controls. Why did a man need so many remotes for one television set?

When Nicholas returned, he hung his hoodie by the door and crossed the room. Crouching, he stared at his sleeping dog.

"She's asleep and not in pain," Emmanuelle assured him. "See? Her tail is twitching. She's probably dreaming about chasing purple pigeons or flopping in the grass at the Cherish Hills Inn. When she wakes up, we'll give her the medicine."

Nicholas nodded. "And I have bad news and good news." He rolled to his feet and handed her a white paper bag. "The bad news is the kiosks were closing. The good news is I managed to plead our upsetting afternoon to my friend from The Grill Room. He was smoking a beef brisket and added coleslaw. I figured you were hungry. I also snagged a couple cups of coffee and two honey-glazed donuts."

She gave an appreciative sniff. "My mouth is watering."

He went to the kitchen and pulled a water from the fridge. "What do you want to drink?"

She followed him and put the kettle on the stove to boil. "Hot tea. Thanks."

He folded his shirtsleeves to his elbows and draped a dishtowel over his shoulder. "My place is a mess, although I used to be fairly neat."

"I think I have enough tidying here to keep me occupied."

"Yeah, for at least a year." He grinned, then grew solemn. "Since my failed engagement to a woman who—"

"You didn't fail." She reached for a thick mug in the cupboard. "Your fiancée did."

They dished out the smoked barbecue brisket and coleslaw and brought stoneware, napkins, and utensils into the living room. She placed the stoneware on the coffee table, set her napkin on her lap, and took a neat bite of brisket. Chewing, she nodded toward Molly Belle. "After she sleeps, she may be sore. Follow the directions on the prescription."

"You'll come ... tomorrow?"

She reached for her tea. "I texted Dorothy to let her know what happened. She and Ryan are still in Stanley. She'll stop in tomorrow to see you and the dog."

"And you?"

"I'll be here on Monday morning, as long as you don't mind leaving the dog by herself to come get me."

"The weatherman calls for a pleasant week. Sunny and highs in the fifties. If you'd prefer to walk—"

"I never walk alone anymore." She gulped her tea and set the mug on the coffee table, and then her napkin alongside it. "Can you drive me to the inn? It's getting late and I'm sure the innkeeper will be worried. Besides, you have his vehicle."

"I phoned Tom, and he knows Molly Belle is fine. He assured me he isn't leaving the inn tonight." He rested his hand lightly on hers. "Please stay a while longer. You haven't finished your brisket, and I could use the company."

Hesitantly, she replaced her napkin in her lap.

Nicholas relished his meal as if he hadn't eaten in a week although she nibbled and pecked at hers. After they finished, he lifted his water for a last pull while she cupped her mug and stared out the narrow window. A splash of light streaked across the black velvet sky.

"You realize we're in full view of your neighbors." She grinned at him over her mug. "One of them is cruising into their driveway."

"Dorothy has reminded me on a weekly basis about buying curtains."

Still holding her mug, she wandered to the window and considered the quiet night covering the sleepy town. The room stilled to a comfortable silence.

"I've been waiting for a beautiful woman to come along who can help me choose the right ones," he said. "Fortunately, I've known her all along."

She pivoted, catching his wicked grin and look of interest as his gaze focused on her face. Her pulse leapt in a disconcerting combination of anticipation and panic.

"Emmanuelle." His voice grew quiet. "I can hardly kiss you when you're standing on the other side of the room."

"Nicholas, we hardly know each other."

"A year ago, we talked regularly. Our bond was strong. Let's be honest. We both know it still is."

She walked to the couch and set down her mug. He set down his water. Their gazes held, the quiet punctuated by the dog's light snores.

Her thoughts scattered. She rearranged them into a semblance of reason. "A year ago we had a common purpose —ensuring your sister made a full recovery."

"Are things so different?" Gently, his fingers curved around her nape, soothing, stroking. "I'll help you make a full recovery from whatever you're struggling with." He bent his head slowly, and his lips met hers with sweet tenderness.

For a moment, she went rigid.

"I'm attracted to you, Emmanuelle," he murmured. "Always have been. I'm here for you."

Her body reacted in a dizzying sensation of emotions she couldn't explain. She didn't want to respond to him. Or perhaps she did because her reaction felt so natural. Trusting a man, feeling safe and cared for in his arms ... She'd thought those feelings happened to other people.

Tentatively, she reached her arms around his neck and returned the kiss.

His mouth deepened as he fit her response to his own. He kissed her fully, insistently, boundlessly, creating a knot of pure awareness in her stomach. The longer his mouth pressed to hers, the more vibrant the sensations became. It was as if a new person had taken the place of the broken Emmanuelle. The new Emmanuelle was sincere and receptive, the former hesitant and uneasy, avoiding any connection with a man.

A sharp woof broke them apart.

Molly Belle lifted her head and regarded them. Before Nicholas could get to her, she laid her head down and went to sleep.

Emmanuelle's lips twitched. "Her injection is wearing off."

He settled on the couch and watched Emmanuelle, his gaze heated. "Shall we continue? We left off at—"

"Your dog may wake up again."

"I'll take my chances." His arms slipped around her, and she reveled in the pleasure of his hard mouth pressed on hers. She kissed him back while his warm hands shifted protectively around her.

Ages later, he lifted his head and cradled her face. Affection smoldered in his hazel eyes. "You came into my life at exactly the right time."

Molly Belle stirred, twitched, woofed to no one in particular, then plunked her nose back on the blanket.

He chuckled. "I think I have a love-hate relationship with that dog." With a sigh, he lowered his hands from Emmanuelle's face. He forked a last bite of coleslaw, leaned against the couch, and stretched out his legs. "Stay a while longer. Please. I'll be sure you make it back to the inn before midnight, Cinderella."

Across the inches of the couch separating them, she met his stare. His striking features were full of hope, almost boyish.

He was an honest man. Genuine and steadfast, his every movement capable, yet easy-going.

"All right, but only because you said 'please,' Prince Charming."

He reached out and gathered her to him. "Remember the night we watched television together when we were Skyping?"

"How did you ever persuade me to stream a documentary

about the Hubble telescope when I had a concert to prepare for the next day?"

He threw back his head and laughed. So good-natured, so familiar. "You should thank me because you learned several new outer-space terms. And all the planets—Mercury, Venus, Earth—"

She laid her hand on his arm. "I'm a musician, not an astronaut."

"Where is your harp, by the way? In New York?"

She kept her features blank and tried to make her voice impassive. "My harp is gone."

His expression was thoughtful as he obviously sensed her bleak mood. A beat passed.

"One of my favorite memories," he said, keeping her in his arms, "is the night you played the harp for me. 'Danny Boy.' Remember? I'd had an argument with Alice, and you said music would soothe me, so you lit candles and darkened your apartment. You had told me your harp was accented in twenty-three karat gold. I remember it shimmered in the candlelight each time you plucked a string. Truly, Emmanuelle, you looked like an angel, and it gave me goose-bumps." He traced her cheekbone with his forefinger.

"You sang while I played," Emmanuelle said. She'd clung to the memory of those shared times, although she'd known he was engaged and never pressed him for anything other than friendship.

Not long afterward, Dorothy had gotten out of rehab for opiate addiction, and Emmanuelle had met George, the wealthy hotel magnate.

And George had taken away her harp. Her pride. Her life.

CHAPTER 7

*N*icholas felt like he danced through the following week, and he wasn't a man who'd ever managed more than a two-step.

Molly Belle improved every day. She had reclaimed her sleeping spot at the foot of his bed, ate regularly, and reveled in her short daily walks with Emmanuelle. She'd even taught the dog to "sit" by holding a treat near the dog's nose. Once Molly Belle was sitting, she'd repeat the command, give the dog the treat, and shower her with affection and praise. She'd repeated the same sequence throughout each day, then demonstrated Molly Belle's progress for Nicholas each evening.

She'd taken Molly Belle to a shop a few doors down from his place and selected a fresh pine wreath, simple and unadorned, that she'd hung on his front door. On another occasion, she purchased curtains in a dazzling shade of lipstick-red and hung them on his bare living room windows. The effect was homey, warm, and Christmassy.

She'd also experimented with cooking new dishes. Thanks to Ryan's *Southern Charms* cookbook, Nicholas never knew quite what to expect for dinner. He only knew an exotic, savory meal waited for him when he got home.

In the evenings, he and Emmanuelle dined in his cozy kitchen, on a wooden table tucked beside a snowy window, polishing off spaghetti carbonara and thick slices of buttery bread accompanied by oven-fried pickles.

"Surprise me," he'd tell her each morning after she'd arrived.

And she did.

He enjoyed her companionship, her considerate nature, the way her dimples flashed whenever she was amused. He hadn't found a word to put to his feelings, especially since he hadn't wanted to become romantically involved with a woman after his breakup with Alice.

With Emmanuelle, though, the word *love* came to mind.

On the last day of the work week, Nicholas issued his customary thank you to her as soon as he strode through his apartment door. Molly Belle wriggled with delight, bounded to his side and greeted him with a continuous train of wet doggy kisses.

He scrubbed a hand along the dog's ears.

Emmanuelle was seated on the couch, intent on studying a page from Ryan's cookbook.

"I've been thinking about dinner all day," he said. He'd been thinking about her too, although he didn't mention that part. For a celebratory end-of-the-week supper, Emmanuelle had declared she was experimenting with a different fix on a traditional Christmas recipe—roasted turkey and sweet potatoes garnished with a fancy topping Nicholas had forgotten the name of.

He slid his gun from his holster, took off his badge. "How was your day?"

"Busy. Despite her size, Molly Belle thinks she's a lap dog." Emmanuelle kept her head down, busy flipping pages.

"And Dorothy and Ryan invited us for Christmas dinner so I tried a new dessert recipe tonight too."

He breathed in a lungful of smoky air just as the smoke alarm went off. "Is something burning?"

"Oh, no!" The cookbook fell from her lap as she jumped to her feet. "I forgot to set the timer."

They sprinted toward the kitchen. The dog whined and raced in the opposite direction, scratching at the door to be let out.

"I was testing a fruitcake recipe," Emmanuelle said as he opened a kitchen window to let out the smoke, and then turned off the alarm.

Not a dreaded fruitcake. Since Nicholas was fairly intelligent, he kept the comment to himself as he retrieved the burnt cake from the oven and set it on the counter. He commiserated with Emmanuelle, sighed, and tried to look regretful. He wanted to joke about the fruitcake making a good doorstop and wisely changed his mind.

"The cake can't be salvaged, so I'll phone for pizza delivery," he said. "Sound good?"

"If you stopped to look around, you'd see I cooked a twelve-pound turkey and sweet potatoes. Is pizza your fix for whatever comes your way?"

"There's no such thing as bad pizza. So …yes." He lifted the foil off the potatoes and pointed accusingly. "What's this white stuff on top?"

"Goat cheese and scallions."

"Sounds awful …" He caught her scowl. … "fancy." He congratulated himself for thinking so quickly on his feet. "Sounds awful fancy. Do you think I'll like it?"

"Fifty-fifty."

He suppressed a chuckle. She looked positively intoxicating, even with her heart-shaped mouth twisted into a grimace as she beheld the burnt cake.

He left the kitchen to check on the dog, who'd resumed her place at the foot of his bed.

When he returned to the kitchen, he drew off the hair-band she'd used to secure her hair when she cooked, brought her closer, and embraced her for a lengthy kiss. "We're beginning to sound as if we're a couple, and I like the sound of it."

She drew an unsteady breath and dropped her gaze, but not before he noticed the warmth kindling in her vivid blue eyes, the flush of heat tinting her creamy complexion a soft pink.

"We can't be a couple."

"Why not?"

She kept her gaze rooted on his bare wood floor. "Because I won't be a burden to you." She placed her arm between them, an effective wedge.

He'd half expected her reaction.

Anything to do with Molly Belle's care prompted an easy conversation. So did the latest recipe in the cookbook. Or classical music, especially her favorite composer, Beethoven. She responded to his kisses, molding herself to him. But any talk of a serious relationship put her off-balance.

He drew her to the couch and took a seat beside her. In an attempt to lighten the mood, he teasingly bumped her shoulder with his. "Tomorrow is Molly Belle's vet appointment. I'm hoping you'll go with me."

"Absolutely."

He smiled, relieved. He'd come to rely on her for emotional support.

"Afterward," he went on, "I'd like to buy a Christmas tree. My apartment is begging for a dose of holiday cheer, so are you up for a stop at a Christmas tree farm outside of town? In the past I've cut my own tree." He gestured to the dog. "Because she's still recovering, we'll buy a precut tree from one of the lots in town."

"Perfect." Her smile was luminous and lit his small apartment with merriment.

The attraction sizzled between them. Soon, he thought, when she was ready, she'd tell him her trepidation, and he'd assure her she was safe. Mutually, they'd dismiss her worries. She was in Cherish where life was secure. He'd keep her out of harm's way—whether real or imagined.

Trying to tamp down his eagerness, he reached into his shirt pocket and withdrew a small box wrapped in gold paper with a red satin ribbon. "Thank you, Emmanuelle, for everything you've done for me this week. On my lunch hour today, I stopped at Musically Yours and bought you something." He held the box out to her.

Lightly, she touched her hand to his. "Nicholas, you didn't have to buy me anything. I wanted to take care of Molly Belle."

His senses buzzed, alive to the brush of her fingertips, the thickened skin where calluses had formed. Once she had told him she was proud of those calluses, a badge for practicing long hours to pursue her dream of becoming a professional harpist.

And she had.

He'd taken her suggestion to give God his attention and had begun praying every night. Lately, he'd lifted a plea that she'd make Cherish her permanent home.

She could build a life here. *They* could build a future together.

He slipped an arm around her waist, delighting in her nearness, staring at her for a long moment. "I wanted to buy you a gift. It was my pleasure."

"Nicholas …" She ran a hand through her unruly blonde curls. Her chin trembled. Although they'd known each other for over a year, she grew unexpectedly shy.

"Please open it." He stilled her hand and kissed her

temple. He was giving her what he could. He wanted to give her so much more.

Nodding brightly, she rapidly undid the paper and unlatched a plain gray box. A tiny harp dangling from a solid-gold chain shot emerald green and diamond prisms across his plain white ceiling.

"The harp charm is from Ireland, from Dublin. I wanted an Irish harp fit for the most gifted woman I've ever known." He brushed his knuckles over her flawless cheek, brushed away a stray tear.

"Happy tears," she said.

He nodded. "Our conversation from the other day about the night you played 'Danny Boy' brought back good memories. I want this necklace to do the same."

"It brought back good memories for me too." She fingered the necklace. Her eyes shimmered a soft blue velvet. "I haven't bought a piece of clothing or jewelry for myself in months. Thank you."

"I looked for a twenty-three-karat necklace to match your harp, but this was the best I could afford. My salary as a deputy sheriff isn't much, though I plan to work my way up to a position of management." He drew her to him and she rested her cheek against his chest. "Someday I'll buy you a real harp."

He spoke above her, breathing in her floral perfume, citrus and violets and expectation.

"Money isn't important," she said. "I know this gift is from your heart."

She was splendid. She made him feel alive again, brought him out of his sadness. After his fiancée had left him, he'd grieved, focusing on his scars. But a new emotion was rising over the scars, allowing him to become again the man he once was—one of faith, free from cynicism, free to open his heart once more.

They avoided eye contact. The moment held too much emotion for her, for him.

"I know how much your harp meant to you," he murmured. "You once let me in on a secret, that your parents surprised you with a harp for your twelfth birthday. They'd saved money for years to buy the best. A Lyon and Healy harp, correct?"

"You remembered." Her tears came hard, sudden, and she let them.

He soothed her, crooning, rocking her. "You're not alone anymore, Emmanuelle."

Any further conversation was forgotten as she wept. When she withdrew, she wiped at her eyes with the handkerchief he provided. "I'm sorry. I mean, crying was uncalled for and I put you in an awkward—"

"Don't apologize. You're the best thing that's ever happened to me." He swept wisps of hair from her nape and secured the delicate gold chain around her throat, then ushered her to the bathroom mirror. "Dorothy assured me you'd fall in love with this necklace."

At first, Emmanuelle kept her gaze downcast before staring at herself. Carefully, she slid a finger along the fine chain and then found the exquisite detailing of the harp. "I haven't worn anything this pretty in many months. Thanks to you, I'm beginning to feel like a woman again. Someone who matters." Her smile sparkled in the mirror reflection.

He stood behind her and rested his hands on her shoulders. "You matter very, very much. More than you can ever imagine."

He stared at her, a vision of beauty with the heirloom-quality necklace shimmering against her creamy skin above her navy-blue cashmere sweater. At that moment he knew. It had returned, his love for a woman.

Only this time it was real.

CHAPTER 8

*A*fter Dr. Troutman's nod of approval, Nicholas and Emmanuelle set off for the Christmas tree farm. Molly Belle waited in Nicholas's car while they chose the last fir tree on the lot. The tree wasn't perfectly shaped; in fact, it wasn't shaped at all. Nicholas named the tree Charlie Brown since the branches jutted out in random angles.

"Every underdog needs a loving home," he declared, and Emmanuelle wholeheartedly agreed.

One of the employees at the farm shook the tree to remove any loose needles, then wrapped it for transport. A short drive later, Emmanuelle and Nicholas hoisted the scraggly tree up his flight of stairs and into his apartment.

"The tree looks better already," she said as Nicholas secured the tree in a sturdy metal stand. "It's just begging for lots of care and plenty of water. And we'll trim your whole apartment to resemble an old-fashioned Christmas. Ryan's book features all sorts of inspiring ideas."

Nicholas pushed himself to his feet after pouring water into the base of the tree stand. "I thought it was a cookbook focused on recipes."

"Recipes and decorating tips. And there's a thought-provoking article on empowering women that provides tips on how to keep safe in dangerous circumstances. The entire book is highly motivating."

"Quite the cookbook," he observed.

They referenced a "traditional Christmas" article as a guide and spent the afternoon decorating. Using heavy embroidery floss, they strung popcorn and cranberries. Nicholas found a set of multicolored lights stuffed in his hall closet. He began at the tree trunk and moved upward, wrapping the lights taut by weaving them from side to side.

"There isn't much of a tree to light," he said with a laugh. "The branches are beyond sparse!"

"I'm always drawn to these types of trees." She stepped back to assess the tree. "In the end, it's all about hope, isn't it?"

"True. And few people are as hopeful as Charlie Brown."

"Multicolored lights remind me of happy times with my family in Remsen. Call me nostalgic and old-fashioned."

"Then I'm old-fashioned too. Nothing is better than colored lights on a green pine tree to get you in the mood for Christmas."

"Last year, my ex wanted white lights and neon-blue bulbs on the tree he'd purchased for his swanky condo in a high-rise. I argued for colored lights. He didn't agree, of course, saying white lights were chic and modern. I like modern." She hesitated, combed nervous fingers through her hair. "No that's wrong. I just told him that."

"You lied?"

"I had no choice. He had two switches, calm or angry. I knew better than to disagree and kept my opinion to myself. He'd trained me like we're training Molly Belle—to obey commands." She watched the dog, resting on a blanket in the corner. The dog returned her stare with steady, shining eyes.

"I understand my former situation now," she went on. "It's easier at a distance."

"What's your ex's name?"

She took a moment to adjust her fire-red tunic, fussing and fidgeting, as if the tunic didn't fit correctly over her jeans. "George."

"That's it? George? George who?"

"Just George." She shrugged, shivered. Slight, but he saw it.

"Where's George now?"

Another shrug. She looked around, rubbed her hands together. "I assume he's in New York."

Her ex had evidently hurt her, and the realization brought anger bubbling to Nicholas's throat. When he found him, *and he would,* he'd silence George with a good stiff jab and a command of his own. *Stay away from Emmanuelle.*

He wrapped an arm around her shoulders and she leaned into him. Each time they were with each other, his need to protect her grew stronger.

He turned to the next page in the book to change the subject. She might get too upset if they continued discussing her ex. "The next round of decorating is to find red and green bulbs for our quirky tree. Do you prefer glass bulbs or—"

"I prefer family vintage bulbs and pinecones and silver tinsel. But ..." She dug in her tote bag and drew out a tiny angel ornament, brandishing it in the air. "I've carried this with me ever since I left New York. The clerk at the airport told me it was a good luck charm. It belongs on your tree."

"*Our* tree," he corrected her, and hung the ornament on a thin lower branch. "All this decorating warrants a celebration, so let's call out for pizza."

"Again? Is pizza your remedy for everything?"

With a laugh, he pulled his phone from his jeans pocket

and placed an order for a large cheese and pepperoni pizza, with a side of barbecue for Emmanuelle.

After pocketing his phone, he took her hands. "Let's wait for the delivery on the porch steps. The weather is mild, so we can go outside without jackets." He glanced at Molly Belle, sleeping soundly, then eased open the door.

They sat on the stoop. It was one of those inviting South Carolina evenings, when the sun had warmed everything in its path, including his front porch.

The view of his charming cul-de-sac lit with strings of festive lights, the nearby clip-clop of a horse-drawn carriage, filled him with gratitude. He imagined the residents inside their homes, savoring steaming cups of hot cocoa, sitting beside their cozy fireplaces.

From a few streets away came the last strains of "We Three Kings." Sung, he surmised, by the Cherish Church ladies' caroling group. He grinned, envisioning the women, young and elderly, dressed in their traditional Victorian costumes, complete with big bonnets and hand muffs.

The day had been perfect. Ending the evening with Emmanuelle by his side brought a quiet, joyous peace, and he whispered a prayer of thanksgiving. Tenderly, he pressed a kiss on her palms. "Two weeks from today is the Musically Yours holiday concert," he said. "Ryan is leading the elementary school chorus in a Christmas carol singalong and then singing a couple solos."

She rested her cheek on his shoulder. "Cherish is like a picture out of a Christmas card."

He chuckled and went back to appreciating the street decorations. Several neighbors had run animated light displays in a scalloped pattern along their fences.

Yes, this was the ideal town to live, to work, to raise a family.

He put an arm around her and she snuggled nearer, the

warmth of her body reaching out to his. He could get used to this. A delightful woman, her breathing soft and even, whose slight body had grown heavier because she was … sleeping?

He grinned. She'd fallen asleep quickly, even quicker than he usually did. Between taking care of his dog and creating nightly meals fit for a food connoisseur, she was clearly exhausted. He considered her profile, her small turned-up nose, the light sprinkling of freckles on her cheeks. Several times during the past week, he'd caught her staring at her cell phone as it rang. She never answered a call, and a few times her face had turned bone-white when she'd glimpsed the screen.

"Unknown caller," she always said, dropping the phone back into her tote bag. Whenever he pressed for details, she just chewed her bottom lip and stubbornly stayed silent.

He reached into his pocket for his phone and canceled the pizza. No sense in waking her when the delivery person arrived. Surely that frozen pizza was sitting somewhere in his freezer.

From inside the apartment, Molly Belle barked.

Emmanuelle woke with a start and rubbed her eyes. She peered at him, darted a peek at her watch. "Sorry, I didn't realize I dozed. I haven't rested well in several months."

"Because of George?"

A noticeable gap hung in the air as she scanned the street and its bright decorations. Distractedly, she nodded.

He went to brush pine needles from her shoulder and she flinched. He let out a whistled sigh and pulled back his hand. "Don't. You insult me when you do that."

"Do what?"

"Treat me as if I'm your ex. Just because I raise my hand doesn't mean I'm going to hit you." He deliberated, but only for a second. "What's really going on with you?"

"Too much." She eased up, then sat back down. "Nicholas,

I can't give you the relationship you want. I'm not the right woman for you."

"How do you know?"

She closed her eyes. Tears escaped. "Because you're a good man and my life is complicated."

"I like complicated."

"No, no, you don't." She opened her eyes, a deep shimmery blue. They stared at each other.

"It's odd," he mused.

"What?"

"The fact you're a harpist and you don't have a harp. Did you sell it?"

"My harp was smashed to pieces." She didn't pause for his sympathy, didn't bury her face in her hands. "George destroyed it."

"Why?"

He hadn't meant to ask the question because he knew the answer. As a law enforcement officer, he'd come across men like George. Domestic violence was the leading cause of injury to women. He'd read the statistics, recognized an abuser's behaviors and characteristics. After the honeymoon phase, they became controlling and jealous, and oftentimes sought to isolate their partner.

"Why?" Emmanuelle repeated. "Why would a man who supposedly cared for me take away something I loved, something so meaningful? To break me, I suppose." She shook her head; she'd answered her own question. "He knew precisely which buttons to press. He was exceptionally charming and people were attracted to him. Me included."

Nicholas's anger was sharp. He pulled it in. "How did you meet him?"

"His secretary booked me to play the harp for one of his office functions, the grand opening of his tenth boutique hotel in the New York area." Her voice caught. "After we became a couple, he always reminded me I was beneath him and how thankful I should be an important man like him was interested in someone like me … someone who was little more than a street performer."

"You know that's not true. You're a skilled professional."

She trailed her fingers along the edge of the porch railing and let out a sigh.

"When are you deserting me for New York?" he asked.

"I'm not deserting you. I happen to live there." She smiled and broke off, apparently waiting for his rejoinder. When he didn't offer one, she added, "I don't have a definite date in mind. Dorothy offered me a job at her music conservatory. I've considered finding a place in town and teaching harp lessons." She shrugged and blew out a breath. "Although I know it's better if I keep moving."

The last part of her answer didn't register because he'd fixated on the first part. His heart had leapt when she'd mentioned living in Cherish.

"Is he the reason you came here? Is he the reason you choose to keep running?"

"I have no choice and I'm not running." Her fingers nervously worked the hem of her tunic before she propped her chin in her hands. "Okay, yes, maybe I am. If George O'Donnell finds me, I don't know what he'll do."

George O'Donnell. Piercing rage sliced Nicholas like a knife. "He won't do anything to harm you. I'll make sure of it."

"You don't know him. He's well-off and powerful."

He joined her cold hands with his warm ones. "And I'm in law enforcement."

"That's why I'm afraid. If you go after him, you'll get hurt. He operates in influential circles with big-city types."

"In our quiet town, you'll be safe. You must know I'll always protect you."

"Our town," she repeated.

"Yes. And our life."

"Nicholas?" A smile ghosted her lips as an errant tear streamed down her cheek. "Will you do something for me?"

He gazed at her enchanting face, her over-bright eyes. He would protect her with his life.

"Anything," he said.

"Will you hold me for a minute?"

CHAPTER 9

$\mathcal{I}$n the ensuing two weeks Emmanuelle slept poorly, despite the inn's exquisitely appointed room and her luxurious queen-sized bed. Nightmares chased her and were always the same: the dim outline of a man with flat black eyebrows above dull gray eyes, trailing her every move.

George O'Donnell.

She'd scramble through unnamed woods while the flash of something vicious, and corrupt, and overpowering, followed her. The nightmare always ended the same, with her weeping and running farther and farther away from Cherish.

She'd wake beneath her cozy coverlet, her heart hammering, searching the room for something recognizable. Country-green walls, the hand-stitched quilt draped over a rocking chair, the braided rug covering the wide-plank pine floor, helped steady her breathing.

"Only a nightmare," she'd murmur, wiping her sweaty brow. "Vivid, horrible, and not real."

She'd focus out the window at the sprinkling of stars

against the black velvet sky. Then she'd close her eyes and think about Nicholas—his kindness, his easy-going manner, his self-assured confidence. Efficient and calm, whether tidying his home or ministering to Molly Belle, dealing with dangerous circumstances on duty or holding her as if she were a china doll. He was all man, all kindness, all compassion.

"In our quiet town, you'll be safe. You must know I'll always protect you," he'd said.

Only then, imagining his capable arms around her, could she seek the peace of slumber.

* * *

BY THE THIRD week of December, Cherish had become a jubilant fairyland, a kaleidoscope of Yuletide hues. Parades were held every weekend, and quaint mom-and-pop stores were decked out in magical window dressings. Children and adults alike stopped and gaped, mesmerized in child-like fascination.

Illuminated by tiny white lights, Emmanuelle's comfy inn, with its snow-covered roof and wisps of smoke billowing from the chimney, looked like a postcard image of Christmas town, USA.

Tom had taken a liking to Molly Belle and allowed her inside, provided she stayed in the foyer and didn't jump on any of the patrons. Unfortunately, the third day she was allowed in, Molly Belle knocked a teenage boy over when she'd leapt on the boy's legs. Despite Nicholas's explanations that the dog was still a puppy with a playful, silly personality, Tom banished Molly Belle to the porch. Both hands braced on his polished wood desk, he'd leaned forward until his cheaters slid down his nose and declared she wasn't allowed inside until she graduated from dog obedience school.

Considering Nicholas had abandoned the idea of obedience school until Molly Belle was fully recovered, Emmanuelle was certain the dog wouldn't be entering the inn anytime soon.

A cold front had brought snow to Cherish, a white dusting that topped off the winter-wonderland. As the snow fell softly, day after day, Emmanuelle's mood became more hopeful. She spent her time at Nicholas's apartment caring for Molly Belle and cooking delectable meals—a flaky crusted chicken pot pie brimming with roasted chicken and baby carrots one night, a sweet winter corn-bread with a splash of jalapeno the next. Oftentimes, she'd bake a tray of Christmas cookies, oozing chocolate chips, warm from the oven. As she cooked, she'd tune the radio to a Christian holiday station and hum along to every Christmas carol.

In the middle of the afternoon, she'd leash Molly Belle for a walk. Few things outshone walking a devoted dog who loved going outside for a squirrel-chasing adventure, especially when sunlight warmed Emmanuelle's cheeks and bracing air brought remembrances of Christmas in Remsen.

At Dorothy's prodding, the two women spent an evening shopping. Emmanuelle purchased a pair of shiny gold earrings to complement her harp necklace, plus a rose-tinted lip gloss. There was something so feminine about earrings and lip gloss, Dorothy said, that made a woman feel attractive. Regarding her reflection in the shop's mirror, Emmanuelle agreed. She'd caught her hair at the nape and secured it with a lace bow, the result a messy bun highlighted by escaping corkscrews of blonde hair.

She'd also painted two opposite walls of Nicholas's living room in a golden-yellow and convinced him to reupholster his couch in a deep-chocolate brown. He'd grinned his approval, and she too was pleased with the result. After

Christmas, she aimed to tackle his kitchen and paint those walls a cool mint-green.

After Christmas.

Yes, because she'd decided to live in Cherish. She hadn't told Nicholas, not yet. She'd decided to surprise him on Christmas, after they attended a church service with Dorothy and Ryan. She'd accepted Dorothy's offer to give harp lessons at the Musically Yours music conservatory and had begun formulating a plan to buy a new harp. Ryan told her that the nearby city of Stanley boasted an excellent symphony that was actively looking for a principal harpist, and encouraged her to audition. She'd agreed, the idea prompting recollections of how much she enjoyed performing.

On the Saturday of the holiday concert in Cherish, Emmanuelle spent the morning peeling potatoes and carrots for a hearty beef stew she simmered on Nicholas's stove. The weatherman had predicted snow, which had rapidly accumulated to several inches.

Nicholas had had to respond to a domestic-dispute call, and she'd gladly volunteered to stay with Molly Belle. He'd added that one of the other officers, Joseph Hannaford, would be on duty at the concert that evening. Large crowds were expected because of Ryan Edwards's performance.

Done with the stew, she surveyed the living room from the kitchen doorway. The Charlie Brown Christmas tree was delightful, brightly lit and brimming with cheer. Her angel ornament hung from one of the branches, and she laughed out loud, inhaling the scents of pine and promise.

Life was good. Very good. On an even more optimistic note, there'd been no sign of George. After she'd begun watching Molly Belle, every morning she'd received a phone call precisely at eight o'clock, a few minutes after Nicholas left for work.

Whenever she answered, no one spoke.

Once, she'd sworn she'd heard breathing on the other end. Bad connection? Most likely. She rejected her suspicions that it might be George. Merely an over-zealous telemarketer, she'd tell herself.

Still, she told Nicholas, admitting to her uneasiness. He listened thoughtfully before assuring her she was right—a telemarketer had programmed her phone number on speed-dial. After a long, thorough kiss, he assured her there was nothing to worry about.

And then, without warning, the mysterious phone calls had stopped.

As the next few days passed, the realization she was finally free from George renewed her confidence. With a strong handsome deputy by her side, friends who loved her, and a spirited dog ever near, what was there to fear? Truly, Christmas in Cherish promised a happiness she'd never dreamed.

CHAPTER 10

*A*fter they'd eaten stew for an early dinner, Nicholas drove Emmanuelle back to the inn to get ready for the evening concert. They passed tree limbs heavy with snow, bushes dusted with a fine white powder.

At the inn, she gifted Tom with a loaf of her crusty bread, prompting him to taste it. He'd chewed with his eyes closed and exclaimed, "Will you marry me, Emmanuelle?"

Before she could reply, Nicholas draped an arm on her shoulders and assured the innkeeper she was spoken for.

She floated to her room where she ran a warm shower, refreshing herself under a stream of multiple jets. The scents of her soap and shampoo—brown sugar and vanilla—reminded her of hot cinnamon rolls slathered in butter cream frosting.

Her anticipation of the evening rising, she grabbed a fluffy towel for her hair, and wrapped herself in a luxurious white robe. She padded across the wood floor of her room and deliberated on her outfit, ultimately choosing a comfortable pair of colored denims and a red cashmere sweater.

Despite his numerous concert engagements, she'd never

heard Ryan perform live, and she was looking forward to the evening.

At 7:00, a light tap on her door signaled Nicholas's arrival.

When she opened the door, he lifted her to her toes and held her. "Emmanuelle Sumter, you look gorgeous and smell like a cinnamon roll." He frequently remarked on her appearance, always complimentary, always causing her to melt, just melt.

She saw the seductive-green passion in his hazel eyes as their lips met.

"And every time I see you," he went on, "I fall more in love with you." He stated his feelings simply, without preamble or fanfare, his mouth brushing against her ear, his warm breath heating her insides.

She ran her fingers over his nape. His blond hair was thick and curled over his collared parka. His lips were smooth, his mouth perfectly shaped. His well-defined jaw and sharp cheekbones brought a chiseled handsomeness to his cover model features.

It's too soon to talk of love, she wanted to say. But it wasn't too soon, because she was falling in love with him too.

She hugged the realization close. This good-looking, conscientious man loved her, and with each heartfelt embrace, each heady kiss, her defenses were thawing. Slowly, she was shaking off her fears and yielding to him.

"Ready for an amazing concert?" he asked.

"I can't wait." She went to her closet and tugged a pink tasseled hat over her hair. "Dorothy said she'd accompany Ryan on keyboard if they can figure out how to run electrical power on stage."

"So far, they haven't," Nicholas said. As she rummaged through the closet, he added that the afternoon sun had melted much of the morning's snow, so the streets were messy tonight.

"Just let me grab my boots. Where's Molly Belle?"

"She's near the porch."

She swiveled. "Alone?"

"She's on her leash. Tom is playing with her in the snow." Nicholas struggled to keep a straight face. "He won't admit he's got a soft spot for dogs, although you and I know he does." He helped her on with her jacket and exaggeratedly hefted her tote bag from the bureau. "What do you carry in this? Lead?"

"Necessities. You know, my cell phone, wallet, loose change …"

"I wouldn't want to tote this heavy bag around."

"You would if you were a sensible woman." She laughed. "I can't be deprived of my pink lip gloss."

Still bantering, they made their way down the carpeted staircase.

As soon as they strolled onto the porch, Molly Belle scampered around them, feathery tail wagging, as if she hadn't seen them in a month. Nicholas thanked Tom and reached for the leash. Hand in hand, Emmanuelle and Nicholas stepped from the porch.

Although the morning snow had blown in quick and heavy, as Nicholas had said, most had melted under sun-kissed daytime skies. As the evening thermometer plunged, what was left had frozen, causing thin sheets of ice to gloss over the surface of the remaining snow. Tom had shoveled a generous path and covered the steps and sidewalk with rock salt.

"I've never listened to opera," Nicholas said, tucking her hand in the crook of his arm as they started for the town square. "I expect—"

"You've never heard Ryan sing?" Her lips twitched with

amusement. "Your sister is married to one of the most famous opera singers in the world!"

"Once, maybe, when we were teenagers, I overheard him singing an operatic version of Dorothy's favorite top-forty hit. I assumed he was trying to impress her. They used to sit for hours on the side porch of our house." Nicholas's deep voice vibrated with laughter. "But I'm all for the idea of a bonfire and roasting s'mores after the concert."

When they reached the square, Ryan and Dorothy gave an absent-minded wave as they arranged chairs beneath a white canvas tent. A stage had been set up alongside the ten-foot decorated Christmas tree. Various kiosks serving refreshments lined the outer edges of the square, and Nicholas briefly introduced her to his coworker, Joseph Hannaford, the officer on duty. As the crowds thickened, a fine, snowy mist began to fall.

A halcyon town awaiting Christmas, Emmanuelle mused. The entire scene was a miniature version of New York's festive theater district. Cheery memories, she thought, ... until ... until ...

She brought a jittery hand to her forehead.

A few months after she began dating George, she wore her favorite sweater to a theater event, and had left her jacket in the restroom at intermission. When he noticed, he demanded they leave before the show was over. She assumed he was angry because she had been foolish enough to have forgotten her jacket. He was concerned, as the theater was cold, she reasoned.

She was way off the mark. He shouted at her and called her a tramp for strutting around in a clingy sweater that he deemed too provocative.

He was jealous. She got that, and even felt flattered.

At first.

The relationship deepened. She believed she was in love

with him, and he was in love with her. However, he began to erupt when she least expected, no matter how fine a line she walked. Scary remembrances of George's viciousness, his narcissistic behavior, his insincere repentance, brought a quake down her spine.

She forced the chilling memories away and glanced at the rugged man standing beside her.

She was being foolish. She was safe, the town was real, this man was real. And this was the picture she needed to carry in order to move forward in her life. The uncommonly large crowd had simply dredged up memories from her uneasy mind.

As if he'd read her thoughts, Nicholas protectively tightened his arm around her waist. "Are you all right?" His hazel gaze locked on hers.

"Yes, I was thinking about how grateful I am to be here. And I'm happy, truly happy."

"So am I." He spoke quietly, tenderly. "I love you, Emmanuelle."

She beamed up at him, this man of faith whom she'd enjoyed endless conversations with, a man who spoke plainly what was on his heart.

"I love you too, Nicholas."

He smiled at her as if she were incredibly beloved.

She sighed with contentment. Finally, her world was coming together, and she whispered a thank you to God for giving her a promising future alongside the man she loved.

As they wove through the tent to find a good seat, she scanned the tent to see where Dorothy and Ryan had gone.

An exuberant Dorothy was arranging the last row of folding chairs. Her simple, classic black sweater dress showed off every curve of her lithe figure. She'd pinned her dark hair into an understated twist at the back of her head, drawing attention to her emerald-green eyes and pearl stud earrings.

Ryan strode over to her, impressively tall with dark, compelling features, his broad shoulders filling out his navy jacket to perfection. He draped a tweed coat around Dorothy. Something she said made him laugh out loud, and he gathered her in his arms and kissed her.

Their delight in each other was so infectious that Nicholas and Emmanuelle shared a grin.

"Well?" he prompted.

"Well what?"

"Well, if everyone is kissing, then where's my kiss?"

"You're impossible. We're not performing in a concert tonight."

"I plan to sing along to every Christmas carol. Does that count?"

She chuckled. "No. Besides, we're not newlyweds."

"Not yet." A slow, roguish smile moved across his face.

She felt her blood heat from her toes to her temple. "You're thinking to kiss me here, with all these people around?" Coyly, she shook her head, teasingly discouraging him. Then with a mischievous smile, she tilted her head back, inviting a kiss.

Dr. Troutman and Scarlett entered carrying two cups of coffee and a bag of chips. They spotted them, waved, and jostled through the crowd. Molly Belle yipped and tugged on her leash in her attempt at a greeting.

Her red hair springy beneath her leopard ear muffs, Scarlett offered a sparkling smile and opened her chips. She offered them to the group, then began munching.

"How's one of my favorite dogs?" Dr. Troutman rubbed Molly Belle's head as she scrabbled her front paws up his legs. He bent and examined her feet. "Just making sure there's no snow trapped in the pads."

"I've been checking," Emmanuelle said.

He sipped his coffee. "Are you two here for the concert?"

"*I* am," Emmanuelle said and then pointed to Nicholas. "He's here for the s'mores."

Dr. Troutman made a dramatic show of choking on his coffee. "Glad to see you're still in Cherish, Emmanuelle. Don't you live in New York?"

Nicholas pressed a light kiss on her forehead. "I'm trying to talk her into moving permanently to Cherish."

"Well, I could use a knowledgeable person in my office. Scarlett is a wonderful receptionist although she's going to be a little busy, now that we're engaged." His hand reached out to cover Scarlett's, but not before Emmanuelle noticed a three-stone diamond ring in a rose-gold setting on Scarlett's ring finger.

"Congratulations," Emmanuelle and Nicholas said simultaneously.

"Thank you." Scarlett's shimmery, ruby earrings swung sideways as she nodded. Enthusiasm glowing in her face, she turned to Dr. Troutman. "I love animals, but I love you more."

Emmanuelle saw the elation in the veterinarian's smile as he swung his attention back toward her. "If you're looking for a job, Emmanuelle, you can work for me anytime."

"My sister beat you to it." Nicholas said, nodding toward Dorothy. "She asked Emmanuelle to teach music lessons at her conservatory. Did you know Emmanuelle is a professional harpist?"

"I'd like to hear you play," Scarlett said.

"Someday." Emmanuelle grimaced. How's that for evasive? she upbraided herself. She was a professional harpist with no harp.

"I'm sorry. I can see from the expression on your face that

I troubled you." Scarlett swallowed a chip and snapped up another. "Dorothy mentioned you don't have a harp."

Emmanuelle stopped her grimace and turned it into a smile. "Don't apologize. Look what Nicholas bought me. Isn't it beautiful?" She drew out the harp necklace from beneath her jacket for Scarlett to admire.

"Yes, very beautiful, and very thoughtful." Scarlett eyed the necklace. "An early Christmas gift, Nicholas?"

"Nope." He laughed. "It's my gift to Emmanuelle for coming to Cherish. She's a blessing to me."

Emmanuelle's heart gave a funny lurch. Nicholas offered safety and security and he was more considerate than anyone she'd ever known. Not every man was cruel and intimidating, she reminded herself yet again. Healing from abuse was a slow road, and it took time and infinite perseverance. And she'd walk that road with the man she loved.

New beginnings.

"You make a very striking couple," Scarlett was saying. "Two good-looking blonds."

"I agree with one of your observations." With a mile-wide beam toward Emmanuelle, Nicholas said, "We'd better claim a seat, my good-looking blonde."

As people converged, aromas of chocolate fudge and honey roasted almonds lifted into the air.

"The staid doctor and his perky receptionist are engaged?" Emmanuelle asked.

"Apparently." He grinned. "He must be twice her age."

"They're charming together and I'm delighted for them.

"The vet has lived alone on his alpaca farm since his wife's passing. He's a moral Christian man and I'm glad he met someone he can share his life with."

"I hope Scarlett likes alpacas." Emmanuelle laughed. "Do they bite?"

"Not normally. And she can eat her junk food while Dr. Troutman's alpaca herd munches on green plants and grass."

They settled on seats in the last row, just in case Molly Belle spotted another dog and attempted to dash off for an impromptu romp in the snow.

When the audience quieted, the first half of the concert began with the elementary school's children's chorus. The music teacher conducted, and everyone joined in a heart-lifting rendition of "Silent Night." Before intermission, Ryan led the crowd in the "Hallelujah" chorus from Handel's *Messiah*. As tradition dictated, everyone stood.

"I've always wondered," Nicholas said under his breath, "why are we supposed to stand?"

"There are many theories, the principal one being that King George II was so overwhelmed by the 'Hallelujah' chorus that he stood up. And whenever the king stood, so did everyone else."

After a brief intermission, Ryan came on stage for the second half. His bass voice, rich and finely textured, was exactly as Dorothy had described, and Emmanuelle felt as if she couldn't breathe during his entire a cappella rendition of "Away in a Manger."

When the concert finished to thunderous clapping, whistles, and cheers, Ryan held up a hand to quell the applause and extended congratulations to the children's chorus. The children scampered back on stage, bowed low, and then grinned and waved at the audience.

Emmanuelle rose along with Nicholas and announced she'd ferret out the booths serving roasted almonds and fudge. Her nose could only take so much temptation.

He circled an arm around her shoulders. "What about our s'mores? The mayor is building the bonfire and we'll eat in a few minutes."

"I'm adopting Scarlett's motto—to embrace life and

indulge yourself. No worries. I promise I'll eat the fudge and almonds and s'mores." She sighed. "Although I won't be able to fit into the holiday skirt I brought if I keep eating at this rate. Fortunately, I also own a pair of slacks with an elastic waist."

Nicholas didn't appease her with a chuckle. Instead, his fingers tightened on her shoulders. "I'll go with you."

"Why?"

"Those suspicious phone calls you were getting ..." He looked around and nodded at a busload of fans swarming around Ryan. "There're too many people here tonight."

"I'm twenty-five, not five, and I lived in New York, one of the busiest cities in the world. I can certainly navigate a crowd and get my own snacks without an escort. I'm over my fear of walking alone." She shook off his arm and grabbed her tote bag. "Besides, Dorothy's headed our way. Please congratulate her for me. I'll shoot ahead of this next horde and catch up with all of you in a few minutes."

She walked purposefully toward the food kiosks. Out from under the tent, she saw the night was black—no moon or stars, and the shimmer of snow was now a gray mist.

She wound past the busy fudge and caramel-corn stands. The stand that advertised roasted almonds was farther down, and there was no line. Actually, the stand looked deserted. Had they sold out of almonds already and closed shop?

She paused, debating what to do, and sensed someone walking up behind her. "Emmanuelle," a man said, "can you give me directions to the stage?

She was so sure she'd imagined the familiar voice, she started walking toward the stand.

"Emmanuelle."

She froze. Her shoulders tightened, her breathing stopped. *Move*, she commanded her feet.

"Turn around, Emmanuelle."

Obediently, she did. George had always had a hold over her.

The sight of him standing so near was enough to unfreeze her. She shifted, one foot stepping back, but his gaze immediately sharpened on her. If only she could make him believe she was standing stock-still while she slowly moved backward.

"How … how did you find me?" She licked her lips and expelled a quick breath. He couldn't be here. He was locked away in a hidden compartment in her mind, in New York, at a theater festival.

"Didn't take long." He grabbed her arm. "A couple of your so-called friends mentioned you'd gone off to some backwater town in South Carolina for the holidays." He laughed derisively. "'Cherish.' I couldn't even find it on a map."

"You don't know any of my friends." She braced her body against a cold wind and tried not to inhale. He smelled of vodka and anger and day-old sweat.

Despite herself, she couldn't control the shiver that rippled through her. He noticed. She saw the satisfaction in his bloodshot gray eyes. He had foreseen this, her cowering, her clumsiness, as she fingered the straps of her tote bag.

"I hired a few musicians for my office party," he said. His fingers tightened on her arm and she flinched. "They were more than willing to help once I offered a large bonus. You starving performers are always looking for handouts."

She swallowed a terrified scream and eyed her isolated surroundings. Several long sprints lay between her and the roasted-almond stand. She could outrun him.

No, argued her practical self. He was a large man. His pace outmatched hers, and he'd overtake her. All he'd have to do was drag her into the nearby woods, and she'd be alone with him.

Adrenaline consumed her, shaping her terror into a

soundless rage. She wasn't a weak, passive victim, shrinking into herself just because he spoke.

This was her town, not his.

Mentally, she reviewed the article from the *Southern Charms* cookbook. If a woman was confronted by an attacker, one of her first lines of defense was her handbag.

She lifted her chin, straightened her spine. "Well, now that you've seen for yourself I'm here, go slither back to your swanky place in New York."

Momentarily, his composure slipped, his fingers loosened. "Every day, I think about when your broken harp was hauled away. I felt so bad, I decided to buy you a new one. We'll call it my Christmas gift to you. It's expensive. You'll like it."

"Keep it. I don't want it."

His eyebrows lifted in distracted mockery. "What—"

She couldn't be afraid. She couldn't allow herself to cringe and plead, but needed to prevent her fright from taking over.

Don't back away. Use the element of surprise. He won't expect you to fight.

"I said keep it." She lifted her heavy tote bag as a club and swung directly for his face.

She was too slow. He saw the blow coming and shoved her to the ground. A dull roar filled her ears, pain firing through her body as she hit solid ice. He fell on top of her, and she fought him, biting and kicking, jabbing at his eyes, focusing all her energy on getting away.

A shiny, silver knife sliced the air and came at her throat. "I heard you've been seeing an officer in town, Emmanuelle. Did you forget? You were meant only for me."

She shut her eyes to keep out the light-headedness, seeking the safety of somewhere dark and safe and silent.

Heavy, racing footsteps cut through her dizzying thoughts.

"Drop the knife and keep your hands over your head."

"George O'Donnell, you're under arrest for aggravated assault."

Two men's voices. Nicholas. And another man. Officer Joseph Hannaford.

"Emmanuelle? Are you okay?" Nicholas's steady tone reached through her fogged thoughts. She squinted. The color had drained from his face, and even in the darkness she could see his distress.

Tears welled. "Yes, yes. I'm—I'm fine. He didn't hurt ..."

Her brave declaration was diminished by her sobbing. She couldn't contain her tears and reached out to Nicholas for comfort. She wanted to be held, wanted her apprehension quieted, wanted only him. Her legs wobbled as he helped her to her feet, and she sagged against his strong body. His gaze stayed focused on her.

George sneered at her as Officer Hannaford snapped handcuffs on him. "You won't get away with this, Emmanuelle."

She noted that he showed no remorse.

"I already did," she said flatly. "Quit following me and go back to New York. I never want to see you again."

"This one stop-light town is no fun. I was leaving anyway." He didn't look tough or threatening now, not with his hands cuffed behind his back. "Just remember, Emmanuelle. You're an insignificant nobody."

Nicholas tightened his fists. "What did you say, O'Donnell?"

"Nothing, Nicholas," she said quickly. "He can't hurt me anymore."

The slow dance of George's belittlement, his cruelty, had ended. His hurtful comments would no longer snake through

232

her dreams because she refused to carry her resentment anymore. She'd acted with courage, and someday, with God's grace, she'd forgive George. Just not today.

"Mr. O'Donnell," Officer Hannaford said, "we've been monitoring your activities. Lots of illegal narcotics are being siphoned through your hotel deliveries into other states besides New York. Drug trafficking is a felony, a federal one when it's across state lines. And then there's the evidence of money laundering, illegal weapons, and other crimes." His gaze flicked to Emmanuelle, then zeroed in on Nicholas's clenched fists. "Why don't you bring your girl back to your apartment and cool off? I guarantee this guy will be locked away for a good many years."

CHAPTER 11

*E*mmanuelle looked like a dream and cooked like a gourmet chef, Nicholas decided, taking a whiff of something heavenly as he strode into his apartment. He was greeted by Molly Belle's hopeful eyes and madly flapping tail.

He hung his pea coat by the door, took off his deputy badge, and slid the gun from his holster. With the dog on his heels, he locked the gun in his safe.

"No walks, Molly Belle," he said. "Emmanuelle texted me and I know you've been outside twice already."

Molly Belle cocked her silky ears, then followed him into the kitchen.

Nicholas feasted his gaze on Emmanuelle as she blended ingredients for a holiday fruitcake. She was dressed for Christmas Eve in a red velvet top and black pencil skirt that showed off her perfectly toned legs. She'd tied a plaid apron featuring a gingerbread man over her outfit. Her blonde hair tumbled in ringlets around her shoulders.

"Merry Christmas, angel," he said. "You're stunning." He tried not to stare, but she sure had shapely legs. He'd brought home a bouquet of red and white carnations, a festive beginning to the Christmas season, the florist had declared, when she'd snatched his credit card and rung up the sale.

No matter how hard he tried to budget, money seemed to slip out of his fingers faster than water.

"Well, thank you, Deputy Thompson," Emmanuelle said. "You're quite handsome yourself in your deputy uniform." She wiped a hand on her apron and twirled. "I was able to squeeze into this skirt after all, despite the endless barbecue sandwiches I've eaten lately. How do I look?"

"Gorgeous." He grinned approvingly, then held up the flowers.

Her face lit. "For me?"

"For Ryan and Dorothy's house," he amended. "The carnations are a Christmas dinner centerpiece, a thank you gift to them along with your ... fruitcake." He gave himself a silent pat on the back for not grimacing.

He blamed his fruitcake dislike on the media, for the cake was fodder for endless jokes. His favorite was one by Johnny Carson, "There is only one fruitcake in the entire world, and people keep sending it to each other."

He didn't share that quote with Emmanuelle.

"I'm trying a new recipe," she said. "This one was passed down to Ryan by his nana."

"Yes, you'd mentioned it this morning. No *Southern Charms* recipe?"

"This one is better." Emmanuelle grinned and pressed the mixture into a baking pan. "It's so generous of your sister and Ryan to welcome us into their new home for the holidays."

The air smelled subtly of candied cherries and walnuts and dates, and Nicholas sniffed enthusiastically. Should he give fruitcake another chance? Most likely, Emmanuelle's cake would prove as tasty as all the other delicacies she'd prepared the past few weeks.

He set the bouquet on the table and brought her into his arms for a hello kiss.

"I missed you today." He nuzzled her neck. The splendidness of her, her sweet lips pressed to his, her sylphlike form leaning into him, brought him such happiness.

She wiped her hands on her apron and twined her arms around him. When he didn't release her, she shifted. "The fruitcake," she reminded him.

"Fruitcakes are invincible." He kept her close and rested his chin on her shiny blonde curls.

"Nicholas ..." She extracted herself to pop the cake into the oven. "The recipe says the cake takes forty-five minutes to bake, which gives us plenty of time to arrive at Dorothy and Ryan's house by seven for dinner. The church service starts at midnight." She glanced at her watch. "It's five now."

Absently, he rubbed Molly Belle's head and eyeballed Emmanuelle as she pulled off her apron and put the flowers in a vase with water.

"Nicholas, did you hear me?"

"I think so."

"What did I say?"

"Something about Christmas dinner." He'd heard the dinner part and little else. He'd been preoccupied with her gorgeous legs.

"I brewed a pot of coffee. Do you want a cup?"

Before he answered, she brought out two mugs from his glass-front cabinet and poured.

"No donuts?" he teased, rousing her into a smile.

"On Christmas we eat fruitcake for dessert."

He sighed and scratched his head. *How could he forget?* He'd just have to keep hoping for the best.

"Emmanuelle ..." From his shirt pocket, he withdrew a neatly wrapped present tied with a white satin bow. "This is a little gift I bought for you."

She looked surprised. "You're very generous, but my wonderful harp necklace is more than enough."

Which, he'd noticed, she wore every day.

"This is another gift because it's Christmas. And because I appreciate you."

Ever since she'd arrived, his apartment had been transformed. Maybe he hadn't paid attention to the dog hair accumulating on his unswept floors before, but he'd sure appreciated it when his wooden floors gleamed.

She smiled. "I bought gifts for you too. They're wrapped and under our Charlie Brown tree. Let's open them now."

With the dog at their side and coffee cups in hand, they wandered into the living room. She clicked on her favorite Christian radio station, then brought a gold-foil-wrapped box from beneath the tree and handed it to him. "Merry Christmas, Nicholas."

They sat together on the floor, backs against the wall, and stretched out their legs. She was barefoot, free from the restrictions of her former lifestyle—one of control and fear. Now, her smile came easy, her movements unrestrained. The subdued colors of the Christmas tree lights warmed her complexion to a healthy rose hue.

Molly Belle settled beside them, patient, good, eyeing them thoughtfully with shiny black eyes.

Nicholas chuckled. He felt like a kid again, filled with the magic of the season. He felt like singing out loud when a new artist's rendition of "O Come All Ye Faithful" lilted from the radio.

"Well? Why are you waiting?" she teased. Expectantly, she watched him open her gift, an electric travel mug. "Do you like it?"

"I love it. Thank you." He shouted with laughter. "This is perfect."

She grinned. "Now that you're a deputy, you're always

focused on getting a good cup of coffee. If duty calls and pulls you away from the office, your coffee won't be left cold anymore."

"Thank you. I've become attached to my coffee. And I've become even more attached to you." He pressed a kiss to her temple.

Still grinning, she reached behind the tree and produced another box, this one lighter and wrapped in the same metallic-gold foil paper.

"Two gifts?" he asked. "Why?"

"You bought me two, so now we're even." She placed the box on his lap, her expression growing serious.

He unwrapped the foil paper slowly, revealing a large jeweler's box. Then he paused, regarding her for a long moment, wondering why she'd lowered her head and seemed suddenly self-conscious. He unhooked the lid, and a silver pendant hanging from a heavy chain shone back at him.

"Read the words on the front," she encouraged. "It's a prayer."

"All right." He read aloud. "'Lord, keep my deputy safe from morning till night, give him strength in your precious light.'" He turned the pendant over. She'd personalized the back with an engraved script: "'I'm proud of you.'"

He wiped at his eyes as the emotion swept over him. He swallowed and held the pendant up to the light to admire it. "Thank you, Emmanuelle."

"You're very welcome."

He nodded toward his gift. "Now it's your turn."

Her fingers moved more slowly. She set the wrapping paper on the floor and gazed at the silver case she'd revealed. Carefully, she unsnapped the lid. A black velvet bed held a solitaire diamond ring in a twist of fourteen-karat white gold.

She drew an unsteady breath. "It's … it's beautiful." Tears

welled, falling down her cheeks. She wiped at them, laughed as she brushed the wetness away. "These are happy tears," she clarified, laughing and crying at the same time before she sank her head into his chest and gave in to the weeping.

"I know." He held her until her cry had passed. The same joy had gripped him.

Taking her left hand, he slid the diamond engagement ring onto her finger. "Will you marry me, Emmanuelle?"

She stared at her finger, stared at him. "Read the explanation on the box that came with your pendant first."

He gazed at her and pondered her reply. How had the conversation shifted to *her* gift when she wore *his* gift on her finger? If his feelings weren't in such a tangle because she was sitting so close to him, because it was Christmas, because it was so easy to love life again, he would have noticed how her bright eyes shone with anticipation.

He lifted the box and read the inside flap. "'A deputy's wife's prayer.'" He set the box down. Paused. Reflected. "Wait a minute. A *wife's* prayer?"

"I planned on making my home in Cherish, and wanted to tell you on Christmas Eve." She looked almost sheepish. "Then I decided that if you didn't ask me to marry you, I'd ask you."

"Well, my answer is yes." He smothered a laugh and tipped up her face. "What's your answer?"

"Yes, yes, yes. I love you, Nicholas Thompson."

His mouth descended on hers as she pressed closer. "I love you so much," he murmured, and then his mouth captured hers again for a breathtakingly long kiss.

When the kiss ended, she stayed in his arms.

"I've been thinking," she began, snuggling closer.

He brushed a kiss against her hair. "About what?"

"About the past few days, going over and over what happened the night of the concert. You obviously knew my relationship with George wasn't over. I didn't. And then I fought back when he attacked me. I shouldn't have."

"He's a dangerous man. You didn't realize how dangerous."

She blew out a breath. "Afterward, when I thought about how deserted it was back there, I chastised myself. I reacted foolishly for edging him on, and then trying to fight him."

"It was a knee-jerk reaction. You were threatened. You didn't realize how serious the situation would become, and so quickly. Officer Hannaford and I had been running a long background check on George O'Donnell ever since you told me his last name, so I was at fault. I knew how dangerous he was and I should never have let you go off alone."

"I only walked across the square to buy almonds." She sighed. "Although I've been blaming myself. I'm good at that."

"Don't." He kissed her again. "If anyone is responsible, it's me. I knew that George was involved in illegal activities."

She nodded. "And then I thought, through the bad came the good. Because of you—because of me—because of us, I've taken my power back. I didn't deserve his violence, and I felt so bitter and resentful when I arrived in Cherish. I've prayed a lot, and I finally realized if I kept feeling that way, that meant he still controlled me. So, I've let go of it. New beginnings, thanks to the grace of God."

Nicholas knuckled a tear from the corner of her eye.

She'd confronted her shame, her anger at herself, and realized God had helped her through the storm.

Love was here, love was now. Love was the magic of the season. They were standing on the edge of Christmas, waiting for the new year and their new life to begin.

For an eternity, they sat together on the floor, his arms enveloping her and holding her close.

* * *

Nicholas awoke to the sound of Molly Belle's whining as she darted across the living room. The shriek of the smoke alarm had him staring blindly ahead. Smoke rolled out of the kitchen.

"Emmanuelle." He shook her awake. "Are you keeping tabs on the time?"

"Yes, it's—" She gaped at her watch. "It's nearly seven o'clock!"

They raced to the kitchen just in time to extract a burnt fruitcake from the oven.

He shut off the smoke alarm. She winced at the cake.

"Oh no." She blew out a breath. "I hope I have enough ingredients left over to bake another one."

"You mean you're going to try to bake another fruitcake?"

She scanned the counter. "Unfortunately, it's too late tonight."

"Well, there's always tomorrow, although none of the stores will be open on Christmas, so we'll just have to wait."

He tried to sound regretful and knew he didn't.

He opened a kitchen window to let out the smoke and inhaled crisp winter air. A neighbor was inching his car into the driveway, wheels spinning, windshield wipers flapping like a wild bird's wings. Fresh snow was falling to the ground, hugging the landscape in a burst of white potential.

"We may not be going anywhere tonight," Emmanuelle murmured. She stood beside him, peering outside the window.

"What will we eat for Christmas dinner?" he asked.

"Burnt fruitcake and coffee?"

"I'll call Dorothy. Once the roads are plowed, we should be able to get to their house and then attend the midnight church service."

He hugged her. The exquisite feeling of her warm body next to his, made his heart beat stronger. He'd been bitter, just like her. In his bitterness, he hadn't wanted to change. He'd preferred to feed on his own loneliness and feel sorry for himself. And then, God had blessed him with Emmanuelle. He'd brought her into his life at the perfect time.

She was his family now, along with Dorothy and Ryan. And Molly Belle, who'd trotted into the kitchen, plopped beneath the kitchen table and curiously eyed the burnt fruitcake.

By the window, Nicholas kissed Emmanuelle, a kiss full of love and promise. "I love you, Emmanuelle."

Her eyes were wet with tears. "I love you too."

"And I'll take a lifetime to prove it to you, right here in Cherish," he said.

"You don't have to prove anything. I know the man you are, and that's why I love you."

Truly, whatever came their way, they could handle it. His faith had been tested, but these were lessons. He'd bounced back from sadness and adversity. They'd both bounced back.

Because God had them covered. Together and always.

With Emmanuelle in his arms, they were ready to face life's challenges.

And this was a Christmas to cherish.

THE END

A NOTE FROM THE AUTHOR

Dear Friends,

A Christmas To Cherish is set in the charming fictional town of Cherish, South Carolina.

I've always enjoyed reading and writing about small town life, and Christmas is a special time of year.

Because I am a musician and even played the harp for a short while, my heroine, Emmanuelle, is a professional harpist.

The hero, Nicholas, was the heroine's brother in *A Love Song To Cherish,* and I wanted him to have his own happily ever after, so I wrote this book.

A Valentine To Cherish is Book 3 in the Cherish series.

This book is also available in ebook, Paperback, Large Print Paperback, Hardcover, and audiobook.

My Spotify Play List for A Christmas To Cherish is here.

Happy Reading!

Josie Riviera

NANA'S FRUITCAKE RECIPE

Ingredients:

4 eggs
1 cup flour
2 teaspoons baking powder
1 pound candied pineapple
1 pound pitted dates
1 pound candied cherries
8 cups walnuts

Instructions:

Pour flour and baking powder into a large paper bag, shake to mix, then add fruits and nuts. Shake well to coat all pieces with flour.

In a large bowl, beat eggs. Pour the fruits and nuts mixture into the egg mixture and use your hand to mix well. Coat all pieces. Grease a small baking pan and press the mixture firmly into the pan. Bake approximately 45 minutes at 350 degrees or until golden brown.

Enjoy!

USA TODAY BESTSELLING AUTHOR
JOSIE RIVIERA
1-800-CHRISTMAS
A SWEET CONTEMPORARY NOVELLA

CHAPTER 1

$\mathcal{D}$esiree Contando had gained weight. Not a lot, although the extra ten pounds on her five-foot-four-inch frame were enough to make her favorite linen skirt fit snugly around her waist. When she was stressed, she ate pumpkin pie. Lately, she'd eaten a lot of pumpkin pie, and she had blamed it on Thanksgiving.

However, it was more than the delicious turkey dinner her sister, Candee, had served. The cause of Desiree's stress was the rundown Queen-Anne style home she'd purchased that morning.

"Your house is beautiful." Candee's voice came from behind her. "Now we both live on Thompson Lane!"

Desiree swallowed hard. "Maybe my house will be beautiful in a thousand years."

She shouldn't have done this. She should have dashed out of the lawyer's office as soon as the closing papers had been handed over for her to sign.

"Mr. Dunworthy, the former owner, never got around to updating the home, and then Teddy didn't have time," Candee said. "Your house won't take long to restore. My dilapidated Victorian is proof that even the most ramshackle house can be renovated."

Teddy and Candee had met in Roses, North Carolina, when Teddy came from Miami searching for a house to flip. They'd married, and together with Teddy's nephew, Joseph, they'd moved into a sprawling Victorian. Teddy had been granted legal guardianship of Joseph a few months earlier.

Desiree pushed out a tight breath. "Your Victorian still needs tons of work."

"Thankfully, it has come a long way." Candee stepped to Desiree's side and flitted her a once-over. She carried a box of pumpkin muffins. "A housewarming token," she'd declared, with a promise of something better coming on Christmas Eve.

"You've accomplished so much this year," Desiree said.

"I'm following your example. Advocating justice for low-income families and children is a daunting task. Fortunately, you're a talented attorney."

"I'm just doing the best job I can."

"You're ensuring the poorest people receive fairness. I respect you." Candee's gaze wandered to the rambling house. "You have more than enough acreage on your property for horses."

"I'll leave horses to your animal expertise. And puppies."

Months earlier, Candee had adopted Kisses, a pregnant beagle, from the local animal shelter. Of the six puppies Kisses had birthed, only one remained, as Candee had sold the rest.

Candee's emerald eyes glowed. "Boomer is adorable—all black and white and tan. And he loves to eat."

"Are you planning to sell him?"

"He'd make a great companion for a special someone."

"I'm sure you'll find a forever home for him."

"I'm sure I will." Candee smirked. "Speaking of animals,

Teddy finished the stable for Joseph's horse therapy. He converted a large shed, and Joseph loves the Haflinger horse. I did my research and the horse is small, with a calm temperament."

"You're wonderful parents. I'm thrilled for all of you." Desiree stared at her house. It seemed to stare back, taunting her. She took a slight step and pressed her lips together. "I don't know if I can do this."

"Of course you can. You're experiencing buyer's remorse." Candee gave Desiree's hand a gentle squeeze. "Everyone panics after buying their first house. Remember, Teddy and I are only two doors away. If you need anything, text me. Better yet, flag me from your driveway."

"Please thank Teddy for selling the house to me at such a bargain price. I'd never have been able to find such a terrific value on my own." Desiree attempted animation, and knew she wavered.

"You have a successful job, and now a home to call your own." Candee kept her hand on Desiree's. "Look how far you've come."

"We," Desiree corrected, keeping her voice light. If she began reminiscing about their miserable childhood, she'd lose it. If she shared her thoughts, they'd both lose it.

The women had been shuffled to five different foster homes in their teens after the state had deemed their parents unfit. Drugs and drink were only part of the issue, as their parents had also struggled with mental health problems. They had died a short time after landing in jail.

Candee broke the somber mood with an encouraging beam. "Just think, you'll pay off the mortgage in thirty years."

"Thirty years." Desiree groaned. "It'll take me forever to find someone with the expertise to fix this house on my limited budget." She paused, willing herself to say her ex-boyfriend's name aloud. "Scott had promised to help."

Not physically, of course, because Scott never got his hands dirty. Nonetheless, he'd agreed to rent the dormer apartment in her attic. In addition, he'd referred his handyman cousin to tackle the house repairs at a reasonable cost.

Some boyfriend. Some *ex*. Desiree had counted on the rental income to help pay her mortgage, and a jack-of-all-trades guy to get the job done. Finally, she had her own house, but no one to share it with. No happily-ever-after.

"Scott is in the past. Forget him," Candee said. "What's worse than a guy who is only around during the good times?"

"I know. It's just . . ."

It was just that it seemed like years had passed since her and Scott's argument, although the breakup had occurred the previous evening when he'd accompanied her to the final walk-through of the house.

"Are you joking? This tumble-down nightmare is your new house?" he'd shouted.

"Well, if you had taken time out of your day before now to see it, you wouldn't be shocked," Desiree had replied. "The owner before Teddy was elderly, and I told you the house needed a facelift."

"A facelift?" Scott had laughed. "Wow, Desiree. The house is a disaster. Is that your smooth-talking attorney jargon kicking into gear?"

"Are you ready to go inside?" Candee asked.

Desiree shifted and checked her shoulder bag for the house key.

Nope. She didn't have it.

"It's better Scott exited before you made a serious commitment to each other." Candee shuffled forward. "Besides, small-town life didn't fit his high-profile aspirations."

"True."

In Roses, life was slower, and people were friendly. A bandstand featured hometown entertainment. Tony's, the local pizzeria, had been there forever. Quaint and charming, the town hadn't given much thought to modernizing.

And now that Thanksgiving was over, the small town was transformed into a magical Christmas wonderland, a virtual postcard. Soon, snow would dust the pine tree branches and outlying mountaintops with a white sheen. Horse-drawn carriages circled the village green every weekend, and scents of gingerbread and cinnamon courtesy of local artisans filled the air. A holiday baking contest was held every year, and Desiree always entered her pistachio cake. She'd never won, although the twenty-five-dollar entry fee was donated to the local animal shelter.

Certainly, the happy Yuletide season and sense of community were reasons Desiree loved Roses and never wanted to leave.

A gust of icy air swept across the house's expansive front lawn, causing the oak tree branches to sway. The chilliness was a firm reminder that winter would soon secure a foothold on their Blue Ridge Mountain town. The wind was like a physical nudge, blowing across Desiree's thin navy suit jacket and bare legs.

She gripped the blue headband holding her thick blond hair in place.

She was out of luck. Her hair had blown into a mass of unmanageable waves.

Willing herself forward, Desiree stared at the various-shaped slate shingles on the roof necessitating repair, and the patterns of varicolored brick laying up the exterior walls. A century ago, the house had been designed to impress. Regardless, did anyone else use green, red, black, blue, and beige on one house?

She shouldered her red tote bag and matched Candee's steps.

This was a moment that Desiree had envisioned sharing with Scott. A life-changing threshold, embarking on their future together. They'd discuss her vision for the house, spend cozy winter evenings thumbing through decorating magazines, and wander paint stores discussing the perfect shade of dove white.

Velvet red ribbons and vibrant green garlands decorating the home's enormous rooms would celebrate Christmas in department-store style, and glittery white lights strung across the expansive front porch would create festive charm.

Now, all these special yet-to-be created memories would be done without Scott, because he was gone.

Her chest tightened, and she told herself to rein in her disappointment. Quietly to herself, she'd even hoped he'd pop the marriage question, bringing their dating arrangement to a happy-ending conclusion. She'd become Mrs. Scott Black, who lived in the beautiful Queen-Anne home on Thompson Lane.

Wow, had she ever been living in a fantasy world.

Between yesterday and today, the dream had disintegrated, and marriage was no longer in the cards. She was reaching thirty years old and every romantic relationship had resulted in a bad breakup. She was beginning to think she would forever be single and relegated to being addressed as Miss Desiree Contando.

Candee was staring at her, apparently wondering about Desiree's peculiar behavior, and why it was taking her so long to enter her new home.

"Desiree?" Candee tucked a strand of auburn hair beneath her faded baseball cap. "I know you're worried about taking on the house repairs, and I understand. When I mentioned to Teddy about your split with Scott, he made inquiries and found a carpenter for you. The guy's relocating here from Atlanta, Georgia. Apparently, Roses is his hometown. He told Teddy he'd like to give back to the community."

"Why would he leave Atlanta with the holidays a few weeks away?" Desiree asked. "Does his family live in the area?"

"Teddy didn't mention anything."

"And this guy's willing to start giving back by renovating my house?" With an overall sweep of her hands, Desiree gestured to the overgrown lawn, the neglected front porch, the weathered slate shingles on the steeply pitched roof.

"Yes. Teddy talked with him, and the guy will be arriving today."

"Does he know how much work my house demands?" Desiree challenged.

"You'll have to ask him yourself. He's reported to be talented and honest."

"Let's hope he's also cheap."

"He'll give you a good price." Candee firmly grasped Desiree's elbow, guiding her up the gravel driveway. "Teddy wanted to make amends for selling you this house when you clearly have reservations. He knows you're in a bind now with Scott gone."

Right. An understatement, to say the least.

Desiree changed her focus from her home's corner tower to Candee. "Who is this carpenter?"

"Keiran O'Malley."

Keiran O'Malley.

His name lodged in her throat. She had to fight down the feelings stirring within her.

"The O'Malleys owned O'Malley's Irish pub, which shut down many years ago," she managed to say.

The image of a tall, green-eyed guy with wavy dark hair came into Desiree's mind. He'd been on the high school football team, his broad chest and strong shoulders emphasized by his well-fitting jersey. He'd been a couple of years ahead of her, and had never given her a passing glance.

She'd glimpsed him at the homecoming game—the only one she and Candee had ever attended. When you lived in as many foster homes as they had, high school socializing was non-existent. Someone had pointed him out as the wealthiest kid in town. From what Desiree had heard, he sometimes helped his parents with their pub, key word being *sometimes*. Usually he was too busy escorting the current prom queen to country club dances, or driving around in his shiny new Ferrari after football practice.

After the game, she'd thought about talking with him, because her heart skipped a beat as she'd watched him. But, he'd been too engrossed in flirting shamelessly with a pretty cheerleader to notice Desiree.

Talk about a guy being off limits. In any event, they had run in completely different social circles. That is, if living in foster care counted as a circle.

"Teddy believes you can benefit from Keiran's carpentry skills," Candee said.

Panic rose inside Desiree. There would be a huge amount of work involved in transforming this house into her dream, and she remembered Keiran as seeming to be the opposite of ambitious.

Was it too late to sell her house back to Teddy and admit she'd made a mistake?

She pressed back her panic and concentrated on the second-story porch—the bracketed columns and neglected ornamental detail.

And the two words the house screamed: money pit.

She grimaced. "How does Teddy know Keiran?" she asked.

"Keiran remodeled a kitchen and bath in Georgia and

someone from Teddy's crew saw his work and recommended him."

Another gust of wind made the women shiver, and Candee jammed one hand into the pocket of her gray hoodie. "Earlier today, Teddy called Keiran and hired him for your project."

Desiree scowled. "Your husband did all this without asking me first?

"The guy's cheap, remember? He's coming back to his hometown and you'll be his—"

Desiree hesitated to finish the sentence. And then she did. "His first client."

"Exactly." Candee cheerfully ignored Desiree's apprehensive glance. "You want to host Christmas Eve dinner in your new house, correct? You can't do that until your kitchen is in working order."

"Regardless, I've never been known for my culinary skills. Except for my pistachio cake."

Candee laughed. "Um, even that's debatable."

The giggles came easier now, and Desiree's mind raced with trying to find a good reason to refuse Keiran's help before he arrived.

"I'd like to see his work. I have a certain design in mind, shabby chic, and I want it to be flawless," she said.

The laughter faded from Candee's face. "Flawlessness isn't the only thing that matters. Sometimes you take what you can get depending on your budget." She extracted Desiree's house key from her purse.

So that was where the key had gone. Desiree had forgotten she'd given it to Candee for safekeeping. Was this a sign she didn't really want the house?

Don't be ridiculous. If it was a sign of anything, it was that she was absentminded.

Candee lifted the key in the air. "Be content."

"Contentment and flawless should always be part of the same sentence."

"Not in our home-flipping world." Candee did a slow whirl, motioning toward the majestic trees, the worn picket fence, the trampled, overgrown bushes. A recent rain had soaked the lawn, and the grass was smeared with clumps of wet clippings. "Every house is a challenge and yours is no exception." She caught Desiree's hand. "C'mon. We've prolonged the inevitable long enough."

Sharing a chuckle, the women stepped onto the porch. Candee inserted the key into the lock, clicked the brass handle, and held the door open. "After you."

They stepped across a straw welcome mat, leaving footprints in the layer of dust on the aged parquet floor. Candee switched on the lights and offered a bright smile. "Oh, and there's one more thing about Keiran."

Desiree hesitated. "Only tell me if it's good."

"He planned on renting a place in town until he got on his feet," Candee said. "So Teddy recommended your attic apartment. He assumed you wouldn't mind if Keiran lived there for a while. The rent payment will help you with the mortgage."

A light fixture in the hallway swung precariously from an unsightly wire, and Desiree silently grumbled. "Is Keiran also an electrician?"

"Possibly, but he may not be licensed. I'm sure Teddy will know someone who is, though."

"Will a free room equal free labor?" Desiree waved off her sister's assurances. "And will his results be immediate? I want the house presentable by Christmas."

"C'mon, Desiree, don't be impatient. You're obliged to supply him with a salary and money for materials. Celebrate your good fortune because he dropped directly into your lap." Candee checked her watch. "Joseph's school bus will be coming soon. The school has early release because of a teacher planning seminar. I'll text you later."

With a nod signaling agreement, Desiree accepted the muffins and thanked her sister.

She took two paces into the foyer. A bone-deep weariness made her anxious, whereas Candee's enthusiasm was a source of inspiration.

Desiree drew on that inspiration. Taking a deep breath, she marched through the foyer and headed to the living room. The stained gold carpeting was peeling at the edges, and she bent to fold it back. Beneath the carpet were hardwood floors crying out for refinishing.

A large marble fireplace took up half the wall, its wide mantel solid oak. At Christmas, she imagined the mantel transformed, complete with sprigs of holly, miniature tealights and classic quilted stockings.

An unexpected downpour spilled across the bay window, and Desiree hoped that Candee had beaten the rain and reached her house without getting soaked.

She passed her fingers over the mantel, locating several candles and a box of matches, a reminder that Teddy had used the fireplace. He'd mentioned the HVAC unit wasn't operating, which meant no central heating or air conditioning.

The lights in the foyer blinked, then went out.

Already? Desiree massaged her temples. She hadn't been in her new home ten minutes.

Have faith, and everything will fall into place. Practical matters first. The encouraging words from her "forever family" foster mother came to mind.

Certainly, Desiree thought, she should hold fast to that wisdom.

First, deal with the electrical problem. And then the plumbing, then the . . .

The list went on and on.

Whereas now she had Keiran, the playboy turned carpenter who was on some kind of bizarre mission to help the community.

She went to the kitchen and placed the muffin box on the counter. Quickly, she captured her tote bag carrying overnight necessities, climbed the oak staircase to the master bedroom, and changed into an old pair of jeans and a flannel shirt. Although the light would soon fade, she'd begin the first afternoon in her new house by scrubbing the tiled floor.

Fun way to spend a Monday evening, she thought wryly. Fortunately, the plumbing was functional, and Teddy had kept a pail of cleaning supplies beneath the sink.

Although she had a love/hate relationship with scrubbing floors, she rolled up her sleeves and eased into a pair of rubber gloves to protect her hands. She loved the way the floors gleamed after a thorough cleaning, and the fresh lemony smell, barring the exhausting, manual labor that went with it.

Either way, she'd prayed over her decision to purchase the house, and with prayer came peace of mind. So she could do this. And she'd accept Keiran's help, because the financial savings would be tremendous.

That is, as long as he cut her a good deal, stayed in his attic apartment, and they maintained a working relationship.

And if he wasn't happy about that arrangement, he could book a hotel in town.

CHAPTER 2

*A*fter finishing a nitpicky adjustment to a kitchen remodeling project in Atlanta, Keiran O'Malley thanked the customer and gathered his tools as the other crewmen departed.

Done. Finally.

He drove his red pickup truck back to his apartment to finish packing, intentionally shifting his gaze away from the picturesque historic neighborhood of Iredell Park. Trendy and upscale, it had been reported as an up-and-coming neighborhood for young professionals. Many of the apartment buildings featured rooftop terraces, while several others were within walking distance of restaurants and shopping. He'd decided it would be an ideal area to live and raise a family.

And, he'd intended to set up a stand at the annual holiday display and sell his homemade Irish whiskey cake.

That was then, and this was now.

Still, they were everywhere—his shattered dreams. He shook his head, acknowledging that Atlanta held nothing for him anymore.

He slowed for the last turn to his apartment and went over what had happened that morning.

For once, he'd been able to complete a carpentry job on time and wasn't delayed because of Patricia, his ex-girlfriend. When they'd first met, he'd enjoyed her dark, sultry beauty.

Not any longer.

Usually, her compulsions to run in overdrive and make his life difficult were at the top of her priority list. Today she'd seemed preoccupied, although she'd slammed the office door in his face when he told her he was leaving Georgia for good.

Startled, he'd laughed and stared at the door. Really? As if this was all *his* fault?

He'd lifted his hand to knock. And then he'd pivoted and strode away. She was officially gone from his life. It was over. If only he could make peace with the fact that the two people he'd grown closest to—his girlfriend and his best friend, Kyle —had deceived him. They'd found each other and forgotten about him.

He bounded up the last flight of stairs and greeted Georges, his roommate, as he entered their fourth-floor walk-up apartment. They rented a place above a pawn shop, and Georges worked there part time, negotiating prices on the various items. Georges spent the rest of his time attending college online, majoring in international studies.

With a thump, Georges set a pizza box on the kitchen counter.

"I ordered pizza for my new roommate, Oscar." Georges's deep chuckle brought Keiran to the kitchen.

"Glad you found someone to take my place so quickly," Keiran said.

"Yup." Georges snatched a beer from the refrigerator and took a long swallow. "And we're planning to get blindingly drunk tonight."

"I hardly ever drink."

"Fortunately, Oscar drinks all the time. Take heart, *mon ami*. I'll miss your cooking." Georges headed to the living room and Keiran followed.

"That's my takeaway conversation?" Keiran asked.

"Most of it." Chuckling, Georges sank onto an armchair and drained his beer. "Because you're leaving, I'm putting take-out on speed-dial."

"Sorry, I don't deliver. You can always learn how to put together a casserole, or bake potatoes in a crockpot."

"Me? Every kitchen appliance runs when it sees me coming." Georges crooked a grin at the unlikely possibility of preparing a meal. "And I checked. Oscar doesn't even know how to fry an egg. He just drinks."

"Does he work?"

"He works at a law firm in town."

Impressed, Keiran inquired, "Is he a lawyer?"

"Nope. He works outside and struts around with a billboard advertising their current specials—you know, divorces, insurance claims if you've been in an accident—"

"What kind of a lawyer does that?"

Georges barked a laugh. "The kind you call if you're in a jam. His firm is a one-stop shop kind of place. Oscar said the lawyer is also a locksmith. You've probably seen his advertising on TV. His name is Abraham Realgood and his nickname is Honest Abe."

Unsuccessfully, Keiran tried to keep his face straight. "Well, thanks for an oversupply of information I'll never need."

"You never know when a lawyer is required, especially one who gets things done in a hurry." Georges lurched to his feet and the men shook hands, Georges joking all the while that he was charging his new roomie a higher rent for their "luxurious" studio apartment in the ancient building.

"You're a good guy, Keiran, and much more forgiving of Patricia and Kyle than I'd ever be," Georges said.

A good guy? Keiran thought.

Not particularly.

Forgiving?

Well, he embraced his faith. But if push came to shove, the answer would be *no*. He wasn't very forgiving.

"Always take the high road, son," his mother had often said.

I'm trying, Mom.

Wouldn't a good Christian man forgive an infidelity, as Georges believed Keiran had done?

Wishing his roommate well, Keiran packed his bags, hoisted his guitar case over his shoulder, and placed his father's precious football card in its plastic case. He tucked the deed to his family's pub, O'Malley's, into his wallet.

He loaded his belongings into his truck alongside the rest of the luggage he'd packed the evening before. Thirty minutes later, he headed east on I-85 through Georgia. He estimated it would take him less than four hours to reach Roses, North Carolina.

This was his opportunity to go back to his roots after leaving his family's pub far behind. He loved to cook and bake, and his father had discouraged him.

"I know the restaurant business," his father had lectured. "It's hard work, and I don't want you tied to a stove night and day, like me and your mother have been all these years. Pursue football. Go pro."

Keiran didn't have the desire, the instinct, or the talent to play football. He really liked the restaurant business. Each night, he'd link his hands behind his head and stare at the ceiling.

He couldn't follow his father's football dreams.

So instead, he'd reacted like an impetuous eighteen-year-old and left town. He'd follow his own road. He'd show his father he'd become a success without his family's support.

In Atlanta, he'd met Patricia. Soon afterward, she'd encouraged him to become a carpenter in her father's construction business, dreaming of million-dollar homes in stellar neighborhoods. Together, they'd climb the ladder of success. He'd learn the carpentry trade while she'd manage his appointments, advertise, and grow his business.

Young and trying to find his way, he'd responded with an enthusiastic "sure," and shelved the idea of opening a restaurant.

Now Patricia was gone and the ladder had been pulled out from under him.

In Roses, he'd be surrounded by the community that had given him an idyllic childhood. And maybe he could find his balance again—reopen the old family pub, visit Ireland for recipe inspirations. The more he thought about this new direction, the more he knew he had planned for the better.

He'd driven thirty minutes when Teddy Winchester phoned, introduced himself as a home flipper, and offered Keiran a job.

Keiran put his cellphone on speaker as Teddy explained that Desiree Contando, his sister-in-law, had purchased a Queen-Anne style home in Roses that was in a desperate state.

"Are you interested?" Teddy asked.

Keiran gripped the steering wheel. "How much repair?"

"I'm estimating a few months' worth. Do you have anything else lined up?"

"Not in the short term." Keiran reminded himself that there was more to life than dreams, and a steady income until he found his footing wasn't a bad idea.

"So will you take the job?"

"Without viewing it? What if your sister-in-law doesn't like my work?"

"She'll like it. Truth is, she's in a jam. The guy overseeing the project bailed, she's moving into 321 Thompson Lane today, and the place is a mess." Teddy paused. "Are you familiar with the road?"

"No, but I can find it."

"It's a definite fixer-upper. Despite that, the house has curb appeal and endless possibilities," Teddy continued in a distinct Southern drawl. "I learned from one of my crewmen that your craftmanship is excellent."

"Roses is my hometown and I'm headed back there as we speak," Keiran replied.

"Yes, so I've heard."

How had Teddy heard? Probably because men gossiped at twice the speed of women.

"As a bonus, I'll offer you an apartment—a remodel in the top dormer of her house. I lived there until my recent marriage and it's in good shape."

"What's the catch?" Keiran asked.

"I'm asking this favor because I sold Desiree the property," Teddy said. "Plus, I live two doors away."

"And you still want your wife speaking to you in the morning," Keiran finished with a laugh.

"Something like that."

"Sure, then," Keiran said. "I've been thinking a lot about making a difference in Roses."

Now why had he said that? Teddy was a stranger who offered employment, not his new buddy.

Serendipity. Fate. A coincidence. Keiran chose to believe the hand of God was bringing him back to his birthplace. A sign to leave his broken heart and Atlanta memories far behind.

Once the carpentry job was finished, he'd reopen his parents' pub. In the meantime, as a favor to Teddy for leading him to his first client, he'd give Desiree an excellent price.

"Thanks. I'll tell her to expect you," Teddy said. "Oh, and by the way, she works full time, so she won't be around much."

"What does she do?"

"She's a lawyer."

Smiling, Keiran clicked off his phone. A lawyer? Really? Two lawyer mentions in one day. He just hoped he never needed one.

He switched on the radio, bypassing the Christmas carols —the cheery "Santa Claus is Coming to Town" sung by a current rap star.

He settled on a classic contemporary station, and his fingers tapped a beat on the steering wheel as an 80's rock song belted, *"Don't stop believin.'"* He knew the lyrics to the Journey hit by heart and sang along.

While sorting his collection of football cards, his father would hum the song after the pub closed for the evening. One particular card had been autographed by a well-known player, a guy he'd met while trying out for a first-pick college draft. His father hadn't made the cut. When Keiran had tried out for high school football, his father had given the prized card to him.

Keiran couldn't imagine his father as young and carefree, full of dreams and aspirations. He only remembered a man with a resigned look on his tired, worn face, his mother cooking diligently by his side.

Keiran glanced at his backpack holding the plastic-encased football card. "Thanks for giving me material things, Dad. I'm sorry I didn't live up to your ambitions. I only wish I had visited Ireland sooner to spend time with you."

But he hadn't.

"Don't stop believin.'"

When the song ended, Keiran clicked off the radio, flicked on his left blinker, and exited the highway leading to Roses. He remembered the area, although he relied on his GPS to locate Thompson Lane.

He admired the natural scenery, the backdrop of the Blue Ridge Mountains, the celebratory way the town center was decked out for the holidays—the streetlights trimmed in decorative red bows, and the garlands strung along every shop's window box. He remembered his parents' love of Christmas had radiated throughout their pub, along with savory scents of homemade relishes, roasted turkeys, and exquisite caraway-seed-filled Irish desserts.

Once upon a time, he'd loved everything about Christmas. Now he was an adult, and the enchantment was gone. The constant arguments with Patricia had cured him of childhood expectations.

He parked at the curb in front of a ramshackle Queen-Anne style home at 321 Thompson Lane. The house stood like a freeze frame of a forgotten time.

"This must be the place," he murmured. He got out of his truck and surveyed the property. "A real fixer-upper, all right."

With his keen eye, Keiran assessed the exterior of the house against the fading afternoon light, grateful he'd arrived in Roses before dark. Patches of spongy moss grew along the slate roof. The window frames bubbled with fading beige paint. All these outdoor repairs would take hours of labor and he hadn't even stepped inside.

Despite the neglected appearance, the house brought back memories, and unexpected emotions rocked him. He recalled his childhood home in Roses, bordered by a white picket fence. The house had been located on the other side of town and was one of the largest in his neighborhood. In his mind, he heard his friends' laughter as they played kickball. He'd had no siblings, but had never felt lonely.

Beams of late afternoon sunshine streamed through the Queen Anne's front bay window. A recent rainfall brought a reflective gleam to the wavy glass. Raindrops trembled and shined along the yellow leaves on thick branches. The house was set in, canopied by four gigantic oak trees that appeared to be over a hundred years old.

Curb appeal, Teddy Winchester had said.

And a whole lot of work.

Keiran hesitated. He was a carpenter, not a demolition crew.

Unlimited possibilities.

Well, that one was negotiable, and depended on how much repair the house required. It certainly exuded charm and a salute to a bygone era. He just had to have faith that the bygone era wasn't so long ago that the home offered no modern comforts.

He didn't blink, hardly moving, debating. A slight drizzle from the tree leaves coated his cheeks and two days' worth of dark stubble. There were no lights on inside the home, although the flicker of candlelight illuminated a window.

He scrubbed a hand over his face, then retrieved his backpack, guitar, and toolbox from his truck. He'd get the rest of his luggage later.

Again, he stared at the house.

He was here, had driven all afternoon, and it seemed foolish not to see if Desiree was home. He went to the front door and knocked once.

No answer.

Twice.

No answer.

He debated about clicking the brass handle to check if the

door was locked. But, even if it was, he couldn't exactly stroll inside.

On the third knock, the door abruptly opened, and he came face to face with a beautiful woman with deep-set blue eyes. She held a lighted candle, sheltering the flickering glow with her small, cupped hand. She could have stepped out of a fairy tale—Cinderella came to mind. Her thick blond hair was piled on top of her head, held precariously by a blue headband. Her fair complexion was smudged with dirt.

"Desiree Contando?" he asked. He thought she flinched, but assumed he was mistaken.

"Just Desiree, please." The expression on her oval-shaped face was calm, and her hair shone in the last rays of daylight. Slender, she wore a pair of worn denims and a plaid flannel shirt with the sleeves rolled up.

A spin of warmth between them sparked an attraction he hadn't expected.

She was drop-dead gorgeous, especially if a guy was drawn to fairytale princesses.

He apparently was. Although he'd tried dating a princess and had failed spectacularly. Patricia had never been happy, despite his attempts to shower her with compliments, expensive meals, and flowers whenever he could afford them.

In the end, it was obvious their values and interests didn't match, and she'd discarded him for his wealthy best friend. Aye, she wanted the castle and the crown. She didn't have time to waste on a guy trying to figure out if he wanted to be a carpenter or a cook.

"Hi, Desiree." Spellbound, he just stared. She had the prettiest golden hair, framing a perfect complexion and generous mouth.

She blinked and took a step back. "Mr. O'Malley?"

"Keiran."

"I've been expecting you." Her tone was dispassionate as

she gestured with her small chin to the home's worn interior. "My brother-in-law said you were driving from Atlanta."

A breeze shifted, the wind carrying the promise of chilly winter nights to come. "Yes, all afternoon."

The weariness in her blue eyes deepened. "Do you realize what you're getting into here?"

"Absolutely." He nodded reassuringly. "I'm a carpenter, more or less."

"With any luck, it's more rather than less. This house warrants an excellent carpenter, plus a whole lot more." Her expression tightened. "Are you also a licensed electrician? I've lost power."

"No," he admitted.

The candle wavered in her hand, vulnerable to the late afternoon breeze.

She shrugged. "Then your services aren't required tonight."

"I was told I had a place to stay when I got here," he said.

"Yes, once you begin working. However, there's nothing for you to do yet, and because it's my first night in my new home, I'd prefer to spend it alone. I'll see you in the morning —and bring an electrician with you." She stepped back and closed the door.

"Well, that's perfect." He stared at the wooden front door, then down at the sagging porch. Evidently, this was his day for women opting to slam the door in his face. "I came all this way, but because I'm not the acceptable tradesman for this evening, I'm supposed to sleep in my truck," he muttered. His earlier enthusiasm at arriving in Roses was quickly waning.

You were planning to come, anyway, a small voice in his head reminded him. *You were going to take a ride by your parents' deserted pub, then find a place to stay in town.*

Aye, before Teddy's phone call.

Nevertheless . . .

He was still muttering when the door opened.

"Mr. O'Malley, are you talking to my porch?" Desiree asked.

"Just enjoying my visit with your broken-down floor. That is, when I'm not having a conversation with the rusty propane grill in the corner." He kept his focus downward. "This porch is unsteady. You'd better hope it doesn't cave in, or you'll be clamoring for a carpenter faster than you can say Queen-Anne disaster."

"Are you saying my house might collapse?" She laughed, and that amazed him. It was unexpected. She seemed so serious, with her slim shoulders and strong posture, her huge eyes speaking of sadness. Slight shadows beneath her eyes gave her an unconscious vulnerability, and one, he guessed, she would never admit to.

Her laugh seemed stilted, though. Just like his had been that morning with Patricia. An ironic laugh of disbelief.

"Minor setbacks. Everything can be fixed." He plastered on a reassuring grin that he didn't quite feel. "We'll bring your house back to her former majestic state."

"For now, she's a good distance from her former crown." Desiree smiled, and this time her smile seemed more genuine. "Why are you still standing on my porch, Mr. O'Malley?"

He studied the lit candle in her hand, and then her. She looked absolutely exquisite, her high cheekbones accentuated by pink color, her classic beauty understated. She wore no makeup, and reminded him of a master painting by Raphael—*Woman with a Veil* came to mind. Alluringly beautiful.

Before answering, he questioned himself. Why *was* he still here? Did he truly belong in Roses? Was he good enough to transform a house in shambles into splendor? Was he good enough to open his parents' pub, a legacy he didn't deserve?

A part of him said aye, although it had nothing to do with the house. Or the pub, for that matter. He wanted to learn more about Desiree Contando.

Not a good idea. Wrong reasons. He was here to work. Besides, he was spinning off of a bad relationship. Better to wall himself off from all women, especially attractive women with enchanting eyes and enticing lips.

He was amazed by his next response, which had nothing to do with his thoughts. "This is my hometown and I haven't been back in ten years. Give me a chance."

"I will, in the morning."

"I would've booked a room in town if I'd known." He pulled out his cell phone. "I'll call Morrison's Hotel on Main Street."

"They closed five years ago."

He didn't think twice. There was Broad Acres, a bed and breakfast on the outskirts. He told her as much.

"They shut down last year," came her cool reply.

He clapped a hand to his forehead. "So here I stand, wondering where I'll be sleeping tonight. Teddy mentioned he lived a couple of doors down. Last name is Winchester?"

"Yes, and … no. I mean, don't call him." Desiree's tone stayed no-nonsense. "He and my sister, Candee, are newly-weds. Plus, they're raising a young boy."

"I'll snooze in my truck for the night, then." Keiran picked up his things. "I've slept in worse places."

"Have you?" Desiree assessed him. "From what I recall, only the finest was good enough for a guy like you."

He grimaced at her evaluation. "Do we know each other, Desiree?"

"I know *of* you. I first saw you at a high school football game. Your nickname was Richie Rich."

Wow, was he ever tired of people assessing him on the basis of his well-to-do background. Sure, his parents had been wealthy and he'd never lacked for anything, although they'd toiled long hours for their success. With the same work ethic, he'd driven himself hard in order to prove himself among the other tradesmen in Atlanta.

He held her gaze. "Rich doesn't mean lazy."

"Not always." Those two words, a slight concession, an assessment of a guy she'd labeled without any facts. Frustration mushroomed inside him.

"Did we talk?" he asked.

"Where?"

"At the football game."

"Are you kidding?" She avoided his gaze. "You were too busy with the pretty cheerleader."

"I can't remember her name."

Desiree started to scowl, but chuckled when he did.

"Do you remember mine?" she asked.

He held out his hand. "I don't think we were ever formally introduced. Let's try this again. I'm Keiran, Desiree."

She accepted his handshake. Her hand was fine and delicate. The idea of living in her house was becoming incredibly appealing.

"So you're an authority about me based on a high school football game?" He still held her hand. She made no move to let go. Neither did he.

Silence reigned for a beat.

Quietly, she shifted her stance and pulled her hand from his. "True. Sometimes one chapter doesn't mean you read the whole book."

"Precisely."

Sure, he'd made bad choices. He'd been foolish and reckless for leaving a town he loved in order to prove he could make it on his own, falling into a profession totally removed from the restaurant scene.

She trained her attention on him, her deep-set eyes considering. "Teddy predicts this house will take several months to complete. I'm hoping he's wrong."

Keiran hoped Teddy was right.

"Hard to tell until I see it." He stamped his feet on the dog-eared welcome mat, a not-so-subtle hint. "May I come in? It's cold out here."

"Why not?" She brushed those gorgeous waves from her face. "After you, Mr. O'Malley." With a graceful turn, she ushered him inside.

CHAPTER 3

*D*esiree led the way through the foyer, pausing to peer at a silvery spider web, an excuse to gain two seconds to compose herself. She'd been totally unprepared. She needed time for this new development she hadn't expected.

And that development was Keiran O'Malley. The handsome, dashing Irish football player. She was certain he was accustomed to plush surroundings, and her house was the farthest one could get from that scenario.

Seeing him, she'd done a double-take, surprised that he surpassed her adolescent daydreams. In high school, she'd heard that he lived on the south side of town, the wealthy side, where tall privacy hedges bordered the homes.

A decade had passed and he'd grown even more striking. His teen body had filled out, and tiny crinkles had formed around his Prince Charming green eyes. The navy-blue parka he wore accentuated his athletic shoulders.

His family had reached financial success owning their profitable pub until it abruptly closed. After Keiran departed (she'd inquired), the pub had gone into a downward slide and never recovered from the economic recession.

The way her heart had thudded when she saw him reminded her that her youthful crush was alive and well. Definitely, she should keep her distance. Difficult to accomplish when she couldn't keep her eyes off him.

She realized his gaze was assessing her, from her messy hair to her disheveled jeans and oversized flannel shirt.

Ten years. During that time she'd earned a bachelor's degree, followed by three years of law school and passed the arduous bar exam on her first try.

Every day since then, she'd had a single-minded vision of creating a picture-perfect life. Her own childhood had been just the opposite. However, she'd learned that as an adult, she could control her destiny. Especially with perseverance and God's generosity.

At present, she focused on the monumental task ahead—transforming a rapidly deteriorating house into the holiday fantasy of her dreams.

"This is lovely," Keiran said.

She swallowed as her gaze shifted to his finely chiseled features. "You're being serious?"

"Aye. The house has good bones. And we'll be able to build on that."

"Speedily, I hope," came her patented reply.

He lifted a dark eyebrow. "In six months this place will be as good as new."

"Six months? I'm hosting Christmas Eve dinner and the kitchen needs to be ready by then."

He gave her a skeptical look. "Does your oven function?" he asked.

"Function? Hah! Fortunately, Christmas Eve isn't tomorrow. I've . . . *we've* got a few weeks."

"To perform a miracle?" He motioned to the mismatched wallpaper in the foyer, the floorboards desperate for major repair, and narrowed his gaze. For a split second, she thought he might turn around and leave.

Purposefully, she didn't meet his stare. "Only God performs miracles."

"Glad we agree on something," he replied. "Six months is a generous estimate and the renovation may take much longer depending on any unforeseen problems once we get started." He set his backpack, guitar, and toolbox in the foyer. "Many times, remodeling goes weeks slower than a customer anticipates. Unexpected delays and spiraling costs are part of the process. When was this house built?"

She rolled her eyes. "Many years ago."

"Please let me know when you find out." He crossed his arms. Tall, athletic, and vital, with his male-model good looks and utterly appealing smile, he was definitely out of place in her shabby interior. He should have been strolling across a Dublin runway wearing designer clothes, not standing in her rundown foyer in worn jeans and a navy-blue parka.

"Surely the age of a home doesn't determine the renovation," she snapped at him, and felt churlish for snapping. Having him stand a few inches away sent unexpected tingles through her nerves. Long ago, she'd secured a place in her heart for him and only him. To have the object of her affection so near made her want to confess her infatuation. Blurt it out and get it over with, so he wouldn't think she was bad mannered for gaping and hesitating and staring.

Whoa. Hold that thought. They'd been together ten minutes and she wanted to tell him how much she'd dreamed about him ten years ago.

No, no, no. She was obviously overtired.

He didn't reply. Instead, he headed for the kitchen. "Other

tradesmen will factor in their estimates and might not cut you the same once-in-a-lifetime deal I'm giving you, and there may be surprises in older homes." He swiped a finger across the double-paneled wainscoting in the adjoining pantry.

That was one of the reasons she loved this house, because of the exquisite detailing not found in cookie-cutter newer homes.

"What kind of surprises?" she asked.

"Termite damage and rotting plumbing, to name a couple."

She winced. Unexpected problems would put a definite crimp in her bank account. "What is your once-in-a-lifetime deal, by the way?"

He paused to check a loose floorboard. "You'll need to trust me."

Easy to say, but words were cheap. She frowned and eyed his strong shoulders.

"Should I start on the renovations tonight?" He pulled off his parka, exposing thick arm muscles bulging from a cream-colored T-shirt. "I feel like I should at least fix that loose wire in your foyer because you're letting me bunk here a day early."

"Sure. Great. Thanks." She had to stop gazing at him.

He'd be sleeping in the attic, which was one floor above her bedroom. She'd hear his footsteps padding across the floor, the water running in the small shower when he bathed. Her heart beat quicker in her chest. This was her teenage dream come true, except the dream was several years too late.

Determined to ignore his desirability, she swallowed hard. Her gaze transferred to the kitchen counter. "Have you eaten?"

"Nope." He peered past her. "Any chance the stove or microwave works?"

"Both appliances are in terrible shape and should be ripped out. Plus, there's no power tonight so you're out of luck." She drew a breath. "Do you cook?"

"My parents owned a pub."

She knew that and waited for him to elaborate. When he didn't, she offered, "My sister brought muffins."

"What kind?"

"Pumpkin. Now you're being selective?" She pointed to the refrigerator. "And there's bottled water in the fridge."

"Any idea when the power will be back on?"

"I checked my phone for an update. A storm hit farther north and affected the lines in this area. The power company estimated everything should be fixed by nightfall."

"Excellent."

Excellent. Excellent would be reporting to her law firm tomorrow morning and coming back home in the evening to a fixed, finished house all decorated for Christmas. Excellent would be keeping her personal life private by living in her own space, far from the gaze of her swoon-worthy new roommate.

She ran a hand through her disheveled curls, wishing she'd pulled a comb through her hair before he'd arrived. And why hadn't she changed back into the proper business suit she'd worn earlier?

Keiran washed his hands in the sink. He slanted a glance at her while grabbing a bottle of water. "You want anything?"

She shook her head, her gaze dropping to her waistline. "After the Thanksgiving holiday, I intend to eat light for the next few weeks."

His gaze did likewise, and he smiled broadly. "You look great to me."

Her heart took a leap.

All day, her emotions had roller-coasted from exhilaration to anxiety. Now, as she stared up at the rugged dark-haired man who seemed sincere in his compliment, unexpected tears sprang to her eyes.

"This has been a difficult week," she admitted. "Usually I can juggle a lot of things with ease—"

"Difficult because of Thanksgiving and working full time? Teddy said you're a lawyer."

His question was so unexpected, so gentle, she smiled despite the tears. "No. Thanksgiving was wonderful. My sister Candee, or rather Teddy, cooked a Thanksgiving feast —a turkey with all the trimmings." She didn't tell him that she and Candee had never experienced a normal Thanksgiving growing up, so they savored every festive get-together. They knew what it was like to go without.

"Holidays are good." Lightly, he covered her hand with his fingers. "They're meant to be enjoyed with loved ones."

Awareness of his masculine presence stirred her pulse. "Mr. O'Malley—"

"Keiran."

She opened her mouth to object, then thought better of it. "Keiran, then."

"Now we're equals, Desiree." Although his tone teased, his expression turned serious.

They were hardly equals. He'd been born with the proverbial silver spoon in his mouth. She'd been born into squalor.

"I . . . I assume your Thanksgiving in Atlanta was pleasant," she offered.

He hesitated, then let out a brief sigh. "I cooked a turkey, a sweet potato casserole, and a round Irish cake filled with caraway seeds for me and my roommate."

"Wow. You'll be a welcome addition to any gathering."

So he'd had a roommate. A woman? she wondered, although she didn't ask.

"I never learned how to fix a proper meal, and now my life is hectic." Despite her shrug, she couldn't quite hold the apology from her voice, although she questioned what she was apologizing for. She hadn't had the opportunity to cook in her foster homes. More often than not, she'd been relegated to a spare room and ignored.

"My favorite pastime is spending afternoons in the kitchen trying new recipes," he said.

"I thought you were a carpenter. I imagined you crafting items out of wood."

He met her gaze. "A guy can do more than one thing, Desiree."

"But can he do more than one thing well?"

"Can you?"

"Absolutely."

"Then so can I." Approval and mirth brightened his face. His hand still covered hers. "Also, I make a mean Irish whiskey cake."

"I bake a pistachio cake that is usually edible, as long as I don't forget it's in the oven."

"How can you forget a cake? Don't you set a kitchen timer?"

"Sometimes." Another shrug. "Believe me, a cake in the oven is easy to forget, especially when I'm immersed in a court case and bring the work home with me. When that happens, I get sidetracked."

He laughed. "When your oven is fixed, we'll set a timer so your cake won't burn, and then I'll challenge you to a baking contest."

"Oh really. Who will be the judge?"

His gaze lit with sharpened interest. "Does Roses still hold a holiday cake contest on the village green?"

"Yes." She acknowledged his question with a smirk. "And always the weekend before Christmas."

"I thought so."

"I'm certain your cake will be a success."

"And so will yours."

She chuckled. "I highly doubt it."

He nodded.

Why was she able to fall into such easy conversation with him when they'd only talked for a short time? He seemed genuinely interested.

Not romantically, though.

No. Guys from his wealthy background didn't give the time of day to women like her.

Still, what was she doing? The peaceful intimacy of his large hand on hers caused her to relax a little too much. However attractive, this man was her employee, and their arrangement was strictly business.

She jerked her hand away.

He didn't seem to notice.

With a flash of white teeth, he offered that devastating grin again. "Do you accept my challenge?" he asked.

"To bake?"

"Aye. I'll make it official. I challenge you to the Roses Christmas baking contest."

"That's not fair. Your parents owned a pub."

"A pub isn't the corner bakery."

"You have more experience in a kitchen than me."

He winked. "I'll teach you all I know."

Cozy evenings baking homemade Christmas treats with him? Immediately, her heart agreed. Her common sense, however, reminded her this wasn't a good idea.

At any rate, she couldn't keep from chuckling and

accepting the challenge. His enthusiasm was contagious, and besides, what was the problem with gaining another ten pounds? Hah! She'd simply buy the next size up in clothes or scope out an elastic waistband.

"We'll schedule oven rights while you're here," she said.

"Sounds good."

Warmth bloomed in her cheeks as she gazed at him. Keiran O'Malley was a strong-featured, devastatingly attractive man who liked to cook and bake. Heads would certainly turn when he strode through town, especially if he toted a cartful of his homemade Irish whiskey cakes.

Opening the bakery box on the counter, he offered her a muffin. She declined and he chose one for himself. The table held a smattering of stoneware, along with boxes of utensils. She intended to arrange the glass-paned cupboards with an artful display of dishes and decided to get started while he ate.

Carefully, she corralled a stack of plates and mounted a chair. At her petite height, she stood on her toes to reach the top shelf of the cupboard.

"Get rid of the doors," he said.

She twisted toward him. "I'm sorry?"

"And lime green isn't trending these days."

"Just like that?" His confident attitude annoyed her. "Doesn't my opinion count? I *am* the owner."

"Of course." He waved a hand around. "Though in the latest designs, kitchens are painted white. And for a more open quality, remove the cupboard doors."

Plates in hand, she remained standing on the chair. "I've already decided to paint the walls dove white. I may want to leave the cupboard doors intact, though, so don't go throwing anything into the junk pile without my permission."

He nodded. "At least wait a few days before you decide."

Digesting his information, she agreed as he helped her off the chair. She loved an open floor plan, and took notes while she watched the home improvement TV shows for modern-day ideas.

While he leaned against the sink, she relit several candles. His gaze assessed her, assessed her kitchen, assessed the flickering candlelight.

She ran warm, sudsy water into the sink and placed several dusty dishes to soak. "You still haven't told me how much the renovation will cost."

Slowly, he bit into the muffin, chewed, swallowed, and took a swig of water. "I haven't seen your house yet."

"You're standing in the main room. Surely you have a rough estimate in your head."

A winning smile lit his features. "A million dollars, give or take a hundred thousand."

"That's not funny."

"I'll know better after you show me around." He strode into the foyer for his toolbox. "First, I'll fix that loose wire hanging from your ceiling."

"You're not an electrician."

"I learned a few things while working on construction sites all these years." He pulled a screwdriver from his toolbox.

"Do you know what you're doing?" She hurried after him. "I don't want you electrocuted before you begin working tomorrow."

He stopped dead and directed a grin at her. "If that happens, your repair list might be delayed a few days."

"You're brimming with not-so-funny jokes today."

"How's this?" he asked. "Providing I'm okay, I'll whip you up an omelet. I noticed you have a dozen eggs in your refrigerator."

"The stove isn't working."

"There's a grill on your front porch. If you have a cast-iron frying pan in one of those boxes, we're all set."

She burst out laughing as mixed reactions filled her. Keiran O'Malley embodied the best qualities in a man. And no matter how much she'd questioned his expertise, he was rapidly becoming a true blessing.

CHAPTER 4

A week passed, bringing the first Friday in December to a close. Along with record-breaking cold temperatures, the promise of snow was in the air, and daylight hours were rapidly becoming shorter.

Despite her desire to snuggle indoors and eat platefuls of carbohydrates, Desiree's over-filled schedule demanded she spend her days at her law firm filing last-minute appeals. Hours, days, had gone by in a blur, and she hadn't devoted as much time as she'd initially earmarked for remodeling her new home. As a lawyer fighting for those who couldn't afford it, she knew her service was critical. Many parents were without the financial means to support themselves or their children, and some spouses were victims of domestic violence. On numerous occasions, she'd provided free legal assistance by working pro bono.

At half past seven in the evening, she eased her car into her gravel driveway. During the day, a number of pickup trucks parked there, although all the tradesmen clocked out by three-thirty. Not Keiran, of course. Keiran worked nonstop.

A light drizzle wet the streets, and she yearned for snow —to sit lightly on her eyelashes, to gift wrap the magical season of Christmas.

She stepped onto the front porch, which Keiran had fixed, and admired the pine-scented, evergreen wreath strung with holly berries and pinecones.

"The first sign of Christmas." He greeted her with a lopsided grin as she opened the front door and smacked into him. Through the thin denim of his shirt, his body was warm, his broad chest hard and toned. She gazed up at his thick midnight-black hair, his well-defined features, and took in a sharp breath.

The smile on his face changed from humor to something else. Something deeper. He gazed at her lips, and she instinctively held her breath. His daily presence in her life was a sweet enticement she refused to acknowledge, and it took all her effort to resist his magnetism.

He dusted off his hands, then took her wool coat and set it on a hallway chair.

The renovation had come an incredibly long way in the short time since he'd arrived, and she peered around approvingly. Although she'd immediately wanted to shop for paint swatches, he'd advised focusing on the practical rather than the aesthetic. The roof, windows, and masonry repairs came first. The house required secure sealing, especially with winter approaching.

She'd approved, and in the course of a few days he'd taken on the role as general contractor, quickly becoming fast friends with Teddy. Keiran relied on Teddy's expertise, as well as his contacts. Once the house was watertight, he'd enlisted a crew to sand and sheetrock the kitchen walls.

As she did every evening upon entering the foyer, she peered at the ceiling and muttered, "Eventually, I'm getting rid of that hideous gold fixture."

"I like it." Keiran came to stand beside her. The harsh light of the open bulbs splayed across his face, and she reached up to brush a trace of sawdust from his cheeks.

He caught her hand, squeezing it warmly. "How was your day?"

"Busy. Yours?"

"The same. And I wouldn't have it any other way."

They'd come to an amiable understanding. He'd maintained a professional, friendly distance and, consequently, they'd built a trusting friendship. Somehow, he'd known intuitively that that was the relationship she wanted, and he'd quickly adapted to her unspoken request.

Her gaze swept the foyer, coming to rest on the hardwood floor. "Can the unevenness be fixed?" she asked.

"Any problem can be fixed. The question is, can you live with an imbalanced floor? I checked with a professional and the house's structure is okay, so I'd leave it and save the money." He gestured toward the bay window in the living room. "Same with the wavy glass. These qualities add character to an older home."

"Beautiful imperfections," she mused. "Like people."

"Perfectly imperfect, my chaplain in Atlanta preached at Sunday services," Keiran replied. "People are setting their sights on happiness, but searching in the wrong places. None of us, and nothing we create, is perfect. We expect a lot of others, though."

"And of ourselves," she said. "It may be that perfection isn't always the best way."

"Better to get over ourselves and think more about serving the people in our lives."

She nodded, reflecting, knowing she was forever striving to create a textbook world for herself, the one she'd read about in fables when she was a child.

Nonetheless, attaining the accomplishments her friends

often displayed on social media brought about exhaustion. Consequently, she didn't enjoy the here and now.

"Wise words," she replied.

And Keiran personified those words. He acted knowledgeably and humbly, and performed his work with a consideration that made her admire the person he was—kind, steadfast, and capable.

Each evening, he'd help her unpack endless boxes and order takeout, with a promise to cook her a proper meal once the stove and oven were installed. In the meantime, he'd rearranged her meager furniture and added a touch she would have expected more from a professional decorator than a carpenter with no formal design training.

"My chaplain is an inspiring person," he went on. "If you're ever free on a weekend, I can bring you to a church service in Atlanta. The drive takes a few hours, although it's doable in one day."

She gazed at him, and pretended she didn't. Her first inclination was to immediately decline his invitation, to maintain their cool, professional relationship.

But how could she?

She could hardly feign disinterest in this six-foot-two man with sparkling green eyes and an utterly masculine appeal. She loved talking with him, laughing with him. And she was impressed by his attention to elements and setup. He had an excellent discernment for arrangement, and was resourceful and creative, keeping her strict budget in mind at all times.

A fun conversationalist, he sported a keen knowledge in topics ranging from child advocacy to football, and, of course, cooking and baking. All in all, she considered him a Renaissance man, a term she'd once heard applied to a man blessed with intellect and proficient in a wide range of areas.

Although the term had originated in Italy, with his mesmerizing charm, Keiran was the epitome of the quick-witted Irish male.

"How's the kitchen coming?" she asked as she set down her briefcase.

"I was waiting for you to ask. Quicker than I anticipated, thanks to Teddy's efficient crew. The walls are painted, and your new appliances were delivered and installed this morning." As always, every sentence he uttered was enhanced by a hand gesture. "Do you want to see it?"

"Of course."

"Close your eyes." Obediently, she squeezed her eyes shut as he led her down the hallway.

He gave her hand a light squeeze. "Open."

She stopped at the kitchen entryway and gasped. Surely, this wasn't the same kitchen that had resembled a demolition area only a few days before.

As she and Keiran had discussed, the walls had been painted a dove white, and shiny new countertops were set in marbled granite. The white freestanding farmhouse sink was a surprise, paired with an old-world style pull-down faucet. A glossy tiled backsplash completed the ambience, along with open cupboards. She'd taken his advice and discarded the doors, giving the space a fluid, chic design.

He gestured to an empty corner. "A base cabinet is on backorder. Once it arrives, I'll install it. Hopefully it will be here in time for Christmas."

She sighed dreamily. "Thank you."

Her kitchen was exactly how she'd envisioned it, and a trendsetter's dream. Natural light spilled inside, thanks to sliding glass doors leading to her two-acre plot of land. A consistent thread of sunny yellow complemented the shelving rims, which were the colors they'd agreed upon. An oversized island in a high-gloss finish created a work triangle between the stove and refrigerator and seamlessly accommodated gleaming stainless-steel appliances. Her kitchen table and chairs had been tucked beneath a set of framed picture windows.

Awestruck, she put her fingers to her mouth. "All you've done in a week is more than most contractors could accomplish in a month."

He laughed. "The credit goes to Teddy's large, efficient crew. I'm merely one person supervising the project and helping wherever warranted."

"Truly, you are a genius."

He gazed down at her with tender amusement. "And while I was overseeing the renovations, you were protecting innocent children. If anyone deserves praise, Desiree, it's you."

Her heart skipped a beat.

Retrieving her coat, he strode to the hallway closet while she kicked off her black leather pumps, pulled on her favorite cardigan, and claimed a stool at the counter. She breathed in the aroma of seafood chowder simmering on the stove, and the sweet, enticing scent of a cake rising in the oven.

"And, in addition to the remodeling, you cooked?" she asked.

"Seafood chowder was my parents' signature dish. During my lunch hour, I shopped for the ingredients. For dessert, I baked an Irish whiskey cake."

"The very same cake you're challenging me with for the baking contest on the village green? It's totally not fair if you get a head start."

"I'll make it up to you."

She crossed her arms. "How?"

"We'll shop for a Christmas tree tomorrow, and I'm

buying. Only a ten-foot spruce will complement your living room's high ceilings. Aye?"

"Aye." How could she refuse a hardworking Irishman? In fascinated admiration, she watched him snap up a wooden spoon and adeptly stir the chowder.

"We'll eat dinner together after I shower and change?" he asked.

"Sure. Everything is wonderful."

He chuckled. "Brilliant."

A jumble of sensations made her pause. No man had ever cooked dinner for her before, inquired about her day, or taken a sincere interest. His consideration went way beyond their work relationship.

She stood and took a bottled water from the refrigerator. "Don't you have anywhere else you'd rather be on a Friday night?"

He studied her face, came closer, then pressed a light kiss on her forehead. "The more time I spend with you, the more time I want to spend with you. Does that make sense?"

There was no reason to offer a blasé answer, so she nodded a yes, because it made perfect sense. That pure attraction for him, a feeling she couldn't shake. Enjoy the moment, she told herself.

The thought made her absurdly pleased.

As he made for the stairs, she paused to take in the splendor of her polished, cheery kitchen. Previously, Keiran had drawn a sketch on his computer and gotten her approval, and his ideas had panned out. Ensuring the interior wall wasn't load-bearing, Teddy's crew had torn down the wall between the kitchen and dining room to make the most of her square footage.

A large communal area for family and friends was ideal for entertaining, Keiran had said.

She hadn't purchased a dining room set, and didn't foresee one in her immediate future.

Smiling, she arranged place settings on the kitchen island using her good china dishes and silver flatware. She'd started a hope chest when she graduated from college. It was silly, and most people had never heard of one. Despite her difficult upbringing, she believed in love and marriage, and a future with a special man. Starry-eyed dreams, she contemplated, while she folded white cloth napkins.

Keiran was down the stairs fifteen minutes later in his favorite pair of lived-in jeans and a T-shirt that revealed his fit physique. His thick jet-black hair was still wet from a shower, and he hadn't bothered to shave. His stubbled chin and prominent cheekbones made her pause. And his scent . . .

Oh, my. Now he even smelled like an Irishman—like early morning and whistle clean.

He raised a questioning dark eyebrow over his teasing gaze. "You own a service of fine crystal and china, your dining area is large enough for a twenty-person feast, and there's no place to sit and enjoy a meal?"

"Pull up a stool, like I did." She nodded to the island. "Or I'll pile cushions on the floor and we'll sit cross-legged. Someday, when I win the lottery, I'll buy dining room furniture."

He regarded the brass flush-mount light above the island. "What type of fixture do you want there?"

"I love French country design." She bent to a stack of magazines she kept in a wicker basket in the corner, and thumbed through one. "I saw a distressed frame fixture with candelabra detailing. See?"

He peered over her shoulder. "Excellent taste. I approve of all you've done." His breath was warm and tickled her ear.

That pull again, drawing her to him.

"You mean, all *you've* done," she corrected.

His lips twitched. Reaching up to the cupboard, he brought out two wine glasses. "I also bought a bottle of sparkling cider for our date."

"You're categorizing eating seafood chowder together at home as kind of a date?"

"Not kind of a date. It is a date."

"Is it a proper date?"

He sobered. "No. But it's here and now and let's embrace the moment."

Her heart did a double-turn in her chest. She didn't want this. Someday . . . maybe . . . when her house was finished and her career was established. And that would take years. Slowly, she was working her way up the ranks, though she owed thousands of dollars in student loans.

Besides, Keiran lived here. Did that count as a date?

At any rate, the man in question strode to the stove and stirred buttery seafood chowder with a wooden spoon.

"Want a taste?" he asked. "I baked a loaf of soda bread to mop up the soup. It's sitting on the table in a wicker bread basket I found in your cupboard."

"Okay, now you're showing off," she teased.

A chuckle tugged at the corners of his mouth. "Do you like the appliances?" As he stirred, he gestured to the six-burner stove and double oven. "Exactly what you ordered."

She kept herself from staring at him by concentrating on slicing the bread.

"It's impressive," she said. "And the low price Teddy's warehouse supplier gave for the cabinets was a relief. A huge thank you."

She'd taken out a home equity loan in addition to her mortgage to cover the improvements. Although she was realistic enough to understand she wasn't financially equipped to afford a total house renovation, she presumed the kitchen and bathrooms were most important. To save money, they'd concentrated on what Keiran labeled "mid-range renovations." He'd upgraded the countertops and changed the lighting.

"You're welcome," he said. "My pleasure, Desiree."

"A modern kitchen has always been my fantasy."

His gaze locked with hers. "Do you have other . . . fantasies?"

You, she almost said aloud. Swallowing, she pushed her gaze to his Irish whiskey cake baking in the oven. She whistled lightly and adeptly changed the subject. "Tell me again how you managed to get all this done, plus bake a cake."

"I delegate." He lifted a clean spoon from a drawer and scooped several spoonfuls of the chowder into a bowl, then brought the bowl to her for a taste. "I learned the skill from my father. When you own a pub, you can't do everything yourself."

She savored the hearty taste of cream, corn and potatoes blended with tender clams and sweet red peppers. "Mmm," she murmured. "This is delicious."

"A secret family recipe."

"Really? You won't share your recipe?"

"It's been handed down through several generations." He watched her, and his gaze shifted to her mouth. Gently, without warning, he kissed her. "Although I can assure you that the chowder isn't nearly as delicious as you."

The oven timer dinged. Reluctantly, he about-faced and gripped a mitt by the stove. He pulled out the cake and set it on a trivet.

"I'll glaze it in a few days. I'm testing a new glaze recipe." He gestured to the sugar and butter glaze, blended with whiskey, and grabbed a spoon so she could taste it.

"More deliciousness," she said softly.

He didn't mention the kiss. It had been quick and light. And memorable.

They'd fallen into a pattern of spending their evenings together, and her first home-cooked meal in her new home proved a mouthwatering delight. After slicing his cake, still warm from the oven, for a "taste test," they washed and dried Desiree's fine china and crystal by hand.

Afterward, Keiran led her into the living room, where he pointed out the detailing on the marble fireplace. Pausing, he got to his knees and inspected the chimney.

"I thought we'd light a fire again tonight," he said. "Eventually, you'll need a chimney sweep. Until then, the fireplace is safe to use."

"Teddy lit the fireplace several times when he lived here," she said.

Still on his knees, Keiran glanced up at her. "So is that a yes? Aye?" When she nodded, he gestured to the matches on the mantel and she handed them to him.

"The crew and I checked your central heating system too," he said, as he lit a match and checked the draft.

"Don't tell me, let me guess. The entire unit died."

"Aye, but don't worry." He offered a reassuring nod. "Fortunately, a reasonably priced HVAC guy stopped over. He's one of Teddy's crewmen."

"How much does a new HVAC cost?"

"Depends on the square footage of the house." Keiran lit the fire and waited for the logs to burn before standing. "I'd estimate your house is around three thousand square feet."

"You're right on target."

"Then your unit will cost six thousand dollars." He gave her the box of matches, his rough fingers brushing against hers. An electric current passed between them, and she felt that insistent magnetism. Not the youthful yearnings of an adolescent. On the contrary, hers were the dreams of a grown woman.

Instinctively, she pulled her hand away and wandered to the bay window. Outside, the vibrant colors of a Carolina winter day had faded, and twilight merged to darkness. The pavement gleamed with the slickness of a wet evening.

Across the street, Mr. Juno, a graduate student with a young family, had decorated his porch with an impressively lit display. Gold, red, and green boxes, wrapped in dazzling silver ribbons and bows, glowed with Christmas color and light.

She wiped unexpected tears from the corners of her eyes. What was it about Christmas that always got to her? Was it because she'd never experienced a real celebration because of her alcoholic parents? Because she'd never had a truly loving home? When life was bleakest, she'd searched for the warmth of faith and community. The Yuletide season was a time of celebration, just never for her and her sister. At least, not until this past year when Candee had married Teddy, and Desiree had purchased her first home.

"Desiree, I realize you're overwhelmed because of the renovations, but everything will evolve into the home of your dreams. I promise." Keiran came to stand behind her. His voice was sincere and deep, and a heat of longing pulsed in her veins. She blamed it on the romance of the candlelight, the flames flickering in the fireplace, the patter of raindrops on the bay window.

With its poignant reminders of the approaching holiday, she hoped that this house was the answer to her prayers. Finally, her days would be filled with the elusive elation everyone around her seemed to experience.

"Will it?" She wrapped her hands around her arms and didn't turn. He'd see the tears shining in her eyes and he'd ask questions—about her, about her past—that she wasn't prepared to answer.

"Aye. You can trust an Irishman's word."

She saw his reassuring smile reflected in the glass. The expression in his eyes, though, was a mirror of her own. Intense and probing.

And she knew what it meant.

He was beginning to fall for her, just as she was falling for him.

He turned her around to face him, his hands resting loosely on her shoulders. "I'm here for you, and I won't leave until this renovation is finished."

"Thanks. It's just—" A wave of emotion choked her voice, and she couldn't get out any words. Strange. She never lost control. After she and her sister had been passed from one foster home to another, she'd learned to keep her feelings securely bound. Not a single person was interested in two teenage girls with no money and no skills. No one had wanted them.

Not even their own mother and father had cared—so why would anyone else?

A ripple of sadness caused tears to stream down her cheeks. Swiftly, she caught the wetness with her fingertips and avoided Keiran's gaze.

"You're a nobody." The harsh words of one of her foster mothers came to the forefront of Desiree's mind. In her early teens, arriving at a brand-new foster family's home, Desiree had broken a dish by mistake. She'd tried to be useful, drying the dishes. Her foster mother had been furious, reprimanding Desiree about having no respect for other people's things, and shouting that Desiree was a useless girl.

Desiree had cried herself to sleep that night. She remembered the loneliness, the sadness, the sense of never belonging. Feasibly, that was the reason she felt inept in the kitchen.

Keiran watched her closely. He seemed unsure what to say next.

Lightly, he kneaded her shoulders. "Are you okay?" he asked quietly.

Grateful, she accepted his silent comfort, his reassuring presence.

"Of course," she murmured. She averted her gaze and thrust her fingers through her hair, attempting to right her curls into a semblance of order. She hadn't bothered to run a comb through her tangles since she'd gotten home, and probably looked a mess.

I'm not a nobody, she reminded herself. *Lift your chin and compose your features. 'Unsophisticated' and 'unimportant' do not belong in your vocabulary anymore. You're a poised, professional, educated woman.*

Although sometimes, oftentimes—she attempted to convince herself more than anyone else.

Gradually, she realized that Keiran was still staring at her, still had his hands on her shoulders.

She raised her gaze to meet his. "What's the matter?" she asked.

"Nothing." He cleared his throat, his face so near that his clear green eyes reminded her of Irish shamrocks, vivid and vital. "I was thinking that I debated about coming back to Roses and starting over. When I first arrived in Atlanta ten years ago, I assumed I was going to live there forever. And now I'm glad—"

Her heart responded in a slow, steady beat. "Glad about what?"

"And now I'm glad I came back. If I hadn't, I wouldn't have met you."

"I'm glad you came too." He was so close she could feel his sweet breath on her cheek. "I would have spent the week trying to find firewood to keep this fireplace burning."

Clearly amused, he said, "I assume you found enough wood."

"Yes, I brought in a few logs the other night, remember? You had stacked a cord behind the fence."

He didn't respond at first. His amusement was replaced by a slow, simmering intensity.

"So you found the firewood." He lowered his head, his lips meeting hers. "And I found you."

CHAPTER 5

*A*nother week went by, marking the fourteenth day until Christmas.

On Friday evening, Keiran experimented with a new dish, mushroom stroganoff, which delighted Desiree. It was heartening to have a simple, unpretentious meal waiting for her when she came home after an exhausting workday.

Following the meal and clean-up, he shadowed her into the living room carrying two glasses of sparkling cider, plates of another Irish whiskey cake he'd baked, and napkins. He stacked kindling over crumpled newspaper in the fireplace, lit the newspaper first, then added large logs. Satisfied, he took a seat beside her on her gray-fabric sofa.

She gazed at the ten-foot spruce tree he'd purchased. Placed in a corner of the large room, the forest-green pine made a majestic statement.

After visiting several Christmas tree sites the previous weekend, Keiran had maintained that the largest tree on the lot was the ideal size to complement her living room's grand design. The tree seller had assisted Keiran in securing the tree to the roof of his truck, and Keiran had driven back to her house slowly with the tree swinging precariously on top.

Between making creamy eggnog and cranking up Yuletide music on a holiday radio station, Desiree and Keiran had decided on traditional red and green lights and a dazzling angel tree topper. Desiree had insisted on sparkly silver tinsel and a popcorn garland, and Keiran had enhanced the glittery embellishments with an array of wooden toy soldier ornaments he'd carved. The result was vibrant, festive, and in Keiran's words, "a masterpiece."

"I might pick up another tree," he casually said.

"One isn't enough? Completely decorated, this tree is practically taking up half my living room."

He grinned impishly, highlighting his boyish features. "I'd like to sprinkle Christmas all through the house. A small tree for the dining room would look festive."

"Especially because I don't own a dining room table or chairs." Desiree picked up the two glasses of sparkling cider from the end table beside her, handed one to him, and beckoned to the fireplace. "You know, everyone at my law firm is encouraging me to convert my fireplace to gas."

"It's your house and you've worked hard to acquire it. You should do what you want." His encouragement was gracious, and a surge of happiness flowed through her that had nothing to do with the delicious meal, the enchantment of a heartening fire on a cold winter's night, or the approaching holidays.

It was him. It was Keiran.

Seeing him like this, relaxed, wearing dark-wash jeans and a sea-green sweater that hugged his wide shoulders to perfection, he lounged beside her on her ten-year-old sofa. How could she remain unaffected when he was so breathtakingly handsome?

"Yes, this house is mine, and I still can't believe it," she replied. "And . . ." She hesitated, trying not to get ahead of herself. This was just the beginning. This was just a house. He was just a man she loved spending every waking hour with.

Just a man.

"And what?" He sipped his cider, set it on the coffee table, and moved nearer. His male presence was compelling, and a quiver of attraction went through her.

Quickly, she pushed the thoughts away, attempting a composure she didn't quite feel.

"I love the smell of a woodburning fireplace, so I'm passing on the gas insert," she said. "Call me outdated."

He pressed a soft kiss to her cheek and murmured agreement.

She gave him a questioning glance. "Can I ask you something?"

"Sure."

"Why did you leave Roses? You had the world at your feet."

"Did I? Tell that to an impulsive teenager." He reached for his glass and drained the cider. "I'll give you the short version, and please don't be sympathetic."

"And if I am?"

He hesitated, his features unreadable. "Don't be."

"Is my question too personal?"

He gave her a look that said it wasn't. "My father and I didn't agree about what I wanted to do for a living," Keiran said. "So, being reckless and headstrong, I decided my way was best."

"Which was?"

"Moving to Atlanta. I planned to become tops in my profession."

"Doing what?"

"Opening my own restaurant."

"And what was your father's way?"

"He wanted me to become an NFL football player. Trouble is, I didn't have the drive, or the interest, or the talent. I was the tallest on the team, but certainly not the fastest."

"I remember seeing you in your football uniform at the homecoming game I attended," she said. "It was the first time I ever saw you."

He offered an indifferent shrug. "Did you actually watch the game?"

"A little, I think. I don't remember you on the playing field."

"You have an awesome memory."

"Why?"

He hesitated. Her question sat in the space between them.

"Because I hardly ever played and frankly, I was relieved, although I knew my father was disappointed." Regret shadowed Keiran's gaze. "The football coach put me on the team to please my father because our pub was one of the sponsors. Soon after that game, I quit."

"I caught glimpses of you in the high school halls. Quitting didn't seem to affect your popularity."

A statement, not a question.

"I suppose." He shrugged. "Although popularity is a difficult word to define, especially when it's used to categorize people."

Wistfully, she gazed at the twinkling tree lights, the shades of red and green belonging to a simpler time, offset by the muted tones of the rustic toy soldiers. Could Christmas be celebrated without glossy bulbs and the sophisticated backdrop of her living room?

Of course.

As a child, well, she had certainly longed for Christmas, although it had never been celebrated at her house. Beer cans littered the floor and food was scarce. Christmas was a luxury her parents couldn't afford, and Santa Claus had never visited.

As an adult, she couldn't imagine life without Christmas. She loved the gift-giving and feasting, the religious celebration, the sacredness of the special holiday.

Profoundly moved by a feeling she couldn't explain, she blinked as her vision blurred. "In my childhood, I wanted a real home so badly—the picket fence, a cute puppy sitting by a welcoming fire burning in the grate, surrounded by people who loved me. When my mother was well and not drinking, she said she envisioned herself as a grand lady living on a beautiful estate." Desiree's lungs and throat felt sore, and she swallowed. "Considering our two-room shack, my mother had quite the imagination."

Tears pricked Desiree's eyes and she wiped them away. She scolded herself for dredging up emotional memories, better kept sealed in a safe corner of her mind. Inhaling, she sat erect. "So what you're saying is that at the end of your senior year, you took off because you didn't get the opportunity to play on the high school team?"

"C'mon, Desiree. Do I seem as shallow as all that? I said I quit football."

"Sorry." She paused. "I mean, you lived in one of the most expensive communities in Roses. I would have given the world to grow up in your shoes."

"It's never just about the stunning home and expensive neighborhood," he said softly. "There's more to a person's story than what's on the surface. I went to Atlanta to pursue my dream, got sidetracked, and failed."

* * *

DESIREE TIPPED her face back to view him. He expected to see disapproval on her beautiful features. After all, he'd had everything and given it all up, while she'd had nothing.

"You're young and can achieve anything you want." A positive smile played on her lips. "Also, you're one of the most talented people I've ever met. But look, we can talk about something else if you're uncomfortable."

"I don't mind our discussion, Desiree." He nodded his assent.

He'd been undecided about what to say, about his past, his future, although being with her lightened his concerns. With Desiree, everything would be okay.

He realized she was watching him, apparently waiting for him to continue.

He put his hands on his knees and focused on the wood sparking in the fireplace, the frosted pine cones and garland adorning the wide wooden mantel. The stylish adornments gave the room a celebratory spirit.

"My father discouraged me from what I wanted to do with my life," he said. "I intended to own a restaurant. Therefore, I rebelled."

"And here I thought you wanted to be a carpenter," she teased.

He pushed out a sigh. "I like woodworking, although my passion is the restaurant business. It's how I grew up. I love the hustle and bustle, the busy dinner hours, the scents of shepherd's pie, potato and leek soup, and thyme complementing my parents' famous corned beef recipe."

She gazed at him, openly interested. "I'm surprised."

"Mind if I ask why?"

Her unpretentious warmth set her apart from any woman he'd ever known. Was that what captivated him about her? Besides her vivaciousness, her sensational figure, and her utterly polished appearance when she came home each evening.

That is, until she pulled her hair from her severe bun and let the blond waves fall down her back. Then she looked irresistible.

She studied his face with a concerned frown. "Because most parents would have been thrilled their kid wanted to follow in their footsteps."

"Mine weren't. They insisted that owning an eating establishment was too difficult because of the long hours, which included early mornings, late evenings, and most holidays." He forked a corner of cake on his plate and chewed around the lump in his throat. "Did you know only one third of all restaurants succeed?"

"I've heard it's one in ten."

He paused, forming his words while he stared at the pile of sheetrock marking the next space in her home to be renovated—the small study attached to the living room via French doors.

"Living in Roses, you probably heard talk that my parents lived beyond their means," he said. "At first they did well and their pub was a huge success. Sadly, they didn't plan for the lean years."

"Yes. I heard." Despite her polite nod, he could tell she knew more than she let on. It was no secret his parents had neglected the pub after his departure, eventually forcing it to close. Even their most loyal customers could no longer endure the erratic schedule and so-so meals.

"They moved to Ireland soon afterward. Dublin," he clarified, briefly closing his eyes. "Although they reached out to me, I never flew across the pond to see them except to attend their funerals years later. They died within a day of each other. In the end, discouragement broke their hearts."

"Keiran."

He opened his eyes. Her gaze held his.

"I'm genuinely sorry. You realize none of this is your fault," she said. "My parents died while serving sentences for several robberies. They were alcoholics."

He felt a twist of sadness in his gut. For her. For him.

She was so sweet, so vulnerable, so totally gorgeous, he was torn between kissing her and commiserating on their losses.

He decided on the latter, and enfolded her into his arms.

Would kissing her mess things up? They got along brilliantly, although he often felt off balance. Could they keep their relationship casual, yet professional, living under the same roof, coming to terms with their attraction? His thoughts scattered, although he already knew the answer.

Nope.

With Desiree, his feelings were too deep to be casual.

He gazed at her mouth and cupped her chin in his hands, forcing her to gaze at him.

What would it be like to kiss her again and again?

Nope, his conscience chimed in a second time. She'd made her intentions known without saying a word. This was a business relationship.

Then why did life with her seem spot-on? Was the universe telling him something—bringing him back to Roses after all this time to open a pub, and bringing him to her? He was at the tail end of one profession, embarking on another. And she was the bridge in between. Or was she more? Perhaps she was the missing link . . . the real reason he was here.

She drew a sharp breath. "Keiran, I—"

He lowered his head and brushed his lips against hers. If she rejected him, he'd deal with it.

She didn't.

With a whisper of acquiescence, she twined her hands around his neck and pressed her delicate body closer.

He shivered. "Do you know how many times I've wanted to kiss you these past two weeks?" His hands slid down her back. "I mean, really kiss you?"

"Then what were you waiting for?" came her teasing reply.

He hadn't planned to spend Friday evening kissing her, he told his intrusive conscience. He'd planned on conversing with her, bantering with her, comparing recipes and paint samples.

Or had he? Because devoting every minute of his free time to her felt like the most natural thing in the world.

Slowly, tenderly, he took her lips in a lingering, passionate kiss.

Her cell phone chirped.

She always had it near in case one of her clients experienced a family emergency. For a second, she hesitated, then drew away from him. She picked up her phone and read the screen. "It's Candee," she said. "She and Teddy and Joseph want to stop over. Candee is helping me plan my Christmas Eve dinner menu."

"Tonight? Christmas isn't for a while yet." Keiran couldn't hide his disappointment. He wanted to spend the evening alone with Desiree. "When? If they've started walking, they'll be here in two minutes."

"They're still at their house." Desiree tapped a text on her phone. "I'll tell her tomorrow is better. Besides, I'm electing you as head preparer for Christmas Eve dinner. You're much better suited to the task, so you should be the one to talk with her."

He brought Desiree back into his arms, fingering the lustrous texture of her hair, breathing in the scent of vanilla and a fresh winter breeze.

"If you'd like," he said, "I'll teach you everything I know."

"Didn't you already offer me that once? Umm, no thanks. You know way too much about too many things—carpentry, decorating, football—"

He laughed. "I'm hardly an expert on anything, especially football."

Her gorgeous eyes sparkled. "Keiran, I hear you play your guitar every night when I'm in bed. You're also an excellent musician."

He'd forgotten her bedroom was directly below his attic apartment. "Do I disturb you?"

"On the contrary. You play really well."

He placed his hand along the curve of her velvety cheek. "Shall I serenade you sometime, my stunning Queen Anne?"

"You sound like a chivalrous knight, although I'm no queen." She grinned. "You're confusing *me* with my Queen-Anne style *home*."

"You're not a queen?" In exaggerated surprise, he splayed his fingers across his chest.

She laughed. "The bay window and spindle work in my home are—"

"Exquisite. Just like you."

"Hardly." The color rose in her cheeks. She didn't meet his gaze, instead looking toward the wavy glass windowpanes splattered with rain. "Most people define me as a workaholic."

"There's nothing wrong with being a workaholic. I prefer the term 'overachiever,' which is an admirable trait."

She shifted and pulled her blue cardigan closer around her shoulders. "Oftentimes, my work gets in the way of the important things in my life—family, friends, and good times."

"I've been accused of the same."

She nodded, agreeing. "I've always believed my career

came first. I've analyzed myself because I've read that understanding the problem is the best way to heal."

"Overachieving isn't a problem, Desiree."

"In some ways it is." Her smooth forehead knit into a pensive frown. "Candee and I have discussed our childhood. More often than not, we were neglected and now we're trying to compensate."

"By buying dilapidated houses?"

"It seems like that, doesn't it?"

"A little." He tried to think of words to encourage her, because he was picturing her as a young girl with fine blond hair and delicate features, helpless and alone. He realized he hadn't spoken for several moments and reminded himself to keep the conversation going. "And what else did your discussion with your sister uncover?" he asked.

Desiree slumped against the couch. "We were parentless children, raising ourselves the best we knew how."

"You had a mother and father."

"They were absent even when they were around. And the parent-child roles were reversed. Candee and I took care of them."

Gently, he slid his arm around her shoulders. "Candee and I spoke one afternoon, and she mentioned your last set of foster parents became your forever family."

"Yes, they're good people." The pensiveness in Desiree's gaze stirred his heart. "They love Candee and me, and email us regularly since they moved away. I'm grateful they came into our lives and offered love and stability."

But still.

She didn't say it, despite the words hanging in the air. She was trying to make up for the negligence in her childhood by . . . by what? Overachieving?

Something about the desolation on her face made him want to do whatever possible to shape her world for the better. She had a successful career, a lovely home, a caring sister.

And she had his heart.

He paused.

His heart?

Aye—and the realization took a firm place in his gut. He'd been half in love with her since the first day they'd met and she'd slammed the front door in his face, then teased him about talking to her porch.

With great effort, he stopped himself from repeating his thoughts aloud, although the shout-in-his-face awareness of their chemistry made him catch his breath. He liked being with her, conversing and comforting her.

No, it was too soon. He wasn't seeking a romance after his breakup with Patricia.

Better to keep things light. Besides, he didn't plan on staying in Desiree's home much longer. As soon as the holidays were over and her house was in better order, he planned to rent an apartment in town.

Move on.

But now, things were different. Fixing her home, spending memorable evenings beside her, anticipating the joyous holiday, and yes, discussing their childhoods—with all the hurts, all the dreams—was the most natural thing in the world. They were content, and he felt as if he'd known her his entire life. She'd given him a peephole into her past, and he'd done the same.

He cradled her face between his fingers, stroking an errant tear from her cheek.

"I'm grateful you came into my life. Or rather, I'm grateful I came into yours."

The tenderness in her soft eyes and lips tore down his defenses. She sparked a yearning in him he barely recognized, reminding him that there was more to life than successful pubs and impeccable carpentry. And these feelings were new. Not even with Patricia had he felt this utter sense of fulfillment.

His mouth descended on hers. She followed his lead, sliding her hands down his shoulders. Her lips were warm and smooth as velvet, tasting of sweet caramel and Irish whiskey cake.

He told himself to go slowly. His lips said otherwise. Their breaths heated the air around them.

An eternity later, the kiss ended.

As they gazed at each other, longing shown from her intense blue eyes.

Along with another emotion.

Wariness?

"You are beautiful," he whispered. "And that was—" How could he find a phrase to describe it?

"Not a good idea," she said.

"You're kidding!" He jerked his head back. "That's what you were thinking?"

"Keiran, we have a business arrangement. Anything else will only complicate things."

He was still searching for an accurate description of their kiss, while she was headed to the other side of the couch.

As usual, she was spot on. They'd only just met.

"Then will you go on a date with me?" he asked.

"After what I just said?"

"I understand you want to take our relationship slowly and I respect your wishes. Let's start with a real date."

She moistened her lips, just enough to captivate him. "A date where? To the kitchen?"

"I was thinking somewhere a little farther." He laughed. "Lunch or dinner in one of the town's restaurants?" His plan was to get to know her. Sure, he was living in her house and familiar with her daily routine, but it wasn't enough. He wanted to learn more.

She spoke what was on her mind, and she was interesting to be around. She was a brave woman. A Christian possessing a kind spirit. Strong, yet gentle. Courageous, yet yielding. Open, yet unassuming.

And these attributes fascinated him.

"Will you play your guitar for me?" she asked.

He widened his eyes at the unexpected question. "Maybe later," he said.

She granted him an audacious smile. "Please, Keiran?"

He knew he could never deny her anything.

Within minutes, he tromped to the attic and reappeared with his father's acoustic guitar. He tuned the strings and strummed a few chords. "What do you want to hear?"

She sat erect, glancing at him, then his guitar. "Something Christmassy."

He plucked the melody of "Jingle Bells" while she sang the lyrics, her voice light and in tune.

When he finished the final refrain, he broke into the beginning of "Don't Stop Believin'."

"That's the song you play in the attic," she said. "I couldn't place the group."

"Journey," he supplied. "Often, my father played the piece after our pub closed for the evening. My mother used to complain it was the only song he knew."

"I read somewhere the composer of that song was inspired by his father's words of encouragement."

"Aye, and the song held special significance for my father, also," Keiran said. "He came to this town disillusioned after he wasn't picked in the NFL draft, and rose to success when he met my mother and they opened the pub. Sadly, the pub closed when he ran out of funds."

"Why, when the pub was so popular at first?" Waiting, she

surveyed him, giving him the kindhearted expression he was coming to know so well.

"Maybe because all along my father was disheartened. Although he worked hard, his initial dreams of becoming a professional football player didn't pan out," Keiran said. "And then, of course, I left."

He shifted, silent for a beat.

"Did this guitar belong to your father?" Desiree asked, breaking the silence.

"Aye. He bequeathed it to me in his will. This and his abandoned Irish pub in town."

"So you own O'Malley's?"

"There's nothing to own. It's my father's broken legacy. This beat-up guitar, an abandoned pub, and a trading card autographed by a famous football player my father met while he was training."

"Hold on. Is the card worth anything?"

"I checked a few years ago because my former roommate, Georges, works at a pawn shop in Atlanta. The card is a 1976 Topps card, and the player didn't sign many, so the estimated worth is around fifteen thousand dollars."

"Certainly, it's a card to treasure and hold on to."

"And it brings back memories, both good and bad." Keiran released a deep breath and set the guitar to the side. "When I attended my parents' funerals in Dublin, I'm ashamed to tell you I was angry and bitter. My cousin William reassured me that although I wasn't there for them, they were always in my heart."

She squeezed his hand. "I know."

"I didn't walk away from my parents because I didn't care. I walked away because I didn't know if I had it in me to live up to my father's expectations. I knew I couldn't be a pro football player, so I disengaged. I found myself in a state of panic."

Caught in the spell of her captivating blue eyes, he placed his arm around her shoulders.

"Go on," she prompted. "You mentioned your cousin William."

He didn't want to spoil their evening by speaking about sadness. Attempting to recover their former gaiety, he replied with an expressive beam. "William lives in Ireland and has the proverbial Irish philosophy. He connects with people and believes forgiveness is most important. It's called Irish craic."

Desiree shot him a quizzical look. "I'm not following."

"Irish craic is fun and good times. William is humorous and witty and earnestly interested in others. You'll like him."

"I'll like him . . . when? I've never visited Ireland nor do I plan to in the future."

"Someday."

Silence lingered between them.

"With my investment in this house, an overseas trip isn't possible," she quietly replied.

"Never say never," Keiran advised. "My father threatened he wouldn't take me back if I ever appeared in Roses again. And here I am, not certain if I'm moving forward or backward, only knowing I was wrong to leave in the first place."

"Don't feel guilty." She touched his arm. "That's life, isn't it? We make mistakes, we brush ourselves off, and we go on."

"Do we ever forgive ourselves?" His voice came as a whisper.

"It's Christmas, the season of forgiveness," she said. "And the answer is an emphatic yes."

CHAPTER 6

"Tomorrow is the bake-off contest," Keiran reminded Desiree as she entered the foyer.

"It's written in bold on my calendar." Desiree set down her briefcase and joked, "How could I ever forget?"

Finally, it was Friday, the last day of another grueling work week.

"I'm glad to see you, gorgeous." He helped her off with her sunny-yellow raincoat and took her in his arms for a long kiss.

He'd been waiting for her at the foot of the stairs, the sparse lighting glinting over his hair. Thick, wavy, and midnight-black. And he looked oh so incredibly handsome.

He was dressed in a cotton chambray shirt unbuttoned at the neckline, showing a deep vee at his throat. His denims were well fitted. Tall, well-built, and confident, he sent her pulse racing. His physique would stop any woman in her tracks.

She linked her fingers around his nape, thinking all the while that he was the type of man she could easily fall in love with.

Wow. Whoa.

Love was the doorway to sorrow, and she'd had enough disappointment to know better than to risk her heart again.

Still, Keiran might be worth the risk. It was pure bliss having his strong, secure arms around her. Love was a quiet, joyous peace with no barriers. Love was exactly that with this man.

For an instant, she squeezed her eyes closed. *No. No. No.*

As much as she cared for him, they could never be together. Although he was talented and creative, he hadn't decided on a career for himself. Cooking or carpentry?

After her chaotic childhood, she knew stability was her primary goal.

Her feelings warred ferociously, and she considered telling him how much she cared, and what she most feared if they were to go forward in their relationship—that he could easily pick up and leave at any time.

Stability. Stability.

Numbly, she pulled from his arms.

He watched her, his gaze penetrating. He was always in tune with her emotions. "Is everything okay?"

"Of course." She dragged her gaze from his and focused on the authentic tin ceiling tile he'd replaced in the foyer. The edges were trimmed neatly and seamlessly overlapped.

Before she could remark on his excellent workmanship, he brushed a kiss across her temple. "Are you ready for an amazing time tomorrow, gorgeous?"

Gorgeous. No one had ever called her gorgeous. Profoundly touched, she brushed away a tear before his perceptive green-eyed gaze leveled on her. She wasn't used to praises, to his unbending good nature, and didn't know how to react.

"I'm ready to win the cake contest." She gave him her best challenging gaze while she shook lingering droplets from her black pencil skirt. Raindrops had chased each other across her car's windshield all the way home. If only it would snow to complete the holiday season.

"We'll see about that." He hung her raincoat in the foyer closet, then laid a callused hand on her cheek. His touch was reassuring. "So how was your day?"

"Demanding, as usual." Without prompting, she lifted her face for a kiss. "I'm delighted I only have one more work week to go before Christmas. You?"

"Hectic. The study off the living room has been sheetrocked and sanded, and the guys left some of their tools there. All you have to do is choose a paint color."

"My specialty."

"That's my girl." He grinned, drawing her to him. "Desiree, I have a confession."

The way he said her name, low and husky, resembled a loving caress.

Her gaze narrowed on his grin. "What is it?" That feeling, that draw, grew stronger each time they were together. That little flip of exhilaration.

"For the first time in a long time, I'm anticipating an amazing holiday." The sentiment in his voice melted her heart. "And it's all because of you."

"I am too." She was helpless to resist him, moving automatically into his arms. "And I'm glad to be home."

"To see me," he clarified.

"Indeed."

"Did you think about me today?"

"Often," she admitted. *Very often.*

"Good. I thought about you too. See how much we are alike? We both love Christmas and we both love—" He bent his head and kissed her deeply, thoroughly.

Both love what?

Each other?

She'd spent far too long trying to figure out men and relationships, and reveled in his kisses instead. She couldn't pull away from him even if she wanted to.

Excuse me, her conscience kicked in. *You're losing your focus.*

Yes, well, because around him she could hardly think. She wasn't good at this—dating—the entire courting process. Her career had always been most important.

Now she wished for more, wished for him.

He'd never mentioned a girlfriend, dismissing Desiree's inquiry with a wave of his hand. He'd explained that he'd dated in Atlanta, although no one worth mentioning. She'd been relieved he hadn't had a serious affair of the heart, although she'd told him about Scott, her ex. She hadn't said much, but apparently just enough, because Keiran had remarked he was sorry she'd been hurt.

His lips twitched as he drew her closer. "I'm glad you're glad to see me."

"Is that proper English?"

His lips moved within an inch of hers. "It is now."

She felt her cheeks flush as she gazed at his ruggedly handsome face.

"Who is judging our cakes?" she asked.

"Excellent change of subject. What cakes?" Smirking, he took her hand and led her to the kitchen. "First, have a cuppa tea with me. I brewed loose leaf tea using a strainer." He pulled out a stool for her, then poured her a steaming cup. "Sugar? Milk?"

"No thanks." She savored a swallow. Loose leaf tea was definitely more flavorful than tea bags. Again, she asked, "So, who is judging our cakes?"

"Several ladies on the town board, and some guy named Rob who owns a chain of bakeries in Florida," Keiran said.

She gasped and set down her cup. "Rob, as in Rob's Marvelous Muffins?"

"Aye." Keiran claimed the seat across from her. "Is he famous or something?"

"He certainly is famous, at least in Miami." Desiree rested her elbows on the island. "Rob is Teddy's mentor and a good friend. He lent Teddy the money for his start-up real estate business. Rob wants to expand his bakeries to another state and is considering Roses because Teddy and Candee are here."

The subject came up again an hour later, after they'd dined on a savory beef and Guinness stew brimming with carrots, potatoes, onions, and chunks of beef.

"I met him when Teddy and Candee got married." Desiree scraped plates while Keiran loaded the dishwasher. "Rob is great fun. You'll like him. Plus, you're both restauranteurs." She paused. "Is that a word?"

An amused gleam lit Keiran's eyes. "Absolutely, and it means the owner or manager of a restaurant. Although technically, I never owned a restaurant. My parents owned the pub."

"Same difference. And you own the pub now."

"True."

She finished wiping down the kitchen counter. "Who else is participating in the baking contest?"

"It's open to everyone. From what I gather, the town will set up tables for our cakes and an awning is being erected in case of bad weather." A lazy smile graced his face. "By the way, Candee is baking a Christmas cake."

"She's participating? To my knowledge, she's never turned on an oven in her life."

"The cake is a surprise. Or rather, it was a surprise until I spilled the beans." A sheepish grin crossed his lips as he gave an apologetic shrug. "Rob flew in from Miami and is staying with Candee and Teddy. Word is that Rob is baking the cake."

Desiree's competitive spirit jumped into true form. "So I'm competing against Rob, who bakes for a living, and you, the guy who's been basting an Irish whiskey cake for four days?"

He chuckled. "The odds are in your favor, though."

"How?"

"You're the prettiest." He stepped behind her and wrapped his arms around her waist. Nuzzling his lips against her neck, he murmured, "Are you certain you have to work next week?"

"Yes, if you want to get paid."

"I work for next to nothing," he joked. "I want a raise."

She laughed, shook her head, and tugged from his grasp. "Not happening."

That morning, she'd driven with a smile on her face all the way to her law firm in the middle of town. Keiran's parents' pub, O'Malley's, was located a few blocks away. Years earlier, the building had been abandoned and boarded up. A "For Lease" sign had hung on the door for ages.

As she'd walked from her car to her office, she'd tried to stop thinking about Keiran.

The more she'd tried, the more she'd failed. And now, another week had passed and Christmas was closing in. So much had happened since he'd arrived. And it was all good. So, so good.

He was a miracle worker, transforming her home into an enchanting, welcoming place. He spent hours in the kitchen after Teddy's crew knocked off for the day, and often sent Candee his baked goods, which she, Teddy, and Joseph enthusiastically praised.

Each evening, Desiree finished her last client's filing with an eye on the clock, counting the minutes until she could see Keiran.

And tomorrow, a week before Christmas, she and Keiran were participating in a baking contest.

She shook her head and added a grin. Her dashing Irishman, her one-of-a-kind Renaissance man, was as equally at home measuring and marking drywall as he was experimenting with a new recipe, or strumming a melody on his guitar.

She closed her eyes and thanked God. During the most blessed season of the year, when she was worried and despondent, He had brought Keiran into her life.

Certainly, she had much to be thankful for. She was no longer stuck in a bad situation with an ex who didn't care about her.

Have faith, her chaplain had preached numerous times.

But how?

She had wondered—as an orphaned teen, as a grown woman with a broken heart.

God had seemed invisible, but He hadn't been. He'd been working for her good all along.

* * *

THE FOLLOWING morning dawned bright and chilly, and sunlight shone through the wavy glass bay window in the living room.

Keiran and Desiree relished their first cup of coffee for the day. Even when their mornings began before dawn, he brewed a fresh pot of coffee and prepared a hearty cooked breakfast. He loved cooking for her.

"You're staring at me again," Desiree said.

"Am I?" He set down his cup. "I can't help it. You're gorgeous." That figure, dressed in flattering faux-leather leggings, suede ankle boots, and a creamy tweed sweater. And those cornflower-blue eyes, even more fascinating than her legs.

Delight quickened inside him. He'd come to Roses to pick up what he'd abandoned ten years before. A timeworn pub. He'd assumed he'd go it alone, far from Atlanta and Patricia.

Except he wasn't alone anymore.

With Desiree, he instinctively felt a sense of coming home and knew that embarking on this journey without her was unthinkable.

He openly admired her as she picked up their empty cups. Her beauty was stunning.

"I'll finish clearing," he offered, coming to his feet.

She held up a hand. "Keiran, I may not be the world's greatest cook, but I certainly know how to keep things tidy. Please let me do a little something to repay all you've done."

"Okay." His gaze shifted to those figure-hugging leggings before doubling back to her face.

She regarded him with her lovely, shiny eyes and smiled.

He thought about her throughout his day while he multi-tasked, installing molding, cutting and sawing wood, and picking up debris after the other crews clocked out.

She'd asked him once if he ever slept, and he'd teased that he obviously didn't require as much sleep as she did.

"Ready for the contest?" he asked, following her to the kitchen where their cakes sat on the counter.

"I feel anything but ready." She set her coffee cup in the sink. "Otherwise, yes, sure."

He helped her on with her cobalt-blue coat. She'd worn her blond hair loose, and she ran her fingers through the ends in that graceful, unassuming way of hers.

They placed their finished cakes on cake boards, then packed them in sturdy, clean covered boxes.

Desiree insisted on them both driving their vehicles to

the event, as she had to pick up a bag of groceries at her favorite green grocer when they were finished. He drove behind her car and parked in an empty parking space. As they got out of their vehicles, Desiree remarked that she felt motivated by seeing all the small-town celebrations.

Her pistachio cake, garnished with powdered sugar and maraschino cherries, presented an eye-catching display. Although Keiran's Irish whiskey cake didn't appear as vibrant, his baking process had taken longer. He'd carefully wrapped the cake, refrigerated it for three days and added a glaze on the fourth.

The first prize for the event was an apron, stamped with a red and green *Kiss Me, It's Christmas* motif.

He and Desiree set their cakes on a long table beneath an expansive white canvas awning on the green. The judges provided cake stands that elevated the cakes to a magnificent new level.

"I'll be wearing that apron when I cook the Christmas Eve dinner you volunteered me to prepare," Keiran baited.

He expected a teasing rejoinder, and she didn't disappoint.

She leaned toward him and joked, "You'll be wearing that apron because I let you *borrow* it. And don't forget we eat dinner at six o'clock sharp."

He gave a shout of laughter as they wended through the crowd and perused the food kiosks. Near the judges' stand she halted in midstep. Spotting Candee and Teddy, Desiree took hold of Keiran's hand and rushed over to them.

As planned, Candee and Teddy were manning a booth distributing free hot chocolate and candy canes to the participants and attendees. Nearby, Joseph skipped and played tag in an adjacent play area with a couple of new friends.

Teddy had confided to Keiran that the boy had changed

significantly since moving to Roses. His demeanor was perky, his gaze gleaming with delight.

"Uncle Teddy, watch me!" the boy called. He'd settled down to working with his playmates to build a sandcastle in the sandbox.

"There's Rob." Desiree waved gaily to an older, bald-headed man, then brought Keiran over to meet him.

"Hello, I'm Keiran O'Malley, Desiree's carpenter." Keiran extended his hand as they met. "I've heard a lot about you."

"I'm Rob the baker." The man beamed good-naturedly. "Although you've got me beat because you're the baker *and* the carpenter. Do you also make candles?"

Keiran blinked.

"You know, the butcher, the baker, and the candlestick—" Rob laughed heartily, gripped Keiran's hand, and vigorously shook it. "An old nursery rhyme. Mother Goose and whatnot. Never mind. You're too young for rhymes, and I'm too old to be able to recite them correctly."

Keiran nodded. What was Rob getting at? "Sorry, I'm not following."

He glanced at Desiree, who grinned and shrugged. "Rob's not talking about nursery rhymes," she said. "He means—"

"I've heard about your baking and carpentry skills, Keiran," Rob interrupted. "Teddy expounded at length. You're good at one, exceptional at the other."

"That's a fair assessment," Keiran replied. "Should I ask which one is better?"

Rob checked out Keiran's Irish whiskey cake, set on a white platter and topped with spiced chopped pecans. "Your baking won by a landslide. Can you cook too?"

"Lots of down-home food including corned beef and cabbage and shepherd's pie. Although I like experimenting with new recipes, Guinness stew is my specialty."

"I can attest to that," Desiree said with a Mona Lisa smile.

"Excellent. You can experiment on me anytime. I told Teddy I was going on a diet." Rob patted his protruding stomach. "Though I've decided to wait until the New Year. Maybe my local gym will have a special."

Keiran laughed. He liked Rob's responses. He was a good, honest guy. "My parents owned a pub in town. They served authentic Irish food and homemade desserts."

"Oh?" Rob gave the surrounding streets a once-over. "Which one?"

"Walking distance from here. The pub's been empty a long time, although it was once busy with customers lining up outside the door when we opened for the day."

As Keiran pointed in the pub's direction, Desiree and Rob followed his gaze.

"Is the place available for rent?" Rob asked.

Desiree placed a hand on Keiran's arm. "The pub's been boarded up for years, although Keiran inherited it from his parents."

Keiran shifted. She was telling Rob more than he needed to know.

He and Desiree had visited the pub a few days earlier. Peering through grimy windows, he'd been anxious to assess the place when he'd first arrived, although he'd delayed seeing it, wanting to view the property with her, hesitant about coming to grips with the fact that his parents were no longer alive.

With a tight throat, he'd asked Candee, who was a realtor, to install new door locks. The permit had been provided to him, as the owner, when his parents had passed away. Because the pub was historically significant to the town, O'Malley's had been grandfathered in.

As he'd feared, memories had assailed him when he'd stepped inside—the sticky spilled beer beneath his boots, the heady smell of buttery Irish scones, the pennants from the local sports teams hanging on the timbered walls.

The charm and character of a timeless design.

And he was overwhelmed by his emotions—regret, sadness. And aye, excitement.

Fear of failure, fear of not trying. Was he capable of upholding the legacy of his parents' beloved pub?

Although he didn't have enough capital, should he dare hope he could reopen it? The huge project entailed purchasing inventory, cleaning the place, and passing inspections. Since working for Desiree, he'd saved most of his weekly salary. He'd said goodbye to Atlanta with limited funds, anxious to get away from Patricia.

His Atlanta pastor had once said that if you've gone through a storm, then it was a sure sign that God would be coming. Although Keiran's faith was strong, he'd been skeptical. A storm was difficult. How could it make a person stronger?

More important, was he entitled to success after abandoning his parents? In Roses, in Ireland, they had missed him.

He was selfish. He was undeserving.

He looked past Rob and Desiree. "I own nothing," he said.

"You own a piece of Roses' past." Desiree leaned against him. "Someday, you'll make your pub whole again."

Your pub. *Whole.* Like him, with Desiree by his side.

He knew her well enough to know she'd used the terms on purpose, to give him hope, to support his dream.

"Tell the vendors to start showing up again, and get the word out to former customers that you're planning on reopening," Rob put in. "Then roll up your sleeves and get to work."

Keiran glanced from Rob's firm expression to Desiree's unwavering one.

That day, after viewing the pub, they'd held hands on their way back to his truck.

"I want to make a difference in Roses," he'd said softly.

"So I've heard."

"Once the pub is up and running, I'd like to offer a free meal and worship service every Sunday for the homeless in the community."

"I'll help you." A radiant smile brightened her lovely face as she matched his strong steps. "You're the son who wants to set things right again."

"I feel I must do this."

"Good. This is the place, and this is the time."

The quiet tenderness in her tone was all the reassurance he longed for.

Besides, he loved it here in Roses. The slower pace of life, the sound of children's laughter, the colorful display of twinkling lights around each shop's window.

As Keiran conversed with Rob, gaining insights into running an up-and-coming restaurant, Keiran's questions multiplied.

Desiree gave his hand an encouraging squeeze, excusing herself to go chat with Candee at the hot chocolate stand.

"I have a question," Keiran said to Rob. "Can you guide me?"

"Certainly." Rob's cellphone chirped. "Excuse me. One minute." He held up a hand in apology, pulled out his phone from his colorful plaid jacket, and read the text.

He sent a brief reply. "It's always something in the restaurant business." Rob rolled his eyes and swore under his breath as he clicked off the phone and stuffed it back into his pocket. "One of our customers in Miami complained the service at the bakery was too slow. An employee called in sick and we were short-handed."

"How did you handle it?"

"I'm sending the customer a coupon for a free box of muffins, along with a heartfelt apology. In my opinion, the customer is always right"—he chortled—"even when they aren't."

"Will you hire more employees?" Keiran asked.

"Yes, especially with the busy Christmas season heating up. I own a half-dozen bakeries in the Miami area, so when I think about expanding, I'll employ someone reliable who knows the business." Rob motioned toward Teddy, who was talking with Candee and Desiree while refilling the five-gallon hot chocolate container with water. "I hoped to stay in Roses a couple more days. However, between getting married, formally adopting Joseph, plus renovating his new home, Teddy's got enough to do." He glanced in the direction of the judges' stand. "At any rate, I'll head to Miami tomorrow. What's your question, by the way? Do you need start-up money for your pub?" He dug into his chinos pocket and pulled out his wallet.

"Thank you, but no thank you." Keiran motioned to the wad of hundred-dollar bills Rob extracted, and shook his head.

"Well, from what I hear, you have an excellent work ethic. When the times comes, toss your pride aside and phone me."

"Thanks." Keiran hesitated. "If I ever do, I'll consider it a loan. I'll pay every penny back."

"No worries, as long as your pub becomes a Roses sensation. How's the place looking?"

"Like it's crying out for lots of TLC."

"So, what's your question?" Rob glanced at Desiree, his blue eyes shrewd. "If it concerns a gorgeous blond lawyer who bakes pistachio cakes, then I'm no expert. Inquiries about dating women should be posed to men who have successfully dated them."

"Meaning that, from your experience, women split after the first date?"

"Meaning that, from my experience, women are a full-time job."

"Desiree's not like that." Keiran gazed at her while she and Candee served steaming cups of hot chocolate to a group of teenagers. In the midst of conversation with her sister, she combed the green with her gaze, found him, and gave him a secret smile. He glimpsed the fire smoldering in her eyes and drew a wobbly breath. She was an attraction pulling him to her like a magnet.

Realizing Rob's piercing gaze was fixed on him, Keiran carefully composed his features. "She's brainy and successful and we've become good friends."

"And that's not all." Rob stuffed his wallet back into his pocket and directed a meaningful glance toward her.

"Look, we're taking it slow."

"Uh huh." A skeptical smirk crossed Rob's round face. "Do you want my unasked-for advice?"

Keiran shrugged. "Sure. Why not?"

"If she's anything like her sister Candee, don't let her get away." Rob's smirk widened into a grin. "Besides, I can see that she's already got you smitten. Are you up for the challenge of starting a new life and a new career with a new wife? That's a lot of new."

Rob was dead-on. Aye, Keiran was ready. He embraced challenges and he cared about Desiree. More than cared. He was in love with her. He was in love with her snappy humor, intellect, and especially her openness.

"We'll talk further." Rob hung a left when his name was called at the judging stand. Over his shoulder, he said, "I hope I gave you some food for thought. Get it? Food?" He chuckled at his own joke, then added, "Seriously, I hope I answered your question."

Keiran paused, wondering how he'd started to ask Rob one question—whether Irish whiskey cake could be baked in a jar—and ended up receiving guidance about dating and romance. Although the dating advice Rob had offered was far more significant than a whiskey cake.

Don't let her get away.

Desiree gave Keiran a thoughtful glance as she approached him with two cups of hot chocolate. "Well, you two were deep in conversation."

Keiran accepted a steaming, frothy cup topped with miniature marshmallows. "He's extremely knowledgeable and I'm fortunate to have met him."

"He knows the restaurant business and he can give you lots of excellent tips." She sipped her hot chocolate. "He's a blessing to Teddy and Candee, and stepped in many times to help with Joseph after Teddy's brother Christian died."

"I didn't know."

"The pain of losing Christian was almost Teddy's undoing. Candee helped him begin a new chapter of his life here in Roses."

"Teddy's never talked about it." Keiran was beginning to realize that Desiree's sister and brother-in-law were genuinely good people who cared about others above themselves. He'd also noted the camaraderie between Rob and Teddy as Rob paused in his judging duties to joke with Teddy.

Desiree set her cup down on a tray. "Loss is always hard. Nonetheless, the certainty of a blessed future is guaranteed through faith in God."

With a glance at the holiday festival taking place—the face painter and balloon artist for the children, the four-piece brass band playing Christmas carols—Keiran took heart. Truly, God had brought him to Desiree.

He gazed around, entertained by the small town oozing

with big-time charm. Market stalls along the side streets sold ornaments and nutcrackers, and children mailed their letters to Santa at the corner post office. Historic walking tours were scheduled as soon as the judging finished, and the shops were becoming increasingly crowded with holiday customers.

While a pleasurable morning awaited them, he brought his attention back to the main reason they were here. He slung his arm around Desiree's shoulder and guided her to the colorful array of cakes, lovingly made, and the mouthwatering aromas of butter, sugar, and cherries. The contestants had been instructed to stand behind their respective baked goods to answer questions from the judges.

Delight surged through him. This was perfection. His enchanting birthplace, his exquisite Desiree, and the delight of spending Christmas with her family.

By ten o'clock, the event was finished. Although the contest had been close, the judges announced Desiree had won first place, and Keiran had taken second.

Loud cheering erupted and Desiree blushed gorgeously as a judge tied the red and green *Kiss me, It's Christmas* apron around her cobalt-blue coat. Graciously, she thanked the judges and gave a special mention to Keiran for buying her a kitchen timer.

In a last-minute decision, Candee hadn't entered her Christmas cake. Because Rob had baked it and he was one of the judges, it wouldn't have been fair. Consequently, Rob sat at the judges' stand, along with a plate filled with the cake. At last count, Keiran estimated that Rob had eaten at least three slices, along with a thick wedge of fudge from a food kiosk.

Keiran caught up with Desiree in the middle of the congratulatory crowd. In a laughing voice, she said, "All that powdered sugar paid off."

"Well done." Keiran brought her into his arms for a breathless kiss. Truly, the day couldn't have gone any better.

She hesitated. "You're kissing me here, in front of the entire town?"

"I'm just following directions." He glanced at her apron and grinned.

"It's not Christmas yet."

"I've designated the entire month of December for celebrating Christmas."

Chuckling, she said, "I want to catch up with Candee for a minute."

"Hurry back. There's a Christmassy silk scarf in the front window of one of the boutiques, and I immediately thought of you. You mentioned you wanted a scarf for Christmas."

"I did? When?"

"Well, maybe I just thought you did because I plan to buy it for you."

With a laugh, she pulled off the apron, carefully folded it, then scurried off with it securely tucked under her arm.

Out of the corner of his eye, Keiran noticed Rob speaking to a woman near the judges' stand. Although her back was turned, Keiran felt a wave of familiarity.

The crowd began dispersing and he was facing that same woman a minute later.

A woman he'd assumed he'd never see again. His ex-girlfriend, Patricia.

He gaped. His heartbeat raced.

She stared back at him with a cool smile, her dark hair streaked with blond, and her even white teeth. She was dressed in thigh-high boots, a short pink mini skirt, and a coyote-trimmed puffer jacket. He recognized the expensive jacket, as she'd coveted it the previous year. It had taken all the money he'd set aside, five hundred dollars, but she'd been happy. At least for a little while.

"Patricia?" He said her name and heard the shock in his voice.

"Hi, Keiran. Did you get my text this morning?" Deliberately, she perused Desiree, who'd bounced back to snuggle close to him.

"No. I've been busy," he replied.

He wanted to shout that this was his world, not hers. What was she doing here?

Patricia's gaze slid back to his face. "Well, I arrived."

His stomach plummeted. This couldn't be good. "I see that."

"You two know each other?" Desiree inquired.

Keiran nodded. "Aye," was all he could manage.

"We were practically engaged." Patricia directed her response toward Keiran. "You've been missed."

"Our relationship ended in Atlanta, remember?"

"Maybe our personal relationship." She gave him a heavy stare. "Unfortunately, our business relationship has hit a snag."

Heat flushed through his body. "I left you everything."

Before Patricia could reply, Desiree asked, "Were you two in business together?"

Patricia swept her fingers across Keiran's sleeve, a possessive gesture and decidedly intimate. "He worked for my daddy's company."

The way Patricia had always thrown it up to him twisted Keiran's stomach. In the beginning he had worked for her father, until he'd built his own carpentry business.

"I don't punch a clock for your father anymore," Keiran said.

"True," she rejoined with wry exasperation. "I heard you own a pub in Roses. And I want half the proceeds when you sell." She gestured to the street where O'Malley's was located.

"I'm not selling. And besides, the place hasn't been in business for years."

Her response was a derisive sneer. Few people believed Patricia was anything but a sultry, gorgeous female and ultimate charmer. He knew better. She was a woman who always got what she wanted.

And if she didn't?

Then she'd make life exceedingly unpleasant.

"Everything is for sale for a price." She was talking louder, her shrillness drawing the stares of passing shoppers, as she obviously intended. "Earlier, I went by the pub. It's not worth much, though it's worth something."

He sensed the desperation in her tone and looked her straight in the eye. "So you're here for money?"

"Obviously," she said.

"Where's Kyle?"

"He's long gone."

"And your father?"

"He refused to give me any more money." Her voice lowered to a stage whisper. "Now it's time for you to pay up, Keiran. I get half of everything you earn."

He planned to tread carefully before she went into a fresh fit of anger, although he couldn't contain himself. He just couldn't.

"Our verbal agreement ended." He started to pull his hand away.

"What about our written agreement?" Her grip tightened. Sagely, she shook her head. "You never were good at reading the fine print, darling, were you?"

CHAPTER 7

*L*aughter burst from the judges' stand, and Desiree jerked at the sound. Keiran shook from Patricia's grip and grabbed Desiree's elbow. He guided her toward the canvas awning, using the excuse he wanted to admire her cake again.

Under her breath, she asked, "What was that about?"

But it didn't matter, because she already knew. And something was shattering deep inside her. Although she tried, she couldn't tear her thoughts away from the lushly provocative Patricia. The woman had the self-confidence of an exceptionally stunning female who commanded attention.

Keiran heaved a sigh. "Her father owns a construction business in Atlanta, and when I met her she got me a job at his company. I learned the trade and became one of his carpentry men."

Desiree felt her face heat, recalling the conversation between Patricia and Keiran. No doubt, they'd been close. Very close. The thought brought a stab of jealousy, along with recalling how the strikingly gorgeous Patricia had ogled Keiran.

Desiree yanked from his grip. "I think this is about a lot more than carpentry."

Neither of them broke the loaded silence as they advanced toward the cake display.

"She's trouble," Keiran said. "Supposedly, she helped me when I was building my carpentry business."

They'd come to the edge of the awning. Desiree leaned against a makeshift pole and crossed her arms. "Supposedly?"

"Aye. We rented an office together. She answered phone calls from customers, scheduled my jobs, and advertised my business. And, I trusted her with all the bookkeeping duties. Now that I look back, though, there were several times that I suspected money was missing."

"Did you confront her?"

"Are you kidding? Of course, although her answer was always the same. She'd nearly bite my head off and her resultant tantrum would last for days."

Desiree glanced at Teddy and Candee near the judges' stand. Teddy had his arm around Candee, and they chatted amiably with Rob.

Oh, to be able to give her heart to a man she could trust, Desiree thought, a man who loved her unconditionally.

She studied Keiran. "And that was okay with you?"

"Unfortunately, aye. I thought she was a prize—pretty, well-heeled, efficient. And then, she cheated on me with Kyle, a moneyed stockbroker."

The tension in the cold air between them crackled.

"You never told me any of this."

"I should have," he admitted. "Except it's demoralizing for a guy to have his girlfriend cheat on him with his best friend. They became a couple and—"

"And you skipped town to land on my doorstep."

"Patricia and I had a rocky relationship from the start. It's odd. Once the truth hit me, I realized I wanted the happily-ever-after ending. Just not with her."

"And yet, you couldn't bring yourself to tell me these revelations."

"I'm sorry. I should have." For a moment, he closed his eyes and breathed aloud. "Teddy said the same thing."

"You told Teddy, yet you wouldn't confide in me?" The surprise that had seized her when she'd realized who Patricia was to Keiran evaporated, along with the belief he actually cared. In a blinding flare of realization, she tore from his hold. "I'm a good listener, I would have understood. Now . . ."

"Nothing's changed."

The lump in her throat was so thick she could hardly manage any words. "Everything's changed."

"Because you're judgmental?"

"You're blaming me?" To stop from splintering into a million pieces, she shielded herself by opposing him. "You're the one who lied by omission."

"I couldn't admit it, okay? I thought I cared about a woman who was nothing more than a liar and a cheat. And then I realized I never cared at all, but wasn't sure how to make a proper exit."

"So your pride got in the way of your decision-making."

"Look, can I show you the silk scarf I saw earlier?" His jaw set with determination. "I think you'll like it."

"Please tell me you're joking."

"I'm completely serious." He laid his hands over hers. "We've got something good, Desiree. Surely you realize it too."

He didn't understand. He never could, considering his silver-spoon background. She'd been hurt and disappointed her entire life.

She winced. The only way to protect herself was to stay

away from precarious situations—the risk of heartache was too great.

"You don't get it," she said. "You weren't there when Candee and I were growing up. You didn't live where we lived."

A look of persistence passed across his features. "True, but I'm not to blame."

Angrily, she swiped at a tear running down her cheek.

"This isn't about me." He kept hold of her hands. "Or Patricia. It's about you growing up in the foster care system. You're afraid to open your heart because you might get hurt again. You can trust me, Desiree. I made a mistake and I'm genuinely sorry." He took her in his arms, lovingly stroking her hair. "Let's discuss this in a quiet place. We can have lunch at the new Chinese restaurant near my pub, and designate the occasion as our first real date."

"A date? *Now* we're dating?" Methodically, she removed his hands as Patricia headed toward them with sheer determination planted on her porcelain features.

"I'm back, Keiran," Patricia said, plunking dainty hands on her nonexistent hips while she perused the village green. "Where do you suggest we eat in this single-traffic-light town before we drive back to Atlanta together?"

"How about Chinese?" Desiree indicated the street where the restaurant was located. "It's across from the pub."

Keiran regarded Desiree levelly. "I'm buying you a silk scarf, and then I'm treating you to lunch to celebrate your cake victory."

"I've lost my appetite for eggrolls." Desiree cut her gaze to Patricia. "Although you'll love the food. Try the fried rice too. I've heard it's the best in Roses."

"I will, as long as he's buying. He's a generous guy." Patricia's thin eyebrows lifted in amused mockery. "Keiran, we can visit our pub too." Possessively, she touched his sleeve and beamed up at him.

"Desiree, please listen to me." He edged away from Patricia. "I can make everything right between us."

"You can't," Desiree shot back.

Her retort reverberated in her mind.

Or could he? They'd grown so close that they'd even begun finishing each other's sentences. One emotion bombarded her—hope—but hope would leave her broken-hearted if it didn't work out.

No. She couldn't take the chance.

"Enjoy your lunch, Keiran." For a second, Desiree forced herself to look at him. So handsome, so striking, so utterly appealing—and she faltered.

And then she reminded herself she wouldn't allow any more disappointment into her life. "We're done here," she said.

He met her look. "Really? You won't hear me out?"

She shook her head.

His green-eyed gaze froze to solid ice.

She twisted, trying not to recall the times in his arms, the pleasurable, passionate thrill of his kisses. Blindly, she made her way to the judges' stand, feeling the keenly inquisitive stares of strangers.

"We're not finished. I'll see you as soon as I get things sorted," he called out to her. "Back at the house. Wait for me there."

Drowning in sadness she couldn't control, she struggled to keep her shoulders straight and her gait sure. All around her, cheerful festivities rang out. The boutiques were filled to capacity. Shoppers spilled into the streets, and light-hearted conversation abounded.

"There you are." Candee raced through the throng and hauled Desiree to the side. "Teddy and I want to invite you and Keiran to our house for lunch. By the way, where is Keiran?" She peered around Desiree, shaded her eyes, and scowled. "Who is that woman he's walking with? I've never seen her before. Does she live in Roses?"

"She's from Atlanta."

"Why is she here?"

Why, indeed.

Desiree didn't answer her sister's question, although she agreed to lunch. The trembling that had started in her arms had spread to her legs, and later, she couldn't remember how she managed to get to her car, bypassing the green grocer as she drove home.

One fact she knew for sure. She wouldn't be waiting when Keiran arrived at her house. She couldn't bear the thought of facing him, yet she didn't have the prerogative to confront him. They weren't engaged or even officially dating, unless one counted nightly home-cooked meals as dates.

Sure, she'd presumed he'd told her the truth about his life in Atlanta, but he'd omitted a key point. He'd been seriously dating Patricia.

What did a lie by omission mean? Her lawyer brain clicked into gear. *Leaving out an important fact, thus fostering a misconception*, she automatically supplied. Yes, that described it.

As soon as she arrived home, she dashed off a note telling him to pack his things and leave, and set the note on her kitchen table. Then she planned to stay at Candee's house until midnight. Or longer, if Desiree saw his truck parked in her driveway.

CHAPTER 8

*D*esiree needn't have worried, because Keiran came and went while she lunched and spent the afternoon with Candee, Teddy, and Joseph.

Keiran had penned his own note and placed it on the kitchen table next to hers, explaining he was driving back to Atlanta with Patricia.

Not sure when I'll return. Will keep you posted, he'd written in his typical bold script.

She crumpled up his note and tossed it on the floor.

A dire, stabbing ache grew as she climbed the stairs to the attic apartment. Hesitating, she slowly opened the door and stared at the room in silence. His bed was neatly made. His scent pervaded the space—raw wood and the outdoors, a hint of sawdust and pine. All related to his job.

And his belongings had vanished.

She inhaled and leaned weakly against the door. Here it was, a week before Christmas, and he'd abandoned her to be with his former girlfriend. For all Desiree knew, Keiran and Patricia planned to return to Roses and renovate O'Malley's as a team.

Her feverish brain refused to accept that scenario, and she seriously considered moving out of her beloved town if that ever occurred. In comparison to Patricia, Desiree felt like an adolescent girl again—ordinary and inexperienced.

Goodbye Keiran, she thought, coming to terms with the fact that they'd gone in opposite directions.

After arriving in Atlanta, he texted and phoned numerous times.

She replied with a brief text: *Don't contact me. No texts, no calls, okay?*

A date when I return? he immediately countered. *It's Christmas, after all.*

And Christmas brought memories of when she was a little kid, feeling alone and deserted while her parents lay drunk on the living room couch. She knew she must come to grips with her emotions in order to move forward. But, oh, this was so hard. Acceptance and forgetting, these were weaknesses in her life she had a hard time acknowledging, although her favorite pastor had assured in a sermon that weakness led to strength.

When, exactly? Had God brought her a Christmas miracle in Keiran? And if so, was she throwing that miracle away with both hands when she refused to speak with him, allowing pride to dictate her lonely path?

She pressed her cell phone to her heart and asked the empty room, "How can I fight you, Keiran, when I'm warring with myself?"

The sparks between them had flamed with his every touch, his every kiss, and she missed his solid strength, calm reassurances, and good humor.

With a deep sigh, she tried to come to terms with the desolation weighing her down. How could she face another day without him when he made her feel so complete? Finally, she'd had a chance to be happy.

But happiness was a funny thing. The fear of being alone stemmed from her childhood, and she'd proven she could succeed on her own.

She reminded herself of all she'd accomplished, that her colleagues had remarked on her spirited, confident nature. With firm determination, she lifted her chin and pushed her thoughts of Keiran aside.

And then she texted him back. A final, single word: *No*.

By Monday of the following week, she knew he'd departed for good. Still, her heart jumped whenever the doorbell rang. Despite her firm reprimands to herself, she'd hurry to the front door, thinking he'd returned for Christmas after all. A secret fantasy come true, despite her conflicting emotions.

Although the opposite prevailed in her real world, and it turned out to be the postman, or an online store delivery.

Very well, then. The next time the doorbell rang, she would take her time answering it.

By the end of the week, she'd established a pattern. No longer did she live in suspended anticipation that Keiran might stride into her foyer. Nonetheless, neither was she able to anticipate the upcoming holiday with delight. She'd thought she'd find the peace she'd been looking for if she bought her own home.

But she hadn't.

Peace had little to do with the most expensive home, the most beautiful neighborhood, she decided. It was who you shared your home with that mattered most. And now that Keiran was gone, despite her attempts to deny it, the truth hit hard.

At six o'clock on the Friday evening before Christmas Eve, Desiree pulled off her black leather boots, hung her jacket in the hall closet, and pulled her blue cardigan over her silk blouse. She was done working for two weeks, and had won a case involving Julie Wallis, a single mother of two children, who was being jailed and fined for a minor offense. When it was clear the mother couldn't afford to pay, Desiree had argued for another solution. The court had accepted a community service plan, and Julie had cried with relief when she was released.

Cause for celebration, Desiree thought, although the day didn't feel at all celebratory.

It felt empty.

Aimlessly, she wandered the spacious rooms of her home, fingering the prominent wooden staircase, the paneled oak walls, the built-in china cabinets.

She barely glanced at her wristwatch as she stepped across the spacious foyer, although her mouth tightened when she realized the time. Candee was coming over in an hour to finalize their Christmas Eve plans.

As much as Desiree liked talking to Candee, she'd avoided her sister's phone calls because she'd been dreading their imminent discussion. Most likely, the topic would center around Keiran and his notable disappearance.

As Desiree headed for the kitchen, Candee phoned, launching into a lengthy monologue regarding the sweet rolls she was bringing for Christmas Eve dinner. Desiree cut her off, making an excuse that a thorough kitchen organization required her attention, and she'd see Candee at seven o'clock.

She poured herself a glass of sparkling cider, sat on a stool, and rehearsed their upcoming exchange in her mind.

"*What happened?*" Candee would ask, referring to Keiran. Most likely, she'd expected to find Desiree and Keiran acting like an official couple by the time Christmas rolled around.

"What happened?" Desiree would repeat. "Keiran lied to me, knowing I was falling in love with him. And then he went off with Patricia."

An unbearable ache pierced her heart. She set down her glass and perused the kitchen. A box of pots and pans required sorting, and her pantry could be more orderly.

As she arranged a variety of spices closer to the stove, a trio of deliverymen knocked on the kitchen's sliding glass doors. Her base cabinet had arrived, they announced, and her contractor had requested they bring the cabinet through the rear door rather than muddying up the new wood floors.

"Is the cabinet heavy?" She invited the men inside to unbox the cabinet in the earmarked corner near the pantry.

"Just awkward, ma'am," the youngest of the three replied, test-fitting the cabinet by what he clarified was dry-fitting. "Do you have a carpenter to install it?" he asked.

She shook her head.

"We're booked until the first of the year, but you're missing the stainless handle for this cabinet. If it's in stock, I'll make a note for a special delivery before Christmas."

"Thank you, and Merry Christmas," she replied.

As the men cheerfully departed, she bid them good-bye with a quiet smile.

She went into the pantry, intending to declutter the shelves by stacking the flat containers on top of one another. Instead, she found herself rummaging in a drawer to retrieve Keiran's note, which she'd salvaged from the floor.

Not sure when I'll return. Will keep you posted, he'd written.

Rereading the simple sentences, she traced the letters with shaking hands, feeling a pang of longing so intense, her knees weakened. He was so magnificent, so unbearably good-looking, she'd taken unabashed pleasure in spending every spare second with him.

If he phoned her even once more, she might cave and answer his call.

Might? Ruefully, she decided that she would answer.

Of course he hadn't, and her phone had sat silent for two days.

"I thought I had everything worked out," she whispered to the quiet pantry.

Apparently not this time. The storybook life she'd planned out hadn't gone the way she'd expected. And despite reaching her goals—her successful career and a home of her own—happiness remained elusive.

Pivoting, she walked into the living room, taking heart in its remarkable transformation, the Christmas tree illuminated in dazzling splendor. She lit a fire in the fireplace, and the flickering light assured her of comfort through the bitter winter ahead.

All week since Keiran's departure, she hadn't allowed herself to cry, and had accomplished her workdays briskly and efficiently. However, now that she didn't have court cases and clients to occupy her mind, the heavy burden of keeping her feelings bottled up threatened to spill over.

As tears welled, she shuffled back to the kitchen. The wintry December wind whistled through a small opening in the sliding glass doors and burned her eyes. She slid the doors closed as tears streamed freely down her cheeks.

She let them come, weeping until there were no tears left to shed—no more sadness or resentment. The picture in her mind's eye of where she was supposed to live, where the man in her life was supposed to stand, and the children she would be blessed with hadn't happened.

She sank onto a chair, her shoulders drooping with desolation. Why had Keiran refrained from telling her about Patricia? And why hadn't he returned to Roses by now? He'd given up so quickly. Wasn't he interested in knowing how Desiree was faring after their break-up?

Her thoughts went back to the previous weekend, and she

visualized Patricia's seductive eyes as she'd gazed intimately up at Keiran.

We were practically engaged, Patricia had said, her words intended to pierce.

Hurt, confused, and angry, Desiree refused to allow that image to dominate her thoughts. Instead, she recalled how Keiran had held her afterwards, murmuring to her, caressing her hair.

You can trust me, Desiree. I made a mistake and I'm genuinely sorry. His voice had been rough with self-reproach.

And later, the guarded hope in his tone as he'd called out, *I'll see you as soon as I get things sorted. Back at the house. Wait for me there.*

A stinging pain punctured her chest with each memory. He'd sounded sincere, and she remembered the despair that had crossed his handsome features.

She half-rose from her chair as a thought struck her. With surprising clarity, she recognized that the pain she felt was more for Keiran than herself.

Angrily, she swiped her wet cheeks and sprang fully to her feet. Surely this proved she was a besotted fool. How could she feel sorry for him when she was the person who'd been deceived?

Surprisingly, with that realization, her mood began to elevate. In fact, by the time she stood by the table and itemized her to-do list for Christmas Eve, she felt better than she had all week. Her sadness began turning into fortitude.

She opened the refrigerator and brought out two bags of fresh cranberries she intended to frost with sugar for a festive centerpiece. She'd also purchased a variety of prepared side dishes including creamy mashed potatoes and a green bean casserole topped with pecans. In the morning, she'd tackle the fresh turkey preparation.

So, the meal was set, and she'd slated her pistachio cake for dessert.

Her gaze travelled to the adjoining dining room.

Where would they all sit—Teddy, Candee, Joseph, and Desiree?

She paused, considered the lack of furniture, then recalled her conversation with Keiran.

You own a service of fine crystal and china, your dining area is large enough for a twenty-people feast, and there's no place to sit and enjoy a meal? he'd teased.

I'll pile cushions on the floor and we'll sit cross-legged, she'd replied.

Dashing back into the living room, she dragged her coffee table into the dining area. Then she draped a red tartan tablecloth over it and arranged colorful throw pillows around the table.

With great care, she set the table with four place settings using her finest china and silver, embellishing the tablespace with shiny silver candle holders and a string of sparkling white lights.

Pleased with the result, she went into the kitchen and sat in the middle of the tiled floor, eyeing the base cabinet waiting to be anchored.

The deliveryman had stated she needed a carpenter. Well, Keiran wasn't here.

However, she was.

On her phone, she searched tutorials on how to install a cabinet, and selected a step-by-step video that assured installation was easy with the proper tools, which included a level, a screw gun, screws, clamps, and a hammer and nails.

"Carefully measure and draw the exact location," the woman in the video instructed. "Drive screws into the wall studs to anchor the cabinet."

Quickly, Desiree changed into jeans and a sweatshirt,

chose the necessary tools from the study where the crewmen kept their supplies, and set to work.

An hour later, she was kneeling on the floor, concentrating intensely on the installation, when Candee entered the kitchen.

"Sorry I'm late," Candee declared as Desiree jerked back, startled by her sister's voice. "Boomer was doing his favorite thing—eating—and then I took him for a quick walk. You didn't hear the doorbell, so I let myself in." Candee's mouth trembled with laughter as she admired the cabinet. "And now I see why. You look remarkably determined."

"Base cabinets aren't difficult to install if the area has been measured accurately and you have the correct tools," Desiree said, parroting the singsong tone of the woman in the video. She finished driving the last nail into the toe kick beneath the cabinet, set the tools on the floor, then stood.

"Bravo!" Candee gave her a high-five. "The place looks great."

She smiled. "Thanks."

"Have you eaten dinner?" Candee's gaze skimmed the kitchen.

"No, and I'm starving." Desiree reminded herself that she needed to set aside a half hour a day for exercise in order to shed the extra ten pounds she'd gained. Appreciating Keiran's magnificent cooking, she hadn't had the opportunity or the inclination to diet.

"Teddy and I are so busy with Joseph and his horse therapy that I haven't eaten, either." Candee peered into the refrigerator and extracted cold cuts and bread, motioning for Desiree to join her. "I'll make us both a sandwich and brew a pot of tea."

The women enjoyed a cozy light supper at the kitchen table.

"You seem much better than I imagined," Candee said as she poured tea. "I mean, after last Saturday."

"I feel better."

"Care to fill me in on what happened between you and Keiran?" Candee fixed Desiree a mug of tea without milk, and added milk and sugar to her own. "Teddy mentioned he and Keiran have been in touch, but when I pressed him for details he was extremely close-lipped."

Desiree debated, opening her mouth to defend her position, then closing it. Today, for the first time in a week, she'd begun to feel purposeful again. A delicate newfound serenity had emerged through her tears. Should she take the risk of talking about it?

But Candee seemed so resolute, Desiree knew holding back was futile. Besides, who was better to confide in than her dear sister?

"Ask away," Desiree said.

"Tell me everything."

"Well," Desiree sat back in her chair, "I suppose our relationship began when he first arrived and began talking to my front porch."

"You mean talking *to you* on your front porch."

"No, I mean talking *to* my front porch," Desiree said with an amused smile. She couldn't explain her attraction to Keiran from that first moment. At night her dreams had been of him. During the day, she'd daydreamed about him. His capable hands as he cooked, or his bass voice as he sang an Irish tune, had awakened her desire for a secure, centered life with the man she loved. Often in the past weeks, she'd told herself that the uniqueness, the unqualified novelty, of having a charismatic Renaissance man living in her house would pass.

Instead, her feelings had intensified.

Noting Candee's raised eyebrows, Desiree set aside her

teacup. "When Keiran arrived, I told him I needed an electrician, not a carpenter, and to return in the morning. So I shut the door on him and when I reopened it, he was still there, muttering to the porch. I invited him to move into the attic because he had nowhere else to stay."

Candee laughed softly. "And then the relationship began."

"A practical relationship."

"A romantic one."

"At night after dinner, we'd go into the living room and he'd light a fire." Desiree drew her legs up in the chair, curling her arms around them. "He'd play his guitar and . . ."

When she finished her story, Candee dabbed at her eyes. "Truly, your entire courtship is enchanting."

"We've never even been out on a formal date."

"In all those hours you spent together you probably know him better than anyone. Teddy said that just because Keiran moved into your house didn't mean a relationship would develop, especially in a short period of time." A satisfied smile wreathed Candee's face. "But I felt certain he was wrong. I heard Keiran talk endlessly about you whenever he came to the house to confer with Teddy. And I watched you two at the cake judging contest, and I knew. He's deeply in love with you."

Desiree stood and wiped her palms on the folds of her sweatshirt. "He has an odd way of showing it, running off to Atlanta with Patricia."

"Has he tried contacting you?"

"He's called and texted many times."

"Have you responded?"

Desiree stared impassively at the glossy white backsplash above the farmhouse sink Keiran had installed. "Only to tell him not to contact me again."

"Well, that's a brilliant way to go about things."

Desiree gave a guilty start. Her heartbeat raced with a

surge of annoyance. Or was it culpability?

Candee crossed the room and took Desiree's cold hands in hers. "Do you love him?"

Understatement. Sweet memories hastened to her mind. With a rush of happiness, she recalled his attentiveness, his patience, the pride she'd felt when he complimented her for fighting court battles against injustice. This broad-shouldered, rugged man gazed at her with such heartfelt tenderness, sometimes words would lodge in her throat.

"*Did you think about me today?*" he'd asked.

"*Often.*"

"*Good. I thought about you too. See how much we are alike? We both love Christmas and we both love—*" Then he'd drawn her into his arms and kissed her.

Desiree willed herself to say no, she didn't love him. Instead, she heard herself saying, "Yes. I fell in love with him at a high school football game ten years ago."

Candee tightened her grip on Desiree's hands. "I thought I recognized his name when Teddy first brought him up. Then O'Malley's pub was discussed and I recalled you going on and on about him when we were teenagers. So often, in fact, I suspected you had a crush on him."

"You were right," Desiree said. "But now I'm a grown woman."

"Who loves a grown man. And that man loves you very much."

Desiree shook free and peered out the window at the thick dark night, chilly and moonless.

"He's gone," she said quietly.

"He's not gone." Candee went to the sink and ran soapy hot water over a stack of dishes. "He's just waiting for you to give him the opportunity to make amends. You can't repair a relationship if you avoid him."

"He hasn't texted or called in a couple of days."

"He's probably come to accept that you don't want anything to do with him."

"That's not true."

"Then go to him in Atlanta. And tell him face to face."

Desiree's brain frantically groped for a way to refute Candee's argument. Suppose she failed? He was obviously more interested in Patricia.

"I can't. Tomorrow is Christmas Eve. We're attending church service, and I'm cooking. See?" Desiree gestured to the dining room. "The table's all set."

"Then I'll give you a one-day pass because you admitted you love him."

Her love for him was out of reach, but she knew if she admitted her thoughts to Candee, her sister would argue her point a tad too vehemently.

"Yes, I love him," Desiree said. Desperately loved him. And when he gazed at her as if she were the only person in his universe, her pulse surged with excitement.

"Settled. On Christmas Day, you're driving to Atlanta," Candee said. "Teddy knows where Keiran used to live, and you'll start there. Or, you can phone him."

Desiree hesitated. Would Keiran be angry with her, or coolly polite? Or would he be thrilled to see her, because he still cared?

Desiree blew out a breath. "I'll surprise him."

Although, as she closed the door after Candee's departure, she felt a sickening fear of failure straight to her belly.

Suppose she interrupted Keiran while he was with Patricia?

Suppose he didn't want to see her?

With resolve, she pulled her thoughts away from irrational worry and concentrated on their reunion in Atlanta.

Please love me, my affectionate, gentle Renaissance man, she thought, *as much as I love you.*

CHAPTER 9

*K*eiran didn't return to Roses in two days, which was the time frame he'd originally planned. Neither did he spend his days with Patricia.

He'd passed on lunching with her in Roses, and hadn't taken her inside O'Malley's. He'd left her in town, driven back to Desiree's home, and read her note with surprised alarm. She wouldn't hear him out.

He'd been raised a gentleman, and quickly packed his bags as she requested and loaded up his truck. It didn't matter who was right or wrong. He'd kept the truth from her, although not intentionally. He'd simply removed Patricia from his heart and mind because Desiree had taken over his thoughts. When he was with her, everything else fell away.

After a silent four-hour drive with Patricia back to Atlanta, he'd dropped her at her apartment. He intended to get to the bottom of her demands, settle any financial score once and for all, and return to Roses, his true home.

And his true love, Desiree.

When Desiree hadn't answered his phone calls or texts in

the ensuing first hours of his departure, he'd tasted a bitter defeat. But not for long. They weren't finished by a long shot.

He bunked in his former apartment, where he discussed his situation with Oscar and Georges. Oscar made a hasty phone call and booked a consultation with Abraham Realgood, Honest Abe, the lawyer he worked for. Although the lawyer wasn't accepting new clients, he'd offer his consultation services as a favor to Oscar.

The following afternoon, Mr. Realgood's receptionist showed Keiran into a dark-paneled office where the lawyer greeted Keiran with a friendly tilt of his head.

"What can I do for you?" He gestured for Keiran to take a seat across from him.

"I'll come directly to the point." Keiran sank into the cushioned chair. "My former girlfriend, Patricia, believes she's entitled to half my earnings, including a pub I inherited."

A pair of astute hazel eyes measured Keiran. "I've heard some of your story, thanks to Oscar and Georges."

"Then can you advise me? I want Patricia out of my life."

"She's requesting money."

"Yes, and more money than I have." With Patricia, it had always been about an extravagant lifestyle, and when she had a goal in mind there was no stopping her.

"Is she entitled to your money?" the lawyer asked.

"When we were together, we had a verbal agreement that we would split half my earnings. I did the work, and she maintained the office and books. However, I've reviewed the paperwork I held on to, because she implied there was some fine print," Keiran said. "I couldn't find anything written down."

"How much does she want?"

"Twenty thousand dollars. I wish it was less. She found out I inherited a pub and she wants me to sell it and she'll take half the proceeds. However, I'm not willing to sell, and besides, the building isn't worth much in its present condition."

"Not functioning?"

"It hasn't been open in many years."

"Is there a possibility she'd take you to court?"

That was a worrisome and infuriating thought. Keiran stretched out his long legs and blew out a sigh. "Knowing Patricia? Aye, although she couldn't possibly win. Could she?"

"Probably not, if your agreement was verbal, but this battle could go on for years. It all depends how badly you want her out of your life."

Furious with himself for getting involved with her in the first place, Keiran glanced out the window at the overcast sky. "I'd like our relationship to be finished, once and for all."

"Then there's a solution because money talks." The lawyer examined the paperwork on his desk and idly pushed it to the side. "Georges mentioned you inherited an autographed football card that might be valuable."

With a nod, Keiran pulled the card from its protective case, as Georges had urged him to bring it to the meeting. He felt a deep, almost agonizing sadness about giving up the card that had meant so much to his father. He'd prayed about it, and realized he needed to get over the sadness and guilt if he sold it. If he reopened the pub, his parents would undoubtedly be grateful and proud. As much as his father's dream had been football, the pub in Roses was his legacy.

Keiran shifted his gaze to the lawyer's sparsely furnished, dimly lit office. He'd expected an oily charmer with a law degree, but Abraham Realgood seemed on the up and up.

"We appraised the card at the pawn shop Georges works for," Keiran said. "The estimate from the pawnbroker is fifteen thousand dollars."

Seemingly impervious to Keiran's emotional state, the lawyer grinned. "I advise you to sell the card and pay the ex. If your past agreement was verbal, you're in the clear, but it's more the matter of guaranteeing she won't be able to badger you for any more money. Otherwise, she may turn up again. More time. More money. Do you want that?"

Keiran shook his head. "I'd like her gone from my life."

"Then I'll draw up a contract, a full and final release stating clearly she's not entitled to anything else after this payment."

"Do you think she'll accept less than she's asking?"

Mr. Realgood rubbed his jaw. "From you and your friends' descriptions, I'm positive she'll jump at it. Fifteen thousand dollars is a lot, especially around Christmas."

"Excellent." It was all Keiran could do not to burst into an Irish song. This was going to work. "How soon can the contract be drafted?"

"By tomorrow. I'll handle everything from here." Slowly, the gray-haired lawyer leaned back in his chair and folded his hands behind his head. "Now I'm not judging, mind you, but if I were you I'd avoid any further correspondence with your ex—verbal or otherwise."

The lawyer *was* judging, Keiran reflected, although he was too relieved to do anything other than watch Mr. Realgood write out a bill and hand it to him.

Keiran looked over the number and gaped.

"Admittedly, my services are costly on account of the short notice and holiday season," the lawyer said. "But your problem is solved. And if you ever need your locks changed, I'll cut you a good deal."

"Thank you." With a deep, relieved breath, Keiran shook hands with the lawyer and left.

By noon the next day, Abe Realgood phoned to report

that Patricia had received the email and accepted via her electronic signature.

Another deep breath of relief.

"The thing is," Keiran told a frowning but somewhat amused Georges and Oscar, "I can't stay to cook Christmas Eve dinner because I'm driving back to Roses."

Georges flashed Keiran a mischievous grin. "What will we eat then, *mon ami?*"

"Why don't you call the local pizzeria? They deliver on Christmas Eve, and pizza goes great with beer." Keiran chuckled as he hoisted his belongings over his shoulder, thanked the men for their help, and wished them a Merry Christmas.

He glanced at his watch. He had two stops to make in Roses, and one important phone call. He hoped he wouldn't be late for Christmas Eve dinner. They ate at six o'clock sharp.

* * *

"You burned the turkey?" Candee hovered over Desiree, who'd dashed into the kitchen to extract a charred, smoking turkey from the oven. "How can anyone burn a fourteen-pound turkey?"

"Fortunately, it didn't catch fire. When the smoke detector went off, I was worried," Desiree replied. "I went into the living room for a few minutes to start a fire in the fireplace and plug in the Christmas tree lights. Then, while I was lighting the candles on the mantel, I got sidetracked when the radio started playing 'Silent Night' on repeat."

Desiree wore the red and green *Kiss Me, It's Christmas* apron over a red silk blouse and black velvet pants. Christmas Eve was a special occasion, and she planned to slip on suede ankle boots and her cobalt-blue wool coat for midnight church services. To keep her hair away from her face while cooking, she'd pinned it into a chignon secured with a red jeweled clasp.

"I should've helped you with the dinner preparations. Sorry I lost track of time. I love watching Teddy and Joseph play a game of flag football," Candee said. "It's amazing—we haven't gotten any snow this year so the guys are still wearing sweatshirts and jeans."

"The weather forecast predicts a light dusting by midnight." Desiree glanced out the kitchen window at the energetic twosome. They'd decided on another game and were flipping a coin. Then Teddy placed the football in the middle of her large backyard. Starting with a snap, Joseph passed the ball in one fluid motion to a third player.

"Recognize that handsome guy? He looks like he could be a male model." Candee feigned fanning herself as she came to stand by the window with Desiree.

He certainly seemed familiar, with his broad shoulders and midnight-black hair and . . .

Desiree's knees buckled. No, it couldn't be. The guy must be one of the neighborhood men, perhaps Mr. Juno taking a break from his graduate studies.

"I'll try flipping the turkey," Candee suggested. "If I drop it, then we can remember this Christmas as the year you burned the turkey and it fell to the floor."

Desiree laughed. "As long as it doesn't roll into the dining room and—"

The front doorbell rang. The cabinet door handle delivery man, Desiree surmised, because she wasn't expecting any visitors.

Or was she?

She told herself to take her time answering, but scratched the idea as she hastened to the door and swung it open.

It wasn't the delivery man.

He stood on her front porch, tall and lean, his green eyes reminding her of Irish emeralds glimmering in his handsome face. He wore his navy-blue parka, unzipped, accentuating his toned physique. His denim shirt and jeans were rumpled. He was holding a small gift, wrapped in brown paper and tied with a red satin ribbon.

"Keiran." She stepped back and attempted to breathe. Part of her functioning brain reminded her that she should stay calm and composed.

"Merry Christmas, Desiree." He held out the gift.

She kept her hands at her sides. "Why are you here?" Her voice shook. He still offered her the gift, his hands outstretched.

"To finish our discussion from last week. And to tell you what I've wanted to say since we met. Listen—"

"Keiran, you're a little late." Candee approached and gave him a mildly sardonic smile.

"It started to snow in Atlanta and the limited visibility on I-85 slowed traffic," he said. "Plus I stopped in town to buy Desiree's gift, then ducked into my pub. Rob is coming in the morning."

"Rob?" Desiree regarded them both. "Why?"

"Rob and Keiran are reopening the pub. Rob is loaning him the start-up money, much as he did for Teddy when he began his real estate flipping business," Candee said.

"Rob and I will be serving Christmas dinner tomorrow to the homeless in our community," Keiran explained. "Several of the markets in town, including your green grocer, are donating food. We're using the ovens at the local supermarkets to prepare the meals. I hope you'll join us, Desiree."

Blinking, Desiree gaped at Keiran, and then Candee. "And you knew about all this?"

"Only recently," Candee replied. "Teddy and Keiran arranged everything."

"And about Keiran returning here? Tonight?"

Feigning innocence, Candee gushed apologetically. "You wouldn't answer his texts. Tonight, Teddy told me they've been in touch all week. And now I'm going to see to dinner." Candee rolled up the sleeves of her glittery silver blouse and hurried away.

"Keiran." Desiree touched her throat. "I don't know what to say."

His strong fingers were gentle as he pressed them against her lips. "Take my gift and invite me inside."

"Please come in." She accepted his gift. "You didn't need to buy me anything. Thank you."

He stepped inside. "I confess I used the gift as an excuse."

"What? I don't understand."

"I've been working all week to make things right between us. I understand you're hurt and justifiably angry. I met with a lawyer in Atlanta, and Patricia signed a full and final release contract. She's not entitled to half of what I earn anymore. Our former business agreement was verbal, by the way."

Desiree's heart was pounding so hard, he could surely hear each beat. "What do you mean?"

"She was demanding twenty thousand dollars, the estimated proceeds if I sold the pub." He shook his head. "You don't know her the way I do. She would have made our lives miserable. So, I gave her fifteen thousand, and made certain she's out of our life for good."

Desiree's gaze narrowed. "Where did you get the money? Rob?"

"Rob's been great, but no."

She paused for a beat. "Then where?"

"My father's football card. I didn't want to sell it, and I prayed long and hard before agreeing. The pawn shop assured me they'll hold it for a while, in case I can come up with the money to buy it back. I don't see that happening, but you never know. Our pub might become extremely success-ful, just like it once was."

"*Our* pub?"

"I'm hoping you'll help me bring it back to its former glory."

Through tears of happiness, she found her voice. "With you at the helm, how can it fail?"

"And you," he said solemnly. "I hope I'm the man you deserve, and I want to make all my mistakes up to you."

The pain in his voice brought a new swell of tears. "Keiran, please, we all make mistakes and—"

"I'm sorry, Desiree. And I love you."

When she realized he was threading his fingers through her hair, then cupping her face so he could kiss her, she whispered the words bursting from her heart. "I love you too."

All week she'd dreamed of kissing him—the tenderness of his mouth on hers, the elation of being reunited. For a long moment, she felt mesmerized, like she was floating. His kiss was light and sweet, and magnificently poignant.

She snuggled against his warm, hard chest, feeling the solid beat of his heart. There was so much she wanted to tell him—that she'd installed a kitchen cabinet by herself, that she'd won a particularly difficult court case.

Not knowing where to begin, she burst out, "I burned the turkey. But I set a lovely table for dinner and I wasn't going to let a little thing like charred meat stop us from enjoying Christmas."

He chuckled. "Let me survey the damage and see if I can help." He removed his parka and Desiree hung it in the front foyer closet, then placed his gift on a side table in the living room. She crossed to the kitchen, where Keiran was deftly removing the burnt skin from the turkey.

"If everyone likes the legs and thighs, we're golden," he said.

Desiree set out her turkey platter, and Candee artfully arranged sliced lemons and sprigs of rosemary around the carved meat Keiran placed on the platter. He asked Desiree to stir the gravy on the stove.

"You're a little bossy."

His eyes crinkled as a grin touched his lips. "I'm delegating."

Teddy and Joseph joined the group, and they settled, cross-legged, on the cushions Desiree had arranged in the dining room around the makeshift table.

Dinner was a feast that did credit to all of Desiree's preparations. She glanced uncertainly at Keiran as he tasted a slice of turkey. He proclaimed the meat expertly roasted, and she couldn't help but notice he gazed at her with profound pride.

She toyed with the mashed potatoes, wishing she hadn't felt so nervous about entertaining. Keiran assumed the role as host with a casual, gracious elegance.

After her pistachio cake was served for dessert, Joseph turned his attention to her. "We have a present for you, Aunt Desiree!" he burst out. "It's a surprise! Uncle Teddy said we could go back to our house and get him as soon as we were finished." He turned to Candee. "May I be excused?"

Him? Get him? Before Desiree could ask, Candee opened her mouth with the obvious intention of suggesting they wait until Christmas morning, but Teddy forestalled her by grinning at Joseph in agreement.

"This won't take long," Teddy said, as he and Joseph hurried out the door.

They returned ten minutes later holding Boomer, the brown and tan beagle pup.

"Merry Christmas, Desiree!" Candee, Teddy, and Joseph chimed.

The beagle wriggled out of Joseph's arms and lunged for the coffee table laden with food.

"This dog loves to eat, so he must think he's landed in paradise because he can reach the height of this table," Teddy said.

Desiree dissolved with laughter. Her contentment was so real, she thought her chest might burst. This was heaven—a happy home, sharing God's message of joy with the people she loved.

After the meal was cleared, Keiran escorted Desiree to the living room while Candee and her family excused themselves to go back to their house and get ready for church services.

Boomer, apparently full and exhausted, curled up near the fireplace, tail to nose.

"Desiree? There are a few things we need to discuss." Keiran claimed a seat beside her on the sofa. Although he asked gently, she knew by his inquisitive expression that he wanted an explanation for why she refused to accept his phone calls and texts.

She pulled off her apron and smoothed her red silk blouse. Drawing a long breath, she told him her feelings about trust, knowing he'd been correct in surmising her issues had come from early life experiences.

"Trust can be relearned," he said quietly. "It helps if you talk about it. And I'll be here for you, to listen."

"You're moving back in?"

He brushed a wisp of blond hair from her face. "I hope you'll invite me to sleep in your attic. I can't drive back to Atlanta in a blizzard."

"I wouldn't call a few inches of snow a blizzard." She stared out the wavy glass of the front bay window. The snow was starting to fall, its thick wet flakes covering the sidewalks and road in a white blanket.

"You don't want your fiancé to be homeless," he said.

"Fiancé?"

Although his tone was light, she heard the rough tinge in his voice.

Tipping her chin up, he gazed deeply into her eyes. "I love you, Desiree."

She laid a hand on his cheek. "And I love you."

Her Renaissance man. She attempted to smile. "Until now, I felt certain I'd never hear those words from you."

"Desiree, I've loved you since you slammed the door in my face when I first arrived, then berated me for talking to your front porch."

"A bit odd, don't you think? Talking to a porch?"

"Not considering the circumstances." With an arm around her waist, he turned to a side table, picked up his gift and handed it to her.

"I thought about something Christmassy, and it's one of the reasons I stopped in town. Please open it."

She unwrapped the gift and slid a silky scarf between her fingers, admiring the holly design in white and green. "Thank you. It's gorgeous."

"The boutique owner said it's a designer scarf, and the colors will go with everything."

"Ideal for the holidays." She tied the scarf around her throat and smiled. "How does it look?"

"Perfect. Like you." He nodded to the box. "There's something else inside, at the bottom."

"What is it?"

He caught her in a long embrace. "Something special that I hope you'll love."

She unsnapped the lid of a tiny black velvet box and

gasped. An exquisite round-cut diamond ring, styled in yellow gold, reflected sparkling white light across the ceiling.

"I've never seen anything so beautiful," she breathed.

He drew back slightly and regarded her. "Will you marry me?"

From the moment he'd returned, Desiree had known he would ask for an open and honest relationship.

Through tears of bliss, she whispered, "Yes."

His arms closed around her. "Good. Because if you don't mean it, I won't bake any more Irish whiskey cakes."

"Maybe it's better, because I need to lose a few pounds." She laughed through her tears. "Besides, you never shared your secret recipe with me."

He took her hand and led her to the kitchen. "We can start this evening. I promise I'll teach you everything I know."

THE END

RECIPE FOR DESIREE'S PISTACHIO CAKE

Easy, fast, and festive, this recipe is always a treat!

You will need:

1 package of white cake mix- any brand

1 package of pistachio instant pudding – sugar-free may be used instead of regular

½ cup vegetable oil

½ cup water

½ cup milk

5 eggs

Blend cake mix with the package of pudding. Add oil, milk, and water. Add eggs one at a time, beating well with electric mixer after each addition.

Pour into a greased (or sprayed with cooking spray) tube or Bundt pan.

Bake 1 hour at 350 degrees. May be done sooner, as ovens vary.

Cool for 30 minutes, and invert onto favorite cake platter.

For a light and festive topping, sprinkle with sifted confectioners sugar and sliced maraschino cherries.

Optional frosting recipe: (Spread on cooled cake)

½ pint heavy cream

1 package instant pistachio pudding (sugar free may be used)

1 container thawed Cool Whip (fat-free may be used)

Beat heavy cream until thick. Blend in rest of ingredients. Frost as desired.

Enjoy!

A NOTE FROM THE AUTHOR

Dear Friends,

1-800-CHRISTMAS is the second book in my contemporary sweet romance series: *Flipping for You*. I hope you enjoyed it. If you did, please help other people find this book and write a review.

House flipping is a subject I've always been fascinated with. In my spare time, I enjoy watching home-improvement television shows, and several of these programs were an inspiration for my story.

1-800-CHRISTMAS continues the series in the same small town of Roses, North Carolina, and follows 1-800-CUPID.

Desiree, the heroine, is a successful lawyer, and determined to find her Happily Ever After.

Keiran, the Irish hero, faces the decision of whether or not to follow his true calling.

The series continues with 1-800-IRELAND, the third book, and features Kathleen, from Oh Danny Boy, and Rob, a reader favorite, from the 1-800 Series.

Then, take a beach trip with Belle and Andrew to beautiful Wilmington and read 1-800-SUMMER.

It is my hope that you will enjoy their house flipping adventures, and celebrate the joyful holiday season along with these fun, quirky, and endearing characters. This book is available in ebook, Paperback, Large Print Paperback, Hardcover, and audiobook.

Happy Reading!

My Spotify Play List for 1-800-CHRISTMAS is here.

Josie Riviera

ABOUT THE AUTHOR

Josie Riviera is a *USA TODAY* bestselling author of contemporary, inspirational, and historical sweet romances that read like Hallmark movies. She lives in the Charlotte, NC, area with her wonderfully supportive husband. They share their home with an adorable shih tzu, who constantly needs grooming, and live in an old house forever needing renovations.

Become a member of my Read and Review VIP Facebook group for exclusive giveaways and ARCs.

To connect with Josie, visit her webpage and subscribe to her newsletter. As a thank-you, she'll send you a free sweet romance novella directly to your inbox.

josieriviera.com

ALSO BY JOSIE RIVIERA

Seeking Patience

Seeking Catherine (always Free!)

Seeking Fortune

Seeking Charity

Seeking Rachel

The Seeking Series

Oh Danny Boy

I Love You More

A Snowy White Christmas

A Portuguese Christmas

Holiday Hearts Book Bundle Volume One

Holiday Hearts Book Bundle Volume Two

Holiday Hearts Book Bundle Volume Three

Holiday Hearts Book Bundle Volume Four

Candleglow and Mistletoe

Maeve (Perfect Match)

A Love Song To Cherish

A Christmas To Cherish

A Valentine To Cherish

A Christmas Puppy To Cherish

A Homecoming To Cherish

A Summer To Cherish

Romance Stories To Cherish

Romance Stories To Cherish Volume Two

Most books are available in ebook, audiobook, paperback, Large Print paperback and Hardcover.

Many are FREE on Kindle Unlimited!